TALES BEFORE
TOLKIEN

THE ROOTS OF
MODERN FANTASY

Books published by The Random House Publishing Group
are available at quantity discounts on bulk purchases for
premium, educational, fund-raising, and special sales use.
For details, please call 1-800-733-3000.

TALES BEFORE TOLKIEN

THE ROOTS OF MODERN FANTASY

EDITED BY
DOUGLAS A. ANDERSON

BALLANTINE BOOKS • NEW YORK

Sale of this book without a front cover may be unauthorized. If this book is coverless, it may have been reported to the publisher as "unsold or destroyed" and neither the author nor the publisher may have received payment for it.

Tales Before Tolkien is a work of fiction. Names, places, and incidents either are a product of the author's imagination or are used fictitiously.

2005 Del Rey Mass Market Edition

Introduction, headnotes, compilation, and author notes © 2003 by Douglas A. Anderson

All rights reserved.

Published in the United States by Del Rey Books, an imprint of The Random House Publishing Group, a division of Random House, Inc., New York.

DEL REY is a registered trademark and the Del Rey colophon is a trademark of Random House, Inc.

Originally published in hardcover in the United States by Del Rey Books, an imprint of The Random House Publishing Group, a division of Random House, Inc., in 2003.

"Chu-bu and Sheemish" by Lord Dunsany. Copyright © Lord Dunsany. Reprinted by permission of Joe Doyle, Curator, on behalf of the present Lord and Lady Dunsany.

"The Coming of the Terror" by Arthur Machen. Copyright © Arthur Machen. Reprinted by permission of A. M. Heath & Co. Ltd.

"Golithos the Ogre" by E. A. Wyke-Smith, reprinted from *The Marvellous Land of Snergs.* Copyright © 1927 by E. A. Wyke-Smith, © 1996 by Edward S. Wyke-Smith and Nina Wyke-Smith. Reprinted by permission of Edward S. Wyke-Smith and Nina Wyke-Smith.

"A Christmas Play" by David Lindsay. Copyright © 2003 by Mrs. Diana Moon and Mrs. Helen Baz. Printed by permission of the copyright holders.

ISBN 0-345-45856-7

Printed in the United States of America

www.delreybooks.com

OPM 9 8 7 6 5 4 3 2 1

To my sister Sue,
who introduced me to Tolkien's writings

ACKNOWLEDGMENTS

For assistance with various aspects of this anthology, I am grateful to Mike Ashley, David Bratman, Mary Ellen Channon, Joe D'Amico, Joe Doyle, Verlyn Flieger, S. T. Joshi, Tappan King, Colin Manlove, John D. Rateliff, Ray Russell, Gordon Van Gelder, Richard C. West, Benjamin Wright, Nina Wyke-Smith, and Ted Wyke-Smith. A special thanks goes to David Underwood and Betsy Mitchell of Ballantine Books.

CONTENTS

1 .... Introduction

5 .... "The Elves" by Ludwig Tieck
27 .... "The Golden Key" by George MacDonald
59 .... "Puss-cat Mew" by E. H. Knatchbull-Hugessen
111 .... "The Griffin and the Minor Canon" by
Frank R. Stockton
129 .... "The Demon Pope" by Richard Garnett
141 .... "The Story of Sigurd" retold by Andrew Lang
151 .... "The Folk of the Mountain Door" by
William Morris
167 .... "Black Heart and White Heart: A Zulu Idyll" by
H. Rider Haggard
229 .... "The Dragon Tamers" by E. Nesbit
245 .... "The Far Islands" by John Buchan
269 .... "The Drawn Arrow" by Clemence Housman
283 .... "The Enchanted Buffalo" by L. Frank Baum
293 .... "Chu-bu and Sheemish" by Lord Dunsany
299 .... "The Baumoff Explosive" by William
Hope Hodgson
319 .... "The Regent of the North" by Kenneth Morris
333 .... "The Coming of the Terror" by
Arthur Machen
381 .... "The Elf Trap" by Francis Stevens
409 .... "The Thin Queen of Elfhame" by
James Branch Cabell

417 .... "The Woman of the Wood" by A. Merritt
451 .... "Golithos the Ogre" by
      E. A. Wyke-Smith
465 .... "A Christmas Play" by David Lindsay

507 .... Author Notes and Recommended Reading

INTRODUCTION

For many readers, fantasy begins with J. R. R. Tolkien (1892–1973), the world-renowned creator of Middle-earth, whose history is recounted in *The Hobbit* (1937), *The Lord of the Rings* (1954–55), and *The Silmarillion* (1977). Fantasy literature, however, did not begin with Tolkien, though he developed it in a manner such that there exists almost a dividing line between fantasy written before Tolkien and fantasy written afterward.

The roots of fantasy extend back to Homer's *Iliad* and *Odyssey* and on through the medieval literatures that were Tolkien's specialties as a professor at Oxford. The Anglo-Saxon poem *Beowulf*, which concerns a hero and his fight with monsters (including a dragon); the Arthurian romances, including *Sir Gawain and the Green Knight* (which Tolkien edited in Middle English and also translated) and those by Chrétien de Troyes; the medieval legends of Alexander the Great (who discovered the Trees of the Sun and Moon in the Far East, the inspiration of Tolkien's Two Trees in Valinor); and the Icelandic *Eddas* and sagas, these are the cornerstones of the medieval genre of heroic romance, with heroic exploits, quests, interlaced stories, and various intrusions of something beyond the natural—that is, elements of fantasy. Tolkien himself followed in this tradition, and *The Lord of the Rings,* as its author rightly noted, is more properly called a heroic romance than a novel.

Tolkien also drew upon folklore and the folktale traditions, as they were recorded in the eighteenth and nineteenth centuries. After this process of the writing down of oral materials there naturally developed the German *kunstmärchen,* or "literary fairy tales"—that is, fairy tales artistically composed by a single author rather than stories merely recorded from oral tradition. From these folktales and fairy tales came the further development of fairy tales as children's literature and, in addition, of fantasy as a mode of literature for adults.

It is from this latter tradition, beginning with the *kunstmärchen,* that this anthology derives. The stories are arranged in chronological order as to when each item was written. One of the criteria by which I selected stories for this anthology was that each item must have been written before *The Hobbit* was published in 1937. Another guideline that I have followed in a more general sense is that I have wanted each author to be at least slightly older than Tolkien—that is, not one of his contemporaries—so I somewhat arbitrarily restricted myself to writers born at least five years before Tolkien. Some of the stories that I have chosen can be seen specifically to have inspired Tolkien, and these connections are detailed in the headnotes to the appropriate stories. I have also selected some stories whose content seems especially Tolkienian, even though there is little or no evidence that Tolkien knew the writers. And I have also chosen other stories that Tolkien almost certainly did not know in order to show some of the diversity of fantasy as it existed before *The Hobbit.*

This anthology begins with what is perhaps the best of the *kunstmärchen,* "The Elves" by Ludwig Tieck. German romantic fairy tales were a great influence on George MacDonald, and it was through MacDonald that the idea of literary fairy tales entered into English literature. In this anthology MacDonald, along with E. H. Knatchbull-Hugessen, Andrew Lang, E. Nesbit, and E. A. Wyke-Smith, represent British children's writers. British adventure fiction is exemplified in the stories of H. Rider Haggard and John Buchan, while the literary side of British fantasy is seen in the selections by Richard Garnett, William Morris, Clemence Housman, Lord Dunsany, William Hope Hodgson, Kenneth Morris, Arthur Machen, and David Lindsay.

Examples of American children's fantasy are found in the stories by Frank R. Stockton and L. Frank Baum. American adventure fantasy is represented by the tales of Francis Stevens and A. Merritt, while the selections by James Branch Cabell and Austin Tappan Wright exemplify more literary American fantasy.

I have kept my headnotes to the stories in this volume brief, intending them to serve more as guiding directions than as critical analyses. Background information on the various authors can be found in the notes at the end of the book, together with recommendations for further reading.

Tolkien's greatness lies in how he brought together the various existing strands of fantasy—heroic romance, folklore, fairy tales, and adult fantasy—and extended the scope of fantasy across the board in a historical as well as novelistic manner. Doing so brought a new depth to the genre, and Tolkien's elaborate history of three Ages of his invented world has raised the bar for his successors. To better appreciate Tolkien's achievement one needs to better understand Tolkien's own roots and the roots of modern fantasy. This anthology merely represents a first step in doing so, while making a number of fine stories, long unavailable, more easily accessible to readers who will enjoy them.

Douglas A. Anderson
November 2002

The Elves

❧

by Ludwig Tieck

Translated by Thomas Carlyle

In his famous essay "On Fairy-stories" Tolkien wrote that
"Faerie is a perilous land, and in it are pitfalls for the unwary
and dungeons for the overbold." Ludwig Tieck's story of the
young girl Mary and her encounter with the Elves is one of
the very best stories of the German *kunstmärchen,* or "literary fairy tales." Here the otherworldly and perilous nature of
Faerie that Tolkien later described is very evident.

"The Elves" was first published in volume 1 (1812) of
Tieck's three-volume *Phantasus.* The translation into English by Thomas Carlyle first appeared in *German Romance*
(1827).

"WHERE is our little Mary?" said the father.

"She is playing out upon the green there with our
neighbour's boy," replied the mother.

"I wish they may not run away and lose themselves," said
he; "they are so thoughtless."

The mother looked for the little ones, and brought them
their evening luncheon. "It is warm," said the boy; "and
Mary had a longing for the red cherries."

"Have a care, children," said the mother, "and do not run
too far from home, and not into the wood; Father and I are
going to the fields."

Little Andres answered: "Never fear, the wood frightens
us; we shall sit here by the house, where there are people
near us."

The mother went in, and soon came out again with her husband. They locked the door, and turned towards the fields to look after their labourers, and see their hay-harvest in the meadow. Their house lay upon a little green height, encircled by a pretty ring of paling, which likewise enclosed their fruit and flower garden. The hamlet stretched somewhat deeper down, and on the other side lay the castle of the Count. Martin rented the large farm from this nobleman; and was living in contentment with his wife and only child; for he yearly saved some money, and had the prospect of becoming a man of substance by his industry, for the ground was productive, and the Count not illiberal.

As he walked with his wife to the fields, he gazed cheerfully round and said: "What a different look this quarter has, Brigitta, from the place we lived in formerly! Here it is all so green; the whole village is bedecked with thick-spreading fruit-trees; the ground is full of beautiful herbs and flowers; all the houses are cheerful and cleanly, the inhabitants are at their ease: nay, I could almost fancy that the woods are greener here than elsewhere, and the sky bluer; and, so far as the eye can reach, you have pleasure and delight in beholding the bountiful Earth."

"And whenever you cross the stream," said Brigitta, "you are, as it were, in another world, all is so dreary and withered; but every traveller declares that our village is the fairest in the country far and near."

"All but that fir-ground," said her husband; "do but look back to it, how dark and dismal that solitary spot is lying in the gay scene: the dingy fir-trees with the smoky huts behind them, the ruined stalls, the brook flowing past with a sluggish melancholy."

"It is true," replied Brigitta; "if you but approach that spot, you grow disconsolate and sad, you know not why. What sort of people can they be that live there, and keep themselves so separate from the rest of us, as if they had an evil conscience?"

"A miserable crew," replied the young Farmer: "gipsies, seemingly, that steal and cheat in other quarters, and have their hoard and hiding-place here. I wonder only that his Lordship suffers them."

"Who knows," said the wife, with an accent of pity, "but perhaps they may be poor people, wishing, out of shame, to conceal their poverty; for, after all, no one can say aught ill of them; the only thing is, that they do not go to church, and none knows how they live; for the little garden, which indeed seems altogether waste, cannot possibly support them; and fields they have none."

"God knows," said Martin, as they went along, "what trade they follow; no mortal comes to them; for the place they live in is as if bewitched and excommunicated, so that even our wildest fellows will not venture into it."

Such conversation they pursued, while walking to the fields. That gloomy spot they spoke of lay aside from the hamlet. In a dell, begirt with firs, you might behold a hut, and various ruined office-houses; rarely was smoke seen to mount from it, still more rarely did men appear there; though at times curious people, venturing somewhat nearer, had perceived upon the bench before the hut, some hideous women, in ragged clothes, dandling in their arms some children equally dirty and ill-favoured; black dogs were running up and down upon the boundary; and, of an evening, a man of monstrous size was seen to cross the footbridge of the brook, and disappear in the hut; and, in the darkness, various shapes were observed, moving like shadows round a fire in the open air. This piece of ground, the firs and the ruined huts, formed in truth a strange contrast with the bright green landscape, the white houses of the hamlet, and the stately new-built castle.

The two little ones had now eaten their fruit; it came into their heads to run races; and the little nimble Mary always got the start of the less active Andres. "It is not fair," cried

Andres at last: "let us try it for some length, then we shall see who wins."

"As thou wilt," said Mary; "only to the brook we must not run."

"No," said Andres; "but there, on the hill, stands the large pear-tree, a quarter of a mile from this. I shall run by the left, round past the fir-ground; thou canst try it by the right over the fields; so we do not meet till we get up, and then we shall see which of us is swifter."

"Done," cried Mary, and began to run; "for we shall not mar one another by the way, and my father says it is as far to the hill by that side of the gipsies's house as by this."

Andres had already started, and Mary, turning to the right, could no longer see him. "It is very silly," said she to herself: "I have only to take heart, and run along the bridge, past the hut, and through the yard, and I shall certainly be first." She was already standing by the brook and the clump of firs. "Shall I? No; it is too frightful," said she. A little white dog was standing on the farther side, and barking with might and main. In her terror, Mary thought the dog some monster, and sprang back. "Fy! fy!" said she: "the dolt is gone half way by this time, while I stand here considering." The little dog kept barking, and, as she looked at it more narrowly, it seemed no longer frightful, but, on the contrary, quite pretty; it had a red collar round its neck, with a glittering bell; and as it raised its head, and shook itself in barking, the little bell sounded with the finest tinkle. "Well, I must risk it!" cried she, "I will run for life; quick, quick, I am through; certainly to Heaven, they cannot eat me up alive in half a minute!" And with this, the gay, courageous little Mary sprang along the footbridge; passed the dog, which ceased its barking and began to fawn on her; and in a moment she was standing on the other bank, and the black firs all round concealed from view her father's house, and the rest of the landscape.

But what was her astonishment when here! The loveliest, most variegated flower-garden, lay round her; tulips, roses and lilies were glittering in the fairest colours; blue and gold-red butterflies were wavering in the blossoms; cages of shining wire were hung on the espaliers, with many-coloured birds in them, singing beautiful songs; and children, in short white frocks, with flowing yellow hair and brilliant eyes, were frolicking about; some playing with lambkins, some feeding the birds, or gathering flowers, and giving them to one another; some, again, were eating cherries, grapes and ruddy apricots. No hut was to be seen; but instead of it, a large fair house, with a brazen door and lofty statues, stood glancing in the middle of the space. Mary was confounded with surprise, and knew not what to think; but, not being bashful, she went right up to the first of the children, held out her hand, and wished the little creature good-even.

"Art thou come to visit us, then?" said the glittering child; "I saw thee running, playing on the other side, but thou wert frightened at our little dog."

"So you are not gipsies and rogues," said Mary, "as Andres always told me? He is a stupid thing, and talks of much he does not understand."

"Stay with us," said the strange little girl; "thou wilt like it well."

"But we are running a race."

"Thou wilt find thy comrade soon enough. There, take and eat."

Mary ate, and found the fruit more sweet than any she had ever tasted in her life before; and Andres, and the race, and the prohibition of her parents, were entirely forgotten.

A stately woman, in a shining robe, came towards them, and asked about the stranger child. "Fairest lady," said Mary, "I came running hither by chance, and now they wish to keep me."

"Thou art aware, Zerina," said the lady, "that she can be here but for a little while; besides, thou shouldst have asked my leave."

"I thought," said Zerina, "when I saw her admitted across

the bridge, that I might do it; we have often seen her running in the fields, and thou thyself hast taken pleasure in her lively temper. She will have to leave us soon enough."

"No, I will stay here," said the little stranger; "for here it is so beautiful, and here I shall find the prettiest playthings, and store of berries and cherries to boot. On the other side it is not half so grand."

The gold-robed lady went away with a smile; and many of the children now came bounding round the happy Mary in their mirth, and twitched her, and incited her to dance; others brought her lambs, or curious playthings; others made music on instruments, and sang to it.

She kept, however, by the playmate who had first met her; for Zerina was the kindest and loveliest of them all. Little Mary cried and cried again: "I will stay with you forever; I will stay with you, and you shall be my sisters"; at which the children all laughed, and embraced her. "Now we shall have a royal sport," said Zerina. She ran into the palace, and returned with a little golden box, in which lay a quantity of seeds, like glittering dust. She lifted of it with her little hand, and scattered some grains on the green earth. Instantly the grass began to move, as in waves; and, after a few moments, bright rosebushes started from the ground, shot rapidly up, and budded all at once, while the sweetest perfume filled the place. Mary also took a little of the dust, and, having scattered it, she saw white lilies, and the most variegated pinks, pushing up. At a signal from Zerina, the flowers disappeared, and others rose in their room. "Now," said Zerina, "look for something greater." She laid two pine-seeds in the ground, and stamped them in sharply with her foot. Two green bushes stood before them. "Grasp me fast," said she; and Mary threw her arms about the slender form. She felt herself borne upwards; for the trees were springing under them with the greatest speed; the tall pines waved to and fro, and the two children held each other fast embraced, swinging this way and that in the red clouds of the twilight, and kissed each other; while the rest were climbing up and down the trunks with quick dexterity, pushing and teasing one another with loud laughter when they met; if any one fell down in the press, it flew through the air, and sank slowly and surely to the ground. At length Mary was beginning to be frightened; and the other little child sang a few loud tones, and the trees again sank down, and set them on the ground as gradually as they had lifted them before to the clouds.

They next went through the brazen door of the palace. Here many fair women, elderly and young, were sitting in the round hall, partaking of the fairest fruits, and listening to glorious invisible music. In the vaulting of the ceiling, palms, flowers and groves stood painted, among which little figures of children were sporting and winding in every graceful posture; and with the tones of the music, the images altered and glowed with the most burning colours; now the blue and green were sparkling like radiant light, now these tints faded back in paleness; the purple flamed up, and the gold took fire; and then the naked children seemed to be alive among the flower-garlands, and to draw breath, and emit it through their ruby-coloured lips; so that by fits you could see the glance of their little white teeth, and the lighting up of their azure eyes.

From the hall, a stair of brass led down to a subterranean chamber. Here lay much gold and silver, and precious stones of every hue shone out between them. Strange vessels stood along the walls, and all seemed filled with costly things. The gold was worked into many forms, and glittered with the friendliest red. Many little dwarfs were busied sorting the pieces from the heap, and putting them in the vessels; others, hunch-backed and bandy-legged, with long red noses, were tottering slowly along, half-bent to the ground, under full sacks, which they bore as millers do their grain; and, with much panting, shaking out the gold-dust on the ground. Then they darted awkwardly to the right and left, and caught the rolling balls that were like to run away; and it happened now and then that one in his eagerness overset the other, so that both fell heavily and clumsily to the ground. They made angry faces, and looked askance, as Mary laughed at their gestures and their ugliness. Behind them sat an old crumpled little man, whom Zerina reverently greeted; he thanked her with a grave inclination of his head. He held a sceptre in his hand, and wore a crown upon his brow, and all the other dwarfs appeared to regard him as their master, and obey his nod.

"What more wanted?" asked he, with a surly voice, as the children came a little nearer. Mary was afraid, and did not speak; but her companion answered, they were only come to look about them in the chambers. "Still your old child's tricks!" replied the dwarf: "Will there never be an end to idleness?" With this, he turned again to his employment, kept his people weighing and sorting the ingots; some he sent away on errands, some he chid with angry tones.

"Who is the gentleman?" said Mary.

"Our Metal-Prince," replied Zerina, as they walked along.

They seemed once more to reach the open air, for they were standing by a lake, yet no sun appeared, and they saw no sky above their heads. A little boat received them, and Zerina steered it diligently forwards. It shot rapidly along. On gaining the middle of the lake, the stranger saw that multitudes of pipes, channels, and brooks, were spreading from the little sea in every direction. "These waters to the right," said Zerina, "flow beneath your garden, and this is why it blooms so freshly; by the other side we get down into the great stream." On a sudden, out of all the channels, and from every quarter of the lake, came a crowd of little children swimming up; some wore garlands of sedge and water-lily; some had red stems of coral, others were blowing on crooked shells; a tumultuous noise echoed merrily from the dark shores; among the children might be seen the fairest women sporting in the waters, and often several of the children sprang about some one of them, and with kisses hung upon her neck and shoulders. All saluted the strangers; and these steered onwards through the revelry out of the lake, into a little river, which grew narrower and narrower. At last the boat came aground. The strangers took their leave, and Zerina knocked against the cliff. This opened like a door, and a female form, all red, assisted them to mount. "Are you all brisk here?" inquired Zerina. "They are just at work," replied the other, "and happy as they could wish; indeed, the heat is very pleasant."

They went up a winding stair, and on a sudden Mary found herself in a most resplendent hall, so that as she entered, her eyes were dazzled by the radiance. Flame-coloured tapestry covered the walls with a purple glow; and when her eye had grown a little used to it, the stranger saw, to her astonishment, that, in the tapestry, there were figures moving up and down in dancing joyfulness; in form so beautiful, and of so fair proportions, that nothing could be seen more graceful; their bodies were as of red crystal, so that it appeared as if the blood were visible within them, flowing and playing in its courses. They smiled on the stranger, and saluted her with various bows; but as Mary was about approaching nearer them, Zerina plucked her sharply back, crying: "Thou wilt burn thyself, my little Mary, for the whole of it is fire."

Mary felt the heat. "Why do the pretty creatures not come out," said she, "and play with us?"

"As thou livest in the Air," replied the other, "so are they obliged to stay continually in Fire, and would faint and languish if they left it. Look now, how glad they are, how they laugh and shout; those down below spread out the fire-floods everywhere beneath the earth, and thereby the flowers, and fruits, and wine, are made to flourish; these red streams again, are to run beside the brooks of water; and thus the fiery creatures are kept ever busy and glad. But for thee it is too hot here; let us return to the garden."

In the garden, the scene had changed since they left it. The moonshine was lying on every flower; the birds were silent, and the children were asleep in complicated groups, among the green groves. Mary and her friend, however, did not feel fatigue, but walked about in the warm summer night, in abundant talk, till morning.

When the day dawned, they refreshed themselves on fruit and milk, and Mary said: "Suppose we go, by way of change, to the firs, and see how things look there?"

"With all my heart," replied Zerina; "thou wilt see our watchmen too, and they will surely please thee; they are standing up among the trees on the mound." The two proceeded through the flower-garden by pleasant groves, full of nightingales; then they ascended a vine-hill; and at last, after long following the windings of a clear brook, arrived at the firs, and the height which bounded the domain. "How does it come," said Mary, "that we have to walk so far here, when without, the circuit is so narrow?"

"I know not," said her friend; "but so it is."

They mounted to the dark firs, and a chill wind blew from without in their faces; a haze seemed lying far and wide over the landscape. On the top were many strange forms standing: with mealy, dusty faces; their misshapen heads not unlike those of white owls; they were clad in folded cloaks of shaggy wool; they held umbrellas of curious skins stretched out above them; and they waved and fanned themselves incessantly with large bat's wings, which flared out curiously beside the woollen roquelaures. "I could laugh, yet I am frightened," cried Mary.

"These are our good trusty watchmen," said her playmate; "they stand here and wave their fans, that cold anxiety and inexplicable fear may fall on every one that attempts to approach us. They are covered so, because without it is now cold and rainy, which they cannot bear. But snow, or wind, or cold air, never reaches down to us; here is an everlasting spring and summer: yet if these poor people on the top were not frequently relieved, they would certainly perish."

"But who are you, then?" said Mary, while again descending to the flowery fragrance; "or have you no name at all?"

"We are called the Elves," replied the friendly child; "people talk about us in the Earth, as I have heard."

They now perceived a mighty bustle on the green. "The fair Bird is come!" cried the children to them: all hastened to the hall. Here, as they approached, young and old were crowding over the threshold, all shouting for joy; and from within resounded a triumphant peal of music. Having entered, they perceived the vast circuit filled with the most varied forms, and all were looking upwards to a large Bird with glancing plumage, that was sweeping slowly round in the dome, and in its stately flight describing many a circle. The music sounded more gaily than before; the colours and lights alternated more rapidly. At last the music ceased; and the Bird, with a rustling noise, floated down upon a glittering crown that hung hovering in air under the high window, by which the hall was lighted from above. His plumage was purple and green, and shining golden streaks played through it; on his head there waved a diadem of feathers, so resplendent that they glanced like jewels. His bill was red, and his legs of a glancing blue. As he moved, the tints gleamed through each other, and the eye was charmed with their radiance. His size was as that of an eagle. But now he opened his glittering beak; and sweetest melodies came pouring from his moved breast, in finer tones than the lovesick nightingale gives forth; still stronger rose the song, and streamed like floods of Light, so that all, the very children themselves, were moved by it to tears of joy and rapture. When he ceased, all bowed before him; he again flew round the dome in circles, then darted through the door, and soared into the light heaven, where he shone far up like a red point, and then soon vanished from their eyes.

"Why are ye all so glad?" inquired Mary, bending to her fair playmate, who seemed smaller than yesterday.

"The King is coming!" said the little one; "many of us have never seen him, and whithersoever he turns his face, there is happiness and mirth; we have long looked for him, more anxiously than you look for spring when winter lingers with you; and now he has announced, by his fair herald, that he is at hand. This wise and glorious Bird, that has been sent to us by the King, is called Phœnix; he dwells far off in Arabia, on a tree, which there is no other that resembles it on Earth, as in like manner there is no second Phœnix. When he feels himself grown old, he builds a pile of balm and incense, kindles it, and dies singing; and then from the fragrant ashes, soars up the renewed Phœnix with unlessened beauty. It is seldom he so wings his course that men behold him; and when once in centuries this does occur, they note it in their annals, and expect remarkable events. But now, my friend, thou and I must part; for the sight of the King is not permitted thee."

Then the lady with the golden robe came through the throng, and beckoning Mary to her, led her into a sequestered walk. "Thou must leave us, my dear child," said she; "the King is to hold his court here for twenty years, perhaps longer; and fruitfulness and blessings will spread far over the land, but chiefly here beside us; all the brooks and rivulets will become more bountiful, all the fields and gardens richer, the wine more generous, the meadows more fertile, and the woods more fresh and green; a milder air will blow, no hail shall hurt, no flood shall threaten. Take this ring, and think of us: but beware of telling any one of our existence; or we must fly this land, and thou and all around will lose the happiness and blessing of our neighbourhood. Once more, kiss thy playmate, and farewell." They issued from the walk; Zerina wept, Mary stooped to embrace her, and they parted. Already she was on the narrow bridge; the cold air was blowing on her back from the firs; the little dog barked with all its might, and rang its little bell; she looked round, then hastened over, for the darkness of the firs, the bleakness of the ruined huts, the shadows of the twilight, were filling her with terror.

"What a night my parents must have had on my account!"

said she within herself, as she stept on the green; "and I dare not tell them where I have been, or what wonders I have witnessed, nor indeed would they believe me." Two men passing by saluted her; and as they went along, she heard them say: "What a pretty girl! Where can she come from?" With quickened steps she approached the house: but the trees which were hanging last night loaded with fruit were now standing dry and leafless; the house was differently painted, and a new barn had been built beside it. Mary was amazed, and thought she must be dreaming. In this perplexity she opened the door; and behind the table sat her father, between an unknown woman and a stranger youth. "Good God! Father," cried she, "where is my mother?"

"Thy mother!" said the woman, with a forecasting tone, and sprang towards her: "Ha, thou surely canst not—Yes, indeed, indeed thou art my lost, long-lost dear, only Mary!" She had recognised her by a little brown mole beneath the chin, as well as by her eyes and shape. All embraced her, all were moved with joy, and the parents wept. Mary was astonished that she almost reached to her father's stature; and she could not understand how her mother had become so changed and faded; she asked the name of the stranger youth. "It is our neighbour's Andres," said Martin. "How comest thou to us again, so unexpectedly, after seven long years? Where hast thou been? Why didst thou never send us tidings of thee?"

"Seven years!" said Mary, and could not order her ideas and recollections. "Seven whole years?"

"Yes, yes," said Andres, laughing, and shaking her trustfully by the hand; "I have won the race, good Mary; I was at the pear-tree and back again seven years ago, and thou, sluggish creature, art but just returned!"

They again asked, they pressed her; but remembering her instruction, she could answer nothing. It was they themselves chiefly that, by degrees, shaped a story for her: How, having lost her way, she had been taken up by a coach, and carried to a strange remote part, where she could not give the

people any notion of her parents' residence; how she was
conducted to a distant town, where certain worthy persons
brought her up and loved her; how they had lately died, and
at length she had recollected her birthplace, and so returned.
"No matter how it is!" exclaimed her mother; "enough, that
we have thee again, my little daughter, my own, my all!"

Andres waited supper, and Mary could not be at home in
anything she saw. The house seemed small and dark; she felt
astonished at her dress, which was clean and simple, but appeared quite foreign; she looked at the ring on her finger, and
the gold of it glittered strangely, enclosing a stone of burning red. To her father's question, she replied that the ring also
was a present from her benefactors.

She was glad when the hour of sleep arrived, and she hastened to her bed. Next morning she felt much more collected; she had now arranged her thoughts a little, and could
better stand the questions of the people in the village, all of
whom came in to bid her welcome. Andres was there too
with the earliest, active, glad, and serviceable beyond all others. The blooming maiden of fifteen had made a deep impression on him; he had passed a sleepless night. The people
of the castle likewise sent for Mary, and she had once more
to tell her story to them, which was now grown quite familiar to her. The old Count and his Lady were surprised at her
good-breeding; she was modest, but not embarrassed; she
made answer courteously in good phrases to all their questions; all fear of noble persons and their equipage had passed
away from her; for when she measured these halls and forms
by the wonders and the high beauty she had seen with the
Elves in their hidden abode, this earthly splendour seemed
but dim to her, the presence of men was almost mean. The
young lords were charmed with her beauty.

It was now February. The trees were budding earlier than
usual; the nightingale had never come so soon; the spring
rose fairer in the land than the oldest men could recollect it.
In every quarter, little brooks gushed out to irrigate the pas-

tures and meadows; the hills seemed heaving, the vines rose higher and higher, the fruit-trees blossomed as they had never done; and a swelling fragrant blessedness hung suspended heavily in rosy clouds over the scene. All prospered beyond expectation; no rude day, no tempest injured the fruits; the wine flowed blushing in immense grapes; and the inhabitants of the place felt astonished, and were captivated as in a sweet dream. The next year was like its forerunner; but men had now become accustomed to the marvellous. In autumn Mary yielded to the pressing entreaties of Andres and her parents; she was betrothed to him, and in winter they were married.

She often thought with inward longing of her residence behind the fir-trees; she continued serious and still. Beautiful as all that lay around her was, she knew of something yet more beautiful; and from the remembrance of this, a faint regret attuned her nature to soft melancholy. It smote her painfully when her father and mother talked about the gipsies and vagabonds, that dwelt in the dark spot of ground. Often she was on the point of speaking out in defence of those good beings, whom she knew to be the benefactors of the land; especially to Andres, who appeared to take delight in zealously abusing them: yet still she repressed the word that was struggling to escape her bosom. So passed this year; in the next, she was solaced by a little daughter, whom she named Elfrida, thinking of the designation of her friendly Elves.

The young people lived with Martin and Brigitta, the house being large enough for all; and helped their parents in conducting their now extended husbandry. The little Elfrida soon displayed peculiar faculties and gifts; for she could walk at a very early age, and could speak perfectly before she was a twelvemonth old; and after some few years, she had become so wise and clever, and of such wondrous beauty, that all people regarded her with astonishment; and her mother could not keep away the thought that her child resembled one of those shining little ones in the space behind the Firs. Elfrida cared not to be with other children; but seemed to avoid, with a sort of horror, their tumultuous amusements; and liked best to be alone. She would then retire into a corner of the garden, and read, or work diligently with her needle; often also you might see her sitting, as if deep sunk in thought; or violently walking up and down the alleys, speaking to herself. Her parents readily allowed her to have her will in these things, for she was healthy, and waxed apace; only her strange sagacious answers and observations often made them anxious. "Such wise children do not grow to age," her grandmother, Brigitta, many times observed; "they are too good for this world; the child, besides, is beautiful beyond nature, and will never find its proper place on Earth."

The little girl had this peculiarity, that she was very loath to let herself be served by any one, but endeavoured to do everything herself. She was almost the earliest riser in the house; she washed herself carefully, and dressed without assistance: at night she was equally careful; she took special heed to pack up her clothes and washed them with her own hands, allowing no one, not even her mother, to meddle with her articles. The mother humoured her in this caprice, not thinking it of any consequence. But what was her astonishment, when, happening one holiday to insist, regardless of Elfrida's tears and screams, on dressing her out for a visit to the castle, she found upon her breast, suspended by a string, a piece of gold of a strange form, which she directly recognised as one of that sort she had seen in such abundance in the subterranean vault! The little thing was greatly frightened; and at last confessed that she had found it in the garden, and as she liked it much, had kept it carefully: she at the same time prayed so earnestly and pressingly to have it back, that Mary fastened it again on its former place, and, full of thoughts, went out with her in silence to the castle.

Sidewards from the farmhouse lay some offices for the

storing of produce and implements; and behind these there was a little green, with an old grove, now visited by no one, as, from the new arrangement of the buildings, it lay too far from the garden. In this solitude Elfrida delighted most; and it occurred to nobody to interrupt her here, so that frequently her parents did not see her for half a day. One afternoon her mother chanced to be in these buildings, seeking for some lost article among the lumber; and she noticed that a beam of light was coming in, through a chink in the wall. She took a thought of looking through this aperture, and seeing what her child was busied with; and it happened that a stone was lying loose, and could be pushed aside, so that she obtained a view right into the grove. Elfrida was sitting there on a little bench, and beside her the well-known Zerina; and the children were playing, and amusing one another, in the kindliest unity. The Elf embraced her beautiful companion, and said mournfully: "Ah! dear little creature, as I sport with thee, so have I sported with thy mother, when she was a child; but you mortals so soon grow tall and thoughtful! It is very hard: wert thou but to be a child as long as I!"

"Willingly would I do it," said Elfrida; "but they all say, I shall come to sense, and give over playing altogether; for I have great gifts, as they think, for growing wise. Ah! and then I shall see thee no more, thou dear Zerina! Yet it is with us as with the fruit-tree flowers: how glorious the blossoming apple-tree, with its red bursting buds! It looks so stately and broad; and every one, that passes under it, thinks surely something great will come of it; then the sun grows hot, and the buds come joyfully forth; but the wicked kernel is already there, which pushes off and casts away the fair flower's dress; and now, in pain and waxing, it can do nothing more, but must grow to fruit in harvest. An apple, to be sure, is pretty and refreshing; yet nothing to the blossom of spring. So is it also with us mortals: I am not glad in the least at growing to be a tall girl. Ah! could I but once visit you!"

"Since the King is with us," said Zerina, "it is quite impossible; but I will come to thee, my darling, often, often; and none shall see me either here or there. I will pass invisible through the air, or fly over to thee like a bird. O! we will be much, much together, while thou art still little. What can I do to please thee?"

"Thou must like me very dearly," said Elfrida, "as I like thee in my heart. But come, let us make another rose."

Zerina took the well-known box from her bosom, threw two grains from it on the ground; and instantly a green bush stood before them, with two deep-red roses, bending their heads, as if to kiss each other. The children plucked them smiling, and the bush disappeared. "O that it would not die so soon!" said Elfrida; "this red child, this wonder of the Earth!"

"Give it me here," said the little Elf; then breathed thrice upon the budding rose, and kissed it thrice. "Now," said she, giving back the rose, "it will continue fresh and blooming till winter."

"I will keep it," said Elfrida, "as an image of thee; I will guard it in my little room, and kiss it night and morning, as if it were thyself."

"The sun is setting," said the other; "I must home." They embraced again, and Zerina vanished.

In the evening, Mary clasped her child to her breast, with a feeling of alarm and veneration. She henceforth allowed the good little girl more liberty than formerly; and often calmed her husband when he came to search for the child; which for some time he was wont to do, as her retiredness did not please him; and he feared that, in the end, it might make her silly, or even pervert her understanding. The mother often glided to the chink; and almost always found the bright Elf beside her child, employed in sport, or in earnest conversation.

"Wouldst thou like to fly?" inquired Zerina once.

"O well! How well!" replied Elfrida; and the fairy clasped her mortal playmate in her arms, and mounted with her from the ground, till they hovered above the grove. The mother, in alarm, forgot herself, and pushed out her head in terror to look after them; when Zerina, from the air, held up her finger, and threatened yet smiled; then descended with the child, embraced her, and disappeared. After this, it happened more than once that Mary was observed by her; and every time, the shining little creature shook her head, or threatened, yet with friendly looks.

Often, in disputing with her husband, Mary had said in her zeal: "Thou dost injustice to the poor people in the hut!" But when Andres pressed her to explain why she differed in opinion from the whole village, nay, from his Lordship himself; and how she could understand it better than the whole of them, she still broke off embarrassed, and became silent. One day, after dinner, Andres grew more violent than ever; and maintained that, by one means or another, the crew must be packed away, as a nuisance to the country; when his wife, in anger, said to him: "Hush! for they are benefactors to thee and to every one of us."

"Benefactors!" cried the other, in astonishment: "These rogues and vagabonds?"

In her indignation, she was now at last tempted to relate to him, under promise of the strictest secrecy, the history of her youth: and as Andres at every word grew more incredulous, and shook his head in mockery, she took him by the hand, and led him to the chink; where, to his amazement, he beheld the glittering Elf sporting with his child, and caressing her in the grove. He knew not what to say; an exclamation of astonishment escaped him, and Zerina raised her eyes. On the instant she grew pale, and trembled violently; not with friendly, but with indignant looks, she made the sign of threatening, and then said to Elfrida: "Thou canst not help it, dearest heart; but they will never learn sense, wise as they believe themselves." She embraced the little one with stormy haste; and then, in the shape of a raven, flew with hoarse cries over the garden, towards the Firs.

In the evening, the little one was very still; she kissed her
rose with tears; Mary felt depressed and frightened, Andres
scarcely spoke. It grew dark. Suddenly there went a rustling
through the trees; birds flew to and fro with wild screaming,
thunder was heard to roll, the Earth shook, and tones of
lamentation moaned in the air. Andres and his wife had not
courage to rise; they shrouded themselves within the curtains, and with fear and trembling awaited the day. Towards
morning, it grew calmer; and all was silent when the Sun,
with his cheerful light, rose over the wood.

Andres dressed himself; and Mary now observed that the
stone of the ring upon her finger had become quite pale. On
opening the door, the sun shone clear on their faces, but the
scene around them they could scarcely recognise. The freshness of the wood was gone; the hills were shrunk, the brooks
were flowing languidly with scanty streams, the sky seemed
grey; and when you turned to the Firs, they were standing
there no darker or more dreary than the other trees. The huts
behind them were no longer frightful; and several inhabitants of the village came and told about the fearful night, and
how they had been across the spot where the gipsies had
lived; how these people must have left the place at last, for
their huts were standing empty, and within had quite a common look, just like the dwellings of other poor people: some
of their household gear was left behind.

Elfrida in secret said to her mother: "I could not sleep last
night; and in my fright at the noise, I was praying from the
bottom of my heart, when the door suddenly opened, and my
playmate entered to take leave of me. She had a travelling
pouch slung round her, a hat on her head, and a large staff in
her hand. She was very angry at thee; since on thy account
she had now to suffer the severest and most painful punish-
ments, as she had always been so fond of thee; for all of
them, she said, were very loath to leave this quarter."

Mary forbade her to speak of this; and now the ferryman
came across the river, and told them new wonders. As it was

growing dark, a stranger man of large size had come to him, and hired his boat till sunrise; and with this condition, that the boatman should remain quiet in his house, at least should not cross the threshold of his door. "I was frightened," continued the old man, "and the strange bargain would not let me sleep. I slipped softly to the window, and looked towards the river. Great clouds were driving restlessly through the sky, and the distant woods were rustling fearfully; it was as if my cottage shook, and moans and lamentations glided round it. On a sudden, I perceived a white streaming light, that grew broader and broader, like many thousands of falling stars; sparkling and waving, it proceeded forward from the dark Fir-ground, moved over the fields, and spread itself along towards the river. Then I heard a trampling, a jingling, a bustling, and rushing, nearer and nearer; it went forwards to my boat, and all stept into it, men and women, as it seemed, and children; and the tall stranger ferried them over. In the river were by the boat swimming many thousands of glittering forms; in the air white clouds and lights were wavering; and all lamented and bewailed that they must travel forth so far, far away, and leave their beloved dwelling. The noise of the rudder and the water creaked and gurgled between-whiles, and then suddenly there would be silence. Many a time the boat landed, and went back, and was again laden; many heavy casks, too, they took along with them, which multitudes of horrid-looking little fellows carried and rolled; whether they were devils or goblins, Heaven only knows. Then came, in waving brightness, a stately freight; it seemed an old man, mounted on a small white horse, and all were crowding round him. I saw nothing of the horse but its head; for the rest of it was covered with costly glittering cloths and trappings: on his brow the old man had a crown, so bright that, as he came across, I thought the sun was rising there, and the redness of the dawn glimmering in my eyes. Thus it went on all night; I at last fell asleep in the tumult, half in joy, half in terror. In the morning all was still; but the river is, as it were, run off, and I know not how I am to steer my boat in it now."

The same year there came a blight; the woods died away, the springs ran dry; and the scene, which had once been the joy of every traveller, was in autumn standing waste, naked and bald; scarcely showing here and there, in the sea of sand, a spot or two where grass, with a dingy greenness, still grew up. The fruit-trees all withered, the vines faded away, and the aspect of the place became so melancholy, that the Count, with his people, next year left the castle, which in time decayed and fell to ruins.

Elfrida gazed on her rose day and night with deep longing, and thought of her kind playmate; and as it drooped and withered, so did she also hang her head; and before the spring the little maiden had herself faded away. Mary often stood upon the spot before the hut, and wept for the happiness that had departed. She wasted herself away like her child, and in a few years she too was gone. Old Martin, with his son-in-law, returned to the quarter where he had lived before.

The Golden Key

by George MacDonald

In "On Fairy-stories" Tolkien wrote that fairy tales might "be made a vehicle of Mystery. This at least is what George MacDonald attempted, achieving stories of power and beauty when he succeeded, as in 'The Golden Key' (which he called a fairy tale); and even when he partly failed, as in *Lilith* (which he called a romance)." Tolkien also knew well MacDonald's children's books *The Princess and the Goblin* and *The Princess and Curdie,* both of which influenced Tolkien's depiction of goblins in *The Hobbit.*

In 1964, Tolkien was asked to contribute a preface to an illustrated edition of "The Golden Key." As Tolkien reread the story, his opinion of MacDonald changed dramatically, and he found the story "ill-written, incoherent, and bad, in spite of a few memorable passages." Tolkien began the preface, but it quickly took on a life of its own, becoming a story whose protagonist, like the boy in "The Golden Key," lived near the borders of Faerie. Tolkien called his new story *Smith of Wootton Major;* it was published as a small book in 1967. Tolkien never went back to the preface, and to an interviewer in 1965 he said, "I now find that I can't stand George MacDonald's books at any price at all." To another friend he called MacDonald an "old grandmother" who preached instead of writing. This judgment seems unduly harsh, and a fairer assessment of MacDonald would recognize both his strengths as a writer (e.g., imagination and atmosphere) and his weaknesses (e.g., the tendency toward didacticism).

"The Golden Key" was first published in MacDonald's volume *Dealing with the Fairies* (1867).

THERE was a boy who used to sit in the twilight and listen to his great-aunt's stories.

She told him that if he could reach the place where the end of the rainbow stands he would find there a golden key.

"And what is the key for?" the boy would ask. "What is it the key of? What will it open?"

"That nobody knows," his aunt would reply. "He has to find that out."

"I suppose, being gold," the boy once said, thoughtfully, "that I could get a good deal of money for it if I sold it."

"Better never find it than sell it," returned his aunt.

And then the boy went to bed and dreamed about the golden key.

Now all that his great-aunt told the boy about the golden key would have been nonsense, had it not been that their little house stood on the borders of Fairyland. For it is perfectly well known that out of Fairyland nobody ever can find where the rainbow stands. The creature takes such good care of its golden key, always flitting from place to place, lest any one should find it! But in Fairyland it is quite different. Things that look real in this country look very thin indeed in Fairyland, while some of the things that here cannot stand still for a moment, will not move there. So it was not in the least absurd of the old lady to tell her nephew such things about the golden key.

"Did you ever know anybody to find it?" he asked, one evening.

"Yes. Your father, I believe, found it."

"And what did he do with it, can you tell me?"

"He never told me."

"What was it like?"

"He never showed it to me."

"How does a new key come there always?"

"I don't know. There it is."

"Perhaps it is the rainbow's egg."

"Perhaps it is. You will be a happy boy if you find the nest."

"Perhaps it comes tumbling down the rainbow from the sky."

"Perhaps it does."

One evening, in summer, he went into his own room, and stood at the lattice-window, and gazed into the forest which fringed the outskirts of Fairyland. It came close up to his great-aunt's garden, and, indeed, sent some straggling trees into it. The forest lay to the east, and the sun, which was setting behind the cottage, looked straight into the dark wood with his level red eye. The trees were all old, and had few branches below, so that the sun could see a great way into the forest; and the boy, being keen-sighted, could see almost as far as the sun. The trunks stood like rows of red columns in the shine of the red sun, and he could see down aisle after aisle in the vanishing distance. And as he gazed into the forest he began to feel as if the trees were all waiting for him, and had something they could not go on with till he came to them. But he was hungry, and wanted his supper. So he lingered.

Suddenly, far among the trees, as far as the sun could shine, he saw a glorious thing. It was the end of a rainbow, large and brilliant. He could count all the seven colours, and could see shade after shade beyond the violet; while before the red stood a colour more gorgeous and mysterious still. It was a colour he had never seen before. Only the spring of the rainbow-arch was visible. He could see nothing of it above the trees.

"The golden key!" he said to himself, and darted out of the house, and into the wood.

He had not gone far before the sun set. But the rainbow only glowed the brighter. For the rainbow of Fairyland is not dependent upon the sun as ours is. The trees welcomed him. The bushes made way for him. The rainbow grew larger and brighter; and at length he found himself within two trees of it.

It was a grand sight, burning away there in silence, with its gorgeous, its lovely, its delicate colours, each distinct, all combining. He could now see a great deal more of it. It rose high into the blue heavens, but bent so little that he could not tell how high the crown of the arch must reach. It was still only a small portion of a huge bow.

He stood gazing at it till he forgot himself with delight—even forgot the key which he had come to seek. And as he stood it grew more wonderful still: For in each of the colours, which was as large as the column of a church, he could faintly see beautiful forms slowly ascending as if by the steps of a winding stair. The forms appeared irregularly—now one, now many, now several, now none—men and women and children—all different, all beautiful.

He drew nearer to the rainbow. It vanished. He started back a step in dismay. It was there again, as beautiful as ever. So he contented himself with standing as near it as he might, and watching the forms that ascended the glorious colours towards the unknown height of the arch, which did not end abruptly, but faded away in the blue air, so gradually that he could not say where it ceased.

When the thought of the golden key returned, the boy very wisely proceeded to mark out in his mind the space covered by the foundation of the rainbow, in order that he might know where to search, should the rainbow disappear. It was based chiefly upon a bed of moss.

Meantime it had grown quite dark in the wood. The rainbow alone was visible by its own light. But the moment the moon rose the rainbow vanished. Nor could any change of place restore the vision to the boy's eyes. So he threw himself down on the mossy bed, to wait till the sunlight would give him a chance of finding the key. There he fell fast asleep.

When he woke in the morning the sun was looking straight into his eyes. He turned away from it, and the same moment saw a brilliant little thing lying on the moss within a foot of his face. It was the golden key. The pipe of it was of plain gold, as bright as gold could be. The handle was curiously wrought and set with sapphires. In a terror of delight he put out his hand and took it, and had it.

He lay for a while, turning it over and over, and feeding his eyes upon its beauty. Then he jumped to his feet, remembering that the pretty thing was of no use to him yet. Where was the lock to which the key belonged? It must be somewhere, for how could anybody be so silly as to make a key for which there was no lock? Where should he go to look for it? He gazed about him, up into the air, down to the earth, but saw no keyhole in the clouds, in the grass, or in the trees.

Just as he began to grow disconsolate, however, he saw something glimmering in the wood. It was a mere glimmer that he saw, but he took it for a glimmer of rainbow, and went towards it.—And now I will go back to the borders of the forest.

Not far from the house where the boy had lived, there was another house, the owner of which was a merchant, who was much away from home. He had lost his wife some years before, and had only one child, a little girl, whom he left to the charge of two servants, who were very idle and careless. So she was neglected and left untidy, and was sometimes illused besides.

Now it is well known that the little creatures commonly called fairies, though there are many different kinds of fairies in Fairyland, have an exceeding dislike to untidiness. Indeed, they are quite spiteful to slovenly people. Being used to all the lovely ways of the trees and flowers, and to the neatness of the birds and all woodland creatures, it makes them feel miserable, even in their deep woods and on their grassy carpets, to think that within the same moonlight lies a dirty, uncomfortable, slovenly house. And this makes them angry with the people that live in it, and they would gladly drive them out of the world if they could. They want the whole earth nice and clean. So they pinch the maids black and blue, and play them all manner of uncomfortable tricks.

But this house was quite a shame, and the fairies in the forest could not endure it. They tried everything on the maids without effect, and at last resolved upon making a clean riddance, beginning with the child. They ought to have known that it was not her fault, but they have little principle and much mischief in them, and they thought that if they got rid of her the maids would be sure to be turned away.

So one evening, the poor little girl having been put to bed early, before the sun was down, the servants went off to the village, locking the door behind them. The child did not know she was alone, and lay contentedly looking out of her window towards the forest, of which, however, she could not see much, because of the ivy and other creeping plants which had straggled across her window. All at once she saw an ape making faces at her out of the mirror, and the heads carved upon a great old wardrobe grinning fearfully. Then two old spider-legged chairs came forward into the middle of the room, and began to dance a queer, old-fashioned dance. This set her laughing, and she forgot the ape and the grinning heads. So the fairies saw they had made a mistake, and sent the chairs back to their places. But they knew that she had been reading the story of Silverhair all day. So the next moment she heard the voices of the three bears upon the stair, big voice, middle voice, and little voice, and she heard their soft, heavy tread, as if they had had stockings over their boots, coming nearer and nearer to the door of her room, till she could bear it no longer. She did just as Silverhair did, and as the fairies wanted her to do: she darted to the window, pulled it open, got upon the ivy, and so scrambled to the ground. She then fled to the forest as fast as she could run.

Now, although she did not know it, this was the very best way she could have gone; for nothing is ever so mischievous in its own place as it is out of it; and, besides, these mischievous creatures were only the children of Fairyland, as it were, and there are many other beings there as well; and if a wanderer gets in among them, the good ones will always help him more than the evil ones will be able to hurt him.

The sun was now set, and the darkness coming on, but the child thought of no danger but the bears behind her. If she had looked round, however, she would have seen that she was followed by a very different creature from a bear. It was a curious creature, made like a fish, but covered, instead of scales, with feathers of all colours, sparkling like those of a humming-bird. It had fins, not wings, and swam through the air as a fish does through the water. Its head was like the head of a small owl.

After running a long way, and as the last of the light was disappearing, she passed under a tree with drooping branches. It propped its branches to the ground all about her, and caught her as in a trap. She struggled to get out, but the branches pressed her closer and closer to the trunk. She was in great terror and distress, when the air-fish, swimming into the thicket of branches, began tearing them with its beak. They loosened their hold at once, and the creature went on attacking them, till at length they let the child go. Then the air-fish came from behind her, and swam on in front, glittering and sparkling all lovely colours; and she followed.

It led her gently along till all at once it swam in at a cottage-door. The child followed still. There was a bright fire in the middle of the floor, upon which stood a pot without a lid, full of water that boiled and bubbled furiously. The air-fish swam straight to the pot and into the boiling water, where it lay quiet. A beautiful woman rose from the opposite side of the fire and came to meet the girl. She took her up in her arms, and said,—

"Ah, you are come at last! I have been looking for you a long time."

She sat down with her on her lap, and there the girl sat staring at her. She had never seen anything so beautiful. She was tall and strong, with white arms and neck, and a delicate flush on her face. The child could not tell what was the colour of her hair, but could not help thinking it had a tinge of dark green. She had not one ornament upon her, but she looked as if she had just put off quantities of diamonds and emeralds. Yet here she was in the simplest, poorest little cottage, where she was evidently at home. She was dressed in shining green.

The girl looked at the lady, and the lady looked at the girl.

"What is your name?" asked the lady.

"The servants always called me Tangle."

"Ah, that was because your hair was so untidy. But that was their fault, the naughty women! Still it is a pretty name, and I will call you Tangle too. You must not mind my asking you questions, for you may ask me the same questions, every one of them, and any others that you like. How old are you?"

"Ten," answered Tangle.

"You don't look like it," said the lady.

"How old are you, please?" returned Tangle.

"Thousands of years old," answered the lady.

"You don't look like it," said Tangle.

"Don't I? I think I do. Don't you see how beautiful I am?"

And her great blue eyes looked down on the little Tangle, as if all the stars in the sky were melted in them to make their brightness.

"Ah! but," said Tangle, "when people live long they grow old. At least I always thought so."

"I have no time to grow old," said the lady. "I am too busy for that. It is very idle to grow old.—But I cannot have my little girl so untidy. Do you know I can't find a clean spot on your face to kiss?"

"Perhaps," suggested Tangle, feeling ashamed, but not too much so to say a word for herself—"perhaps that is because the tree made me cry so."

"My poor darling!" said the lady, looking now as if the moon were melted in her eyes, and kissing her little face, dirty as it was, "the naughty tree must suffer for making a girl cry."

"And what is your name, please?" asked Tangle.

"Grandmother," answered the lady.

"Is it, really?"

"Yes, indeed. I never tell stories, even in fun."

"How good of you!"

"I couldn't if I tried. It would come true if I said it, and then I should be punished enough."

And she smiled like the sun through a summer-shower.

"But now," she went on, "I must get you washed and dressed, and then we shall have some supper."

"Oh! I had supper long ago," said Tangle.

"Yes, indeed you had," answered the lady—"three years ago. You don't know that it is three years since you ran away from the bears. You are thirteen and more now."

Tangle could only stare. She felt quite sure it was true.

"You will not be afraid of anything I do with you—will you?" said the lady.

"I will try very hard not to be; but I can't be certain, you know," replied Tangle.

"I like your saying so, and I shall be quite satisfied," answered the lady.

She took off the girl's night-gown, rose with her in her arms, and going to the wall of the cottage, opened a door. Then Tangle saw a deep tank, the sides of which were filled with green plants, which had flowers of all colours. There was a roof over it like the roof of the cottage. It was filled with beautiful clear water, in which swam a multitude of such fishes as the one that had led her to the cottage. It was the light their colours gave that showed the place in which they were.

The lady spoke some words Tangle could not understand, and threw her into the tank.

The fishes came crowding about her. Two or three of them got under her head and kept it up. The rest of them rubbed themselves all over her, and with their wet feathers washed her quite clean. Then the lady, who had been looking on all the time, spoke again; whereupon some thirty or forty of the fishes rose out of the water underneath Tangle, and so bore her up to the arms the lady held out to take her. She carried her back to the fire, and, having dried her well, opened a chest, and taking out the finest linen garments, smelling of grass and lavender, put them upon her, and over all a green dress, just like her own, shining like hers, and soft like hers, and going into just such lovely folds from the waist, where it was tied with a brown cord, to her bare feet.

"Won't you give me a pair of shoes too, grandmother?" said Tangle.

"No, my dear; no shoes. Look here. I wear no shoes."

So saying, she lifted her dress a little, and there were the loveliest white feet, but no shoes. Then Tangle was content to go without shoes too. And the lady sat down with her again, and combed her hair, and brushed it, and then left it to dry while she got the supper.

First she got bread out of one hole in the wall; then milk out of another; then several kinds of fruit out of a third; and then she went to the pot on the fire, and took out the fish now nicely cooked, and, as soon as she had pulled off its feathered skin, ready to be eaten.

"But," exclaimed Tangle. And she stared at the fish, and could say no more.

"I know what you mean," returned the lady. "You do not like to eat the messenger that brought you home. But it is the kindest return you can make. The creature was afraid to go until it saw me put the pot on, and heard me promise it should be boiled the moment it returned with you. Then it darted out of the door at once. You saw it go into the pot of itself the moment it entered, did you not?"

"I did," answered Tangle, "and I thought it very strange; but then I saw you, and forgot all about the fish."

"In Fairyland," resumed the lady, as they sat down to the

table, "the ambition of the animals is to be eaten by the people; for that is their highest end in that condition. But they are not therefore destroyed. Out of that pot comes something more than the dead fish, you will see."

Tangle now remarked that the lid was on the pot. But the lady took no further notice of it till they had eaten the fish, which Tangle found nicer than any fish she had ever tasted before. It was as white as snow, and as delicate as cream. And the moment she had swallowed a mouthful of it, a change she could not describe began to take place in her. She heard a murmuring all about her, which became more and more articulate, and at length, as she went on eating, grew intelligible. By the time she had finished her share, the sounds of all the animals in the forest came crowding through the door to her ears; for the door still stood wide open, though it was pitch dark outside; and they were no longer sounds only; they were speech, and speech that she could understand. She could tell what the insects in the cottage were saying to each other too. She had even a suspicion that the trees and flowers all about the cottage were holding midnight communications with each other; but what they said she could not hear.

As soon as the fish was eaten, the lady went to the fire and took the lid off the pot. A lovely little creature in human shape, with large white wings, rose out of it, and flew round and round the roof of the cottage; then dropped, fluttering, and nestled in the lap of the lady. She spoke to it some strange words, carried it to the door, and threw it out into the darkness. Tangle heard the flapping of its wings die away in the distance.

"Now have we done the fish any harm?" she said, returning.

"No," answered Tangle, "I do not think we have. I should not mind eating one every day."

"They must wait their time, like you and me too, my little Tangle."

And she smiled a smile which the sadness in it made more lovely.

"But," she continued, "I think we may have one for supper to-morrow."

So saying she went to the door of the tank, and spoke; and now Tangle understood her perfectly.

"I want one of you," she said,—"the wisest."

Thereupon the fishes got together in the middle of the tank, with their heads forming a circle above the water, and their tails a larger circle beneath it. They were holding a council, in which their relative wisdom should be determined. At length one of them flew up into the lady's hand, looking lively and ready.

"You know where the rainbow stands?" she asked.

"Yes, mother, quite well," answered the fish.

"Bring home a young man you will find there, who does not know where to go."

The fish was out of the door in a moment. Then the lady told Tangle it was time to go to bed; and, opening another door in the side of the cottage, showed her a little arbour, cool and green, with a bed of purple heath growing in it, upon which she threw a large wrapper made of the feathered skins of the wise fishes, shining gorgeous in the firelight. Tangle was soon lost in the strangest, loveliest dreams. And the beautiful lady was in every one of her dreams.

In the morning she woke to the rustling of leaves over her head, and the sound of running water. But, to her surprise, she could find no door—nothing but the moss-grown wall of the cottage. So she crept through an opening in the arbour, and stood in the forest. Then she bathed in a stream that ran merrily through the trees, and felt happier; for having once been in her grandmother's pond, she must be clean and tidy ever after; and, having put on her green dress, felt like a lady.

She spent that day in the wood, listening to the birds and beasts and creeping things. She understood all that they said, though she could not repeat a word of it; and every kind had a different language, while there was a common though more limited understanding between all the inhabitants of the forest. She saw nothing of the beautiful lady, but she felt that she was near her all the time; and she took care not to go out of sight of the cottage. It was round, like a snow-hut or a wigwam; and she could see neither door nor window in it. The fact was, it had no windows; and though it was full of doors, they all opened from the inside, and could not even be seen from the outside.

She was standing at the foot of a tree in the twilight, listening to a quarrel between a mole and a squirrel, in which the mole told the squirrel that the tail was the best of him, and the squirrel called the mole Spade-fists, when, the darkness having deepened around her, she became aware of something shining in her face, and looking round, saw that the door of the cottage was open, and the red light of the fire flowing from it like a river through the darkness. She left Mole and Squirrel to settle matters as they might, and darted off to the cottage. Entering, she found the pot boiling on the fire, and the grand, lovely lady sitting on the other side of it.

"I've been watching you all day," said the lady. "You shall have something to eat by-and-by, but we must wait till our supper comes home."

She took Tangle on her knee, and began to sing to her—such songs as made her wish she could listen to them for ever. But at length in rushed the shining fish, and snuggled down in the pot. It was followed by a youth who had outgrown his worn garments. His face was ruddy with health, and in his hand he carried a little jewel, which sparkled in the firelight.

The first words the lady said were,—

"What is that in your hand, Mossy?"

Now Mossy was the name his companions had given him, because he had a favourite stone covered with moss, on which he used to sit whole days reading; and they said the moss had begun to grow upon him too.

Mossy held out his hand. The moment the lady saw that it was the golden key, she rose from her chair, kissed Mossy on the forehead, made him sit down on her seat, and stood before him like a servant. Mossy could not bear this, and rose at once. But the lady begged him, with tears in her beautiful eyes, to sit, and let her wait on him.

"But you are a great, splendid, beautiful lady," said Mossy.

"Yes, I am. But I work all day long—that is my pleasure; and you will have to leave me so soon!"

"How do you know that, if you please, madam?" asked Mossy.

"Because you have got the golden key."

"But I don't know what it is for. I can't find the key-hole. Will you tell me what to do?"

"You must look for the key-hole. That is your work. I cannot help you. I can only tell you that if you look for it you will find it."

"What kind of a box will it open? What is there inside?"

"I do not know. I dream about it, but I know nothing."

"Must I go at once?"

"You may stop here to-night, and have some of my supper. But you must go in the morning. All I can do for you is to give you clothes. Here is a girl called Tangle, whom you must take with you."

"That *will* be nice," said Mossy.

"No, no!" said Tangle. "I don't want to leave you, please, grandmother."

"You must go with him, Tangle. I am sorry to lose you, but it will be the best thing for you. Even the fishes, you see, have to go into the pot, and then out into the dark. If you fall in with the Old Man of the Sea, mind you ask him whether he has not got some more fishes ready for me. My tank is getting thin."

So saying, she took the fish from the pot, and put the lid on as before. They sat down and ate the fish and then the winged creature rose from the pot, circled the roof, and settled on the lady's lap. She talked to it, carried it to the door, and threw it out into the dark. They heard the flap of its wings die away in the distance.

The lady then showed Mossy into just such another chamber as that of Tangle; and in the morning he found a suit of clothes laid beside him. He looked very handsome in them. But the wearer of Grandmother's clothes never thinks about how he or she looks, but thinks always how handsome other people are.

Tangle was very unwilling to go.

"Why should I leave you? I don't know the young man," she said to the lady.

"I am never allowed to keep my children long. You need not go with him except you please, but you must go some day; and I should like you to go with him, for he has found the golden key. No girl need be afraid to go with a youth that has the golden key. You will take care of her, Mossy, will you not?"

"That I will," said Mossy.

And Tangle cast a glance at him, and thought she should like to go with him.

"And," said the lady, "if you should lose each other as you go through the—the—I never can remember the name of that country,—do not be afraid, but go on and on."

She kissed Tangle on the mouth and Mossy on the forehead, led them to the door, and waved her hand eastward. Mossy and Tangle took each other's hand and walked away into the depth of the forest. In his right hand Mossy held the golden key.

They wandered thus a long way, with endless amusement from the talk of the animals. They soon learned enough of their language to ask them necessary questions. The squirrels were always friendly, and gave them nuts out of their own hoards; but the bees were selfish and rude, justifying themselves on the ground that Tangle and Mossy were not subjects of their queen, and charity must begin at home, though indeed they had not one drone in their poorhouse at the time. Even the blinking moles would fetch them an earth-nut or a truffle now and then, talking as if their mouths, as well as their eyes and ears, were full of cotton wool, or their own velvety fur. By the time they got out of the forest they were very fond of each other, and Tangle was not in the least sorry that her grandmother had sent her away with Mossy.

At length the trees grew smaller, and stood farther apart, and the ground began to rise, and it got more and more steep, till the trees were all left behind, and the two were climbing a narrow path with rocks on each side. Suddenly they came upon a rude doorway, by which they entered a narrow gallery cut in the rock. It grew darker and darker, till it was pitch-dark, and they had to feel their way. At length the light began to return, and at last they came out upon a narrow path on the face of a lofty precipice. This path went winding down the rock to a wide plain, circular in shape, and surrounded on all sides by mountains. Those opposite to them were a great way off, and towered to an awful height, shooting up sharp, blue, ice-enamelled pinnacles. An utter silence reigned where they stood. Not even the sound of water reached them.

Looking down, they could not tell whether the valley below was a grassy plain or a great still lake. They had never seen any space look like it. The way to it was difficult and dangerous, but down the narrow path they went, and reached the bottom in safety. They found it composed of smooth, light-coloured sandstone, undulating in parts, but mostly level. It was no wonder to them now that they had not been able to tell what it was, for this surface was everywhere crowded with shadows. It was a sea of shadows. The mass was chiefly made up of the shadows of leaves innumerable, of all lovely and imaginative forms, waving to and fro, float-ing and quivering in the breath of a breeze whose motion was unfelt, whose sound was unheard. No forests clothed the mountain-sides, no trees were anywhere to be seen, and yet the shadows of the leaves, branches, and stems of all various trees covered the valley as far as their eyes could reach. They soon spied the shadows of flowers mingled with those of the leaves, and now and then the shadow of a bird with open beak, and throat distended with song. At times would appear the forms of strange, graceful creatures, running up and down the shadow-holes and along the branches, to disappear in the wind-tossed foliage. As they walked they waded knee-deep in the lovely lake. For the shadows were not merely lying on the surface of the ground, but heaped up above it like substantial forms of darkness, as if they had been cast upon a thousand different planes of air. Tangle and Mossy often lifted their heads and gazed upwards to descry whence the shadows came; but they could see nothing more than a bright mist spread above them, higher than the tops of the mountains, which stood clear against it. No forests, no leaves, no birds were visible.

After a while, they reached more open spaces, where the shadows were thinner; and came even to portions over which shadows only flitted, leaving them clear for such as might follow. Now a wonderful form, half bird-like, half human, would float across on outspread sailing pinions. Anon an exquisite shadow group of gambolling children would be followed by the loveliest female form, and that again by the grand stride of a Titanic shape, each disappearing in the surrounding press of shadowy foliage. Sometimes a profile of unspeakable beauty or grandeur would appear for a moment and vanish. Sometimes they seemed lovers that passed linked arm in arm, sometimes father and son, sometimes brothers in loving contest, sometimes sisters entwined in gracefullest community of complex form. Sometimes wild horses would tear across, free, or bestrode by noble shadows of ruling men. But some of the things which pleased them most they never knew how to describe.

About the middle of the plain they sat down to rest in the heart of a heap of shadows. After sitting for a while, each, looking up, saw the other in tears: they were each longing after the country whence the shadows fell.

"We *must* find the country from which the shadows come," said Mossy.

"We must, dear Mossy," responded Tangle. "What if your golden key should be the key to *it*?"

"Ah! that would be grand," returned Mossy.—"But we must rest here for a little, and then we shall be able to cross the plain before night."

So he lay down on the ground, and about him on every side, and over his head, was the constant play of the wonderful shadows. He could look through them, and see the one behind the other, till they mixed in a mass of darkness. Tangle, too, lay admiring, and wondering, and longing after the country whence the shadows came. When they were rested they rose and pursued their journey.

How long they were in crossing this plain I cannot tell; but before night Mossy's hair was streaked with gray, and Tangle had got wrinkles on her forehead.

As evening drew on, the shadows fell deeper and rose higher. At length they reached a place where they rose above their heads, and made all dark around them. Then they took hold of each other's hand, and walked on in silence and in some dismay. They felt the gathering darkness, and something strangely solemn besides, and the beauty of the shadows ceased to delight them. All at once Tangle found that she had not a hold of Mossy's hand, though when she lost it she could not tell.

"Mossy, Mossy!" she cried aloud in terror.

But no Mossy replied.

A moment after, the shadows sank to her feet, and down under her feet, and the mountains rose before her. She turned towards the gloomy region she had left, and called once more upon Mossy. There the gloom lay tossing and heaving, a dark, stormy, foamless sea of shadows, but no Mossy rose out of it, or came climbing up the hill on which she stood. She threw herself down and wept in despair.

Suddenly she remembered that the beautiful lady had told

them, if they lost each other in a country of which she could not remember the name, they were not to be afraid, but to go straight on.

"And besides," she said to herself, "Mossy has the golden key, and so no harm will come to him, I do believe."

She rose from the ground, and went on.

Before long she arrived at a precipice, in the face of which a stair was cut. When she had ascended halfway, the stair ceased, and the path led straight into the mountain. She was afraid to enter, and turning again towards the stair, grew giddy at sight of the depth beneath her, and was forced to throw herself down in the mouth of the cave.

When she opened her eyes, she saw a beautiful little creature with wings standing beside her, waiting.

"I know you," said Tangle. "You are my fish."

"Yes. But I am a fish no longer. I am an aëranth now."

"What is that?" asked Tangle.

"What you see I am," answered the shape. "And I am come to lead you through the mountain."

"Oh! thank you, dear fish—aëranth, I mean," returned Tangle, rising.

Thereupon the aëranth took to his wings, and flew on through the long, narrow passage, reminding Tangle very much of the way he had swum on before when he was a fish. And the moment his white wings moved, they began to throw off a continuous shower of sparks of all colours, which lighted up the passage before them.—All at once he vanished, and Tangle heard a low, sweet sound, quite different from the rush and crackle of his wings. Before her was an open arch, and through it came light, mixed with the sound of sea-waves.

She hurried out, and fell, tired and happy, upon the yellow sand of the shore. There she lay, half asleep with weariness and rest, listening to the low plash and retreat of the tiny waves, which seemed ever enticing the land to leave off being land, and become sea. And as she lay, her eyes were fixed upon the foot of a great rainbow standing far away against the sky on the other side of the sea. At length she fell fast asleep.

When she awoke, she saw an old man with long white hair down to his shoulders, leaning upon a stick covered with green buds, and so bending over her.

"What do you want here, beautiful woman?" he said.

"Am I beautiful? I am so glad!" answered Tangle, rising. "My grandmother is beautiful."

"Yes. But what do you want?" he repeated, kindly.

"I think I want you. Are not you the Old Man of the Sea?"

"I am."

"Then grandmother says, have you any more fishes ready for her?"

"We will go and see, my dear," answered the Old Man, speaking yet more kindly than before. "And I can do something for you, can I not?"

"Yes—show me the way up to the country from which the shadows fall," said Tangle.

For there she hoped to find Mossy again.

"Ah! indeed, that would be worth doing," said the Old Man. "But I cannot, for I do not know the way myself. But I will send you to the Old Man of the Earth. Perhaps he can tell you. He is much older than I am."

Leaning on his staff, he conducted her along the shore to a steep rock, that looked like a petrified ship turned upside down. The door of it was the rudder of a great vessel, ages ago at the bottom of the sea. Immediately within the door was a stair in the rock, down which the Old Man went, and Tangle followed. At the bottom the Old Man had his house, and there he lived.

As soon as she entered it, Tangle heard a strange noise, unlike anything she had ever heard before. She soon found that it was the fishes talking. She tried to understand what they said; but their speech was so old-fashioned, and rude, and undefined, that she could not make much of it.

"I will go and see about those fishes for my daughter," said the Old Man of the Sea.

And moving a slide in the wall of his house, he first looked out, and then tapped upon a thick piece of crystal that filled the round opening. Tangle came up behind him, and peeping through the window into the heart of the great deep green ocean, saw the most curious creatures, some very ugly, all very odd, and with especially queer mouths, swimming about everywhere, above and below, but all coming towards the window in answer to the tap of the Old Man of the Sea. Only a few could get their mouths against the glass; but those who were floating miles away yet turned their heads towards it. The Old Man looked through the whole flock carefully for some minutes, and then turning to Tangle, said,—

"I am sorry I have not got one ready yet. I want more time than she does. But I will send some as soon as I can."

He then shut the slide.

Presently a great noise arose in the sea. The Old Man opened the slide again, and tapped on the glass, whereupon the fishes were all as still as sleep.

"They were only talking about you," he said. "And they do speak such nonsense!—To-morrow," he continued, "I must show you the way to the Old Man of the Earth. He lives a long way from here."

"Do let me go at once," said Tangle.

"No. That is not possible. You must come this way first."

He led her to a hole in the wall, which she had not observed before. It was covered with the green leaves and white blossoms of a creeping plant.

"Only white-blossoming plants can grow under the sea," said the Old Man. "In there you will find a bath, in which you must lie till I call you."

Tangle went in, and found a smaller room or cave, in the further corner of which was a great basin hollowed out of a rock, and half-full of the clearest sea-water. Little streams were constantly running into it from cracks in the wall of the cavern. It was polished quite smooth inside, and had a carpet of yellow sand in the bottom of it. Large green leaves and white flowers of various plants crowded up over it, draping and covering it almost entirely.

No sooner was she undressed and lying in the bath, than she began to feel as if the water were sinking into her, and she were receiving all the good of sleep without undergoing its forgetfulness. She felt the good coming all the time. And she grew happier and more hopeful than she had been since she lost Mossy. But she could not help thinking how very sad it was for a poor old man to live there all alone, and have to take care of a whole seaful of stupid and riotous fishes.

After about an hour, as she thought, she heard his voice calling her, and rose out of the bath. All the fatigue and aching of her long journey had vanished. She was as whole, and strong, and well as if she had slept for seven days.

Returning to the opening that led into the other part of the house, she started back with amazement, for through it she saw the form of a grand man, with a majestic and beautiful face, waiting for her.

"Come," he said; "I see you are ready."

She entered with reverence.

"Where is the Old Man of the Sea?" she asked, humbly.

"There is no one here but me," he answered, smiling. "Some people call me the Old Man of the Sea. Others have another name for me, and are terribly frightened when they meet me taking a walk by the shore. Therefore I avoid being seen by them, for they are so afraid, that they never see what I really am. You see me now.—But I must show you the way to the Old Man of the Earth."

He led her into the cave where the bath was, and there she saw, in the opposite corner, a second opening in the rock.

"Go down that stair, and it will bring you to him," said the Old Man of the Sea.

With humble thanks Tangle took her leave. She went down the winding-stair, till she began to fear there was no end to it.

Still down and down it went, rough and broken, with springs of water bursting out of the rocks and running down the steps beside her. It was quite dark about her, and yet she could see. For after being in that bath, people's eyes always give out a light they can see by. There were no creeping things in the way. All was safe and pleasant, though so dark and damp and deep.

At last there was not one step more, and she found herself in a glimmering cave. On a stone in the middle of it sat a figure with its back towards her—the figure of an old man bent double with age. From behind she could see his white beard spread out on the rocky floor in front of him. He did not move as she entered, so she passed round that she might stand before him and speak to him. The moment she looked in his face, she saw that he was a youth of marvellous beauty. He sat entranced with the delight of what he beheld in a mirror of something like silver, which lay on the floor at his feet, and which from behind she had taken for his white beard. He sat on, heedless of her presence, pale with the joy of his vision. She stood and watched him. At length, all trembling, she spoke. But her voice made no sound. Yet the youth lifted up his head. He showed no surprise, however, at seeing her—only smiled a welcome.

"Are you the Old Man of the Earth?" Tangle had said.

And the youth answered, and Tangle heard him, though not with her ears:—

"I am. What can I do for you?"

"Tell me the way to the country whence the shadows fall."

"Ah! that I do not know. I only dream about it myself. I see its shadows sometimes in my mirror: the way to it I do not know. But I think the Old Man of the Fire must know. He is much older than I am. He is the oldest man of all."

"Where does he live?"

"I will show you the way to his place. I never saw him myself."

So saying, the young man rose, and then stood a while gazing at Tangle.

"I wish I could see that country too," he said. "But I must mind my work."

He led her to the side of the cave, and told her to lay her ear against the wall.

"What do you hear?" he asked.

"I hear," answered Tangle, "the sound of a great water running inside the rock."

"That river runs down to the dwelling of the oldest man of all—the Old Man of the Fire. I wish I could go to see him. But I must mind my work. That river is the only way to him."

Then the Old Man of the Earth stooped over the floor of the cave, raised a huge stone from it, and left it leaning. It disclosed a great hole that went plumb-down.

"That is the way," he said.

"But there are no stairs."

"You must throw yourself in. There is no other way."

She turned and looked him full in the face—stood so for a whole minute, as she thought: it was a whole year—then threw herself headlong into the hole.

When she came to herself, she found herself gliding down fast and deep. Her head was under water, but that did not signify, for, when she thought about it she could not remember that she had breathed once since her bath in the cave of the Old Man of the Sea. When she lifted up her head a sudden and fierce heat struck her, and she dropped it again instantly, and went sweeping on.

Gradually the stream grew shallower. At length she could hardly keep her head under. Then the water could carry her no farther. She rose from the channel, and went step for step down the burning descent. The water ceased altogether. The heat was terrible. She felt scorched to the bone, but it did not touch her strength. It grew hotter and hotter. She said, "I can bear it no longer." Yet she went on.

At the long last, the stair ended at a rude archway in an all

but glowing rock. Through this archway Tangle fell exhausted into a cool mossy cave. The floor and walls were
covered with moss—green, soft, and damp. A little stream
spouted from a rent in the rock and fell into a basin of moss.
She plunged her face into it and drank. Then she lifted her
head and looked around. Then she rose and looked again.
She saw no one in the cave. But the moment she stood upright she had a marvellous sense that she was in the secret
of the earth and all its ways. Everything she had seen, or
learned from books; all that her grandmother had said or
sung to her; all the talk of the beasts, birds, and fishes; all
that had happened to her on her journey with Mossy, and
since then in the heart of the earth with the Old Man and the
Older Man—all was plain: she understood it all, and saw that
everything meant the same thing, though she could not have
put it into words again.

The next moment she descried, in a corner of the cave, a
little naked child, sitting on the moss. He was playing with
balls of various colours and sizes, which he disposed in
strange figures upon the floor beside him. And now Tangle
felt that there was something in her knowledge which was
not in her understanding. For she knew there must be an infinite meaning in the change and sequence and individual
forms of the figures into which the child arranged the balls,
as well as in the varied harmonies of their colours, but what
it all meant she could not tell.* He went on busily, tirelessly,
playing his solitary game, without looking up, or seeming to
know that there was a stranger in his deep-withdrawn cell.
Diligently as a lace-maker shifts her bobbins, he shifted and
arranged his balls. Flashes of meaning would now pass from
them to Tangle, and now again all would be not merely obscure, but utterly dark. She stood looking for a long time, for
there was fascination in the sight; and the longer she looked
the more an indescribable vague intelligence went on rous-

* I think I must be indebted to Novalis for these geometrical figures.

ing itself in her mind. For seven years she had stood there watching the naked Child with his coloured balls, and it seemed to her like seven hours, when all at once the shape the balls took, she knew not why, reminded her of the Valley of Shadows, and she spoke:—

"Where is the Old Man of the Fire?" she said.

"Here I am," answered the Child, rising and leaving his balls on the moss. "What can I do for you?"

There was such an awfulness of absolute repose on the face of the Child that Tangle stood dumb before him. He had no smile, but the love in his large gray eyes was deep as the centre. And with the repose there lay on his face a shimmer as of moonlight, which seemed as if any moment it might break into such a ravishing smile as would cause the beholder to weep himself to death. But the smile never came, and the moonlight lay there unbroken. For the heart of the child was too deep for any smile to reach from it to his face.

"Are you the oldest man of all?" Tangle at length, although filled with awe, ventured to ask.

"Yes, I am. I am very, very old. I am able to help you, I know. I can help everybody."

And the Child drew near and looked up in her face so that she burst into tears.

"Can you tell me the way to the country the shadows fall from?" she sobbed.

"Yes. I know the way quite well. I go there myself sometimes. But you could not go my way; you are not old enough. I will show you how you can go."

"Do not send me out into the great heat again," prayed Tangle.

"I will not," answered the Child.

And he reached up, and put his little cool hand on her heart.

"Now," he said, "you can go. The fire will not burn you. Come."

He led her from the cave, and following him through another archway, she found herself in a vast desert of sand and rock. The sky of it was of rock, lowering over them like solid thunder-clouds; and the whole place was so hot that she saw, in bright rivulets, the yellow gold and white silver and red copper trickling molten from the rocks. But the heat never came near her.

When they had gone some distance, the Child turned up a great stone, and took something like an egg from under it. He next drew a long curved line in the sand with his finger, and laid the egg in it. He then spoke something Tangle could not understand. The egg broke, a small snake came out, and, lying in the line in the sand, grew and grew till he filled it. The moment he was thus full-grown, he began to glide away, undulating like a sea-wave.

"Follow that serpent," said the Child. "He will lead you the right way."

Tangle followed the serpent. But she could not go far without looking back at the marvellous Child. He stood alone in the midst of the glowing desert, beside a fountain of red flame that had burst forth at his feet, his naked whiteness glimmering a pale rosy red in the torrid fire. There he stood, looking after her, till, from the lengthening distance, she could see him no more. The serpent went straight on, turning neither to the right nor left.

Meantime Mossy had got out of the lake of shadows, and, following his mournful, lonely way, had reached the sea-shore. It was a dark, stormy evening. The sun had set. The wind was blowing from the sea. The waves had surrounded the rock within which lay the Old Man's house. A deep water rolled between it and the shore, upon which a majestic figure was walking alone.

Mossy went up to him and said,—

"Will you tell me where to find the Old Man of the Sea?"

"I am the Old Man of the Sea," the figure answered.

"I see a strong kingly man of middle age," returned Mossy.

Then the Old Man looked at him more intently, and said,—

"Your sight, young man, is better than that of most who take this way. The night is stormy: come to my house and tell me what I can do for you."

Mossy followed him. The waves flew from before the footsteps of the Old Man of the Sea, and Mossy followed upon dry sand.

When they had reached the cave, they sat down and gazed at each other.

Now Mossy was an old man by this time. He looked much older than the Old Man of the Sea, and his feet were very weary.

After looking at him for a moment, the Old Man took him by the hand and led him into his inner cave. There he helped him to undress, and laid him in the bath. And he saw that one of his hands Mossy did not open.

"What have you in that hand?" he asked.

Mossy opened his hand, and there lay the golden key.

"Ah!" said the Old Man, "that accounts for your knowing me. And I know the way you have to go."

"I want to find the country whence the shadows fall," said Mossy.

"I dare say you do. So do I. But meantime, one thing is certain.—What is that key for, do you think?"

"For a keyhole somewhere. But I don't know why I keep it. I never could find the keyhole. And I have lived a good while, I believe," said Mossy, sadly. "I'm not sure that I'm not old. I know my feet ache."

"Do they?" said the Old Man, as if he really meant to ask the question; and Mossy, who was still lying in the bath, watched his feet for a moment before he replied.

"No, they do not," he answered. "Perhaps I am not old either."

"Get up and look at yourself in the water."

He rose and looked at himself in the water, and there was not a gray hair on his head or a wrinkle on his skin.

"You have tasted of death now," said the Old Man. "Is it good?"

"It is good," said Mossy. "It is better than life."

"No," said the Old Man: "it is only more life.—Your feet will make no holes in the water now."

"What do you mean?"

"I will show you that presently."

They returned to the outer cave, and sat and talked together for a long time. At length the Old Man of the Sea, arose and said to Mossy,—

"Follow me."

He led him up the stair again, and opened another door. They stood on the level of the raging sea, looking towards the east. Across the waste of waters, against the bosom of a fierce black cloud, stood the foot of a rainbow, glowing in the dark.

"This indeed is my way," said Mossy, as soon as he saw the rainbow, and stepped out upon the sea. His feet made no holes in the water. He fought the wind, and clomb the waves, and went on towards the rainbow.

The storm died away. A lovely day and a lovelier night followed. A cool wind blew over the wide plain of the quiet ocean. And still Mossy journeyed eastward. But the rainbow had vanished with the storm.

Day after day he held on, and he thought he had no guide. He did not see how a shining fish under the waters directed his steps. He crossed the sea, and came to a great precipice of rock, up which he could discover but one path. Nor did this lead him farther than half-way up the rock, where it ended on a platform. Here he stood and pondered.—It could not be that the way stopped here, else what was the path for? It was a rough path, not very plain, yet certainly a path.—He examined the face of the rock. It was smooth as glass. But as his eyes kept roving hopelessly over it, something glittered, and he caught sight of a row of small sapphires. They bordered a little hole in the rock.

"The keyhole!" he cried.

He tried the key. It fitted. It turned. A great clang and clash, as of iron bolts on huge brazen caldrons, echoed thunderously within. He drew out the key. The rock in front of him began to fall. He retreated from it as far as the breadth of the platform would allow. A great slab fell at his feet. In front was still the solid rock, with this one slab fallen forward out of it. But the moment he stepped upon it, a second fell, just short of the edge of the first, making the next step of a stair, which thus kept dropping itself before him as he ascended into the heart of the precipice. It led him into a hall fit for such an approach—irregular and rude in formation, but floor, sides, pillars, and vaulted roof, all one mass of shining stones of every colour that light can show. In the centre stood seven columns, ranged from red to violet. And on the pedestal of one of them sat a woman, motionless, with her face bowed upon her knees. Seven years had she sat there waiting. She lifted her head as Mossy drew near. It was Tangle. Her hair had grown to her feet, and was rippled like the windless sea on broad sands. Her face was beautiful, like her grandmother's, and as still and peaceful as that of the Old Man of the Fire. Her form was tall and noble. Yet Mossy knew her at once.

"How beautiful you are, Tangle!" he said, in delight and astonishment.

"Am I?" she returned. "Oh, I have waited for you so long! But you, you are like the Old Man of the Sea. No. You are like the Old Man of the Earth. No, no. You are like the oldest man of all. You are like them all. And yet you are my own old Mossy! How did you come here? What did you do after I lost you? Did you find the key-hole? Have you got the key still?"

She had a hundred questions to ask him, and he a hundred more to ask her. They told each other all their adventures, and were as happy as man and woman could be. For they were younger and better, and stronger and wiser, than they had ever been before.

It began to grow dark. And they wanted more than ever to reach the country whence the shadows fall. So they looked about them for a way out of the cave. The door by which Mossy entered had closed again, and there was half a mile of rock between them and the sea. Neither could Tangle find the opening in the floor by which the serpent had led her thither. They searched till it grew so dark that they could see nothing, and gave it up.

After a while, however, the cave began to glimmer again. The light came from the moon, but it did not look like moon-light, for it gleamed through those seven pillars in the middle, and filled the place with all colours. And now Mossy saw that there was a pillar beside the red one, which he had not observed before. And it was of the same new colour that he had seen in the rainbow when he saw it first in the fairy forest. And on it he saw a sparkle of blue. It was the sapphires round the key-hole.

He took his key. It turned in the lock to the sounds of Æolian music. A door opened upon slow hinges, and disclosed a winding stair within. The key vanished from his fingers. Tangle went up. Mossy followed. The door closed behind them. They climbed out of the earth; and, still climbing, rose above it. They were in the rainbow. Far abroad, over ocean and land, they could see through its transparent walls the earth beneath their feet. Stairs beside stairs wound up together, and beautiful beings of all ages climbed along with them.

They knew that they were going up to the country whence the shadows fell.

And by this time I think they must have got there.

Puss-cat Mew

by E. H. Knatchbull-Hugessen

In a letter from 1971, Tolkien recalled that as a child ("before 1900") he used to be read to from an old collection that "contained one story I was then very fond of called 'Puss-cat Mew.'" The tale has several Tolkienian resonances. It purports to give the story behind the nursery rhyme of the same title—something that Tolkien himself would do years later in his two "Man in the Moon" poems, one of which gives the background to the familiar childhood rhyme "Hey diddle diddle, the cat and the fiddle" while the other tells the story behind why "The Man in the Moon came down too soon." Both of Tolkien's poems are collected in *The Adventures of Tom Bombadil*, but the first poem will be familiar to readers of *The Lord of the Rings*, for it is the one that Frodo sings in the inn at Bree.

"Puss-cat Mew" tells the story of a young man named Joe Brown who journeys into a large and gloomy forest where Ogres, Dwarfs, and Fairies dwell. One scene, where by trickery Joe keeps two Ogres and a Dwarf fighting, is similar to the scene in *The Hobbit* where Gandalf keeps the three trolls quarreling. One illustration found in the original publication of the story depicts an Ogre disguised as a tree, uncannily foreshadowing Tolkien's Ents in *The Lord of the Rings*. (This illustration is reprinted with note 23 to chapter 2 in the revised edition, published in 2002, of *The Annotated Hobbit*.)

"Puss-cat Mew" by E. H. Knatchbull-Hugessen first appeared in his collection *Stories for My Children* (1869).

EVERY child knows the sweet nursery rhyme of "Puss-cat Mew,"—

> "Puss-cat Mew jumped over a coal;
> In her best petticoat burnt a great hole;
> Puss-cat Mew shan't have any milk
> Till her best petticoat's mended with silk."

But very few children, or big people either, know *who* Puss-cat Mew was, or what was the history upon which those lines were made. I do not know that I should ever have found it out, only that I happened to overhear the White Stable Cat talking to the Brown Kitten that lives in the cottage over the road. I was lying down on the croquet-ground bank, smoking my cigarette, and thinking of the pretty blue sky up at which I was looking, and watching the fleecy white clouds that slowly followed each other over the face of it, and wondering whether it would rain next day, or be fine and bright enough for Ned's cricket-match, when I heard soft voices talking near me. I raised myself on my elbow to listen, and soon discovered whence they came. The White Cat had got the Brown Kitten into the arbour between the croquet-ground and the kitchen-garden, and, whilst they were watching the young robins which had just been fledged, and plainly expecting that one would hop within reach before long, they were talking over old times and old legends, and the White Cat was telling the whole story about Puss-cat Mew—which by this means I am able to tell to you.

There was, so she said, many years ago a worthy couple who had an only son, to whom they were tenderly attached. The boy grew up strong and hearty, and was withal of a clever turn of mind and a right cheerful disposition. But, somehow or other, he could never fancy his father's trade, which was that of a miller, and was seized with a great desire to see more of the world than he could do by remaining at home. His parents did not appear (so far as the White Cat knew) to have offered any great opposition to his wishes; so after the usual kissing and crying on the part of his mother, and good advice on the part of the honest old father, our young friend boldly started off on his travels.

He journeyed on merrily enough for a year or more, during which time he had many adventures, but none worth relating, until one day he came to a large and gloomy forest, in which he hoped to find shade and rest, and possibly some adventures worth telling when he got home again. The first thing, however, which met his eye was a large board nailed against a tree, with an inscription upon it. He walked up, no doubt expecting to see "Trespassers, beware!" written up, or "Whosoever is found trespassing in these woods will be prosecuted according to law," or some other gratifying announcement, such as usually greets the eyes of a weary traveller just as he is proposing to himself a pleasant change from the dusty highway to the soft moss of the shady wood before him.

No such words, however, greeted the eyes of *our* traveller. Something much more curious and unusual did he read. This was the inscription:

"Within this wood do Ogres dwell,
And Fairies here abide as well;
Go back, go back, thou miller's son,
Before thy journey is begun."

"Well," exclaimed the young man, when he had read these words, "this beats cock-fighting! How can they know here that I am a miller's son? and how could they have found out that I was coming just to this place, and so have got this board put up all ready? However, if they know as much as this, they might also have known that Joe Brown is not the chap to turn back for a trifle when he has once started. Go back, indeed! Not for Joe! None of my noble name ever yet knew what fear was, and I am quite resolved that I will never disgrace my family!"

With these brave words on his lips and noble sentiments in his heart, Joe Brown marched forward boldly into the wood, and proceeded for some considerable distance without meeting anything to annoy him in the slightest degree. The turf was soft under his feet, the trees above his head afforded the most welcome shade, and the birds poured forth their sweet melody in a manner which rejoiced his heart, and made him think that he had never heard better music in his life. At last, however, he came to a rather open space, when he saw immediately before him, some thirty or forty yards off, an old dead Oak, with two great branches, with scarce a leaf upon them, spreading out right and left. Almost as soon as he noticed the Tree, he perceived, to his intense surprise, that it was visibly agitated, and trembled all over. Gradually, as he stood stock-still with amazement, this trembling rapidly increased, the bark of the tree appeared to become the skin of a living body, the two dead limbs became the gigantic arms of a man, a head popped up from the trunk, and an enormous Ogre stood before the astonished traveller. Stood, but only for an instant; for, brandishing a stick as big as a young tree, he took a step forward, uttering at the same moment such a tremendous roar as overpowered the singing of all the birds, and made the whole forest re-echo with the awful sound.

There was no time for Joe to think of escape, and the difficulty would have been great had he had plenty of time; but at the very moment of the giant's advance, and before the echo of his roar had died away, a low, sweet voice whispered in the wayfarer's ear, in soothing and reassuring accents, "Stand hard, Joey"; and he had scarcely time to look down and perceive that the words came from a beautifully-marked Tortoiseshell Cat before he began to find his legs stiffen, his body harden; and almost before he could say "Jack Robinson" (which, by the way, was an expression he would probably never have thought of), he was turned into a Hawthorn-tree of apparent age and respectability, having a hollow place in its trunk, into which the Cat quietly crept and lay perfectly still.

With another roar, the Ogre made two or three strides forward, taking about ten yards in each stride, and then suddenly pulled up short, and stared around stupidly.

"I saw a Mortal," he growled, in a voice that made the Hawthorn-tree feel as if every berry would fall off him—"I swear I saw a Mortal, but I don't see him now! It's those bothering Fairies again—I know it is—confound them and their tricks!"

And he stamped so hard on the ground that every mole and rabbit for a mile round felt it; and, in fact, there was a paragraph in the *Mole Chronicle* next day, stating that the shock of an earthquake had been distinctly felt at that particular time on that very day.

"Spiflicate those Fairies!" again said the Ogre in an angry tone, using the worst word he knew of, which had the great merit of being understood by nobody. "Here have I been waiting in my oak dress for hours to catch a Mortal, and spank my great grandfather if those Fairies haven't sold me again! It is really too bad that this should go on!" And he then moved sulkily off, muttering the well-known "Fe-fi-fo-fum," which is so popular a song among Ogres.

As soon as he was well out of sight, the Tortoiseshell Cat stepped purring out of the hole in the Hawthorn-tree, and began to rub herself gently against the trunk. Joe Brown felt his bark again becoming skin, his sap blood, and his branches arms, and in a few moments was again himself. He stretched immediately, yawned and sneezed, to be sure that he was just as he had been before, and, having satisfied himself in this respect, turned to thank his friend and deliverer the Cat. But there was no Cat there. He stood transfixed with amazement. How had she disappeared? Where had she gone to? "And what the dickens was he to do?" He uttered these last words audibly, and had scarcely done so when a voice near him exclaimed—

"Don't say 'dickens,' Joe Brown; it is merely a substitute for a worse word, which your friends in this wood much object to."

And, as he turned round to see who or what had now spoken to him, the same voice, which appeared to proceed from an old Hornbeam Pollard which stood near, chanted these words in a low but clear voice:

"Within this forest Ogres dwell,
And Fairies here abide as well:
If these two races could agree,
No chance of life, O man, for thee.
But, though the Ogres of the wood
Eat human flesh, and thirst for blood,
An honest man will ever find
The Fairies friendly to his kind.
In vain the Ogres rage and fume,
And form of trees in fraud assume,
The Fairies watch by night and day
To rob them of expected prey.
And you, poor mortal, only must
To fairy aid entirely trust;
For if you on yourself rely,
By Ogre cruelty you'll die.
So if in danger or in doubt,
On Fairies call to help you out,
And, all your scrapes to pull you through,
Call—and at once—for 'Puss-cat Mew.' "

"Well, I never!" said Joe, when the voice ceased. And no more he ever had, nor any one else that I ever heard of. And there he stood for a minute, thinking what to do next. It was plainly a place in which there was plenty to be found in the way of adventures, and, of course, it was highly satisfactory to think that there would be always a friend at hand, in the shape of a Fairy, to get you out of any difficulty. On the other hand, he thought it rather beneath him to have to be turned into a tree—or anything else; for, as far as he could see, he might as well be turned next time into a thistle, or a fungus, or any other unpleasant thing, and he didn't quite like the idea. Besides, he had only the word of a voice—evidently belonging to a partisan of the Fairies—to tell him that his friends were really the stronger: and from what he had already seen it appeared to him that unless a Fairy was there in the very nick of time, an Ogre of the kind which he had seen might destroy him in a moment before help could come. He thought therefore that, after all, he was better out of the forest than in it; for although he did not desire to shun danger, he was wise enough to know that it is no proof of a brave man to run blindly into it; and he therefore determined to leave the forest, and keep round the outside till he got beyond it on his journey. He then turned round to retrace his steps, when, to his astonishment, he again heard a voice singing to him in these words—

"Of courage we know that Joe Brown has no lack,
　Fa de jo dum, fol de rol do;
He chose to go on when he *might* have gone back,
　Fa de jo dum, fol de rol lo.
But his choice it was made when he entered the wood,
　Fa de jo dum, fol de rol do,
And he *can't* go back now—don't he wish that he could?
　Fa de jo dum, fol de rol lo."

"All right," rejoined Joe, "my name's Easy" (which was an entire falsehood, as we know that it was "Brown"). "If I can't go back, I'll go forward." And on he marched with a firm step, for he thought this voice seemed to be chaffing him, and he didn't like to be chaffed by a fellow whom he couldn't even see to chaff back again! So he pushed on for a little way, and then sat down under a fir-tree, and began to eat some bread and cheese which he had brought with him.

As everything seemed perfectly quiet around him, and he experienced no interruption, he began to think that what had happened must really have been a dream, and that, after all, a bold heart and his own right arm were the best things to rely on, and that it was nonsense to suppose that any Fairy could really help him, or that any danger would occur to him from which he could not extricate himself by his own caution and courage. As this thought took full possession of his mind, he could not help finishing it aloud with the remark—

"And as to 'Puss-cat Mew,' what good can it possibly be to me to call out such a name as *that* if I was in trouble?"

Scarcely were the words out of his mouth when a low sigh reached his ears, and he plainly heard the sound of some creature running away over the dead leaves; but though he turned quickly, he could see no one.

He finished his bread and cheese, and was just thinking of lighting his pipe, when, to his great surprise, he felt a light tap on his shoulder, followed by a cuff on the side of the head, which knocked his wide-awake off, and made his ears tingle for a long time afterwards. Looking up in surprise and rage, he beheld, close to him, a most decided Ogre. Ten feet or more was he in height—with a fur-cap on his head, a grim and most forbidding countenance, very red nose, eyes bloodshot and set deep in his head, prominent teeth looking uncomfortably sharp, and a chin with a bristly beard, which had evidently not been shaved for a fortnight. Wishing to act upon the plan which he had laid down for himself, and determined not to lose heart, Joe put the best face upon the matter at once.

"Come," said he, "leave off, will you? None of that! Hit one of your own size!"

"Fool!" exclaimed the Giant moodily; "a truce to your idle jesting. This is no time or place for it. *You've* put your foot in it nicely."

"I don't see why," replied Joe. "I've a right to be here as

much as any other fellow, and——. Come, I say, you let me go, will you?"

For the other cut his speech short by seizing him, and, in spite of all his struggles, tied his hands and feet with a bit of whipcord which he drew out of his pocket. He then put his finger to his mouth and gave a whistle, which Joe thought was the most fearful sound he ever heard, like seventeen railway trains screeching at the same time, as they entered their tunnels. A crunching of sticks followed, as if some heavy animals were approaching, and two Ogres, who could be little less than sixteen or eighteen feet high, came running up, and touched their hats to the Ogre who had captured Joe.

"I've got one, my men," said this monster, who was evidently an Ogre of superior rank; "and I think he looks young and tender. Carry him up to the castle, and when I come home I'll give orders about him. I shan't want any luncheon to-day, for since I caught those school-children at the picnic the other morning, and rather over-ate myself with the tender dears, crunch my jawbones if I haven't been off my feed."

Joe Brown now felt exceedingly uncomfortable, but had no means whatever of resisting. The servant Ogres produced a large game-bag, into which they popped the unfortunate young miller; and there he lay at the bottom of it, along with an old woman and a young girl, both of whom appeared half dead with fright. The old woman would say but little, and was evidently of no friendly disposition, although in like misfortune with the two others. But the young girl was more communicative, and said that she was a teacher in a school not far from the forest, and having joined the children in a picnic a day or two before, had been surprised by the sudden appearance of a terrible Ogre. Those of the children who bore the best characters escaped with comparative ease; the idle ones were less fortunate, and three, who had neglected to learn their collects the Sunday before, and had fidgeted notably during the whole of the sermon, were instantly devoured before the eyes of their affrighted Teacher. She had made her escape at the time, but as several of her little lambs were still missing, had ventured into the forest again that day to search for them, and had just been seized by the cruel Ogres. She added, that the old woman was a noted Witch of the neighbourhood, who had done as much harm to mankind as the Ogres, but that it was well known that Witches had no power in any forest in which Ogres and Fairies both lived. The old lady, therefore, having foolishly entered the forest in search of a particular herb of great value, with which she wished to make some magic broth, had been caught by the Ogres, and would certainly find no mercy at their hands. Joe listened with attention, and, in return, told his story to the poor School-teacher.

Thus they whiled away the time until their bearers came to a stop, and taking the game-bags off their shoulders, opened them, and let the captives out. They were in a small room paved with stones, a beam across the top of it, and rows of hooks fastened in the beam, which bore fruit by no means likely to inspire them with hope. A stout farmer, in boots and breeches, quite dead, hung by the chin from one hook, and from his appearance was evidently nearly fit for dressing. A priest hung next, with his throat cut from ear to ear, who did not seem to have been long dead; and these two were the sole occupants of the Ogre's larder.

Joe Brown began to dislike the look of things very much, especially when one of the Ogres said to the other, "Did the Prince say they was to be killed and hung up directly?" "No, you duffer," replied the other; "to wait till he came home." And with these words the three wretched Mortals were left alone. The old Witch now began to use the most fearful language, abusing Ogres, Fairies, and even her two companions, whom she said she would tear to pieces if she had but got them out of the wood; but as she hadn't, and could do nothing where she was, they cared but little for her threats.

Presently the door opened, and one of the two servant Ogres entered, and cut the cord which bound Joe's arms and legs, at the same time driving him and his fellow-captives before him through the door. They passed along a cold damp passage till they came to a door at the end of it, on the left hand. This being opened, they found themselves in a large hall, with a big fire at one end, and a table before it, at each side of which sat an Ogre in an enormous arm-chair. At a glance Joe saw that whilst one of these Ogres was the one who had caught him, the other was the Oak-tree Ogre from whom he had escaped in the morning.

"Ho, ho" laughed the latter, when he saw the captives enter. "Man's marrow-bones and liver! this is the Mortal whom I saw this morning, and who unaccountably gave me the slip! Girls' pettitoes! we've got him now, though! And, as I live, here's the old Witch. Ha! my pet, my duckling, my tender love, don't I long to fix my teeth in your giblets! How good they will be!"

And he leered horribly at the old woman, who thereupon burst out into a torrent of abuse:

"You bloodthirsty brute—you cannibal—you wretch—you detestable monster—you anthropophagous demon——"

But she got no further; for the Giant, who had risen as he finished his own speech, cut hers short by such a terrific kick as doubled the old Witch up like a ball, and sent her up with such force towards the roof, that striking a beam, which broke her back directly, she was as dead as mutton before she reached the ground again: the Giant's foot, however, caught her again, and she went up once more, and then fell with a dull thud against the pavement.

"Take her away, and dress her directly," said the Ogre; "there is nothing so good to eat as your real Witch, but they should always be dressed the same day, or they become tough, and don't get tender again for an age. As for these other two, as we have game already hanging in the larder, we might keep them for a day or two, only there's no knowing what tricks those confounded Fairies might play—perhaps they'd better be killed and hung up at once; take them down, bleed the girl to death, that her flesh may be as white as possible, and cut the man's throat in the back yard."

The School-teacher instantly fainted, and Joe heard with very disagreeable feelings; for no one likes the prospect of being killed like a pig, and afterwards eaten by an Ogre; though it must be allowed that if the former fate happened to any of us, the latter would cause us little pain or trouble. But the reason of the Ogre's order for his slaughter brought back to our traveller's mind the voice and the warning which he had heard. How foolish had he been! He had trusted to his own strength and courage, and this was the result! What could he do? Was it now too late? There was certainly no time to lose; for as soon as the Ogre's order had been given, the servants raised the unhappy School-teacher from the ground, and giving Joe a push, drove him along the passage down which they had just before passed, at the end of which was a small yard, which they had crossed on leaving the larder, and which had every appearance of being the very back yard in which his throat was to be cut. He was half-way down the passage when these thoughts came into his head, and in a voice of regret and despair he sighed forth the words, "O for my Puss-cat Mew to help me now!"

Scarcely were the words out of his mouth, when there came down the passage a soft breath of air from the fresh woodlands which he had so lately left; it seemed to carry with it the most delicious perfume you can imagine—so sweet, and yet not too sweet; so strong, and yet not too strong—that nothing was ever so perfectly exquisite. And with the perfume there came a sweet, soft, clear voice—

> "Faithless child of mortal race,
> Courage take, and heart of grace;
> Banish doubt, away with fear,
> Puss-cat Mew is ever near!"

The servant Ogres did not seem to hear the voice, at least they paid no attention to it; but the perfume was hateful to their blood-spoiled and brutalized senses.

"Ugh! what a horrible smell!" they each exclaimed; and immediately fell down in a fainting-fit. At the same moment Joe saw the Tortoiseshell Cat standing at the end of the passage, and beckoning to him, and you may well believe that he lost no time in hurrying up to her. But he stopped when he came close, for he remembered his poor fellow-captive, and he could not bear the thoughts of leaving her to perish.

"Oh, Puss-cat Mew," said he, "pray save that girl too!"

The Cat drew herself up with an angry kind of purr, and made no movement; upon which Joe, being a brave fellow, and too chivalrous to neglect a lady in distress, declared that he must go back and bring the poor creature out. The Cat set up her back and looked cross, but the same low voice came floating over the yard from the free forest—

"Fear not for the maiden left,
Though of human aid bereft;
Yet she Ogres need not dread,
Saints and angels guard her head;
Spirits of the children taught,
And to know religion brought,
To her rescue soon will fly,
Nought her danger here to die."

This somewhat reassured Joe, but that which did so even more was to see the School-teacher rise from the place where the fainting Giants had dropped her, and follow him into the yard. A door stood open from the yard into the forest, through which the three passed, and the Teacher turned down a path to the left, which she said she somehow felt quite certain would lead her right. The Cat said not a word, but moved quietly along till the Teacher was gone, when she came up to

Joe, and rubbed herself against his legs, seeming almost to smile as she looked up into his face.

"O you little darling!" he exclaimed; "you dear, good, charming little Puss-cat Mew! there never was, and never will be, such another Cat in the world as you. How shall I ever thank you enough for getting me out of that horrible place!"

Still the Cat spoke not, probably because cats don't generally speak, except under peculiar circumstances; but then Joe thought that his circumstances *were* rather peculiar, and expected this Cat might perhaps make an exception in his favour. But she kept on, still without speaking, till they had gone for some distance; then, without a word, good, bad, or indifferent, she disappeared behind a large old oak-tree, near which they were passing.

Joe was terribly puzzled, for he didn't know which way to go, or what to do; and, moreover, he began to feel rather hungry, which was not surprising, as it was now getting late, and he had tasted nothing since that bread and cheese which he had just finished before his capture by the Ogre. He searched his pockets over and over again, but could only find a few crumbs, which went but a very little way towards satisfying his hunger; and he therefore sat down under the old oak, and began to consider what was the best thing to do next. He had not sat there long, however, before a loud shout at no very great distance convinced him that his flight had been discovered, and that the Ogres were in pursuit. However, he felt no alarm this time, being quite sure that his friends would not desert him. Nor indeed did they do so, for on a second roar being heard, evidently nearer than the first, a noise inside the tree immediately followed, and a passage opened, apparently of itself, in the tree, through which Joe instantly entered. What was his surprise and joy to find within the large hollow space inside the tree a small table with a white cloth upon it, which displayed a still further attraction in the shape of a fine beefsteak, with rich yellow fat and steaming gravy, to-

gether with a foaming pot of porter by its side. At the same
time came the old, friendly voice—

"Son of Mortal, do not fear,
    Fairies will no harm allow;
Eat thy steak and drink thy beer,
    Ogres shall not hurt thee now."

Joe needed no second invitation, but, sitting down at once,
made as good a dinner as he had ever made in his life. Whilst
he was eating, he heard the Ogres trampling through the
wood, and peeping out through a hole in the oak, saw no less
than seven of these monsters passing by, and heard them
talking about his escape, and abusing the Fairies as the
cause. Presently, however, their voices died away, and all
sounds in the forest ceased. The inside of the oak was large,
and, looking round, Joe perceived a comfortable bed made
up in a corner.

"Well," said he, "this is the very thing for me!" and without more ado he tumbled into it, and was fast asleep in a very
few moments.

How long he slept I cannot say, but it was late in the
evening when he laid down, and when he opened his eyes it
was broad daylight. He jumped up, and rubbed his eyes two
or three times before he could remember where he was, but
after a while he began to recollect all that had happened, and
to think that it was high time to take some steps to escape
from the neighbourhood of such unpleasant people as the
Ogres, from whom he had taken refuge in his present curious
quarters. Accordingly, he got up, and was charmed to see
that a bath stood near him, ready filled with water, of which
he speedily availed himself, and, after a good wash, found
himself fresh enough to be quite ready to start upon another
day's adventures.

The first thought that occurred to him was how to get
out of the oak. This, however, did not trouble him long, for

scarcely had he laid his hand against the inside of the tree, when a door flew open for him of its own accord, and he passed out into the forest. All was quiet, and the morning sun lit up the woodland scenery with its bright rays; the birds were singing, and everything appeared as beautiful and joyous as if there were no such beings as Ogres in the world. Uncertain whether to turn to the right or the left, he got rid of the difficulty by going straight on, and, as he did so, began to wonder whether he should now be allowed to leave the forest, or be still as unable to do so as he was the day before.

As he walked along, meditating upon this point, he came suddenly upon a very little man, sitting on a faggot, and sharpening a stick with a penknife. Little indeed was his body, but his head was enormously big; his hair was red, his nose was hooked, and he squinted fearfully. Joe didn't like the looks of him a bit, but he thought to himself that it was wrong to judge by appearances, and that, if the worst came to the worst, he could manage to get the better of such a chap as that in a fair stand-up fight. So he bowed civilly, and without more ado asked the little man if he could show him the way out of the forest.

The little man instantly jumped up, squinting more than ever, and, looking Joe straight in the face, exclaimed, in a voice so harsh and unpleasant as to increase the feeling of distrust which had already taken possession of the traveller—

"Out of the forest? Eggs and nuts! that I can, my fine fellow. Follow me, and I'll soon put you right"; and so saying, he set off at a short trot, stopping every moment to beckon Joe to follow. Joe began to do so; but scarcely had he gone a step, before a low sigh seemed to steal across his ear, like that which he had heard under the fir-tree the day before, and, being wiser by experience, he immediately came to a full stop. His companion turned round upon this, and sharply asked him what he was about?

"It strikes me," replied Joe, "that you are not leading me the right way out of the wood."

"Strikes you?" answered the little man, angrily; "*what* strikes you, and *who* strikes you, and what do you mean by it? If you know the way better than I do, you had better go first; and if not, follow me without any nonsense. Don't suppose that *I'm* to be humbugged; come on!" and with these words he walked close up to Joe Brown, and taking hold of his coat with one hand, pointed with the other in the direction he had been going.

Joe still hesitated. "You see," he said, "this is a queer sort of place, and I've been in one bad scrape already."

"You'll be in another in half a minute," said his guide, "if you're such a fool as to stand shilly-shallying here"; and without more to-do he gave Joe such a pull by the coat as nearly threw him off his balance, and made him aware that there was more strength in the little man than he had thought possible in so small a body.

"I wish I could consult Puss-cat Mew," he said, almost without meaning to speak; and the words were scarcely out of his mouth, when a low, angry purr was heard, and, springing in suddenly between Joe and his companion, Puss-cat Mew, without the least warning, gave the latter such a scratch down his ugly face, that the blood followed the marks of her claws immediately, and the victim roared aloud, and struck a fearful blow at the Cat. This, however, she easily avoided, and in the short battle which followed not once could the little man strike her; whilst she, darting in at every opportunity, so scratched his head and face, that he presently fled bellowing into the wood with all possible speed, and left the astonished Joe alone with his faithful friend.

Joe now hoped that he should receive some explanation from the Cat as to what had just occurred, and some plain directions as to what course he was to pursue in order to get out of the forest; for although it was undoubtedly a fine thing to have such good friends there to save him from Ogres and other enemies, he by no means desired to spend the rest of his life in that particular place.

Puss-cat Mew, however, said never a word; and yet Joe thought she must be able to speak, because he was very sure that it was from her that the words "Stand hard, Joey," came when they first met. All she did, after looking up at him in a friendly manner, and rubbing against his leg, was to trot on into the wood, and beckon with her fore-paw for him to follow, which he did without the least hesitation. They went on and on under the high trees for some little way, until, as they were slowly descending a hill where the underwood was somewhat thicker, Joe thought he heard again the distant shout of an Ogre. He pulled up short, but, as the Cat beckoned to him and seemed to frown, soon went on again, and at the bottom of the hill saw that the wood fell away gradually from an open grassy space, in the middle of which bubbled up a clear spring of water, from which a stream seemed to take its birth, and to flow merrily forward into the woods below.

Puss-cat Mew paused at the edge of the wood, where the open space began, and without entering it herself, pointed to Joe, and made signs that he should do so; which he immediately did. Hardly had he set foot within the space and trod upon the green grass, than there sprang up around him a myriad Fairy forms, like those that children see in the Christmas pantomimes, only smaller and prettier; and oh! so graceful in every movement that it was marvellous to see them. They formed a circle round the astonished Joe, and began a dance, the like of which he had never seen or heard of before, whilst at the same time they were accompanied by the sweetest possible music, which proceeded from invisible minstrels.

Joe stood entranced and delighted; this was indeed Fairyland, and to have seen such a sight and heard such sounds was really worth the dangers which he had encountered. After the dancing had continued for some little time, the Fairy forms fell back behind the fountain, in front of which Joe was standing, and ranged themselves in a semicircle, whilst one of their number, coming forward and standing under the very spray of the water as it bubbled up, sang sweetly forth the following words:—

"Seldom is a Mortal seen
On the magic Fairy Green;
Seldom will the Fairies rise
Thus to dance for mortal eyes;
Seldom may a Mortal hear
Strains to Fairy minstrel dear.
Mortal! since to thee kind Fate
Gives these glades to penetrate,
Listen with an awe profound
Whilst I tell of foes around;
Listen, ere thou longer stray,
Hear my mandate—and obey.
Wherefore didst thou come to roam
All around the Ogres' home?
Daring Mortal! were it not
Plot is met by counterplot,
Ere thou reach'dst Fairy Green
Food for Ogres thou hadst been.
Seven Ogres, fierce and strong,
Terrify this forest long;
Slaves to whom there likewise be
Dwarfs of might—in number three.
Then beware, thou miller's son,
Of these Dwarfs speak thou to none;
Trust alone to Fairies true
And the faithful Puss-cat Mew.
Thus I give thee, on our green,
Message from the Fairy Queen!"

Here the Fairy stopped; and Joe, who was no great poet, but of a practical turn of mind, took off his hat, as civilly as he could, and with great respect addressed her in the following words:—

"If you please, ma'am, *would* you be kind enough to speak for once without rhyme, and tell me how I can get out of this forest?"

With a gracious smile, the Fairy instantly replied.

"Joe Brown," said she, "you must be well aware that the universal custom of Fairies all over the world, and at all times, has been to speak in verse, and to address by the general term 'Mortal' the individual whom they honoured by speaking to him. But as you are a good sort of fellow, and I am directed by our Queen to do what I can for you, I have no objection to give you a little information in English prose. You must know that the seven Ogres who inhabit a castle in the middle of this wood are about the worst Ogres, as well as the greatest scamps, in the country. Old Grindbones is the chief one; and Smashman, his nephew, is every bit as bad as he: the other five are of an inferior class; but no man, woman, or child is safe within half a mile of any of them. We Fairies have done, and still do, everything that can be done, to protect the unhappy people who *will* keep coming into the forest; but, of course, we have other things to do, and we cannot be always bothering ourselves with these matters, which really ought to be settled by the Rural Police. What makes it much worse is the recent arrival of three Dwarfs, who have bound themselves to serve the Ogres for a certain payment, and who do their best to entice travellers to the castle of their masters. The names of these dwarfs are Juff, Jumper, and Gandleperry; and, fortunately for you, it was Jumper whom you lately met, and whose very appearance set you upon your guard. Had it been Gandleperry, I would not have answered for the consequences, for a slyer or more arrant knave doesn't exist. However, all you have now to do is, to walk quite straight forward, and on no account either scratch your left leg or turn your head round for a moment. If you do, evil may follow; if not, half a mile will bring you to the edge of the wood; when, if you stand upon your head whilst you count ten, throw up your hat in the air twice, and take off your boots and carry them in your hand, you will find yourself able to leave the forest and go where you will."

Having made this speech, which the White Cat told the Brown Kitten was supposed to be the very longest ever made by a Fairy, the pretty creature gracefully waved her hand to Joe, and in a moment the whole of the party vanished from his sight. He stood for a moment plunged in thought, and then boldly stepped forward, determined, at all hazards, to get out of the wood. Half a mile was no great distance, and he thought it would be easy enough to do as he had been told by his kind adviser. He had not gone ten yards, however, before his right leg began to itch violently, just as happens to people when they walk across the corn-fields directly after harvest. Without a thought, he stooped down, and relieved it by a violent and comfortable scratching. Then his left leg began to itch horribly too; but just as he was going to treat it in the same manner, he remembered the Fairy's warning, and stopped himself in time. Oh! how he longed to scratch his leg! but he bravely bore it, and went on as fast as he could. He was half-way to the edge of the wood, when he heard a voice behind him, calling out—

"Joe! Joe Brown! stop a minute, will ye?"

But the warning had been so lately given, that he never turned his head and only hurried on all the faster. He was actually within twenty yards of the outside, and in another minute would have been there—and this story, for all I know, would never have been written—when, close behind him, he heard a scream, a loud scream, which startled him so as to make him forget everything he had been thinking of before. It was the voice of a woman in distress, and, to his ears, sounded as if it was certainly the voice of his own mother.

"Oh Joe, dear Joe," it said, in heartrending accents, "don't leave me behind, *please* don't. I'm caught in the brambles here, and can't get on anyhow."

Joe loved his mother dearly, and without thinking for a
moment of anything else, turned round, head and all, and
made for the thicket whence the sound had come. He reached
it, but could see no mother, nor indeed any woman at all.
What he *did* see, however, was more remarkable than com-
forting. A Dwarf was sitting upon a fallen tree, with his two
thumbs one in each of his waistcoat-pockets, peering into
the thicket, as if he was looking for something. Very unlike the Dwarf whom Joe had met before was this little man.
He was older, had a black coat and buff waistcoat on, and his
face was by no means disagreeable to look at, if there had
not been a certain odd appearance about his eyes, which
made Joe feel at once that he was a deep old fellow, who
knew what was what as well as most people.

"Did you scream, sir?" said Joe.

"Scream, sir?—no, sir: I did *not* scream," answered the
Dwarf, with perfect politeness; "but I certainly *heard* a
scream, sir, and a woman's scream. In fact, I was just looking
for the person who *did* scream, sir. I think it must have been
in the thicket beyond, sir, and not here. Perhaps you will aid
me in my search, since we are both on the same errand?"

Joe, who smelt mischief, would have given the world to
refuse, but hardly knew how to do so, and, accordingly, took
a step or two towards the other thicket, into which he and the
Dwarf carefully looked, but could see no woman, principally
because no woman was there. For you must know that the
scream had really proceeded from the little man himself,
who was none other than the celebrated Dwarf Gandleperry,
who had come out to entrap the unfortunate Joe, and to deliver him to the Ogres. The Dwarfs' bargain with the Ogres
was that they should have the head of every other Mortal
whom they brought to the Ogres—for there is nothing Dwarfs
like so much as brains, and they will go any distance, and
play any trick, in order to secure this delicacy.

Of course, I say, they found no woman, and heard no more
screams; but the Dwarf began to talk to Joe in such a pleas-

ant and amusing manner, that he soon lost his first feeling of
mistrust, and began to think that he had found an agreeable
companion. Instead of walking straight back, however, the
little man bore to the left, so that they soon left the Fairy
Green behind them on the right. Joe asked what was the
sound of falling water which he heard; to which his companion replied, that there was a spring which rose down there,
but that the ground was so wet and soft about it, that it was
best to go someway round. Joe ought to have known from
this that something was wrong, since he had so recently
crossed the place himself; but somehow his senses were
lulled to rest, and he seemed to walk on in a kind of dream,
listening to the Dwarf, and being only half awake to the reality of the scene. He was roughly awakened, however, before long; for, as they entered the thicker part of the wood,
beyond the Fairy Green, two other Dwarfs suddenly sprang
out of a neighbouring thicket, each armed with a thick stick,
and fell upon Joe in a moment. His companion, too, ceasing
from his pleasant conversation, joined in the attack, and
shouted loudly at the same time—

"Well done, Juff! down with him, Jumper!" and then, as
Joe recognised in one of the new-comers the ill-looking
Dwarf from whom Puss-cat Mew had before delivered him,
he became suddenly aware that he had fallen into the hands
of three rascals who would certainly deliver him to the Ogres
if he could not escape. Joe was a strong man, and a bold, and
he fought bravely; but three to one is fearful odds. He knocked
one of Juff's teeth down his throat, and caught Jumper a
regular stinger on his red rose; but Gandleperry evaded his
blows, and struck him such a tremendous crack over the head
with a life-preserver, that he sank down senseless on the
ground, whilst the other two Dwarfs rained blows upon him
with their sticks till they felt pretty sure they had left no
breath in his body. Then they all three stood a few yards off,
and burst into a roar of savage laughter.

"So much for the Fairies' pet," said Jumper. "It's worth all the scratches on my face to have caught this ugly brute"; and he laughed again.

"Well," said Gandleperry, "I thought I could manage it, and so I have. Now you two fellows had better carry him up to the castle."

"Thank you for nothing," answered Juff; "do you expect us to go and carry a great lumbering carcase like that, whilst you go lounging about and amusing yourself? Not a yard will I carry him, unless you help."

"You forget yourself strangely," said Gandleperry; "but I have no time for disputes. Bring the carrion up or not, as you please. I shall go on to the castle and tell Grindbones that the Mortal is caught and killed, and he will probably come and meet you, or at least send one of his servants to bring the game in." And with these words he quietly walked away.

"This won't do," said Juff to Jumper, as soon as he was gone. "I'll tell you what the old boy means to do. He'll tell his story first, and get all the credit with the old Ogre, and then, whilst we are bringing the booty in, *he* will get the promise of the head, and our share will be but small. Don't let us be done by old Gandleperry like this! Let us slip off and get to the castle before him, and the Ogres can send their own servants to fetch the Mortal's body."

This proposal appeared to please Jumper, and off they both set as fast as they could go.

Poor Joe lay still enough, and no one would have given much for his life at that moment. But the Dwarfs had scarcely left the place when something so cold and refreshing touched his forehead, that it brought back his senses directly. He slowly opened his eyes, and beheld a sight the most welcome that could have met his gaze. Puss-cat Mew was leaning over him, and bathing his face and head with some mixture of so refreshing a character, that it seemed to put new life into him every moment. She looked very grave and sad, and was evidently quite alive to the danger he was in. Drawing from her apron pocket a small box, she took out

of it a very little bottle, which she gave to him, and made
signs that he should drink its contents. Having done so, he
found himself so much better that he was able, though with
difficulty, to stand upright, and very slowly to creep along
after his faithful friend, who kept beckoning and urging him
along, until they came to the very selfsame oak in which he
had slept the night before. Luckily it was at no great distance
from the place where he had been so cruelly beaten by the
three Dwarfs, for, had it been much further, he could not
have struggled so far before his enemies would have overtaken him. As it was, the back door had scarcely opened to
receive him before he heard the roar of the infuriated Ogres,
who had come back with the Dwarfs and found their prey
gone. Their shouts of rage rent the forest air, and poor Joe
trembled as he lay on his bed and listened to the fearful
sounds.

When he was safely in bed, Puss-cat Mew brought a pot of
wonderful ointment, which she ordered him to rub carefully
into every part of him that had been bruised by the blows of
the Dwarfs; which he did, and experienced great relief.

For three days and three nights, however, the poor fellow
remained in the oak, carefully nursed by his kind friend, and
requiring nothing except that she should speak to him, which
she never did, by any accident. On the fourth morning he felt
so well and strong that he expressed his desire to go out, and,
touching the bark as before, found himself again in the forest. His guide showed him the same way as before, and he
arrived quite safely at the Fairy Green, where she again disappeared.

He boldly stepped into the open space, as he had done
upon his first visit, but no Fairy forms arose around him. Perhaps they were angry at his foolish disobedience of the directions given him; but still that could hardly be the case, or
why had they allowed Puss-cat Mew to help him again? And
as he came near the spring, the old, soft, low voice stole
gently through the air, and said to him, in friendly tones—

"Remember, Mortal, thou hast seen
The revels of the Fairy Green;
Hast heard the words of warning true
From one who falsehood never knew.
Unchanged is truth, so ponder o'er
The same directions as before.
Obey—and never count the cost;
But disobey, and thou art lost!"

Joe heard with attention, and determined that, come what
might, he would not be tempted again to forget the directions
which he had received. He set off from the Fairy Spring, and
walked briskly towards the edge of the forest. His legs both
itched violently as before, but not a scratch did they get, and
he arrived within a few yards of the edge without the slightest adventure of any kind. Then, suddenly, he heard a voice
calling to him loudly—

"Joe, Joe," it said, "turn round, you rascal Joe! You coward! are you afraid of an old man? I'll fight ye for half-a-
crown, Joe! Turn and come on! don't run away like a cur with
his tail between his legs."

Joe heard plainly enough, and recognised the tones of the
wily Gandleperry, but was resolved to make no mistake this
time; so, although the Dwarf called him all the bad names he
could lay his tongue to, he kept boldly on until he reached
the edge of the forest. Then he immediately stood upon his
head and counted ten, as he had been told by the Fairy. Next
he threw his hat in the air, and then began to take off his
boots. All this time the angry Dwarf was abusing him with
all his might, but to no purpose. Off came Joe's boots; he
took them in his hand, and in another moment was outside
the forest. Hardly was he there when he boldly turned round,
knowing that the spell was broken, and there he saw, not only
Gandleperry gnashing his teeth in rage and fury, but three of
the Ogres running up behind him, and showing plainly
enough their fury and disappointment. But, luckily for him,

the magic power which had kept him so long in the wood
was even more powerful over them, and they were not able to
pass the edge of the forest. They were therefore compelled to
content themselves with yells and threats, which did Joe not
the slightest harm, and he walked off, highly delighted at
having at last been able to leave the scene of his troubles. He
began to whistle a merry tune, which he had not done all the
morning before, having been told, I suppose, by some wise
person or another, that "you should never whistle till you
are out of the wood."

As Joe walked onwards, he cast many a thought back to
his friends the Fairies, and especially to that kind and faithful Puss-cat Mew to whom, as he rightly felt, he owed everything; and he sighed heavily as he thought that perhaps he
might never more see one who had become so dear to him,
and in whom he had begun to take the deepest interest. His
path lay over rough ground, with brakes and briars growing
around on every side, for several hundred yards after he had
left the forest; and it then led him suddenly into a broad
track, on one side of which was a fence of tangled thorns,
through which no human being could ever have forced his
way; whilst on the other was a steep precipice, over which if
a fellow fell, his friends would have found him in several
pieces if they took the trouble to go round, and down to the
bottom, to look after him. As, however, the pathway was at
least a dozen yards wide, Joe thought little about these obsta-
cles to his going right or left, and trudged steadily on.

All at once he became aware of another obstacle of a different nature. The path, at a short distance before him, sloped
rapidly down to the valley below; and just where it began to
do so, nearly in the middle of the path, sat an old woman in
a red cloak; while, to his great astonishment, a broad—very
broad—bar of iron, perfectly red-hot, stretched completely
across the path right and left of her. As turning back was out
of the question, Joe boldly advanced; but when he got within
a couple of yards of the bar, it began to fizz and glow, and

threw out such a strong heat that he stepped back a pace or two, quite unable to proceed.

"Well, Dame," he said, addressing the old woman, "what's the matter *here*? Do you keep a toll-bar? or why mayn't I pass on?"

The person he addressed had her back to him, but, turning round when he spoke, disclosed a face very much wrinkled, the nose of which was like the beak of a hawk, and the chin at least a yard and a half long.

"I am sure you are welcome to pass," said she; "but *I* have nothing to do with it. I am only here to see whether anybody burns themselves. In fact, you know, I'm not the master, but the Bar-maid."

Joe thought she was the queerest-looking barmaid *he* had ever seen, and didn't quite believe her story; however, he did not say so, but went again up to the bar, with the same result. The old woman said no more, but sat still, knitting away at a pair of stockings all the time with the greatest composure. Joe was fairly puzzled, and at last, in despair, exclaimed—

"Well, it really does seem a strange thing, that after escaping the Ogres and Dwarfs, I am to be stopped here by a bar of iron. Oh, Puss-cat Mew! can't you help me now?"

At that very moment he turned his head, and, to his great delight, perceived his friend sitting down behind him in the middle of the pathway.

"O you beauty!—you darling!" he cried: "now I shall be all right again!"

And kneeling down, he took her in his arms, and kissed her again and again with joy and gratitude; whilst she softly purred, as if by no means displeased at the attention. But when he put her down, she no longer led the way, as she had done in the forest, but merely rubbed against his leg, and kept on purring. Joe was fairly puzzled for some time, till at last he thought he understood that she wanted to be carried; and accordingly he took her up in his arms again, and walked up to the bar. To his great surprise, as he neared it, it quietly sank into the earth, leaving a black, burnt mark where it had descended, over which he stepped, and found himself free to go down the grassy slope of the hill before him, which he now saw with astonishment would lead him right down upon the river, upon which, but a short distance off, stood his father's mill. He had hardly time, however, to remark this, when his surprise was increased tenfold. Puss-cat Mew sprang out of his arms the very moment they crossed the black line; her skin fell off, her whole appearance changed, and she stood before him the most charming young Lady he had ever seen. I cannot attempt to describe her; but let everybody that reads this story think who is the prettiest person he or she has ever seen, and Puss-cat Mew was just like *her*. All I do know is, that, under a gown which was quite smart enough for the occasion, she had the most magnificently embroidered petticoat you can imagine.

But this was not all that happened. The red cloak of the old woman fell off her shoulders, her head with the ugly face disappeared, and there stood in her place a grand and lovely Lady, small, but exquisitely made, and with something so noble and royal in her appearance, that Joe Brown took off his hat directly, and made a very low bow.

"Joe Brown," said the Lady, in a voice so sweet and yet so dignified that it filled Joe with admiration—"Joe Brown, the time is come when you may be told much which you might not know before. I am the Queen of the Fairies, and Puss-cat Mew is my favourite daughter. As you are a good young man, I am willing to bestow her hand upon you, and a better wife could no man wish; but it is necessary to tell you several things which it is most important for you to know. Owing to circumstances which I must not explain, the destiny of Fairies and of mankind is linked together in a curious way, and both of them have something akin to the mere animals. For instance, it is well known that the face of every man who comes into the world wears, when he grows up, an

expression like the face of some animal—a horse, a sheep, a
dog, a fox, or some other creature of the same sort. Now, in
Fairies, destiny takes a different turn. We are liable to be
obliged actually to take the shape of some animal during a
portion of our lives; and thus it is that my daughter has appeared to you as a Cat. The only way in which she could hope
permanently to resume her own shape was by marrying a
Mortal, and you are the fortunate object of her choice. The
bar which you have just passed, and which will rise again
after you have descended the hill, prevents any one from
leaving the outskirts of this forest and descending into the
valley. The Ogres cannot leave the forest; and although
Fairies can of course do more than such wretches as they, yet
no Fairy can pass this bar unless carried by a Mortal, except
on very special occasions, and for a short time only. You
could not have passed the bar without Fairy aid, nor could
Puss-cat Mew have done so without you. Take her, then, Joe,
and make her a good husband. Remember, however, that you
obey the directions which I now give you. Once every year,
on the anniversary of the day on which you are married,
Puss-cat Mew must wear that garment which she now has
on, her best embroidered petticoat. That would seem to you
a simple thing enough, but you little know how much depends upon it. It is necessary that, for three years to come,
my dear daughter should daily drink a bason of milk; at the
end of that time, no rules will be necessary, and she will
be quite safe, and beyond the power of evil. But if, during the
three years, she omits for one day to drink her milk, and for-
gets to wear the petticoat on her marriage anniversary, her
enemies will have power over her, and she will have to become a Cat again. And one more thing I must tell you,
namely, that if during the time that she is wearing her petticoat it gets the least bit torn or burnt, no one but a Fairy can
mend it, and it must be mended in this forest, and with Fairy
silk. Until this is done, she will be lost to you, and you may
fancy the difficulty of getting it done in a place where our

enemies are so continually on the watch. Here there is no
milk, so that no Fairy has a chance of drinking for three
years, and thus being able to keep a Mortal shape. Puss-cat
Mew, therefore, will depend upon your care and attention,
and I am sure you will never repent the day on which she becomes your wife."

Joe listened with respectful attention to the words of the
Fairy Queen, and faithfully promised that which was required. He didn't the least object to marry the young lady
who stood blushing before him, for not only was he exceedingly grateful for all the services she had rendered him as
Puss-cat Mew, but he had really become exceedingly fond of
her; and this fondness was by no means diminished when he
looked upon the great beauty of her present appearance. The
Fairy Queen now kissed her daughter; and bidding them both
farewell, disappeared from their sight; whilst Joe tenderly
embraced his bride, and they descended the hill together, and
made the best of their way to the old miller's house.

Joe's father and mother were delighted to see him again,
and still more so with the beautiful wife whom he had
brought with him. Puss-cat Mew was welcomed with the
greatest tenderness, which she returned with an affection
which greatly pleased the old couple. Moreover, they soon
found that it was a great advantage to have a Fairy for a
daughter-in-law, for she was the handiest creature imagin-
able, and everything she laid her hand to seemed to prosper.
The mill went merrily, and money came so fast into the
miller's pocket, that he was able to enlarge his house, which
he made very comfortable, and to greatly increase his business.

So time rolled on, and Joe began to think himself the happiest fellow in the world,—and so I dare say he was while
those jolly days lasted. He never forgot the cup of milk for
his wife—it was placed every morning on a little table by her
bedside; and, in case of any accident, the miller had three

fine cows in his meadow by the river, so that there might always be a good supply of the delicious fluid.

At last the year passed away, and the day dawned which was the first anniversary of Joe's wedding-day. Puss-cat Mew did not forget the embroidered petticoat, which had been carefully put away the year before. She took it out of the wardrobe with great care, and put it on just as it was; and very well she looked in it. They had had many consultations as to how she had better pass the day so as most surely to avoid any danger to the important garment, and at last it was determined that Puss-cat Mew should remain all day in the front room, and keep as quiet as possible. So she did, and the day passed off without any particular occurrence till quite towards the evening. Then, as it grew chilly, the fire was lighted and blazed up merrily. The old people were sitting on one side of it, Joe and his wife on the other, when suddenly a large coal, all alight, bounced from the fire and fell close to Joe's mother. They all started up, but Puss-cat Mew was quicker than any of them, and springing over the coal, caught the old lady's dress and pulled it away lest it should catch fire. Unlucky action! In so doing she either touched the coal with her own dress, or the wind of her dress in passing over it made it flare up; whatever was the cause, however, the sad result was the same; in one instant her petticoat caught light, and, although Joe extinguished it in a moment, a large and undeniable hole was burnt in it! Her face grew deadly pale at the same moment, her dress fell from her, and in the twinkling of an eye Joe and his parents saw nothing before them but a Tortoiseshell Cat, which, with a melancholy mew, vanished from their sight, whilst at the same moment a harsh and cruel voice was heard to exclaim the fatal words—

"Puss-cat Mew jumped over a coal,
In her best petticoat burnt a great hole;
Puss-cat Mew shan't have any milk
Till her best petticoat's mended with silk."

They all three looked round, and beheld the hateful face of
Jumper, gleaming with malicious pleasure. Joe rushed out,
but the Dwarf was off at the top of his speed, and there was
no chance of catching him. Poor Joe Brown! He threw himself on the ground in the deepest misery, and his parents' efforts to console him were all in vain. His loved, his beautiful
wife was gone—gone for ever—and probably in the power
of her enemies. He felt that life without her was impossible,
and his first impulse was to kill himself in the quickest way
he could. However, on reflection, he remembered that this
would do neither himself nor Puss-cat Mew the slightest
good, and would, moreover, please her enemies more than
anything else. He took a second and a better resolution, and
this was to devote the rest of his life to the endeavour to recover his lost and loved one.

From what the Fairy Queen had told him, it was evident
that the forest was the place in which alone this could be accomplished, and the question was whether he could manage
to get the petticoat mended in the forest without being slain
by the Ogres or entrapped by the crafty Dwarfs. His old father had often told him that "courage overcame difficulties,"
and although both father and mother were very much averse
to his leaving them again, yet when they saw that he was
quite determined to do so, and remembered how much he
owed to Puss-cat Mew, they could say no more; and, after
tenderly embracing and blessing him, bade him farewell.

This was a very different starting from his last, when he
had nothing to think of but the adventures of which he was
in search, and was as light-hearted and merry as could be.
Now, his heart was heavy enough, and his hopes were all set
upon the recovery of his lost treasure. The petticoat was
safely tied up and fastened to his waist, and with a stout
oaken staff in his hand he set out for the forest.

As he walked along, however, he thought long and anxiously as to what would be the best course to pursue; for,
after all, he could hardly hope to escape his enemies and suc-

ceed in recovering his wife, unless some help could be
found. Whilst he was thinking, he drew nearer and nearer to
the forest, until he was quite close to it; and at that moment
he perceived a Fox standing at the edge of the wood, and
looking steadily at him. The animal did not run away, or appear the least frightened, but, on his coming near, sat up on
its hind-legs and began to talk to him at once—

"Joe Brown," it said, "you are come upon a dangerous
business. I know your story, and am come to give you all the
aid in my power; for I pity you from the bottom of my heart."

"Thank you, Mr. Fox," replied poor Joe; "if you really *can*
help me, I shall never forget your kindness."

"Well," rejoined the animal, "you know that foxes are by
no means fools, and I hope to show you that I am not a friend
to be despised. Take these three hairs from my brush, and
be careful to remember what I now tell you. These are the
means by which your dearest wishes may be accomplished;
but first you must place each one separately upon the palm of
your left hand, and pronounce the magic word 'Leeneitz.' "

Joe took the three hairs as he was told, and laying the first
one upon the palm of his left hand, pronounced the word as
the Fox had done, when the hair immediately turned into a
bright steel dagger, sharp and strong.

"This," said the Fox, "is a dagger which even the tough
hide of an Ogre cannot turn aside; it will stand you in good
stead in the hour of need."

Joe then tried the second hair, which, upon the magic
word being spoken, changed into a snuff-box, full of such
strong snuff, that, even though the lid was shut, it set Joe
sneezing at once.

"Now," said the Fox, "this snuff makes you sneeze, it is
true, but it also sends any one who smells it to sleep very
shortly; and if your enemies have once taken a good pull at
it, they will be quiet enough for a few hours, I'll warrant
you."

Joe then tried the third hair, which, somewhat to his surprise, became a left-hand glove.

"Do not despise it, Joe Brown," said the Fox; "when this glove is upon your left hand, you will be invisible. Thus you have three powerful weapons to use against your foes, although you must remember that you can only use one of them at a time; but as I notice that your oaken staff there is tipped with lead, I think you are really so well armed, that only common courage and caution are needful to give you every hope of success."

"I thank you," said Joe, "from the bottom of my heart; but, oh! can you tell me where I shall be likely to find my wife— my own beloved Puss-cat Mew?"

The Fox shook his head solemnly, and replied—"That belongs to others to tell. I have performed my part, as directed by One who has a right to direct me, and I can say and do no more for you." With which words he darted after a hare which was sauntering by at the moment, and was out of sight instantly. But Joe felt more cheerful after what he had heard and the gifts which he had received. He boldly entered the wood, and shaped his course towards where he supposed the Fairy Spring to be. As he went along, however, something suddenly dropped upon him from a tree and lighted on his shoulders, with its legs one on each side of his neck, while a voice at the same time exclaimed, in rough tones of exultation—

"I've nabbed him! I've nabbed him!"

In an instant Joe recognised the voice of one of the Dwarfs, and, dropping suddenly upon his knees, sent the little man flying over his head; but, not knowing how near the other Dwarfs might be, he then put on the left-hand glove as fast as he could, determined to try its powers. The Dwarf jumped up in a fury, but his face expressed blank astonishment as he looked at where Joe had been standing, and where indeed he was really standing still, but the Dwarf could not see him. It was Juff who had made this attack and

been so roughly thrown on the ground, and he now exclaimed, in a voice of mingled anger and surprise—

"Why, where on earth has the fellow got to? Vile Mortal—
where are you?"

Joe stood quite still, delighted to have proved the power of
his glove, and the truth of the Fox.

"This must be seen to," said Juff, and ran growling off in
a rage.

Joe could have probably slain him, as the little villain
seemed to be all alone, but he was full of anxiety to reach the
Fairy Spring, where he hoped to hear news of his dear one;
so he thought not of pursuit, but pushed forward till he came
close to the spot. He stepped sadly on to the green space. The
fountain seemed no longer to sparkle so brightly and play so
merrily as it had done when he first saw it. There was something mournful in its appearance, and the stream seemed to
sigh as it slowly trickled away into the forest.

Joe sat down upon the ground, and fairly sobbed aloud. At
last, in a sad tone of voice, he said—

"Oh, Fairies, tell me of my darling! tell me how to recover
my adorable Puss-cat Mew!"

Soft and low came the voice this time, in sweet but plain-
tive strain, and Joe clasped his hands tightly and listened:—

"Puss-cat Mew in dungeon pines:
Every day the Ogre grim
On the flesh of Mortal dines,
Boasting none can conquer him:
Boasts he too, that villain dread,
Shortly he will capture you,
And will lay your bleeding head
At the feet of Puss-cat Mew.
Should this monster, whom we hate,
In the forest take thy life,
Know the solemn doom of Fate—
Puss-cat Mew must be his wife!

Speaking only Ogre tongue,
Fairy music all forgot,
Doomed to nourish Ogres young—
Can there be more cruel lot?
Mortal! steel thy gallant heart,
Be thou cautious, bold, and true,
From the forest ne'er depart
Till thou rescue Puss-cat Mew!"

Joe jumped up with a bound, and raised his oak-staff high
in the air.

"By everything I hold dear!" he cried, "never will I turn
back from this venture till I rescue my true love from so terrible a fate. Courage! I should be a recreant knave indeed if
I had it not. The blood of all the Browns foams and boils in
my veins. I am ready for the fray!" and without more to say
or do, he walked out of the green and marched boldly forward.

He had not gone far before he heard footsteps, and looking round, having first put on his glove, he perceived the
Dwarf Juff, with two of the Ogres, talking eagerly.

"Why don't he eat her?" said the Dwarf.

"You little hop-o'-my-thumb!" growled one of the Giants,
"you can't eat a Fairy, you know, or he'd have made but a
mouthful of her. But if he catches that lout of a Mortal
whom she is so sweet on, he can eat *him,* and then he has the
right to marry her. But I know one thing—*I* wouldn't marry
such a squalling Cat for ninepence-halfpenny. The row she
makes after that Joe! I wish I had him here! I'd Joe him!
Wouldn't you, Mumble-chumps?"

"Yes," returned the other Ogre, to whom he had spoken;
"yes, brother Munch'emup, I think we could show him a
trick or two worth mentioning."

"Why don't you do it, then?" said a loud voice close to
them; and Joe, with his glove on, hit Juff such a crack on the
head that the little wretch rolled over like a ninepin.

"Help, oh, help me!" he roared in agony, as Joe dealt him another blow; but the Ogres could see nobody, and therefore did nothing, whilst Juff lay there bellowing.

However, Joe, finding how well he was concealed by his glove, and being highly indignant with the Ogre Munch'emup, who had spoken so disrespectfully of Puss-cat Mew, dealt him a blow across the shins with his staff, which made him jump.

"What do you mean by kicking me, Mumble-chumps?" asked he.

"I didn't touch you," answered the other, to whom Joe at the same time administered a like blow.

"But I'm not going to stand being kicked by you!" and as Joe dealt them another blow apiece, the two monsters furiously attacked each other, each believing that his friend had assaulted him.

Joe stepped back and watched the fight with interest, until a blow from Mumble-chumps felled Munch'emup to the ground, where he lay senseless. Joe now thought that he had better play out *his* part in the game, so he saluted the other Ogre with a tremendous stroke on the wrist, which was nearly broken by the lead-tipped staff.

The Giant roared with fury, but could see no one to strike, and another blow on the inside of the kneecap brought him on his knees. Then Joe struck him on the head with his full force, crying out as he did so—

"Puss-cat Mew sends you this!" and the Ogre toppled over with a groan.

To make matters safe, Joe (having taken off his glove) took his steel dagger, and put an end to the two murdering villains who lay there. As to the wretch Juff, he begged hard for mercy, and Joe was inclined to spare him on account of his size, and would probably have done so had not the old voice at that moment sounded in his ears, less softly and sweetly than ever before—

"Spare not the Dwarfs! for they are sent
    Down to that dungeon day by day;
With jeers they Puss-cat Mew torment;
    Wherefore 'tis justice bids thee slay!"

"Say you so?" cried Joe; "then, by my grandmother's petticoat, *this* rascal jeers no more!" and he raised his staff over his head.

"Oh dear, oh dear!" yelled Juff, "I didn't do it—I didn't mean to—I wasn't there—it was somebody else." And he howled in abject terror; but Joe, having once invoked his grandmother's petticoat, which was the most solemn form of adjuration known among the Brown family, hesitated no longer, but dashed out the brains of the miserable Dwarf with his staff immediately.

But the mention of the garment which had caused all his troubles made Joe recollect that it was still fastened to his waist, and indeed he had found it rather inconvenient during his late exertions. Moreover, he had now fully made up his mind to attack the Ogres in their castle, but he did not see how he was likely to get the petticoat mended with Fairy silk *there,* and he determined to retrace his steps to the Fairy Green and there leave it. The spring appeared to bubble up rather more merrily when he stepped upon the green, but there was still a melancholy look about the place. Joe spread the garment carefully out before the spring, and, as he found the Fairies always spoke in rhyme, thought he would try his own hand at it, and accordingly spoke thus—

"With Fairy silk this petticoat,
    They tell me, must be mended;
And thus the girl on whom I doat
    Will find her sorrows ended.
To get it mended therefore now
    My one incessant care is;

So please inform me where and how,
    You dear delightful Fairies!"

And Joe felt rather proud of himself after this first attempt at rhyming, which was duly answered by the friendly voice—

"Leave the sacred garment here;
Leave it, youth, and never fear.
To the fight thyself devote,
Leave to us the petticoat!"

Thus reassured, Joe left the petticoat on the green, shouldered his oaken staff, and marched on. Through the wood he toiled up the gradual ascent, till, without interruption, he came very near to the castle of the Ogres.

As he came up to the gate, he heard a great noise, and having put on his glove, he quietly entered the courtyard, in which he found the two Ogres, Grindbones and Smashman, playing at bowls with petrified men's heads; whilst their three remaining servants, whose names were Grimp, Grump, and Gruby, were in attendance, and the two Dwarfs, seated on a low stone bench, looking on. There, then, were all his enemies at once; but Joe knew that caution was necessary. When invisible, he could only use his staff, or his course might have been easier; but no two of the three gifts could be used at the same time: moreover, he mistrusted Gandleperry, whose cunning was evidently superior to that of all the rest. He therefore remained quiet, silently turning over in his mind what was the best thing to do next, when, to his disgust, Grindbones presently turned round and said aloud—

"Now, you Dwarfs, it is time for you to go and tease Pusscat Mew. Where's that fellow Juff? Man's eyes and cheeks! he is never here to the time!"

With a wily leer Gandleperry replied—

"He is out after that poor fool of a Mortal, whom he will probably entice here soon; but Jumper and I are enough to tease that conceited Fairy minx. I wish our power was great enough to allow us to touch her; wouldn't we tear her flesh for her, and make that pretty face rather different!"

And with a fearful scowl he and Jumper left the seat and entered the house.

Joe instantly perceived that this was his chance of discovering his darling. Keeping on his glove, he followed the two Dwarfs into the house, down a stone passage, till they came to a flight of stairs—at the top of which Gandleperry suddenly stopped, and exclaimed to his companion:

"Did you hear anything, Jumper? I thought I heard a step; and there's an uncommon smell of Mortal here, too!"

"No," replied Jumper, "I heard nothing; and as to a smell of Mortal, I should be surprised if there wasn't, for don't you remember how the alderman, whom the Ogres caught yesterday, was chased up and down by the servant Ogres to make him tender? Here it was they worried him at last, and I should think the place would smell for a week."

Gandleperry made no reply, but taking a lucifer-box from a shelf in the wall, struck a light, and, with candle in hand, descended the steps, and Jumper after him. Joe cautiously followed, and counted thirty steps, at the bottom of which they came to a low door, which Gandleperry opened by means of a key which he took from Jumper, who carried it at his belt. They all three entered, and Joe could hardly restrain his passion at the sight which met his eyes. On a low chair, in the middle of a vaulted room, lighted only by a dim lamp fixed in the wall, sat Puss-cat Mew. She seemed only the wreck of her former self. Her tortoiseshell skin was no longer bright and glossy, her eyes no longer sparkled with their old joyous, loving light; she sat with her head supported by one of her paws, and sorrow and suffering were written on her countenance. A tin can of cold water was by her side, and an untasted loaf with it.

"Now, prisoner," said Jumper, "how are you to-day, my minnikin Miss?"

Then Gandleperry seated himself cross-legged opposite her on the floor, put a thumb into each waistcoat-pocket, approached his face so near to her that Joe longed to attack him, and with a malicious grin, leering up into her face, thus accosted her—

"Pettikin, dear, how is she this nice, bright day? Oh, how lovely it is in the forest! Birds are singing, the sun is shining, flowers are blossoming—oh, *so* delightful it is! And here is poor Pussy sitting all alone in a nasty damp dungeon! Where's her Joe now, eh? You little meek-faced beast!—you can't get out!—no, not a bit of it! And, I say, what do you think? Here's a bit of news for you! Joe's caught! Oh yes, he is! Such a go! Ain't the Ogres just pleased! Joe-giblets for soup! Joe's feet and ears cold for breakfast! Roast loin of Joe for dinner! Joe and onions for the servant Ogres, and Joe's head and brains for the dear little Dwarfs! And then Puss-cat Mew will have to marry the nice, kind, handsome old Ogre that beats all his wives till their bones are broken and their flesh is tender, and then has them made into pies to take but for luncheon when he goes shooting! O you pet Puss-cat!—Miaw-aw-aw."

And the Dwarf put out his tongue at the poor victim, and imitated the mewing of a cat. Joe was fearfully enraged, but he felt that everything depended upon his prudence, and he therefore restrained himself, and waited.

Puss-cat Mew made no answer to these taunts at first, but only sighed. As Gandleperry, however, continued, and Jumper chimed in with even coarser insults, she spoke at last in a soft voice and said,—

"You do well, wretched creatures, to abuse one who is permitted for a time to be in your power, but your own hour of sorrow and misfortune may be near, and then you will remember Puss-cat Mew."

This remark had but little effect upon the Dwarfs, and they continued to tease and revile the poor Lady for half an hour, during which time Joe stood still near the door, grinding his teeth with vexation. It was, however, fortunate for him that he had waited, for an event now occurred, than which nothing could have served him better. The crafty Gandleperry had long been dissatisfied with his position in the Ogres' castle with respect to the two other Dwarfs, whose presence deprived him of the large share of Mortal heads and brains which he desired, and who, moreover, were inclined to side together against the superiority over them which he claimed. He had therefore long determined to get rid of one or other of them upon the first opportunity, and the time seemed to him to have now arrived. When they had tormented poor Puss-cat Mew till they could think of nothing else, Gandleperry told Jumper to go before him up the stairs, and he would fasten the door; and as the latter did so, Joe saw with horror that Gandleperry drew a sharp knife from his belt, and struck his brother Dwarf a fearful blow over the shoulder into the neck. With an unearthly yell, Jumper fell to the ground; but he never yelled again, for Gandleperry jumped on him and cut his throat in a moment, as if he had been a pig! He then dragged him back into the dungeon, and making a horrible face at Puss-cat Mew, said to her—

"Here is a nice companion for you, Pettikin; pray be kind to him till I have time to fetch him away or bury him! He won't make a noise or disturb you! Ta-ta!"

And he kissed his hand to the poor creature in fearful mockery! But his triumph was short. Joe now saw the opportunity he had so long waited for, and a tremendous blow upon the head stretched Gandleperry senseless and bleeding upon the body of his murdered mate, and avenged the insults he had heaped upon the unfortunate prisoner.

Joe drew off his glove in a moment, and with a purr of joy Puss-cat Mew rushed into his arms. They had, however, no time to talk or to think of happy things. Five deadly enemies were alive, and there was no safety yet.

Puss-cat Mew told Joe that she had no power to help him now, and that he must judge and act for himself. "No one," she said, "would come near her dungeon again till late in the evening, when one or both of the chief Ogres, after their dinner, might probably come down to laugh at her."

Joe could not bear to leave her with the bodies of the Dwarfs, neither could he take her up where she would be seen by the Ogres; he therefore locked the door of the dungeon, and left her at the bottom of the stairs till she should hear of him again, telling her at the same time to come up directly if she heard him call. Then, again putting on his glove, he ascended the stairs. In the dining-room, which was on the first floor, and a pleasant room enough, sat the two chief Giants, each on one side of a round table, with dishes and plates before them. Joe just peeped in, and then creeping down again, saw the three servant Ogres sitting sleepily over the fire in the servants' hall. He advanced very quietly, and, after a few moments, found that the lazy fellows were really all dozing. He therefore took off his glove, and, taking out his snuff-box, went behind the chair of one, and, opening the box, held it so immediately under his nose that its strength actually prevented his sneezing, and sent him to sleep more soundly than ever. Joe had previously stuffed his own nose quite full of the cotton-wool in which the box had been wrapped; and thus feeling secure from the effects of the snuff, he held the box under the nose of each of the servant Ogres until they were all buried in slumbers which would render them harmless for some time to come. Then Joe put on his glove again, and walked up to the dining-room, where the two chief Ogres were at dinner. They were very merry, for they were feasting off the alderman of whose fate Joe had lately heard, and who seemed to have been fat enough to have been Lord Mayor. There was a smoking haunch of alderman upon the table, to which both the Ogres seemed to have paid great attention, and they were accompanying the meal with deep draughts of some strong spirit. Joe advanced slowly to the table, and stood for a short time watching the monsters.

"Flesh and brains!" said the elder of the two, "but this Mortal was fat and well-to-do. I wish all Mortals were as fat and juicy."

"Yes," replied the other; "they would be choice morsels then, and not like that vile pedlar the other day, who was all skin and bone."

And so ran the discourse of the creatures upon their dreadful meal, until Joe sickened with disgust. Having eaten and drunk heartily, the Ogres threw themselves back in their chairs, extended their legs, and in a few moments snored loudly, making so hideous a noise that Joe could compare it to nothing but a hundred fat hogs rolled into one, and all grunting at the same time. When he saw them thus, Joe boldly drew off his glove, and taking a full handful of the snuff in his hands, instantly flung it into the face and eyes, one after the other, of both his enemies. And so much more went into their eyes than up their noses, the effect was not to send them to sleep, but to half-blind them, and put them in a furious passion. Quick as lightning Joe had his glove on again, whilst the Giants, both jumping up at the same moment, overset the table with a tremendous crash, and roared for their servants, who, however, could not awake if they wished to, and therefore never came.

"Did you throw something at me, nephew?" asked old Grindbones.

"Certainly not," replied the young Ogre.

"Then the Fairies have played us some trick! What is it? Where are they? Confound this stuff!" said Grindbones, and he stamped violently on the floor, and roared again for Grimp, Grump, and Gruby. "Stay," said he; "man's marrow-bones! I will know the cause of this!" and he walked through a door which led into a room close by, whilst the younger Ogre sank back into his chair, growling to himself and, not having had so much snuff as his uncle, being rather more disposed for sleep; and having withal drunk heavily of the spirits, he began to nod again.

But the old Ogre had gone to fetch something in which he
had great trust. It was a tame Magpie, from whom nothing
was invisible, and who would soon tell him if anything was
wrong. He took her out of her cage, and hastened back to the
room where he had left his nephew. But no Magpie was
needed to tell him what was going on. As soon as Smashman
began to show signs of sleep, Joe, feeling that there was
no time to lose, drew off his glove, drew out his steel dagger, and, stepping speedily but quietly behind his chair,
plunged the weapon up to the hilt in his throat. The Ogre
gave a loud sobbing sound, half screech, half speech, and as
Joe plucked out the dagger, his head fell forward and the
blood gushed from a fearful wound. It was at this moment
that the old Ogre entered the room from the side door by
which he had left it, and saw in a moment what had happened. In an instant he rushed upon Joe with a dreadful
howl, but Joe sheathed his dagger and popped on his glove
just in time to escape him, and made for the door. As he
rushed towards it, however, the Magpie, seated on the Ogre's
shoulder, shouted out to him—

"This way, Master, to the door that opens on to the stairs.
I can see him,—quick! quick!" And so well did the old fellow follow her directions, that Joe only just got through the
door in time, and dashed down stairs, calling at the top of
his voice for Puss-cat Mew to follow him out of the castle.
Down he rushed, out of the door, into the yard; but as ill-
luck would have it, a nail in the doorpost caught his glove,
which fell from his hand, and as he rushed from the yard the
Ogre saw him, and, no longer wanting the eyes of the Magpie to help him, rushed furiously in pursuit, making the forest re-echo with his hideous cries of rage.

If he had not eaten and drunk so much, nothing could
have saved Joe, since the monster could go twice as fast as he
could; but the quantity of alderman and spirits which he had
taken caused old Grindbones to go somewhat slower and less
steadily than usual, and gave Joe a good chance for his life.

He rushed forward at the top of his speed in a straight line for the Fairy Green, the Ogre furiously blundering after him, and the Magpie flying by his side and chuckling with excitement as she encouraged her master. Joe saw the green and the spring before him, and strained every nerve to reach it. The enemy gained upon him at each stride, and actually stretched out his hand to seize him at the very instant that he stepped within the green space.

Here, however, occurred something which Joe had never thought of, but which the Giant, if he had not been mad with rage and drink, would probably have recollected. The spot, sacred to the Fairies and beloved by them, received a friendly Mortal kindly, and Joe hastened forward as usual to the spring. But the huge Ogre had no sooner advanced upon it for a couple of yards, than the whole space began to quiver and shake like a quicksand, and the monster found himself sinking in at every step. He strove to turn and fly, but it was too late. In an instant, a myriad Fairy forms were dancing around him with light laughs of derision. He struck at them in vain; deeper and deeper he sank, till the soft earth had drawn him down, so that only the upper half of his body was visible. Then he uttered an awful yell, which scared every creature in the forest, and his struggles were tremendous; but they only seemed to cause him to sink deeper. And as he slowly sank down, making the most horrible faces and contortions, the soft, sweet voice sang once more from the Fairy Spring—

"See where the monster Ogre lies
    At mercy of the Fairy race;
In vain his bulky form he tries
    To move across th' enchanted space.
A mass of wickedness so great
    No Fairy Green could e'er endure;
And here the wretch must meet his fate,
    And here his punishment is sure.

So happiness to all the wood
   And all the Fairies shall accrue;
His death shall work for wondrous good,
   And triumph to our Puss-cat Mew!"

And as the voice sounded, the Giant still sank, and he threw
up his arms in despair above his head; and when only his
waving arms and his head were seen, so that it was plain he
could not escape and his end was certain, the cruel and
wicked Magpie flew down and perched upon her master's
head, and began to have a peck at his eyes. But such ingrati-
tude was not allowed, and when a Fairy came near to drive
her away, the bird flew off chattering to a neighbouring tree,
in the branches of which was hid an Adder, who dealt her a
mortal wound as she sat there abusing the Fairies for spoiling
her fun.

And now there were only the head and neck and one hand
of the Ogre to be seen above the ground; and Joe was anxiously waiting and gazing, when, looking up, he perceived
his own beloved Puss-cat Mew approaching from the forest,
and drawing near to the green. At the same moment spoke
the old voice in his ear—

"Mortal! do thou lightly tread,
   And, with dagger keen and true,
Take the monster Ogre's head
   To the feet of Puss-cat Mew!"

Joe could not hesitate to obey the command given by one
who had proved so true an adviser. He seized his dagger, and
advancing lightly over the green, raised it in his hand, and
was about to strike the wretched Grindbones, when all of a
sudden the terrific sound of a fearful explosion rent the air,
and, looking towards the hill on which the Ogres' castle had
stood, he perceived stones and rockwork, earth and trees,
filling the air, whilst the terrible noise deadened every other

sound, and was succeeded by a dread stillness even more alarming.

What do you think had happened? The truth is, that Gandleperry had not been killed, but only stunned by the blow which Joe had given him. After a while, he had come to himself again, and sitting up, found himself in a very uncomfortable position. There was Jumper's body unpleasantly close, and the dungeon door fast locked, and after thinking for a little while, he began to feel pretty certain that the Fairies were at the bottom of it all. Puss-cat Mew was gone, and how to get out he did not know. However, groping about the floor, he came upon his lucifer-match box, which he had brought down with the candle, and, immediately striking a light, began to search every corner of the dungeon, to find some means of getting out. At last he perceived a low door in one corner of the room, and at the handle of this he tugged, and then he pushed as hard as he could against it; and at last it suddenly gave way, so that, candle in hand, he stumbled forward into another vault.

Now, many years before, when the Ogres had first taken possession of that castle, it had belonged to a band of robbers, whom the monsters had killed, eaten, or dispersed. These robbers had stored all their gunpowder in one of the vaults below the castle, and there it had been left; for gunpowder is not a thing which Ogres use, except occasionally to flavour their soup. In the course of time some of the casks which held the powder had decayed and burst, and so the vault was half full of loose gunpowder, strewn about over the floor.

Into this vault Gandleperry stumbled, and the candle which was in his hand fell on the powder. There was so much of it that the whole castle was blown to the skies in the explosion that followed. The wretched Gandleperry was of course blown to atoms, and the three Ogres, Grimp, Grump, and Gruby, who were sleeping off the effects of Joe's snuff in the room above, flew all in different directions—heads,

arms, and legs being torn off and driven through the air with
the masses of wood and stone which were sent up.

In one minute no living thing remained in the castle of the
Ogres, and the castle itself was one vast blackened ruin! The
dying Grindbones heard the noise, and a fearful groan which
he gave seemed to show that he understood that it betokened
the downfall of the power and pride of his race. That groan,
however, was his last, for Joe hesitated no longer, but, in obedience to the Fairy's command, plunged his steel dagger into
the monster's throat, and had just time to sever his head from
his body before the latter disappeared for ever, swallowed up
by the fatal quicksand of the Fairy Green. The ground, having closed over the Ogre's carcase, immediately resumed its
former placid appearance. Joe hastened to meet Puss-cat
Mew, and laid the head of her enemy at her feet. Then leading her on to the green space, upon which she now came with
him readily, they saw the spring bubbling up more merrily
than ever, and the stream seemed to laugh and chuckle with
joy as it darted on. And then, as they came close to the
spring, once more the soft, clear voice spoke in sweet and
happy accents—

> "The hour is come: the foe is slain,
> And Puss-cat Mew is free again;
> Again has Fortune blest the Right,
> And Wrong has perished in the fight.
> Go, happy Mortal, take the Bride
> Who stands all blushing by your side,
> And Heaven be merciful to you,
> As you are kind to Puss-cat Mew!"

And, as the voice concluded, Puss-cat Mew lightly bounded
forward and disappeared behind the spring. In one moment,
however, she reappeared, but no longer in the shape of a cat,
which she had lately worn. Clad in the same dress which she
had on when he first saw her in mortal form at the iron bar,

and with her embroidered petticoat mended and as good as new, Joe saw his own dear beautiful wife standing before him, whilst the Fairy Queen led her by the hand, and Fairy forms danced around in gay and festive merriment. Then the Queen addressed the happy Joe in these words—

"Joe Brown, you have borne your trials well, and right gallantly have you fought, and thus deserved the success which has attended your efforts. There is no longer any difficulty in leaving the forest; the iron bar has perished with the Ogres and the Dwarfs, and Puss-cat Mew is able at once to resume her human form, and to become yours again. Take her, then, and remember the conditions on which alone you can keep her. Observe them carefully, and many years of happy life will be before you both. Bless you, my children!"

Then Joe and Puss-cat Mew knelt before the Fairy Queen, who solemnly blessed them; and the Fairies sang sweet songs as the loving pair walked away; and as they turned round to cast a lingering look of regret at the dear old Fairy Green and Spring, they saw the Fairy mother just mounting on a rainbow to have a last look at them as they left the forest!

Safely they reached the hill, and safely descended; and you may fancy the delight of the old miller and his wife when they saw them enter the house again, and heard all the wonderful adventures that had happened to Joe.

I am sure you can guess the rest of the story. The three years passed over without any accident. Puss-cat Mew took her milk regularly (which people should always do when they have any medicine, nice or nasty, to take), and everything went on as well as possible. They had sons who were strong, and daughters who were beautiful; and, though nobody knows it, *for certain,* it is strongly suspected that the "Miller's Daughter," about whom Mr. Tennyson wrote such pretty poetry, was descended directly from our dear Puss-cat Mew.

The Ogres' castle became a well-known ruin, visited by

many people, who wondered when it was built, and what it had been. Well, Stonehenge is a vast ruin, and no one knows what it was, or when it was built; and if I should tell you that the Ogres' castle is Stonehenge, and that Stonehenge is the Ogres' castle, who is to contradict me?

Now, children, go and find out all about Stonehenge directly; but whether you agree with this part of the story or not, remember that you now know the true history of Puss-cat Mew; and I am glad to say that, in spite of all their former trials and troubles, she and Joe Brown lived very happily together all the rest of their lives!

There! that is all the White Cat told the Brown Kitten; and you see how lucky it is that I understand the language of the animals!

The Griffin
and the Minor Canon
-*-
by Frank R. Stockton

Frank R. Stockton was the first great American writer of original fairy tales. Stockton's style is gentle and droll, and his stories frequently show an inquisitive questioning of society's norms. There is no evidence as to whether or not Tolkien knew Stockton's tales; in the late nineteenth century and the first half of the twentieth they were widely available.

"The Griffin and the Minor Canon" appeared in the October 1885 issue of *St. Nicholas* and was included in *The Bee-Man of Orn and Other Fanciful Tales* (1887).

OVER the great door of an old, old church which stood in a quiet town of a far-away land there was carved in stone the figure of a large griffin. The old-time sculptor had done his work with great care, but the image he had made was not a pleasant one to look at. It had a large head, with enormous open mouth and savage teeth; from its back arose great wings, armed with sharp hooks and prongs; it had stout legs in front, with projecting claws; but there were no legs behind,—the body running out into a long and powerful tail, finished off at the end with a barbed point. This tail was coiled up under him, the end sticking up just back of his wings.

The sculptor, or the people who had ordered this stone figure, had evidently been very much pleased with it, for little copies of it, also in stone, had been placed here and there along the sides of the church, not very far from the ground, so that people could easily look at them, and ponder on their curious forms. There were a great many other sculptures on the outside of this church,—saints, martyrs, grotesque heads of men, beasts, and birds, as well as those of other creatures which can not be named, because nobody knows exactly what they were; but none were so curious and interesting as the great griffin over the door, and the little griffins on the sides of the church.

A long, long distance from the town, in the midst of dreadful wilds scarcely known to man, there dwelt the Griffin whose image had been put up over the church-door. In some way or other, the old-time sculptor had seen him, and afterward, to the best of his memory, had copied his figure in stone. The Griffin had never known this, until, hundreds of years afterward, he heard from a bird, from a wild animal, or in some manner which it is not now easy to find out, that there was a likeness of him on the old church in the distant town. Now, this Griffin had no idea how he looked. He had never seen a mirror, and the streams where he lived were so turbulent and violent that a quiet piece of water, which would reflect the image of any thing looking into it, could not be found. Being, as far as could be ascertained, the very last of his race, he had never seen another griffin. Therefore it was, that, when he heard of this stone image of himself, he became very anxious to know what he looked like, and at last he determined to go to the old church, and see for himself what manner of being he was. So he started off from the dreadful wilds, and flew on and on until he came to the countries inhabited by men, where his appearance in the air created great consternation; but he alighted nowhere, keeping up a steady flight until he reached the suburbs of the town which had his image on its church. Here, late in the afternoon, he alighted in a green meadow by the side of a brook, and stretched himself on the grass to rest. His great wings were tired, for he had not made such a long flight in a century, or more.

The news of his coming spread quickly over the town, and the people, frightened nearly out of their wits by the arrival of so extraordinary a visitor, fled into their houses, and shut themselves up. The Griffin called loudly for some one to come to him, but the more he called, the more afraid the people were to show themselves. At length he saw two laborers hurrying to their homes through the fields, and in a terrible voice he commanded them to stop. Not daring to disobey, the men stood, trembling.

"What is the matter with you all?" cried the Griffin. "Is there not a man in your town who is brave enough to speak to me?"

"I think," said one of the laborers, his voice shaking so that his words could hardly be understood, "that—perhaps— the Minor Canon—would come."

"Go, call him, then!" said the Griffin; "I want to see him."

The Minor Canon, who filled a subordinate position in the old church, had just finished the afternoon services, and was coming out of a side door, with three aged women who had formed the weekday congregation. He was a young man of a kind disposition, and very anxious to do good to the people of the town. Apart from his duties in the church, where he conducted services every weekday, he visited the sick and the poor, counseled and assisted persons who were in trouble, and taught a school composed entirely of the bad children in the town with whom nobody else would have anything to do. Whenever the people wanted anything done for them, they always went to the Minor Canon. Thus it was that the laborer thought of the young priest when he found that some one must come and speak to the Griffin.

The Minor Canon had not heard of the strange event, which was known to the whole town except himself and the three old women, and when he was informed of it, and was told that the Griffin had asked to see him, he was greatly amazed, and frightened.

"Me!" he exclaimed. "He has never heard of me! What should he want with *me*?"

"Oh! you must go instantly!" cried the two men. "He is very angry now because he has been kept waiting so long; and nobody knows what will happen if you don't hurry to him."

The poor Minor Canon would rather have had his hand cut off than go out to meet an angry griffin; but he felt that it was his duty to go, for it would be a woeful thing if injury should come to the people of the town because he was not brave enough to obey the summons of the Griffin. So, pale and frightened, he started off.

"Well," said the Griffin, as soon as the young man came near, "I am glad to see that there is some one who has the courage to come to me."

The Minor Canon did not feel very courageous, but he bowed his head.

"Is this the town," said the Griffin, "where there is a church with a likeness of myself over one of the doors?"

The Minor Canon looked at the frightful figure of the Griffin and saw that it was, without doubt, exactly like the stone image on the church. "Yes," he said, "you are right."

"Well, then," said the Griffin, "will you take me to it? I wish very much to see it."

The Minor Canon instantly thought that if the Griffin entered the town without the people knowing what he came for, some of them would probably be frightened to death, and so he sought to gain time to prepare their minds.

"It is growing dark, now," he said, very much afraid, as he spoke, that his words might enrage the Griffin, "and objects on the front of the church cannot be seen clearly. It will be better to wait until morning, if you wish to get a good view of the stone image of yourself."

"That will suit me very well," said the Griffin. "I see that you are a man of good sense. I am tired, and I will take a nap here on this soft grass, while I cool my tail in the little stream that runs near me. The end of my tail gets red-hot when I am angry or excited, and it is quite warm now. So you may go, but be sure and come early tomorrow morning, and show me the way to the church."

The Minor Canon was glad enough to take his leave, and hurried into the town. In front of the church he found a great many people assembled to hear his report of his interview with the Griffin. When they found that he had not come to spread ruin and devastation, but simply to see his stony likeness on the church, they showed neither relief nor gratification, but began to upbraid the Minor Canon for consenting to conduct the creature into the town.

"What could I do?" cried the young man. "If I should not bring him he would come himself and, perhaps, end by setting fire to the town with his red-hot tail."

Still the people were not satisfied, and a great many plans were proposed to prevent the Griffin from coming into the town. Some elderly persons urged that the young men should go out and kill him; but the young men scoffed at such a ridiculous idea. Then some one said that it would be a good thing to destroy the stone image so that the Griffin would have no excuse for entering the town; and this idea was received with such favor that many of the people ran for hammers, chisels, and crowbars, with which to tear down and break up the stone griffin. But the Minor Canon resisted this plan with all the strength of his mind and body. He assured the people that this action would enrage the Griffin beyond measure, for it would be impossible to conceal from him that his image had been destroyed during the night. But the people were so determined to break up the stone griffin that the Minor Canon saw that there was nothing for him to do but to stay there and protect it. All night he walked up and down in front of the church-door, keeping away the men who brought ladders, by which they might mount to the great stone griffin, and knock it to pieces with their hammers and crowbars. After many hours the people were obliged to give up their attempts, and went home to sleep; but the Minor Canon remained at his post till early morning, and then he hurried away to the field where he had left the Griffin.

The monster had just awakened, and rising to his fore-legs and shaking himself, he said that he was ready to go into the town. The Minor Canon, therefore, walked back, the Griffin flying slowly through the air, at a short distance above the head of his guide. Not a person was to be seen in the streets, and they proceeded directly to the front of the church, where the Minor Canon pointed out the stone griffin.

The real Griffin settled down in the little square before the church and gazed earnestly at his sculptured likeness. For a long time he looked at it. First he put his head on one side, and then he put it on the other; then he shut his right eye and gazed with his left, after which he shut his left eye and gazed with his right. Then he moved a little to one side and looked at the image, then he moved the other way. After a while he said to the Minor Canon, who had been standing by all this time:

"It is, it must be, an excellent likeness! That breadth between the eyes, that expansive forehead, those massive jaws! I feel that it must resemble me. If there is any fault to find with it, it is that the neck seems a little stiff. But that is nothing. It is an admirable likeness,—admirable!"

The Griffin sat looking at his image all the morning and all the afternoon. The Minor Canon had been afraid to go away and leave him, and had hoped all through the day that he would soon be satisfied with his inspection and fly away home. But by evening the poor young man was utterly exhausted, and felt that he must go away to eat and sleep. He frankly admitted this fact to the Griffin, and asked him if he would not like something to eat. He said this because he felt obliged in politeness to do so, but as soon as he had spoken the words, he was seized with dread lest the monster should demand half a dozen babies, or some tempting repast of that kind.

"Oh, no," said the Griffin, "I never eat between the equinoxes. At the vernal and at the autumnal equinox I take a good meal, and that lasts me for half a year. I am extremely regular in my habits, and do not think it healthful to eat at odd times. But if you need food, go and get it, and I will return to the soft grass where I slept last night and take another nap."

The next day the Griffin came again to the little square before the church, and remained there until evening, steadfastly regarding the stone griffin over the door. The Minor Canon came once or twice to look at him, and the Griffin seemed very glad to see him; but the young clergyman could not stay as he had done before, for he had many duties to perform. Nobody went to the church, but the people came to the Minor Canon's house, and anxiously asked him how long the Griffin was going to stay.

"I do not know," he answered, "but I think he will soon be satisfied with regarding his stone likeness, and then he will go away."

But the Griffin did not go away. Morning after morning he came to the church, but after a time he did not stay there all day. He seemed to have taken a great fancy to the Minor Canon, and followed him about as he pursued his various avocations. He would wait for him at the side door of the church, for the Minor Canon held services every day, morning and evening, though nobody came now. "If any one *should* come," he said to himself, "I must be found at my post." When the young man came out, the Griffin would accompany him in his visits to the sick and the poor, and would often look into the windows of the school-house where the Minor Canon was teaching his unruly scholars. All the other schools were closed, but the parents of the Minor Canon's scholars forced them to go to school, because they were so bad they could not endure them all day at home,—griffin or no griffin. But it must be said they generally behaved very well when that great monster sat up on his tail and looked through the school-room window.

When it was perceived that the Griffin showed no sign of going away, all the people who were able to do so left the town. The canons and the higher officers of the church had fled away during the first day of the Griffin's visit, leaving behind only the Minor Canon and some of the men who opened the doors and swept the church. All the citizens who could afford it shut up their houses and traveled to distant parts, and only the working people and the poor were left behind. After a while these ventured to go about and attend to their business, for if they did not work they would starve. They were getting a little used to seeing the Griffin, and having been told that he did not eat between equinoxes, they did not feel so much afraid of him as before.

Day by day the Griffin became more and more attached to the Minor Canon. He kept near him a great part of the time, and often spent the night in front of the little house where the young clergyman lived alone. This strange companionship was often burdensome to the Minor Canon; but, on the other hand, he could not deny that he derived a great deal of benefit and instruction from it. The Griffin had lived for hundreds of years, and had seen much; and he told the Minor Canon many wonderful things.

"It is like reading an old book," said the young clergyman to himself; "but how many books I would have had to read before I would have found out what the Griffin has told me about the earth, the air, the water, about minerals, and metals, and growing things, and all the wonders of the world!"

Thus the summer went on, and drew toward its close. And now the people of the town began to be very much troubled again.

"It will not be long," they said, "before the autumnal equinox is here, and then that monster will want to eat. He will be dreadfully hungry, for he has taken so much exercise since his last meal. He will devour our children. Without doubt, he will eat them all. What is to be done?"

To this question no one could give an answer, but all agreed that the Griffin must not be allowed to remain until the approaching equinox. After talking over the matter a great deal, a crowd of the people went to the Minor Canon, at a time when the Griffin was not with him.

"It is all your fault," they said, "that that monster is among us. You brought him here, and you ought to see that he goes away. It is only on your account that he stays here at all, for, although he visits his image every day, he is with you the greater part of the time. If you were not here, he would not stay. It is your duty to go away and then he will follow you, and we shall be free from the dreadful danger which hangs over us."

"Go away!" cried the Minor Canon, greatly grieved at being spoken to in such a way. "Where shall I go? If I go to some other town, shall I not take this trouble there? Have I a right to do that?"

"No," said the people, "you must not go to any other town. There is no town far enough away. You must go to the dreadful wilds where the Griffin lives; and then he will follow you and stay there."

They did not say whether they expected the Minor Canon to stay there also, and he did not ask them anything about it. He bowed his head, and went into his house, to think. The more he thought, the more clear it became to his mind that it was his duty to go away, and thus free the town from the presence of the Griffin.

That evening he packed a leathern bag full of bread and meat, and early the next morning he set out on his journey to the dreadful wilds. It was a long, weary, and doleful journey, especially after he had gone beyond the habitations of men, but the Minor Canon kept on bravely, and never faltered. The way was longer than he had expected, and his provisions soon grew so scanty that he was obliged to eat but a little every day, but he kept up his courage, and pressed on, and, after many days of toilsome travel, he reached the dreadful wilds.

When the Griffin found that the Minor Canon had left the town he seemed sorry, but showed no disposition to go and look for him. After a few days had passed, he became much annoyed, and asked some of the people where the Minor Canon had gone. But, although the citizens had been so anxious that the young clergyman should go to the dreadful wilds, thinking that the Griffin would immediately follow him, they were now afraid to mention the Minor Canon's destination, for the monster seemed angry already, and, if he should suspect their trick he would, doubtless, become very much enraged. So every one said he did not know, and the Griffin wandered about disconsolately. One morning he looked into the Minor Canon's school-house, which was always empty now, and thought that it was a shame that everything should suffer on account of the young man's absence.

"It does not matter so much about the church," he said, "for nobody went there; but it is a pity about the school. I think I will teach it myself until he returns."

It was just about school-time, and the Griffin went inside and pulled the rope which rang the school-bell. Some of the children who heard the bell ran in to see what was the matter, supposing it to be a joke of some one of their companions; but when they saw the Griffin they stood astonished, and scared.

"Go tell the other scholars," said the monster, "that school is about to open, and that if they are not all here in ten minutes, I shall come after them."

In seven minutes every scholar was in place.

Never was seen such an orderly school. Not a boy or girl moved, or uttered a whisper. The Griffin climbed into the master's seat, his wide wings spread on each side of him, because he could not lean back in his chair while they stuck out behind, and his great tail coiled around, in front of the desk, the barbed end sticking up, ready to tap any boy or girl who might misbehave. The Griffin now addressed the scholars, telling them that he intended to teach them while their master was away. In speaking he endeavored to imitate, as far as possible, the mild and gentle tones of the Minor Canon, but it must be admitted that in this he was not very successful. He had paid a good deal of attention to the studies of the school, and he now determined not to attempt to teach them anything new, but to review them in what they had been studying; so he called up the various classes, and questioned them upon their previous lessons. The children racked their brains to remember what they had learned. They were so afraid of the Griffin's displeasure that they recited as they had never recited before.

One of the boys, far down in his class, answered so well that the Griffin was astonished.

"I should think you would be at the head," said he. "I am sure you have never been in the habit of reciting so well. Why is this?"

"Because I did not choose to take the trouble," said the boy, trembling in his boots. He felt obliged to speak the truth, for all the children thought that the great eyes of the Griffin could see right through them, and that he would know when they told a falsehood.

"You ought to be ashamed of yourself," said the Griffin. "Go down to the very tail of the class, and if you are not at the head in two days, I shall know the reason why."

The next afternoon the boy was number one.

It was astonishing how much these children now learned of what they had been studying. It was as if they had been educated over again. The Griffin used no severity toward them, but there was a look about him which made them unwilling to go to bed until they were sure they knew their lessons for the next day.

The Griffin now thought that he ought to visit the sick and the poor; and he began to go about the town for this purpose.

The effect upon the sick was miraculous. All, except those who were very ill indeed, jumped from their beds when they heard he was coming, and declared themselves quite well. To those who could not get up, he gave herbs and roots, which none of them had ever before thought of as medicines, but which the Griffin had seen used in various parts of the world; and most of them recovered. But, for all that, they afterward said that, no matter what happened to them, they hoped that they should never again have such a doctor coming to their bed-sides, feeling their pulses and looking at their tongues.

As for the poor, they seemed to have utterly disappeared. All those who had depended upon charity for their daily bread were now at work in some way or other; many of them offering to do odd jobs for their neighbors just for the sake of their meals,—a thing which had been seldom heard of before in the town. The Griffin could find no one who needed his assistance.

The summer had now passed, and the autumnal equinox was rapidly approaching. The citizens were in a state of great alarm and anxiety. The Griffin showed no signs of going away, but seemed to have settled himself permanently among them. In a short time, the day for his semi-annual meal would arrive, and then what would happen? The monster would certainly be very hungry, and would devour all their children.

Now they greatly regretted and lamented that they had sent away the Minor Canon; he was the only one on whom they could have depended in this trouble, for he could talk freely with the Griffin, and so find out what could be done. But it would not do to be inactive. Some step must be taken immediately. A meeting of the citizens was called, and two old men were appointed to go and talk to the Griffin. They were instructed to offer to prepare a splendid dinner for him on equinox day,—one which would entirely satisfy his hunger. They would offer him the fattest mutton, the most tender beef, fish, and game of various sorts, and anything of the kind that he might fancy. If none of these suited, they were to mention that there was an orphan asylum in the next town.

"Anything would be better," said the citizens, "than to have our dear children devoured."

The old men went to the Griffin, but their propositions were not received with favor.

"From what I have seen of the people of this town," said the monster, "I do not think I could relish anything that was ever prepared by them. They appear to be all cowards, and, therefore, mean and selfish. As for eating one of them, old or young, I couldn't think of it for a moment. In fact, there was only one creature in the whole place for whom I could have had any appetite, and that is the Minor Canon, who has gone away. He was brave, and good, and honest, and I think I would have relished him."

"Ah!" said one of the old men very politely, "in that case I wish we had not sent him to the dreadful wilds!"

"What!" cried the Griffin. "What do you mean? Explain instantly what you are talking about!"

The old man, terribly frightened at what he had said, was obliged to tell how the Minor Canon had been sent away by the people, in the hope that the Griffin might be induced to follow him.

When the monster heard this, he became furiously angry. He dashed away from the old men and, spreading his wings, flew backward and forward over the town. He was so much excited that his tail became red-hot, and glowed like a meteor against the evening sky. When at last he settled down in the little field where he usually rested, and thrust his tail into the brook, the steam arose like a cloud, and the water of the stream ran hot through the town. The citizens were greatly frightened, and bitterly blamed the old man for telling about the Minor Canon.

"It is plain," they said, "that the Griffin intended at last to go and look for him, and we should have been saved. Now who can tell what misery you have brought upon us."

The Griffin did not remain long in the little field. As soon as his tail was cool he flew to the town-hall and rang the bell. The citizens knew that they were expected to come there, and although they were afraid to go, they were still more afraid to stay away; and they crowded into the hall. The Griffin was on the platform at one end, flapping his wings and walking up and down, and the end of his tail was still so warm that it slightly scorched the boards as he dragged it after him.

When everybody who was able to come was there, the Griffin stood still and addressed the meeting.

"I have had a contemptible opinion of you," he said, "ever since I discovered what cowards you were, but I had no idea that you were so ungrateful, selfish, and cruel, as I now find you to be. Here was your Minor Canon, who labored day and night for your good, and thought of nothing else but how he might benefit you and make you happy; and as soon as you imagine yourselves threatened with a danger,—for well I know you are dreadfully afraid of me,—you send him off, caring not whether he returns or perishes, hoping thereby to save yourselves. Now, I had conceived a great liking for that young man, and had intended, in a day or two, to go and look him up. But I have changed my mind about him. I shall go and find him, but I shall send him back here to live among you, and I intend that he shall enjoy the reward of his labor and his sacrifices. Go, some of you, to the officers of the church, who so cowardly ran away when I first came here, and tell them never to return to this town under penalty of death. And if, when your Minor Canon comes back to you, you do not bow yourselves before him, put him in the highest place among you, and serve and honor him all his life, beware of my terrible vengeance! There were only two good things in this town: the Minor Canon and the stone image of myself over your church-door. One of these you have sent away, and the other I shall carry away myself."

With these words he dismissed the meeting, and it was

time, for the end of his tail had become so hot that there was danger of its setting fire to the building.

The next morning, the Griffin came to the church, and tearing the stone image of himself from its fastenings over the great door, he grasped it with his powerful fore-legs and flew up into the air. Then, after hovering over the town for a moment, he gave his tail an angry shake and took up his flight to the dreadful wilds. When he reached this desolate region, he set the stone griffin upon a ledge of a rock which rose in front of the dismal cave he called his home. There the image occupied a position somewhat similar to that it had had over the church-door; and the Griffin, panting with the exertion of carrying such an enormous load to so great a distance, lay down upon the ground, and regarded it with much satisfaction. When he felt somewhat rested he went to look for the Minor Canon. He found the young man, weak and half starved, lying under the shadow of a rock. After picking him up and carrying him to his cave, the Griffin flew away to a distant marsh, where he procured some roots and herbs which he well knew were strengthening and beneficial to man, though he had never tasted them himself. After eating these the Minor Canon was greatly revived, and sat up and listened while the Griffin told him what had happened in the town.

"Do you know," said the monster, when he had finished, "that I have had, and still have, a great liking for you?"

"I am very glad to hear it," said the Minor Canon, with his usual politeness.

"I am not at all sure that you would be," said the Griffin, "if you thoroughly understood the state of the case, but we will not consider that now. If some things were different, other things would be otherwise. I have been so enraged by discovering the manner in which you have been treated that I have determined that you shall at last enjoy the rewards and honors to which you are entitled. Lie down and have a good sleep, and then I will take you back to the town."

As he heard these words, a look of trouble came over the young man's face.

"You need not give yourself any anxiety," said the Griffin, "about my return to the town. I shall not remain there. Now that I have that admirable likeness of myself in front of my cave, where I can sit at my leisure, and gaze upon its noble features and magnificent proportions, I have no wish to see that abode of cowardly and selfish people."

The Minor Canon, relieved from his fears, now lay back, and dropped into a doze; and when he was sound asleep the Griffin took him up, and carried him back to the town. He arrived just before day-break, and putting the young man gently on the grass in the little field where he himself used to rest, the monster, without having been seen by any of the people, flew back to his home.

When the Minor Canon made his appearance in the morning among the citizens, the enthusiasm and cordiality with which he was received was truly wonderful. He was taken to a house which had been occupied by one of the banished high officers of the place, and every one was anxious to do all that could be done for his health and comfort. The people crowded into the church when he held services, and the three old women who used to be his week-day congregation could not get to the best seats, which they had always been in the habit of taking; and the parents of the bad children determined to reform them at home, in order that he might be spared the trouble of keeping up his former school. The Minor Canon was appointed to the highest office of the old church, and before he died, he became a bishop.

During the first years after his return from the dreadful wilds, the people of the town looked up to him as a man to whom they were bound to do honor and reverence; but they often, also, looked up to the sky to see if there were any signs of the Griffin coming back. However, in the course of time, they learned to honor and reverence their former Minor

Canon without the fear of being punished if they did not do so.

But they need never have been afraid of the Griffin. The autumnal equinox day came round, and the monster ate nothing. If he could not have the Minor Canon, he did not care for anything. So, lying down, with his eyes fixed upon the great stone griffin, he gradually declined, and died. It was a good thing for some of the people of the town that they did not know this.

If you should ever visit the old town, you would still see the little griffins on the sides of the church; but the great stone griffin that was over the door is gone.

The Demon Pope

*

by Richard Garnett

Richard Garnett was for many years associated with the library of the British Museum, eventually rising to be Keeper of Printed Books (in effect, the head librarian), a position that he held for nearly ten years before his retirement. A man of profound learning, he was also a prolific author of scholarly works. His quiet erudition is evident in his sole work of fiction, a collection of short stories called *The Twilight of the Gods and Other Tales*. It was first published in 1888; an expanded edition appeared in 1903. "The Demon Pope" first appeared in the 1888 edition.

"So you won't sell me your soul?" said the devil.

"Thank you," replied the student, "I had rather keep it myself, if it's all the same to you."

"But it's not all the same to me. I want it very particularly. Come, I'll be liberal. I said twenty years. You can have thirty." The student shook his head.

"Forty!"

Another shake.

"Fifty!"

As before.

"Now," said the devil, "I know I'm going to do a foolish thing, but I cannot bear to see a clever, spirited young man throw himself away. I'll make you another kind of offer. We won't have any bargain at present, but I will push you on in the world for the next forty years. This day forty years I come back and ask you for a boon; not your soul, mind, or anything not perfectly in your power to grant. If you give it, we are quits; if not, I fly away with you. What say you to this?"

The student reflected for some minutes. "Agreed," he said at last.

Scarcely had the devil disappeared, which he did instantaneously, ere a messenger reined in his smoking steed at the gate of the University of Cordova (the judicious reader will already have remarked that Lucifer could never have been allowed inside a Christian seat of learning), and, inquiring for the student Gerbert, presented him with the Emperor Otho's nomination to the Abbacy of Bobbio, in consideration, said the document, of his virtue, and learning, well-nigh miraculous, in one so young. Such messengers were frequent visitors during Gerbert's prosperous career. Abbot, bishop, archbishop, cardinal, he was ultimately enthroned Pope on April 2, 999, and assumed the appellation of Silvester the Second. It was then a general belief that the world would come to an end in the following year, a catastrophe which to many seemed the more imminent from the election of a chief pastor whose celebrity as a theologian, though not inconsiderable, by no means equalled his reputation as a necromancer.

The world, notwithstanding, revolved scatheless through the dreaded twelvemonth, and early in the first year of the eleventh century Gerbert was sitting peacefully in his study, perusing a book of magic. Volumes of algebra, astrology, alchemy, Aristotelian philosophy, and other such light reading filled his bookcase; and on a table stood an improved clock of his invention, next to his introduction of the Arabic numerals his chief legacy to posterity. Suddenly a sound of wings was heard, and Lucifer stood by his side.

"It is a long time," said the fiend, "since I have had the pleasure of seeing you. I have now called to remind you of our little contract, concluded this day forty years."

"You remember," said Silvester, "that you are not to ask anything exceeding my power to perform."

"I have no such intention," said Lucifer. "On the contrary, I am about to solicit a favour which can be bestowed by you alone. You are Pope, I desire that you would make me a Cardinal."

"In the expectation, I presume," returned Gerbert, "of becoming Pope on the next vacancy."

"An expectation," replied Lucifer, "which I may most reasonably entertain, considering my enormous wealth, my proficiency in intrigue, and the present condition of the Sacred College."

"You would doubtless," said Gerbert, "endeavour to subvert the foundations of the Faith, and, by a course of profligacy and licentiousness, render the Holy See odious and contemptible."

"On the contrary," said the fiend, "I would extirpate heresy, and all learning and knowledge as inevitably tending thereunto. I would suffer no man to read but the priest, and confine his reading to his breviary. I would burn your books together with your bones on the first convenient opportunity. I would observe an austere propriety of conduct, and be especially careful not to loosen one rivet in the tremendous yoke I was forging for the minds and consciences of mankind."

"If it be so," said Gerbert, "let's be off!"

"What!" exclaimed Lucifer, "you are willing to accompany me to the infernal regions!"

"Assuredly, rather than be accessory to the burning of Plato and Aristotle, and give place to the darkness against which I have been contending all my life."

"Gerbert," replied the demon, "this is arrant trifling. Know you not that no good man can enter my dominions? That, were such a thing possible, my empire would become intolerable to me, and I should be compelled to abdicate?"

"I do know it," said Gerbert, "and hence I have been able to receive your visit with composure."

"Gerbert," said the devil, with tears in his eyes, "I put it to you—is this fair, is this honest? I undertake to promote your interests in the world; I fulfil my promise abundantly. You obtain through my instrumentality a position to which you could never otherwise have aspired. Often have I had a hand in the election of a Pope, but never before have I contributed to confer the tiara on one eminent for virtue and learning. You profit by my assistance to the full, and now take advantage of an adventitious circumstance to deprive me of my reasonable guerdon. It is my constant experience that the good people are much more slippery than the sinners, and drive much harder bargains."

"Lucifer," answered Gerbert, "I have always sought to treat you as a gentleman, hoping that you would approve yourself such in return. I will not inquire whether it was entirely in harmony with this character to seek to intimidate me into compliance with your demand by threatening me with a penalty which you well knew could not be enforced. I will overlook this little irregularity, and concede even more than you have requested. You have asked to be a Cardinal. I will make you Pope——"

"Ha!" exclaimed Lucifer, and an internal glow suffused his sooty hide, as the light of a fading ember is revived by breathing upon it.

"For twelve hours," continued Gerbert. "At the expiration of that time we will consider the matter further; and if, as I anticipate, you are more anxious to divest yourself of the Papal dignity than you were to assume it, I promise to bestow upon you any boon you may ask within my power to grant, and not plainly inconsistent with religion or morals."

"Done!" cried the demon. Gerbert uttered some cabalistic words, and in a moment the apartment held two Pope Silvesters, entirely indistinguishable save by their attire, and the fact that one limped slightly with the left foot.

"You will find the Pontifical apparel in this cupboard," said Gerbert, and, taking his book of magic with him, he retreated through a masked door to a secret chamber. As the door closed behind him he chuckled, and muttered to himself, "Poor old Lucifer! Sold again!"

If Lucifer was sold he did not seem to know it. He approached a large slab of silver which did duty as a mirror, and contemplated his personal appearance with some dissatisfaction.

"I certainly don't look half so well without my horns," he soliloquised, "and I am sure I shall miss my tail most grievously."

A tiara and a train, however, made fair amends for the deficient appendages, and Lucifer now looked every inch a Pope. He was about to call the master of the ceremonies, and summon a consistory, when the door was burst open, and seven cardinals, brandishing poinards, rushed into the room.

"Down with the sorcerer!" they cried, as they seized and gagged him.

"Death to the Saracen!"

"Practises algebra, and other devilish arts!"

"Knows Greek!"

"Talks Arabic!"

"Reads Hebrew!"

"Burn him!"

"Smother him!"

"Let him be deposed by a general council," said a young and inexperienced Cardinal.

"Heaven forbid!" said an old and wary one, *sotto voce*.

Lucifer struggled frantically, but the feeble frame he was doomed to inhabit for the next eleven hours was speedily exhausted. Bound and helpless, he swooned away.

"Brethren," said one of the senior cardinals, "it hath been delivered by the exorcists that a sorcerer or other individual in league with the demon doth usually bear upon his person some visible token of his infernal compact. I propose that we forthwith institute a search for this stigma, the discovery of which may contribute to justify our proceedings in the eyes of the world."

"I heartily approve of our brother Anno's proposition," said another, "the rather as we cannot possibly fail to discover such a mark, if, indeed, we desire to find it."

The search was accordingly instituted, and had not proceeded far ere a simultaneous yell from all the seven cardinals indicated that their investigation had brought more to light than they had ventured to expect.

The Holy Father had a cloven foot!

For the next five minutes the Cardinals remained utterly stunned, silent, and stupefied with amazement. As they gradually recovered their faculties it would have become manifest to a nice observer that the Pope had risen very considerably in their good opinion.

"This is an affair requiring very mature deliberation," said one.

"I always feared that we might be proceeding too precipitately," said another.

"It is written, 'the devils believe,' " said a third: "the Holy Father, therefore, is not a heretic at any rate."

"Brethren," said Anno, "this affair, as our brother Benno well remarks, doth indeed call for mature deliberation. I therefore propose that, instead of smothering his Holiness with cushions, as originally contemplated, we immure him for the present in the dungeon adjoining hereunto, and, after spending the night in meditation and prayer, resume the consideration of the business to-morrow morning."

"Informing the officials of the palace," said Benno, "that his Holiness has retired for his devotions, and desires on no account to be disturbed."

"A pious fraud," said Anno, "which not one of the Fathers would for a moment have scrupled to commit."

The Cardinals accordingly lifted the still insensible Lucifer, and bore him carefully, almost tenderly, to the apartment appointed for his detention. Each would fain have lingered in hopes of his recovery, but each felt that the eyes of his six brethren were upon him: and all, therefore, retired simultaneously, each taking a key of the cell.

Lucifer regained consciousness almost immediately afterwards. He had the most confused idea of the circumstances which had involved him in his present scrape, and could only say to himself that if they were the usual concomitants of the Papal dignity, these were by no means to his taste, and he wished he had been made acquainted with them sooner. The dungeon was not only perfectly dark, but horribly cold, and the poor devil in his present form had no latent store of infernal heat to draw upon. His teeth chattered, he shivered in every limb, and felt devoured with hunger and thirst. There is much probability in the assertion of some of his biographers that it was on this occasion that he invented ardent spirits; but, even if he did, the mere conception of a glass of brandy could only increase his sufferings. So the long January night wore wearily on, and Lucifer seemed likely to expire from inanition, when a key turned in the lock, and Cardinal Anno cautiously glided in, bearing a lamp, a loaf, half a cold roast kid, and a bottle of wine.

"I trust," he said, bowing courteously, "that I may be excused any slight breach of etiquette of which I may render myself culpable from the difficulty under which I labour of determining whether, under present circumstances, 'Your Holiness,' or 'Your Infernal Majesty' be the form of address most befitting me to employ."

"Bub-ub-bub-boo," went Lucifer, who still had the gag in his mouth.

"Heavens!" exclaimed the Cardinal, "I crave your Infenal Holiness's forgiveness. What a lamentable oversight!"

And, relieving Lucifer from his gag and bonds, he set out the refection, upon which the demon fell voraciously.

"Why the devil, if I may so express myself," pursued Anno, "did not your Holiness inform us that you *were* the devil? Not a hand would then have been raised against you. I have myself been seeking all my life for the audience now happily vouchsafed me. Whence this mistrust of your faithful Anno, who has served you so loyally and zealously these many years?"

Lucifer pointed significantly to the gag and fetters.

"I shall never forgive myself," protested the Cardinal, "for the part I have borne in this unfortunate transaction. Next to ministering to your Majesty's bodily necessities, there is nothing I have so much at heart as to express my penitence. But I entreat your Majesty to remember that I believed myself to be acting in your Majesty's interest by overthrowing a magician who was accustomed to send your Majesty upon errands, and who might at any time enclose you in a box, and cast you into the sea. It is deplorable that your Majesty's most devoted servants should have been thus misled."

"Reasons of State," suggested Lucifer.

"I trust that they no longer operate," said the Cardinal. "However, the Sacred College is now fully possessed of the whole matter: it is therefore unnecessary to pursue this department of the subject further. I would now humbly crave leave to confer with your Majesty, or rather, perhaps, your Holiness, since I am about to speak of spiritual things, on the important and delicate point of your Holiness's successor. I am ignorant how long your Holiness proposes to occupy the Apostolic chair; but of course you are aware that public opinion will not suffer you to hold it for a term exceeding that of the pontificate of Peter. A vacancy, therefore, must one day occur; and I am humbly to represent that the office could not be filled by one more congenial than myself to the present incumbent, or on whom he could more fully rely to carry out in every respect his views and intentions."

And the Cardinal proceeded to detail various circumstances of his past life, which certainly seemed to corroborate his assertion. He had not, however, proceeded far ere he was disturbed by the grating of another key in the lock, and had just time to whisper impressively, "Beware of Benno," ere he dived under a table.

Benno was also provided with a lamp, wine, and cold viands. Warned by the other lamp and the remains of Lucifer's repast that some colleague had been beforehand with him, and not knowing how many more might be in the field, he came briefly to the point as regarded the Papacy, and preferred his claim in much the same manner as Anno. While he was earnestly cautioning Lucifer against this Cardinal as one who could and would cheat the very Devil himself, another key turned in the lock, and Benno escaped under the table, where Anno immediately inserted his finger into his right eye. The little squeal consequent upon this occurrence Lucifer successfully smothered by a fit of coughing.

Cardinal No. 3, a Frenchman, bore a Bayonne ham, and exhibited the same disgust as Benno on seeing himself forestalled. So far as his requests transpired they were moderate, but no one knows where he would have stopped if he had not been scared by the advent of Cardinal No. 4. Up to this time he had only asked for an inexhaustible purse, power to call up the Devil *ad libitum,* and a ring of invisibility to allow him free access to his mistress, who was unfortunately a married woman.

Cardinal No. 4 chiefly wanted to be put into the way of poisoning Cardinal No. 5; and Cardinal No. 5 preferred the same petition as respected Cardinal No. 4.

Cardinal No. 6, an Englishman, demanded the reversion of the Archbishoprics of Canterbury and York, with the faculty of holding them together, and of unlimited non-residence. In the course of his harangue, he made use of the phrase *non obstantibus,* of which Lucifer immediately took a note.

What the seventh Cardinal would have solicited is not known, for he had hardly opened his mouth when the twelfth hour expired, and Lucifer, regaining his vigour with his shape, sent the Prince of the Church spinning to the other end of the room, and split the marble table with a single

stroke of his tail. The six crouched and huddling Cardinals
cowered revealed to one another, and at the same time enjoyed the spectacle of his Holiness darting through the stone
ceiling, which yielded like a film to his passage, and closed
up afterwards as if nothing had happened. After the first
shock of dismay they unanimously rushed to the door, but
found it bolted on the outside. There was no other exit, and
no means of giving an alarm. In this emergency the de-
meanour of the Italian Cardinals set a bright example to their
ultramontane colleagues. *"Bisogna pazienzia,"* they said, as
they shrugged their shoulders. Nothing could exceed the mu-
tual politeness of Cardinals Anno and Benno, unless that of
the two who had sought to poison each other. The Frenchman was held to have gravely derogated from good manners
by alluding to this circumstance, which had reached his ears
while he was under the table: and the Englishman swore so
outrageously at the plight in which he found himself that the
Italians then and there silently registered a vow that none of
his nation should ever be Pope, a maxim which, with one exception, has been observed to this day.

Lucifer, meanwhile, had repaired to Silvester, whom he
found arrayed in all the insignia of his dignity; of which, as
he remarked, he thought his visitor had probably had enough.

"I should think so indeed," replied Lucifer. "But at the
same time I feel myself fully repaid for all I have undergone
by the assurance of the loyalty of my friends and admirers,
and the conviction that it is needless for me to devote any
considerable amount of personal attention to ecclesiastical
affairs. I now claim the promised boon, which it will be in no
way inconsistent with thy functions to grant, seeing that it is
a work of mercy. I demand that the Cardinals be released,
and that their conspiracy against thee, by which I alone suffered, be buried in oblivion."

"I hoped you would carry them all off," said Gerbert, with
an expression of disappointment.

"Thank you," said the Devil. "It is more to my interest to leave them where they are."

So the dungeon-door was unbolted, and the Cardinals came forth, sheepish and crestfallen. If, after all, they did less mischief than Lucifer had expected from them, the cause was their entire bewilderment by what had passed, and their utter inability to penetrate the policy of Gerbert, who henceforth devoted himself even with ostentation to good works. They could never quite satisfy themselves whether they were speaking to the Pope or to the Devil, and when under the latter impression habitually emitted propositions which Gerbert justly stigmatised as rash, temerarious, and scandalous. They plagued him with allusions to certain matters mentioned in their interviews with Lucifer, with which they naturally but erroneously supposed him to be conversant, and worried him by continual nods and titterings as they glanced at his nether extremities. To abolish this nuisance, and at the same time silence sundry unpleasant rumours which had somehow got abroad, Gerbert devised the ceremony of kissing the Pope's feet, which, in a grievously mutilated form, endures to this day. The stupefaction of the Cardinals on discovering that the Holy Father had lost his hoof surpasses all description, and they went to their graves without having obtained the least insight into the mystery.

The Story of Sigurd

Retold by Andrew Lang

As a child, Tolkien found delight in the variously colored fairy-tale books of Andrew Lang. Especially he enjoyed *The Red Fairy Book*, for it contained Lang's retelling of one of the greatest dragon stories in northern literature, that of Fafnir from the Old Norse *Völsunga Saga*. To an interviewer in 1965 Tolkien said, "Dragons always attracted me as a mythological element. They seemed to be able to comprise human malice and bestiality together so extraordinarily well, and also a sort of malicious wisdom and shrewdness—terrifying creatures!"

"The Story of Sigurd," as retold by Andrew Lang, first appeared in *The Red Fairy Book* (1890).

[*This is a very old story: the Danes who used to fight with the English in King Alfred's time knew this story. They have carved on the rocks pictures of some of the things that happen in the tale, and those carvings may still be seen. Because it is so old and so beautiful the story is told here again, but it has a sad ending—indeed it is all sad, and all about fighting and killing, as might be expected from the Danes.*]

ONCE upon a time there was a King in the North who had won many wars, but now he was old. Yet he took a new wife, and then another Prince, who wanted to have married her, came up against him with a great army. The old King went out and fought bravely, but at last his sword broke, and he was wounded and his men fled. But in the night, when the battle was over, his young wife came out and searched for him among the slain, and at last she found him, and asked whether he might be healed. But he said "No," his luck was gone, his sword was broken, and he must die. And he told her that she would have a son, and that son would be a great warrior, and would avenge him on the other King, his enemy. And he bade her keep the broken pieces of the sword, to make a new sword for his son, and that blade should be called Gram.

Then he died. And his wife called her maid to her and said, "Let us change clothes, and you shall be called by my name, and I by yours, lest the enemy finds us."

So this was done, and they hid in a wood, but there some strangers met them and carried them off in a ship to Denmark. And when they were brought before the King, he thought the maid looked like a Queen, and the Queen like a maid. So he asked the Queen, "How do you know in the dark of night whether the hours are wearing to the morning?"

And she said:

"I know because, when I was younger, I used to have to rise and light the fires, and still I waken at the same time."

"A strange Queen to light the fires," thought the King.

Then he asked the Queen, who was dressed like a maid, "How do you know in the dark of night whether the hours are wearing near the dawn?"

"My father gave me a gold ring," said she, "and always, ere the dawning, it grows cold on my finger."

"A rich house where the maids wore gold," said the King. "Truly you are no maid, but a King's daughter."

So he treated her royally, and as time went on she had a son called Sigurd, a beautiful boy and very strong. He had a tutor to be with him, and once the tutor bade him go to the King and ask for a horse.

"Choose a horse for yourself," said the King; and Sigurd

went to the wood, and there he met an old man with a white beard, and said, "Come! help me in horse-choosing."

Then the old man said, "Drive all the horses into the river, and choose the one that swims across."

So Sigurd drove them, and only one swam across. Sigurd chose him: his name was Grani, and he came of Sleipnir's breed, and was the best horse in the world. For Sleipnir was the horse of Odin, the God of the North, and was as swift as the wind.

But a day or two later his tutor said to Sigurd, "There is a great treasure of gold hidden not far from here, and it would become you to win it."

But Sigurd answered, "I have heard stories of that treasure, and I know that the dragon Fafnir guards it, and he is so huge and wicked that no man dares to go near him."

"He is no bigger than other dragons," said the tutor, "and if you were as brave as your father you would not fear him."

"I am no coward," says Sigurd; "why do you want me to fight with this dragon?"

Then his tutor, whose name was Regin, told him that all this great hoard of red gold had once belonged to his own father. And his father had three sons—the first was Fafnir, the Dragon; the next was Otter, who could put on the shape of an otter when he liked; and the next was himself, Regin, and he was a great smith and maker of swords.

Now there was at that time a dwarf called Andvari, who lived in a pool beneath a waterfall, and there he had hidden a great hoard of gold. And one day Otter had been fishing there, and had killed a salmon and eaten it, and was sleeping, like an otter, on a stone. Then someone came by, and threw a stone at the otter and killed it, and flayed off the skin, and took it to the house of Otter's father. Then he knew his son was dead, and to punish the person who had killed him he said he must have the Otter's skin filled with gold, and covered all over with red gold, or it should go worse with him. Then the person who had killed Otter went down and caught the Dwarf who owned all the treasure and took it from him.

Only one ring was left, which the Dwarf wore, and even that was taken from him.

Then the poor Dwarf was very angry, and he prayed that the gold might never bring any but bad luck to all the men who might own it, for ever.

Then the otter skin was filled with gold and covered with gold, all but one hair, and that was covered with the poor Dwarf's last ring.

But it brought good luck to nobody. First Fafnir, the Dragon, killed his own father, and then he went and wallowed on the gold, and would let his brother have none, and no man dared go near it.

When Sigurd heard the story he said to Regin:

"Make me a good sword that I may kill this Dragon."

So Regin made a sword, and Sigurd tried it with a blow on a lump of iron, and the sword broke.

Another sword he made, and Sigurd broke that too.

Then Sigurd went to his mother, and asked for the broken pieces of his father's blade, and gave them to Regin. And he hammered and wrought them into a new sword, so sharp that fire seemed to burn along its edges.

Sigurd tried this blade on the lump of iron, and it did not break, but split the iron in two. Then he threw a lock of wool into the river, and when it floated down against the sword it was cut into two pieces. So Sigurd said that sword would do. But before he went against the Dragon he led an army to fight the men who had killed his father, and he slew their King, and took all his wealth, and went home.

When he had been at home a few days, he rode out with Regin one morning to the heath where the Dragon used to lie. Then he saw the track which the Dragon made when he went to a cliff to drink, and the track was as if a great river had rolled along and left a deep valley.

Then Sigurd went down into that deep place, and dug

many pits in it, and in one of the pits he lay hidden with his sword drawn. There he waited, and presently the earth began to shake with the weight of the Dragon as he crawled to the water. And a cloud of venom flew before him as he snorted and roared, so that it would have been death to stand before him.

But Sigurd waited till half of him had crawled over the pit, and then he thrust the sword Gram right into his very heart.

Then the Dragon lashed with his tail till stones broke and trees crashed about him.

Then he spoke, as he died, and said:

"Whoever thou art that hast slain me this gold shall be thy ruin, and the ruin of all who own it."

Sigurd said:

"I would touch none of it if by losing it I should never die. But all men die, and no brave man lets death frighten him from his desire. Die thou, Fafnir," and then Fafnir died.

And after that Sigurd was called Fafnir's Bane, and Dragon-slayer.

Then Sigurd rode back, and met Regin, and Regin asked him to roast Fafnir's heart and let him taste of it.

So Sigurd put the heart of Fafnir on a stake, and roasted it. But it chanced that he touched it with his finger, and it burned him. Then he put his finger in his mouth, and so tasted the heart of Fafnir.

Then immediately he understood the language of birds, and he heard the Woodpeckers say:

"There is Sigurd roasting Fafnir's heart for another, when he should taste of it himself and learn all wisdom."

The next bird said:

"There lies Regin, ready to betray Sigurd, who trusts him."

The third bird said:

"Let him cut off Regin's head, and keep all the gold to himself."

The fourth bird said:

"That let him do, and then ride over Hindfell, to the place where Brynhild sleeps."

When Sigurd heard all this, and how Regin was plotting to betray him, he cut off Regin's head with one blow of the sword Gram.

Then all the birds broke out singing:

"We know a fair maid,
A fair maiden sleeping;
Sigurd, be not afraid,
Sigurd, win thou the maid
Fortune is keeping.

"High over Hindfell
Red fire is flaming,
There doth the maiden dwell
She that should love thee well,
Meet for thy taming.

"There must she sleep till thou
Comest for her waking
Rise up and ride, for now
Sure she will swear the vow
Fearless of breaking."

Then Sigurd remembered how the story went that somewhere, far away, there was a beautiful lady enchanted. She was under a spell, so that she must always sleep in a castle surrounded by flaming fire; there she must sleep for ever till there came a knight who would ride through the fire and waken her. There he determined to go, but first he rode right down the horrible trail of Fafnir. And Fafnir had lived in a cave with iron doors, a cave dug deep down in the earth, and full of gold bracelets, and crowns, and rings; and there, too, Sigurd found the Helm of Dread, a golden helmet, and whoever wears it is invisible. All these he piled on the back of the good horse Grani, and then he rode south to Hindfell.

Now it was night, and on the crest of the hill Sigurd saw a red fire blazing up into the sky, and within the flame a castle, and a banner on the topmost tower. Then he set the horse Grani at the fire, and he leaped through it lightly, as if it had been through the heather. So Sigurd went within the castle door, and there he saw someone sleeping, clad all in armour. Then he took the helmet off the head of the sleeper, and behold, she was a most beautiful lady. And she wakened and said, "Ah! is it Sigurd, Sigmund's son, who has broken the curse, and comes here to waken me at last?"

This curse came upon her when the thorn of the tree of sleep ran into her hand long ago as a punishment because she had displeased Odin the God. Long ago, too, she had vowed never to marry a man who knew fear, and dared not ride through the fence of flaming fire. For she was a warrior maid herself, and went armed into the battle like a man. But now she and Sigurd loved each other, and promised to be true to each other, and he gave her a ring, and it was the last ring taken from the dwarf Andvari. Then Sigurd rode away, and he came to the house of a King who had a fair daughter. Her name was Gudrun, and her mother was a witch. Now Gudrun fell in love with Sigurd, but he was always talking of Brynhild, how beautiful she was and how dear. So oneday Gudrun's witch mother put poppy and forgetful drugs in a magical cup, and bade Sigurd drink to her health, and he drank, and instantly he forgot poor Brynhild and he loved Gudrun, and they were married with great rejoicings.

Now the witch, the mother of Gudrun, wanted her son Gunnar to marry Brynhild, and she bade him ride out with Sigurd and go and woo her. So forth they rode to her father's house, for Brynhild had quite gone out of Sigurd's mind by reason of the witch's wine, but she remembered him and loved him still. Then Brynhild's father told Gunnar that she would marry none but him who could ride the flame in front

of her enchanted tower, and thither they rode, and Gunnar
set his horse at the flame, but he would not face it. Then Gunnar tried Sigurd's horse Grani, but he would not move with
Gunnar on his back. Then Gunnar remembered witchcraft
that his mother had taught him, and by his magic he made
Sigurd look exactly like himself, and he looked exactly like
Gunnar. Then Sigurd, in the shape of Gunnar and in his mail,
mounted on Grani, and Grani leaped the fence of fire, and
Sigurd went in and found Brynhild, but he did not remember
her yet, because of the forgetful medicine in the cup of the
witch's wine.

Now Brynhild had no help but to promise she would be
his wife, the wife of Gunnar as she supposed, for Sigurd
wore Gunnar's shape, and she had sworn to wed whoever
should ride the flames. And he gave her a ring, and she gave
him back the ring he had given her before in his own shape
as Sigurd, and it was the last ring of that poor dwarf Andvari. Then he rode out again, and he and Gunnar changed
shapes, and each was himself again, and they went home to
the witch Queen's, and Sigurd gave the dwarf's ring to his
wife, Gudrun. And Brynhild went to her father, and said that
a King had come called Gunnar, and had ridden the fire, and
she must marry him. "Yet I thought," she said, "that no man
could have done this deed but Sigurd, Fafnir's bane, who was
my true love. But he has forgotten me, and my promise I
must keep."

So Gunnar and Brynhild were married, though it was not
Gunnar but Sigurd in Gunnar's shape, that had ridden the fire.

And when the wedding was over and all the feast, then the
magic of the witch's wine went out of Sigurd's brain, and he
remembered all. He remembered how he had freed Brynhild
from the spell, and how she was his own true love, and how
he had forgotten and had married another woman, and won
Brynhild to be the wife of another man.

But he was brave, and he spoke not a word of it to the others to make them unhappy. Still he could not keep away the

curse which was to come on every one who owned the treasure of the dwarf Andvari, and his fatal golden ring.

And the curse soon came upon all of them. For one day, when Brynhild and Gudrun were bathing, Brynhild waded farthest out into the river, and said she did that to show she was Gudrun's superior. For her husband, she said, had ridden through the flame when no other man dared face it.

Then Gudrun was very angry, and said that it was Sigurd, not Gunnar, who had ridden the flame, and had received from Brynhild that fatal ring, the ring of the dwarf Andvari.

Then Brynhild saw the ring which Sigurd had given to Gudrun, and she knew it and knew all, and she turned as pale as a dead woman, and went home. All that evening she never spoke. Next day she told Gunnar, her husband, that he was a coward and a liar, for he had never ridden the flame, but had sent Sigurd to do it for him, and pretended that he had done it himself. And she said he would never see her glad in his hall, never drinking wine, never playing chess, never embroidering with the golden thread, never speaking words of kindness. Then she rent all her needlework asunder and wept aloud, so that everyone in the house heard her. For her heart was broken, and her pride was broken in the same hour. She had lost her true love, Sigurd, the slayer of Fafnir, and she was married to a man who was a liar.

Then Sigurd came and tried to comfort her, but she would not listen, and said she wished the sword stood fast in his heart.

"Not long to wait," he said, "till the bitter sword stands fast in my heart, and thou will not live long when I am dead. But, dear Brynhild, live and be comforted, and love Gunnar thy husband, and I will give thee all the gold, the treasure of the dragon Fafnir."

Brynhild said:

"It is too late."

Then Sigurd was so grieved and his heart so swelled in his breast that it burst the steel rings of his shirt of mail.

Sigurd went out and Brynhild determined to slay him. She mixed serpent's venom and wolf's flesh, and gave them in one dish to her husband's younger brother, and when he had tasted them he was mad, and he went into Sigurd's chamber while he slept and pinned him to the bed with a sword. But Sigurd woke, and caught the sword Gram into his hand, and threw it at the man as he fled, and the sword cut him in twain. Thus died Sigurd, Fafnir's bane, whom no ten men could have slain in fair fight. Then Gudrun wakened and saw him dead, and she moaned aloud, and Brynhild heard her and laughed; but the kind horse Grani lay down and died of very grief. And then Brynhild fell a-weeping till her heart broke. So they attired Sigurd in all his golden armour, and built a great pile of wood on board his ship, and at night laid on it the dead Sigurd and the dead Brynhild, and the good horse, Grani, and set fire to it, and launched the ship. And the wind bore it blazing out to sea, flaming into the dark. So there were Sigurd and Brynhild burned together, and the curse of the dwarf Andvari was fulfilled.

The Folk
of the Mountain Door

~

by William Morris

William Morris was an enormous influence on Tolkien in terms of the general shape of his literary interests. Morris was a poet who translated *Beowulf* and a number of the Icelandic sagas. He was also a writer of prose romances tinged with a medieval flavor and style. Tolkien discovered Morris's translations in his teens, and his interest in Morris deepened at Exeter College, Oxford, where Morris had also been an undergraduate. Tolkien's earliest stories of his Middle-earth legendarium, published posthumously as *The Book of Lost Tales*, show a decided influence of Morris in their archaism and style.

Although written in the early 1890s, "The Folk of the Mountain Door" first appeared in volume 21 (1914) of *The Collected Works of William Morris*. The story itself was left untitled by Morris, and the title was given to it by his daughter, May Morris.

OF old time, in the days of the kings, there was a king of folk, a mighty man in battle, a man deemed lucky by the wise, who ruled over a folk that begrudged not his kingship, whereas they knew of his valour and wisdom and saw how by his means they prevailed over other folks, so that their land was wealthy and at peace save about its uttermost borders. And this folk was called the Folk of the Mountain Door, or more shortly, of the Door.

Strong of body was this king, tall and goodly to look on,

so that the hearts of women fluttered with desire when he passed them by. In the prime and flower of his age he wedded a wife, a seemly mate, a woman of the Earl-kin, tall and white-skinned, golden haired and grey-eyed; healthy, sweet-breathed, and soft-spoken, courteous of manners, wise of heart, kind to all folk, well-beloved of little children. In early spring-tide was the wedding, and a little after Yule she was brought to bed of a man-child of whom the midwives said they had never seen a fairer. He was sprinkled with water and was named Host-lord after the name of his kindred of old.

Great was the feast of his name-day, and much people came thereto, the barons of the land, and the lords of the neighbouring folk who would fain stand well with the king; and merchants and craftsmen and sages and bards; and the king took them with both hands and gave them gifts, and hearkened to their talk and their tales, as if he were their very earthly fellow; for as fierce as he was afield with the sword in his fist, even so meek and kind he was in the hall amongst his folk and the strangers that sought to him.

Now amongst the guests that ate and drank in the hall on the even of the Name-day, the king as he walked amidst the tables beheld an old man as tall as any champion of the king's host, but far taller had he been, but that he was bowed with age. He was so clad that he had on him a kirtle of lambs-wool undyed and snow-white, and a white cloak, lined with ermine and welted with gold; a golden fillet set with gems was on his head, and a gold-hilted sword by his side; and the king deemed as he looked on him that he had never seen any man more like to the Kings of the Ancient World than this man. By his side sat a woman old and very old, but great of stature, and noble of visage, clad, she also, in white wool raiment embroidered about with strange signs of worms and fire-drakes, and the sun and the moon and the host of heaven.

So the king stayed his feet by them, for already he had noted that at the table whereat they sat there had been this long time at whiles greater laughter and more joyous than anywhere else in the hall, and whiles the hush of folk that hearken to what delights the inmost of their hearts. So now he greeted those ancients and said to them: "Is it well with you, neighbours?" And the old carle hailed the king, and said, "There is little lack in this house today."

"What lack at all do ye find therein?" said the king. Then there came a word into the carle's mouth and he sang in a great voice:

> Erst was the earth
> Fulfilled of mirth:
> Our swords were sheen
> In the summer green;
> And we rode and ran
> Through winter wan,
> And long and wide
> Was the feast-hall's side.
> And the sun that was sunken
> Long under the wold
> Hung ere we were drunken
> High over the gold;
> And as fowl in the bushes
> Of summer-tide sing
> So glad as the thrushes
> Sang earl-folk and king.
> Though the wild wind might splinter
> The oak-tree of Thor,
> The hand of mid-winter
> But beat on the door.

"Yea," said the king, "and dost thou say that winter hath come into my hall on the Name-day of my first-born?" "Not so," said the carle.

"What is amiss then?" said the king. Then the carle sang again:

Were many men
In the feast-hall then,
And the worst on bench
Ne'er thought to blench
When the storm arose
In the war-god's close;
And for Tyr's high-seat,
Were the best full meet:
And who but the singer
Was leader and lord,
I steel-god, I flinger
Of adder-watched hoard?
Aloft was I sitting
Amidst of the place
And watched men a-flitting
All under my face.
And hushed for mere wonder
Were great men and small
As my voice in rhyme-thunder
Went over the hall.

"Yea," said the king, "thou hast been a mighty lord in days
gone past, I thought no less when first I set eyes on thee. And
now I bid thee stand up and sit on the high-seat beside me,
thou and thy mate. Is she not thy very speech-friend?"

Therewith a smile lit up the ancient man's face, and the
woman turned to him and he sang:

Spring came of old
In the days of gold,
In the thousandth year
Of the thousands dear,
When we twain met
And the mead was wet
With the happy tears
Of the best of the years.

But no cloud hung over
The eyes of the sun
That looked down on the lover
Ere eve was begun.
Oft, oft came the greeting
Of spring and her bliss
To the mead of our meeting,
The field of our kiss.
Is spring growing older?
Is earth on the wane
As the bold and the bolder
That come not again?

"O king of a happy land," said [the ancient man], "I will
take thy bidding, and sit beside thee this night that thy wisdom may wax and the days that are to come may be better for
thee than the days that are."

So he spake and rose to his feet, and the ancient woman
with him, and they went with the king up to the high-seat,
and all men in the feast-hall rose up and stood to behold
them, and they deemed them wonderful and their coming a
great thing.

But now when they were set down on the right hand and
the left hand of the king, he turned to the ancient man and
said to him: "O Lord of the days gone past, and of the battles that have been, wilt thou now tell me of thy name, and
the name of thy mate, that I may call a health for thee first of
all great healths that shall be drunk tonight."

But the old man said and sang:

King, hast thou thought
How nipped and nought
Is last year's rose
Of the snow-filled close?
Or dost thou find
Last winter's wind

Will yet avail
For thy hall-glee's tale?
E'en such and no other
If spoken tonight
Were the name of the brother
Of war-gods of might.
Yea the word that hath shaken
The walls of the house
When the warriors half waken
To battle would rouse
Ye should drowse if ye heard it
Nor turn in the chair.
O long long since they feared it
Those foemen of fear!
Unhelpful, unmeaning
Its letters are left;
For the man overweening
Of manhood is reft.

This word the king hearkened, and found no word in his mouth to answer: but he sat pondering heavy things, and sorrowful with the thought of the lapse of years, and the waning of the blossom of his youth. And all the many guests of the great feast-hall sat hushed, and the hall-glee died out amongst them.

But the old man raised his head and smiled, and he stood on his feet, and took the cup in his hand and cried out aloud: "What is this my masters, are ye drowsy with meat and drink in this first hour of the feast? Or have tidings of woe without words been borne amongst you, that ye sit like men given over to wanhope, awaiting the coming of the doom that none may gainsay, and the foe that none may overcome? Nay then, nay; but if ye be speechless I will speak; and if ye be joyless I will rejoice and bid the good wine welcome home. But first will I call a health over the cup:

Pour, white-armed ones,
As the Rhine flood runs!
And O thanes in hall
I bid you all
Rise up, and stand
With the horn in hand,
And hearken and hear
The old name and the dear.
To HOST-LORD the health is
Who guarded of old
The House where the wealth is
The Home of the gold.
And again the Tree bloometh
Though winter it be
And no heart of man gloometh
From mountain to sea.
Come thou Lord, the rightwise,
Come Host-lord once more
To thy Hall-fellows, fightwise
The Folk of the Door!

Huge then was the sudden clamour in the hall, and the shouts of men and clatter of horns and clashing of weapons as all folk old and young, great and little, carle and quean, stood up on the Night of the Name-day. And once again there was nought but joy in the hall of the Folk of the Door.

But amidst the clamour the inner doors of the hall were thrown open, and there came in women clad most meetly in coloured raiment, and amidst them a tall woman in scarlet, bearing in her arms the babe new born clad in fine linen and wrapped in a golden cloth, and she bore him up thus toward the high-seat, while all men shouted even more if it were possible, and set down cup and horn from their lips, and took up sword and shield and raised the shield-roar in the hall.

But the [king] rose up with a joyful countenance, and got him from out of his chair, and stood thereby: and the women

stayed at the foot of the dais all but the nurse, who bore up
the child to the king, and gave it into his arms; and he looked
fondly on the youngling for a short space, and then raised
him aloft so that all men in the hall might see him, and so
laid him on the board before them and took his great spear
from the wall behind him and drew the point thereof across
and across the boy's face so that it well nigh grazed his flesh:
at the first and at the last did verily graze it as little as might
be, but so that the blood started; and while the babe wailed
and cried, as was to be looked for, the king cried aloud with
a great voice:

"Here mark I thee to Odin even as were all thy kin marked
from of old from the time that the Gods were first upon the
earth."

Then he took the child up in his arms and laid him in his
own chair, and cried out: "This is Host-lord the son of Host-
lord King and Duke of the Folk of the Door, who sitteth in
his father's chair and shall do when I am gone to Odin, unless any of the Folk gainsay it."

When he had spoken there came a man in at the door of
the hall clad in all his war-gear with a great spear in his hand,
and girt with a sword, and he strode clashing through the hall
up to the high-seat and stood by the chair of the king and
lifted up his helm a little and cried out:

"Where are now the gainsayers, or where is the champion
of the gainsayers? Here stand I Host-rock of the Falcons of
the Folk of the Door, ready to meet the gainsayers."

And he let his helm fall down again so that his face was
hidden. And a man one-eyed and huge rose up from the
lower benches and cried out in a loud voice: "O champion,
hast thou hitherto foregone thy meat and drink to sing so idle
a song over the hall-glee? Come down amongst us, man, and
put off thine armour and eat and drink and be merry; for [of]
thine hunger and thirst am I full certain. Here be no gainsayers, but brethren all, the sons of one Mother and one Father, though they be grown somewhat old by now."

Then was there a clamour again, joyous with laughter and many good words. And some men say, that when this man had spoken, the carle and quean ancient of days who sat beside the king's chair, were all changed and seemed to men's eyes as if they were in the flower of their days, mighty, and lovely and of merry countenance: and it is told that no man knew that big-voiced speaker, nor whence he came, and that presently when men looked for him he was gone from the hall, and they knew not how.

Be this as it may, the two ancient ones each stooped down over the chair whereas lay the little one and kissed him; and the old man took his cup and wetted the lips of the babe with red wine, and the old woman took a necklace from her neck of amber and silver and gold and did it on the youngling's neck and spake; and her voice was very sweet though she were old; and many heard the speech of her:

"O Host-lord of this even, Live long and hale! Many a woman shall look on thee and few that see thee shall forbear to love thee."

Then the nurse took up the babe again and bore him out to the bower where lay his mother, and the folk were as glad as glad might be, and no man hath told of mirth greater and better than the hall-glee of that even. And the old carle sat yet beside the king and was blithe with him and of many words, and told him tales that he had never known before; and all these were of the valiant deeds and the lives of his fathers before him, and strange stories of the Folk of the Door and what they had done, and the griefs which they had borne and the joys which they had won from the earth and the heavens and the girdling waters of the world. And the king waxed exceeding glad as he heard it all, and thought he would try to bear it in mind as long as he lived; for it seemed to him that when he had parted from those two ancient ones, that night, he should never see them again.

So wore the time and the night was so late, that had it been summer-tide, it had been no night but early day. And the king

looked up from the board and those two old folk, and beheld
the hall, that there were few folk therein, save those that lay
along by the walls of the aisles, so swiftly had the night gone
and all folk were departed or asleep. Then was he like a man
newly wakened from a dream, and he turned about to the two
ancients almost looking to see their places empty. But they
abode there yet beside him on the right hand and on the left;
so he said: "Guests, I give you all thanks for your company
and the good words and noble tales wherewith ye have be-
guiled this night of winter, and surely tomorrow shall I rise
up wiser than I was yesterday. And now meseemeth ye are
old and doubtless weary with the travel and the noisy mirth
of the feast-hall, nor may I ask you to abide bedless any
longer, though it be great joy to me to hearken to your speech.
Come then to the bower aloft and I will show you the best of
beds and the soft and kind place to abide the uprising of to-
morrow's sun; and late will he arise, for this is now the very
midwinter, and the darkest of all days in the year."

Then answered the old man: "I thank thee, O son of the
Kindred; but so it is that we have further to wend than thou
mightest deem; yea, back to the land whence we came many
a week of years ago and before the building of houses in the
land, between the mountain and the sea. Wherefore if thou
wouldest do aught to honour us, come thou a little way on the
road and see us off in the open country without the walls of
thy Burg: then shall we depart in such wise that we shall be
dear friends as long as we live, thou and thine, and I and
mine."

"This is not so great an asking," said the king, "but that I
would do more for thee; yet let it be as thou wilt."

And he arose from table and they with him, and they went
down the hall amidst the sleeping folk and the benches
that had erst been so noisy and merry, and out a-doors they
went all three and into the street of the Burg. Open were the
Burg-gates and none watched there, for there was none to
break the Yule-tide peace; so the king went forth clad in his

feasting-raiment, and those twain went, one on either side of him. The mid-winter frost was hard upon the earth, so that few waters were running, and all the face of the world was laid under snow: high was the moon and great and round in a cloudless sky, so that the stars looked but little.

The king set his face toward the mountains and strode with great strides over the white highway betwixt the hidden fruitfulness of the acres, and he was as one wending on an errand which he may not forego; but at last he said: "Whither wend we and how far?" Then spake the old man: "Whither should we wend save to the Mountain Door, and the entrance to the land whence the folk came forth, when great were its warriors and little was the tale of them."

Then the king spake no more, but it seemed to him as if his feet sped on faster than their wont was, and as if those twain bore him up so that his feet were but light on the face of the earth.

Thuswise they passed the plain and the white-clad ridges at the mountain feet in no long while, and were come before the yawning gap and strait way into the heart of the mountains, and there was no other way thereinto save this; for otherwhere, the cliffs rose like a wall from the plain-country. Grim was that pass, and high were the sides of it beneath the snow, which lay heaped up high, so now there were smooth white slopes on either side of the narrow road of the pass; while the wind had whistled the said road in most places well nigh clear of snow, which even now went whirling and drifting about beneath the broad moon. For the wind yet blew though the night was old, and the sound of it in the clefts of the rocks and the windings of the pass was like the rolling of the summer thunder.

Up the pass they went till it widened, and there was a wide space before them, the going up whereto was as by stairs, and also the going up from it to the higher pass; and all around it the rocks were high and sheer, so that there was no way over them save for the fowl flying; and were it not winter there had been a trickling stream running round about the eastern side of the cliff wall which lost itself in the hollow places of the rocks at the lower end of that round hall of the mountain, unroofed and unpillared. Amidmost the place the snow was piled up high; for there in summer was a grassy mound amidst of a little round meadow of sweet grass, treeless, bestrewn here and there with blocks that had been borne down thitherward by the waters from the upper mountain; and for ages beyond what the memory of men might tell of this had been the Holy place and Motestead of the Folk of the Door.

Now all three went up on to the snow-covered mound, and those two turned about and faced the king and he saw their faces clearly, so bright as the moon was, and now it was so that they were no more wrinkled and hollow-cheeked and sunken-eyed, though scarce might a man say that they looked young, but exceeding fair they were, and they looked on him with eyes of love, and the carle said: "Lord of the Folk of the Door, father of the son new born whom the Folk this night have taken for their father, and the image of those that have been, we have brought thee to the Holy Place that we might say a word to thee and give thee a warning of the days to come, so that if it may be thou mightest eschew the evil and ensue the good. For thou art our dear son, and thy son is yet dearer to us, since his days shall be longer if weird will so have it. Hearken to this by the token that under the grass, beneath this snow, lieth the first of the Folk of the Door of those that come on the earth and go thence; and this was my very son begotten on this woman that here standeth. For wot thou that I am Host-lord of the Ancient Days, and from me is all the blood of you come; and dear is the blood of my sons and my name even as that which I have seen spilt on field and in fold, on grass and in grange, without the walls of the watches and about the lone wells of the desert places. Hearken then, Host-lord the Father of Host-lord, for we have looked into the life of thy son; and this we say is the weird of him; childless shall he be unless he wed as his will is; for of all his kindred none is wilfuller than he. Who then shall he wed, and where is the House that is lawful to him that thou hast not heard of? For as to wedding with his will in the House whereof thou wottest, and the Line of the Sea-dwellers, look not for it. Where then is the House of his wedding, lest the Folk of the Door lose their Chieftain and become the servants of those that are worser than they? I may not tell thee; and if I did, it would help thee nought. But this I will tell thee, when thy fair son is of fifteen winters, until the time that he is twenty winters and two, evil waylayeth on him: evil of the sword, evil of the cord, evil of the shaft, evil of the draught, evil of the cave, evil of the wave. O Son and father of my son, heed my word and let him be so watched that while as none hath been watched and warded of all thy kindred who have gone before, lest when his time come and he depart from this land he wander about the further side of the bridge that goeth to the Hall of the Gods, for very fear of shaming amongst the bold warriors and begetters of kindred and fathers of the sons that I love, that shall one day sit and play at the golden tables in the Plains of Ida."

So he spake, but the king spake: "O Host-lord of the Ancients I had a deeming of what thou wert, and that thou hadst a word for me. Wilt thou now tell me one thing more? In what wise shall I ward our son from the evil till his soul is strengthened, and the Wise-wights and the Ancients are become his friends, and the life of the warrior is in his hands and the days of a chieftain of our folk?"

Then the carle smiled on him and sang:

Wide is the land
Where the houses stand,
There bale and bane
Ye scarce shall chain;
There the sword is ground
And wounds abound;

And women fair
Weave the love-nets there.

Merry hearts in the Mountain
Dales shepherd-men keep,
And about the Fair Fountain
Need more than their sheep.
Of the Dale of the Tower
Where springeth the well
In the sun-slaying hour
They talk and they tell;
And often they wonder
Whence cometh the name
And what tale lies thereunder
For honour or shame.
For beside the fount welling
No castle now is;
Yet seldom foretelling
Of weird wends amiss.

Quoth the king, "I have heard tell of the Fair Fountain and
the Dale of the Tower; though I have never set eyes thereon,
and I deem it will be hard to find. But dost thou mean that
our son who is born the Father of the Folk shall dwell there
during that while of peril?"

Again sang the carle:

Good men and true,
They deal and do
In the grassy dales
Of that land of the tales;
Where dale and down
Yet wears the crown
Of the flower and fruit
From our kinship's root.
There little man sweateth

In trouble and toil,
And in joy he forgetteth
The feud and the foil.
The weapon he wendeth
Achasing the deer,
And in peace the moon endeth
That endeth the year.
Yet there dwell our brothers,
And should they but know
They thy stem of all others
Were planted to grow
Beside the Fair Fountain,
How fain were those men
Of the God of the Mountain
So come back again.

Then the king said: "Shall I fulfill the weird and build a
Tower in the Dale for our Son? And deemest thou he shall
dwell there happily till the time of peril is overpast?"

But the carle cried out, "Look, look! Who is the shining
one who cometh up the pass?"

And the king turned hastily and drew his sword, but beheld neither man nor mare in the mountain, and when he
turned back again to those twain, lo! they were clean gone,
and there was nought in the pass save the snow and the wind,
and the long shadows cast by the sinking moon. So he turned
about again and went down the pass; and by then he was
come into the first of the plain-country once more, the moon
was down and the stars shone bright and big; but even in the
dead mid-winter there was a scent abroad of the coming of
the dawn. So went the king as speedily as he might back to
the Burg and his High House; and he was glad in his inmost
heart that he had seen the God and Father of his Folk.

Black Heart and White Heart:
A Zulu Idyll

✦

by H. Rider Haggard

Tolkien was born of English parents in Bloemfontein, South Africa, where his father was a bank manager. As a small child Tolkien was briefly stolen by the houseboy, who wanted to show off a white baby to his native kraal. At the age of three, Tolkien, with his mother and his younger brother, traveled to England, and during this visit his father died in South Africa. Tolkien never returned, but the country of his birth held a fascination for him, as did the romances of H. Rider Haggard, many of which have an African setting and some of which, like "Black Heart and White Heart," deal with native South African traditions and history. Roger Lancelyn Green, who was a student of Tolkien's in the 1940s and who became a close friend of C. S. Lewis, has recalled that Tolkien, like C. S. Lewis and Green himself, ranked Haggard very highly. Green was pleased to be able to lend Tolkien at least one Haggard novel he had never read. Various writers on Tolkien have seen in Haggard's two most famous novels, *She* and *King Solomon's Mines,* some direct influences on Tolkien.

"Black Heart and White Heart" has a historical setting—it is set in Zulu territory in 1878, just prior to the Zulu massacre of British troops at Isandhlwana (a few hundred miles to the east of Bloemfontein) in January of the following year. It was first published in the *African Review* in January 1896 and included in *Black Heart and White Heart and Other Stories* (1900).

CHAPTER I
Philip Hadden and King Cetywayo

AT the date of our introduction to him, Philip Hadden was a transport-rider and trader in "the Zulu." Still on the right side of forty, in appearance he was singularly handsome; tall, dark, upright, with keen eyes, short-pointed beard, curling hair and clear-cut features. His life had been varied, and there were passages in it which he did not narrate even to his most intimate friends. He was of gentle birth, however, and it was said that he had received a public school and university education in England. At any rate he could quote the classics with aptitude on occasion, an accomplishment which, coupled with his refined voice and a bearing not altogether common in the wild places of the world, had earned for him among his rough companions the *soubriquet* of "The Prince."

However these things may have been, it is certain that he had emigrated to Natal under a cloud, and equally certain that his relatives at home were content to take no further interest in his fortunes. During the fifteen or sixteen years which he had spent in or about the colony, Hadden followed many trades, and did no good at any of them. A clever man, of agreeable and prepossessing manner, he always found it easy to form friendships and to secure a fresh start in life. But, by degrees, the friends were seized with a vague distrust of him; and, after a period of more or less application, he himself would close the opening that he had made by a sudden disappearance from the locality, leaving behind him a doubtful reputation and some bad debts.

Before the beginning of this story of the most remarkable episodes in his life, Philip Hadden was engaged for several years in transport-riding—that is, in carrying goods on ox waggons from Durban or Maritzburg to various points in the interior. A difficulty such as had more than once confronted him in the course of his career, led to his temporary aban-

donment of this means of earning a livelihood. On arriving
at the little frontier town of Utrecht in the Transvaal, in
charge of two waggon loads of mixed goods consigned to a
storekeeper there, it was discovered that out of six cases of
brandy five were missing from his waggon. Hadden explained the matter by throwing the blame upon his Kaffir
"boys," but the storekeeper, a rough-tongued man, openly
called him a thief and refused to pay the freight on any of the
load. From words the two men came to blows, knives were
drawn, and before anybody could interfere the storekeeper
received a nasty wound in his side. That night, without waiting till the matter could be inquired into by the landdrost or
magistrate, Hadden slipped away, and trekked back into
Natal as quickly as his oxen would travel. Feeling that even
here he was not safe, he left one of his waggons at Newcas-
tle, loaded up the other with Kaffir goods—such as blankets,
calico, and hardware—and crossed into Zululand, where in
those days no sheriff's officer would be likely to follow him.

Being well acquainted with the language and customs of
the natives, he did good trade with them, and soon found
himself possessed of some cash and a small herd of cattle,
which he received in exchange for his wares. Meanwhile
news reached him that the man whom he had injured still
vowed vengeance against him, and was in communication
with the authorities in Natal. These reasons making his return to civilisation undesirable for the moment, and further
business being impossible until he could receive a fresh
supply of trade stuff, Hadden like a wise man turned his
thoughts to pleasure. Sending his cattle and waggon over the
border to be left in charge of a native headman with whom
he was friendly, he went on foot to Ulundi to obtain permission from the king, Cetywayo, to hunt game in his country.
Somewhat to his surprise, the Indunas or headmen, received
him courteously—for Hadden's visit took place within a few
months of the outbreak of the Zulu war in 1878, when Cetywayo was already showing unfriendliness to the English

traders and others, though why the king did so they knew not.

On the occasion of his first and last interview with Cetywayo, Hadden got a hint of the reason. It happened thus. On the second morning after his arrival at the royal kraal, a messenger came to inform him that "the Elephant whose tread shook the earth" had signified that it was his pleasure to see him. Accordingly he was led through the thousands of huts and across the Great Place to the little enclosure where Cetywayo, a royal-looking Zulu seated on a stool, and wearing a kaross of leopard skins, was holding an *indaba,* or conference, surrounded by his counsellors. The Induna who had conducted him to the august presence went down upon his hands and knees, and, uttering the royal salute of *Bayéte,* crawled forward to announce that the white man was waiting.

"Let him wait," said the king angrily; and, turning, he continued the discussion with his counsellors.

Now, as has been said, Hadden thoroughly understood Zulu; and, when from time to time the king raised his voice, some of the words he spoke reached his ear.

"What!" Cetywayo said, to a wizened and aged man who seemed to be pleading with him earnestly; "am I a dog that these white hyenas should hunt me thus? Is not the land mine, and was it not my father's before me? Are not the people mine to save or to slay? I tell you that I will stamp out these little white men; my *impis* shall eat them up. I have said!"

Again the withered aged man interposed, evidently in the character of a peacemaker. Hadden could not hear his talk, but he rose and pointed towards the sea, while from his expressive gestures and sorrowful mien, he seemed to be prophesying disaster should a certain course of action be followed.

For a while the king listened to him, then he sprang from his seat, his eyes literally ablaze with rage.

"Hearken," he cried to the counsellor; "I have guessed it

for long, and now I am sure of it. You are a traitor. You are Sompseu's* dog, and the dog of the Natal Government, and I will not keep another man's dog to bite me in my own house. Take him away!"

A slight involuntary murmur rose from the ring of *indunas,* but the old man never flinched, not even when the soldiers, who presently would murder him, came and seized him roughly. For a few seconds, perhaps five, he covered his face with the corner of the kaross he wore, then he looked up and spoke to the king in a clear voice.

"O King," he said, "I am a very old man; as a youth I served under Chaka the Lion, and I heard his dying prophecy of the coming of the white man. Then the white men came, and I fought for Dingaan at the battle of the Blood River. They slew Dingaan, and for many years I was the counsellor of Panda, your father. I stood by you, O King, at the battle of the Tugela, when its grey waters were turned to red with the blood of Umbulazi your brother, and of the tens of thousands of his people. Afterwards I became your counsellor, O King, and I was with you when Sompseu set the crown upon your head and you made promises to Sompseu— promises that you have not kept. Now you are weary of me, and it is well; for I am very old, and doubtless my talk is foolish, as it chances to the old. Yet I think that the prophecy of Chaka, your great-uncle, will come true, and that the white men will prevail against you and that through them you shall find your death. I would that I might have stood in one more battle and fought for you, O King, since fight you will, but the end which you choose is for me the best end. Sleep in peace, O King, and farewell. *Bayéte!*"†

For a space there was silence, a silence of expectation while men waited to hear the tyrant reverse his judgment.

---

* Sir Theophilus Shepstone's.
† The royal salute of the Zulus.

But it did not please him to be merciful, or the needs of policy outweighed his pity.

"Take him away," he repeated. Then, with a slow smile on his face and one word, "Good-night," upon his lips, supported by the arm of a soldier, the old warrior and statesman shuffled forth to the place of death.

Hadden watched and listened in amazement not unmixed with fear. "If he treats his own servants like this, what will happen to me?" he reflected. "We English must have fallen out of favour since I left Natal. I wonder whether he means to make war on us or what? If so, this isn't my place."

Just then the king, who had been gazing moodily at the ground, chanced to look up. "Bring the stranger here," he said.

Hadden heard him, and coming forward offered Cetywayo his hand in as cool and nonchalant a manner as he could command.

Somewhat to his surprise it was accepted. "At least, White Man," said the king, glancing at his visitor's tall spare form and cleanly cut face, "you are no 'umfagozan' (low fellow); you are of the blood of chiefs."

"Yes, King," answered Hadden, with a little sigh, "I am of the blood of chiefs."

"What do you want in my country, White Man?"

"Very little, King. I have been trading here, as I daresay you have heard, and have sold all my goods. Now I ask your leave to hunt buffalo, and other big game, for a while before I return to Natal."

"I cannot grant it," answered Cetywayo, "you are a spy sent by Sompseu, or by the Queen's Induna in Natal. Get you gone."

"Indeed," said Hadden, with a shrug of his shoulders; "then I hope that Sompseu, or the Queen's Induna, or both of them, will pay me when I return to my own country. Meanwhile I will obey you because I must, but I should first like to make you a present."

"What present?" asked the king. "I want no presents. We are rich here, White Man."

"So be it, King. It was nothing worthy of your taking, only a rifle."

"A rifle, White Man? Where is it?"

"Without. I would have brought it, but your servants told me that it is death to come armed before the 'Elephant who shakes the Earth.'"

Cetywayo frowned, for the note of sarcasm did not escape his quick ear.

"Let this white man's offering be brought; I will consider the thing."

Instantly the Induna who had accompanied Hadden darted to the gateway, running with his body bent so low that it seemed as though at every step he must fall upon his face. Presently he returned with the weapon in his hand and presented it to the king, holding it so that the muzzle was pointed straight at the royal breast.

"I crave leave to say, O Elephant," remarked Hadden in a drawling voice, "that it might be well to command your servant to lift the mouth of that gun from your heart."

"Why?" asked the king.

"Only because it is loaded, and at full cock, O Elephant, who probably desires to continue to shake the Earth."

At these words the "Elephant" uttered a sharp exclamation, and rolled from his stool in a most unkingly manner, whilst the terrified Induna, springing backwards, contrived to touch the trigger of the rifle and discharge a bullet through the exact spot that a second before had been occupied by his monarch's head.

"Let him be taken away," shouted the incensed king from the ground, but long before the words had passed his lips the Induna, with a cry that the gun was bewitched, had cast it down and fled at full speed through the gate.

"He has already taken himself away," suggested Hadden, while the audience tittered. "No, King, do not touch it rashly;

it is a repeating rifle. Look——" and lifting the Winchester, he fired the four remaining shots in quick succession into the air, striking the top of a tree at which he aimed with every one of them.

"*Wow,* it is wonderful!" said the company in astonishment.

"Has the thing finished?" asked the king.

"For the present it has," answered Hadden. "Look at it."

Cetywayo took the repeater in his hand, and examined it with caution, swinging the muzzle horizontally in an exact line with the stomachs of some of his most eminent Indunas, who shrank to this side and that as the barrel was brought to bear on them.

"See what cowards they are, White Man," said the king with indignation; "they fear lest there should be another bullet in this gun."

"Yes," answered Hadden, "they are cowards indeed. I believe that if they were seated on stools they would tumble off them just as it chanced to your Majesty to do just now."

"Do you understand the making of guns, White Man?" asked the king hastily, while the Indunas one and all turned their heads, and contemplated the fence behind them.

"No, King, I cannot make guns, but I can mend them."

"If I paid you well, White Man, would you stop here at my kraal, and mend guns for me?" asked Cetywayo anxiously.

"It might depend on the pay," answered Hadden; "but for awhile I am tired of work, and wish to rest. If the king gives me the permission to hunt for which I asked, and men to go with me, then when I return perhaps we can bargain on the matter. If not, I will bid the king farewell, and journey to Natal."

"In order to make report of what he has seen and learned here," muttered Cetywayo.

At this moment the talk was interrupted, for the soldiers who had led away the old Induna returned at speed, and prostrated themselves before the king.

"Is he dead?" he asked.

"He has travelled the king's bridge," they answered grimly; "he died singing a song of praise of the king."

"Good," said Cetywayo, "that stone shall hurt my feet no more. Go, tell the tale of its casting away to Sompseu and to the Queen's Induna in Natal," he added with bitter emphasis.

"*Baba!* Hear our Father speak. Listen to the rumbling of the Elephant," said the Indunas taking the point, while one bolder than the rest added: "Soon we will tell them another tale, the white Talking Ones, a red tale, a tale of spears, and the regiments shall sing it in their ears."

At the words an enthusiasm caught hold of the listeners, as the sudden flame catches hold of dry grass. They sprang up, for the most of them were seated on their haunches, and stamping their feet upon the ground in unison, repeated:—

Indaba ibomwu—indaba ye mikonto
Lizo dunyiswa nge impi ndhlebeni yaho.
(A red tale! A red tale! A tale of spears,
And the *impis* shall sing it in their ears.)

One of them, indeed, a great fierce-faced fellow, drew near to Hadden and shaking his fist before his eyes—fortunately being in the royal presence he had no assegai—shouted the sentences at him.

The king saw that the fire he had lit was burning too fiercely.

"Silence," he thundered in the deep voice for which he was remarkable, and instantly each man became as if he were turned to stone, only the echoes still answered back: "And the *impis* shall sing it in their ears—in their ears."

"I am growing certain that this is no place for me," thought Hadden; "if that scoundrel had been armed he might have temporarily forgotten himself. Hullo! who's this?"

Just then there appeared through the gate of the fence a splendid specimen of the Zulu race. The man, who was about thirty-five years of age, was arrayed in a full war dress

of a captain of the Umcityu regiment. From the circlet of
otter skin on his brow rose his crest of plumes, round his
middle, arms and knees hung the long fringes of black ox-
tails, and in one hand he bore a little dancing shield, also
black in colour. The other was empty, since he might not appear before the king bearing arms. In countenance the man
was handsome, and though just now they betrayed some anxiety, his eyes were genial and honest, and his mouth sensitive. In height he must have measured six foot two inches,
yet he did not strike the observer as being tall, perhaps because of his width of chest and the solidity of his limbs, that
were in curious contrast to the delicate and almost womanish
hands and feet which so often mark the Zulu of noble blood.
In short the man was what he seemed to be, a savage gentleman of birth, dignity and courage.

In company with him was another man plainly dressed in
a moocha and a blanket, whose grizzled hair showed him to
be over fifty years of age. His face also was pleasant and
even refined, but the eyes were timorous, and the mouth
lacked character.

"Who are these?" asked the king.

The two men fell on their knees before him, and bowed till
their foreheads touched the ground—the while giving him
his *sibonga* or titles of praise.

"Speak," he said impatiently.

"O King," said the young warrior, seating himself Zulu
fashion, "I am Nahoon, the son of Zomba, a captain of the
Umcityu, and this is my uncle Umgona, the brother of one of
my mothers, my father's youngest wife."

Cetywayo frowned. "What do you here away from your
regiment, Nahoon?"

"May it please the king, I have leave of absence from the
head captains, and I come to ask a boon of the king's
bounty."

"Be swift, then, Nahoon."

"It is this, O King," said the captain with some embarrassment: "A while ago the king was pleased to make a *keshla* of me because of certain service that I did out yonder——" and he touched the black ring which he wore in the hair of his head. "Being now a ringed man and a captain, I crave the right of a man at the hands of the king—the right to marry."

"Right? Speak more humbly, son of Zomba; my soldiers and my cattle have no rights."

Nahoon bit his lip, for he had made a serious mistake.

"Pardon, O King. The matter stands thus: My uncle Umgona here has a fair daughter named Nanea, whom I desire to wife, and who desires me to husband. Awaiting the king's leave I am betrothed to her and in earnest of it I have paid to Umgona a *lobola* of fifteen head of cattle, cows and calves together. But Umgona has a powerful neighbour, an old chief named Maputa, the warden of the Crocodile Drift, who doubtless is known to the king, and this chief also seeks Nanea in marriage and harries Umgona, threatening him with many evils if he will not give the girl to him. But Umgona's heart is white towards me, and towards Maputa it is black, therefore together we come to crave this boon of the king."

"It is so; he speaks the truth," said Umgona.

"Cease," answered Cetywayo angrily. "Is this a time that my soldiers should seek wives in marriage, wives to turn their hearts to water? Know that but yesterday for this crime I commanded that twenty girls who had dared without my leave to marry men of the Undi regiment, should be strangled and their bodies laid upon the cross-roads and with them the bodies of their fathers, that all might know their sin and be warned thereby. Ay, Umgona, it is well for you and for your daughter that you sought my word before she was given in marriage to this man. Now this is my award: I refuse your prayer, Nahoon, and since you, Umgona, are troubled with one whom you would not take as son-in-law, the old chief Maputa, I will free you from his importunity. The girl, says Nahoon, is fair—good, I myself will be gracious to her, and she shall be numbered among the wives of the royal house. Within thirty days from now, in the week of the next new moon, let her be delivered to the *Sigodhla,* the royal house of the women, and with her those cattle, the cows and the calves together, that Nahoon has given you, of which I fine him because he has dared to think of marriage without the leave of the king."

CHAPTER II
The Bee Prophesies

" 'A Daniel come to judgment' indeed," reflected Hadden, who had been watching this savage comedy with interest; "our love-sick friend has got more than he bargained for. Well, that comes of appealing to Cæsar," and he turned to look at the two suppliants.

The old man, Umgona, merely started, then began to pour out sentences of conventional thanks and praise to the king for his goodness and condescension. Cetywayo listened to his talk in silence, and when he had done answered by reminding him tersely that if Nanea did not appear at the date named, both she and he, her father, would in due course certainly decorate a cross-road in their own immediate neighbourhood.

The captain, Nahoon, afforded a more curious study. As the fatal words crossed the king's lips, his face took an expression of absolute astonishment, which was presently replaced by one of fury—the just fury of a man who suddenly has suffered an unutterable wrong. His whole frame quivered, the veins stood out in knots on his neck and forehead, and his fingers closed convulsively as though they were grasping the handle of a spear. Presently the rage passed away—for as well might a man be wroth with fate as with a Zulu despot—to be succeeded by a look of the most hopeless misery. The proud dark eyes grew dull, the copper-coloured face sank in and turned ashen, the mouth drooped, and down one corner of it there trickled a little line of blood springing from the lip bitten through in the effort to keep silence. Lifting his hand in salute to the king, the great man rose and staggered rather than walked towards the gate.

As he reached it, the voice of Cetywayo commanded him to stop. "Stay," he said, "I have a service for you, Nahoon, that shall drive out of your head these thoughts of wives and marriage. You see this white man here; he is my guest, and would hunt buffalo and big game in the bush country. I put him in your charge; take men with you, and see that he comes to no hurt. So also that you bring him before me within a month, or your life shall answer for it. Let him be here at my royal kraal in the first week of the new moon—when Nanea comes—and then I will tell you whether or no I agree with you that she is fair. Go now, my child, and you, White Man, go also; those who are to accompany you shall be with you at the dawn. Farewell, but remember we meet again at the new moon, when we will settle what pay you shall receive as keeper of my guns. Do not fail me, White Man, or I shall send after you, and my messengers are sometimes rough."

"This means that I am a prisoner," thought Hadden, "but it will go hard if I cannot manage to give them the slip somehow. I don't intend to stay in this country if war is declared, to be pounded into *mouti* (medicine), or have my eyes put out, or any little joke of that sort."

Ten days had passed, and one evening Hadden and his escort were encamped in a wild stretch of mountainous country lying between the Blood and Unvunyana Rivers, not more than eight miles from that "Place of the Little Hand" which within a few weeks was to become famous throughout the world by its native name of Isandhlwana. For three days they had been tracking the spoor of a small herd of buffalo that still inhabited the district, but as yet they had not come up with them. The Zulu hunters had suggested that they should follow the Unvunyana down towards the sea where game was more plentiful, but this neither Hadden, nor the captain, Nahoon, had been anxious to do, for reasons which each of them kept secret to himself. Hadden's object was to work gradually down to the Buffalo River across which he hoped to effect a retreat into Natal. That of Nahoon was to linger in the neighbourhood of the kraal of Umgona, which was situated not very far from their present camping place, in the vague hope that he might find an opportunity of speaking with or at least of seeing Nanea, the girl to whom he was affianced, who within a few weeks must be taken from him, and given over to the king.

A more eerie-looking spot than that where they were encamped Hadden had never seen. Behind them lay a tract of land—half-swamp and half-bush—in which the buffalo were supposed to be hiding. Beyond, in lonely grandeur, rose the mountain of Isandhlwana, while in front was an amphitheatre of the most gloomy forest, ringed round in the distance by sheer-sided hills. Into this forest there ran a river which drained the swamp, placidly enough upon the level. But it was not always level, for within three hundred yards of them it dashed suddenly over a precipice, of no great height but very steep, falling into a boiling rock-bound pool that the light of the sun never seemed to reach.

"What is the name of that forest, Nahoon?" asked Hadden.

"It is named *Emagudu,* The Home of the Dead," the Zulu replied absently, for he was looking towards the kraal of Nanea, which was situated at an hour's walk away over the ridge to the right.

"The Home of the Dead! Why?"

"Because the dead live there, those whom we name the *Esemkofu,* the Speechless Ones, and with them other Spirits, the *Amahlosi,* from whom the breath of life has passed away, and who yet live on."

"Indeed," said Hadden, "and have you ever seen these ghosts?"

"Am I mad that I should go to look for them, White Man? Only the dead enter that forest, and it is on the borders of it that our people make offerings to the dead."

Followed by Nahoon, Hadden walked to the edge of the cliff and looked over it. To the left lay the deep and dreadful-looking pool, while close to the bank of it, placed upon a narrow strip of turf between the cliff and the commencement of the forest, was a hut.

"Who lives there?" asked Hadden.

"The great *Isanusi*—she who is named *Inyanga* or Doctoress; she who is named Inyosi (the Bee), because she gathers wisdom from the dead who grow in the forest."

"Do you think that she could gather enough wisdom to tell me whether I am going to kill any buffalo, Nahoon?"

"Mayhap, White Man, but," he added with a little smile, "those who visit the Bee's hive may hear nothing, or they may hear more than they wish for. The words of that Bee have a sting."

"Good; I will see if she can sting me."

"So be it," said Nahoon; and turning, he led the way along the cliff till he reached a native path which zig-zagged down its face.

By this path they climbed till they came to the sward at the foot of the descent, and walked up it to the hut which was surrounded by a low fence of reeds, enclosing a small court-yard paved with ant-heap earth beaten hard and polished. In this court-yard sat the Bee, her stool being placed almost at the mouth of the round opening that served as a doorway to the hut. At first all that Hadden could see of her, crouched as she was in the shadow, was a huddled shape wrapped round with a greasy and tattered catskin kaross, above the edge of which appeared two eyes, fierce and quick as those of a leopard. At her feet smouldered a little fire, and ranged around it in a semi-circle were a number of human skulls, placed in pairs as though they were talking together, whilst other bones, to all appearance also human, were festooned about the hut and the fence of the court-yard.

"I see that the old lady is set up with the usual properties," thought Hadden, but he said nothing.

Nor did the witch-doctoress say anything; she only fixed her beady eyes upon his face. Hadden returned the compliment, staring at her with all his might, till suddenly he became aware that he was vanquished in this curious duel. His brain grew confused, and to his fancy it seemed that the woman before him had shifted shape into the likeness of a colossal and horrid spider sitting at the mouth of her trap, and that these bones were the relics of her victims.

"Why do you not speak, White Man?" she said at last in a slow clear voice. "Well, there is no need, since I can read your thoughts. You are thinking that I who am called the Bee should be better named the Spider. Have no fear; I did not kill these men. What would it profit me when the dead are so many? I suck the souls of men, not their bodies, White Man. It is their living hearts I love to look on, for therein I read much and thereby I grow wise. Now what would you of the Bee, White Man, the Bee that labours in this Garden of Death, and—what brings *you* here, son of Zomba? Why are you not with the Umcityu now that they doctor themselves for the great war—the last war—the war of the white and the black—or if you have no stomach for fighting, why are you not at the side of Nanea the tall, Nanea the fair?"

Nahoon made no answer, but Hadden said:—

"A small thing, mother. I would know if I shall prosper in my hunting."

"In your hunting, White Man; what hunting? The hunting of game, of money, or of women? Well, one of them, for a-hunting you must ever be; that is your nature, to hunt and be hunted. Tell me now, how goes the wound of that trader who tasted of your steel yonder in the town of the Maboon (Boers)? No need to answer, White Man, but what fee, Chief, for the poor witch-doctoress whose skill you seek," she added in a whining voice. "Surely you would not that an old woman should work without a fee?"

"I have none to offer you, mother, so I will be going," said Hadden, who began to feel himself satisfied with this display of the Bee's powers of observation and thought-reading.

"Nay," she answered with an unpleasant laugh, "would you ask a question, and not wait for the answer? I will take no fee from you at present, White Man; you shall pay me later on when we meet again," and once more she laughed. "Let me look in your face, let me look in your face," she continued, rising and standing before him.

Then of a sudden Hadden felt something cold at the back of his neck, and the next instant the Bee had sprung from him, holding between her thumb and finger a curl of dark hair which she had cut from his head. The action was so instantaneous that he had neither time to avoid nor to resent it, but stood still staring at her stupidly.

"That is all I need," she cried, "for like my heart my magic is white. Stay—son of Zomba, give me also of your hair, for those who visit the Bee must listen to her humming."

Nahoon obeyed, cutting a little lock from his head with the sharp edge of his assegai, though it was very evident that he did this not because he wished to do so, but because he feared to refuse.

Then the Bee slipped back her kaross, and stood bending over the fire before them, into which she threw herbs taken from a pouch that was bound about her middle. She was still a finely-shaped woman, and she wore none of the abominations which Hadden had been accustomed to see upon the persons of witch-doctoresses. About her neck, however, was a curious ornament, a small live snake, red and grey in hue, which her visitors recognised as one of the most deadly to be found in that part of the country. It is not unusual for Bantu witch-doctors thus to decorate themselves with snakes, though whether or not their fangs have first been extracted no one seems to know.

Presently the herbs began to smoulder, and the smoke of them rose up in a thin, straight stream, that, striking upon the face of the Bee, clung about her head enveloping it as though with a strange blue veil. Then of a sudden she stretched out her hands, and let fall the two locks of hair upon the burning herbs, where they writhed themselves to ashes like things alive. Next she opened her mouth, and began to draw the fumes of the hair and herbs into her lungs in great gulps; while the snake, feeling the influence of the medicine, hissed and, uncoiling itself from about her neck, crept upwards and took refuge among the black *saccaboola* feathers of her head-dress.

Soon the vapours began to do their work; she swayed to and fro muttering, then sank back against the hut, upon the straw of which her head rested. Now the Bee's face was turned upwards towards the light, and it was ghastly to behold, for it had become blue in colour, and the open eyes were sunken like the eyes of one dead, whilst above her forehead the red snake wavered and hissed, reminding Hadden of the Uraeus crest on the brow of statues of Egyptian kings. For ten seconds or more she remained thus, then she spoke in a hollow and unnatural voice:—

"O Black Heart and body that is white and beautiful, I look into your heart, and it is black as blood, and it shall be black with blood. Beautiful white body with black heart, you shall find your game and hunt it, and it shall lead you into the House of the Homeless, into the Home of the Dead, and it shall be shaped as a bull, it shall be shaped as a tiger, it shall be shaped as a woman whom kings and waters cannot harm. Beautiful white body and black heart, you shall be paid your wages, money for money, and blow for blow. Think of my word when the spotted cat purrs above your breast; think of it when the battle roars about you; think of it when you grasp your great reward, and for the last time stand face to face with the ghost of the dead in the Home of the Dead.

"O White Heart and black body, I look into your heart and it is white as milk, and the milk of innocence shall save it. Fool, why do you strike that blow? Let him be who is loved of the tiger, and whose love is as the love of a tiger. Ah! what face is that in the battle? Follow it, follow it, O swift of foot; but follow warily, for the tongue that has lied will never plead for mercy, and the hand that can betray is strong in war. White Heart, what is death? In death life lives, and among the dead you shall find the life you lost, for there awaits you she whom kings and waters cannot harm."

As the Bee spoke, by degrees her voice sank lower and lower till it was almost inaudible. Then it ceased altogether and she seemed to pass from trance to sleep. Hadden, who had been listening to her with an amused and cynical smile, now laughed aloud.

"Why do you laugh, White Man?" asked Nahoon angrily.

"I laugh at my own folly in wasting time listening to the nonsense of that lying fraud."

"It is no nonsense, White Man."

"Indeed? Then will you tell me what it means?"

"I cannot tell you what it means yet, but her words have to do with a woman and a leopard, and with your fate and my fate."

Hadden shrugged his shoulders, not thinking the matter worth further argument, and at that moment the Bee woke up shivering, drew the red snake from her head-dress and coiling it about her throat wrapped herself again in the greasy kaross.

"Are you satisfied with my wisdom, *Inkoos?*" she asked of Hadden.

"I am satisfied that you are one of the cleverest cheats in Zululand, mother," he answered coolly. "Now, what is there to pay?"

The Bee took no offence at this rude speech, though for a

second or two the look in her eyes grew strangely like that which they had seen in those of the snake when the fumes of the fire made it angry.

"If the white lord says I am a cheat, it must be so," she answered, "for he of all men should be able to discern a cheat. I have said that I ask no fee;—yes, give me a little tobacco from your pouch."

Hadden opened the bag of antelope hide and drawing some tobacco from it, gave it to her. In taking it she clasped his hand and examined the gold ring that was upon the third finger, a ring fashioned like a snake with two little rubies set in the head to represent the eyes.

"I wear a snake about my neck, and you wear one upon your hand, *Inkoos*. I should like to have this ring to wear upon my hand, so that the snake about my neck may be less lonely there."

"Then I am afraid you will have to wait till I am dead," said Hadden.

"Yes, yes," she answered in a pleased voice, "it is a good word. I will wait till you are dead and then I will take the ring, and none can say that I have stolen it, for Nahoon there will bear me witness that you gave me permission to do so."

For the first time Hadden started, since there was something about the Bee's tone that jarred upon him. Had she addressed him in her professional manner, he would have thought nothing of it; but in her cupidity she had become natural, and it was evident that she spoke from conviction, believing her own words.

She saw him start, and instantly changed her note.

"Let the white lord forgive the jest of a poor old witchdoctoress," she said in a whining voice. "I have so much to do with Death that his name leaps to my lips," and she glanced first at the circle of skulls about her, then towards the waterfall that fed the gloomy pool upon whose banks her hut was placed.

"Look," she said simply.

Following the line of her outstretched hand Hadden's eyes fell upon two withered mimosa trees which grew over the fall almost at right angles to its rocky edge. These trees were joined together by a rude platform made of logs of wood lashed down with *riems* of hide. Upon this platform stood three figures; notwithstanding the distance and the spray of the fall, he could see that they were those of two men and a girl, for their shapes stood out distinctly against the fiery red of the sunset sky. One instant there were three, the next there were two—for the girl had gone, and something dark rushing down the face of the fall, struck the surface of the pool with a heavy thud, while a faint and piteous cry broke upon his ear.

"What is the meaning of that?" he asked, horrified and amazed.

"Nothing," answered the Bee with a laugh. "Do you not know, then, that this is the place where faithless women, or girls who have loved without the leave of the king, are brought to meet their death, and with them their accomplices. Oh! they die here thus each day, and I watch them die and keep the count of the number of them," and drawing a tally-stick from the thatch of the hut, she took a knife and added a notch to the many that appeared upon it, looking at Nahoon the while with a half-questioning, half-warning gaze.

"Yes, yes, it is a place of death," she muttered. "Up yonder the quick die day by day and down there"—and she pointed along the course of the river beyond the pool to where the forest began some two hundred yards from her hut—"the ghosts of them have their home. Listen!"

As she spoke, a sound reached their ears that seemed to swell from the dim skirts of the forests, a peculiar and unholy sound which it is impossible to define more accurately than by saying that it seemed beastlike, and almost inarticulate.

"Listen," repeated the Bee, "they are merry yonder."

"Who?" asked Hadden; "the baboons?"

"No, *Inkoos,* the *Amatongo*—the ghosts that welcome her who has just become of their number."

"Ghosts," said Hadden roughly, for he was angry at his own tremors, "I should like to see those ghosts. Do you think that I have never heard a troop of monkeys in the bush before, mother? Come, Nahoon, let us be going while there is light to climb the cliff. Farewell."

"Farewell *Inkoos,* and doubt not that your wish will be fulfilled. Go in peace *Inkoos*—to sleep in peace."

CHAPTER III

The End of the Hunt

The prayer of the Bee notwithstanding, Philip Hadden slept ill that night. He felt in the best of health, and his conscience was not troubling him more than usual, but rest he could not. Whenever he closed his eyes, his mind conjured up a picture of the grim witch-doctoress, so strangely named the Bee, and the sound of her evil-omened words as he had heard them that afternoon. He was neither a superstitious nor a timid man, and any supernatural beliefs that might linger in his mind were, to say the least of it, dormant. But do what he might, he could not shake off a certain eerie sensation of fear, lest there should be some grains of truth in the prophesyings of this hag. What if it were a fact that he was near his death, and that the heart which beat so strongly in his breast must soon be still for ever—no, he would not think of it. This gloomy place, and the dreadful sight which he saw that day, had upset his nerves. The domestic customs of these Zulus were not pleasant, and for his part he was determined to be clear of them so soon as he was able to escape the country.

In fact, if he could in any way manage it, it was his intention to make a dash for the border on the following night. To do this with a good prospect of success, however, it was necessary that he should kill a buffalo, or some other head of game. Then, as he knew well, the hunters with him would feast upon meat until they could scarcely stir, and that would be his opportunity. Nahoon, however, might not succumb to this temptation; therefore he must trust to luck to be rid of him. If it came to the worst, he could put a bullet through him, which he considered he would be justified in doing, seeing that in reality the man was his jailor. Should this necessity arise, he felt indeed that he could face it without undue compunction, for in truth he disliked Nahoon; at times he even hated him. Their natures were antagonistic, and he knew that the great Zulu distrusted and looked down upon him, and to be looked down upon by a savage "nigger" was more than his pride could stomach.

At the first break of dawn Hadden rose and roused his escort, who were still stretched in sleep around the dying fire, each man wrapped in his kaross or blanket. Nahoon stood up and shook himself, looking gigantic in the shadows of the morning.

"What is your will, *Umlungu* (white man), that you are up before the sun?"

"My will, *Muntumpofu* (yellow man), is to hunt buffalo," answered Hadden coolly. It irritated him that this savage should give him no title of any sort.

"Your pardon," said the Zulu reading his thoughts, "but I cannot call you *Inkoos* because you are not my chief, or any man's; still if the title 'white man' offends you, we will give you a name."

"As you wish," answered Hadden briefly.

Accordingly they gave him a name, *Inhlizin-mgama,* by which he was known among them thereafter, but Hadden was not best pleased when he found that the meaning of those soft-sounding syllables was "Black Heart." That was how the *inyanga* had addressed him—only she used different words.

An hour later, and they were in the swampy bush country

that lay behind the encampment searching for their game. Within a very little while Nahoon held up his hand, then pointed to the ground. Hadden looked; there, pressed deep in the marshy soil, and to all appearance not ten minutes old, was the spoor of a small herd of buffalo.

"I knew that we should find game to-day," whispered Nahoon, "because the Bee said so."

"Curse the Bee," answered Hadden below his breath. "Come on."

For a quarter of an hour or more they followed the spoor through thick reeds, till suddenly Nahoon whistled very softly and touched Hadden's arm. He looked up, and there, about two hundred yards away, feeding on some higher ground among a patch of mimosa trees, were the buffaloes— six of them—an old bull with a splendid head, three cows, a heifer and a calf about four months old. Neither the wind nor the nature of the veldt were favourable for them to stalk the game from their present position, so they made a detour of half a mile and very carefully crept towards them up the wind, slipping from trunk to trunk of the mimosas and when these failed them, crawling on their stomachs under cover of the tall *tambuti* grass. At last they were within forty yards, and a further advance seemed impracticable; for although he could not smell them, it was evident from his movements that the old bull heard some unusual sound and was growing suspicious. Nearest to Hadden, who alone of the party had a rifle, stood the heifer broadside on—a beautiful shot. Remembering that she would make the best beef, he lifted his Martini, and aiming at her immediately behind the shoulder, gently squeezed the trigger. The rifle exploded, and the heifer fell dead, shot through the heart. Strangely enough the other buffaloes did not at once run away. On the contrary, they seemed puzzled to account for the sudden noise; and, not being able to wind anything, lifted their heads and stared round them.

The pause gave Hadden space to get in a fresh cartridge

and to aim again, this time at the old bull. The bullet struck him somewhere in the neck or shoulder, for he came to his knees, but in another second was up and having caught sight of the cloud of smoke he charged straight at it. Because of this smoke, or for some other reason, Hadden did not see him coming, and in consequence would most certainly have been trampled or gored, had not Nahoon sprung forward, at the imminent risk of his own life, and dragged him down behind an ant-heap. A moment more and the great beast had thundered by, taking no further notice of them.

"Forward," said Hadden, and leaving most of the men to cut up the heifer and carry the best of her meat to camp, they started on the blood spoor.

For some hours they followed the bull, till at last they lost the trail on a patch of stony ground thickly covered with bush, and exhausted by the heat, sat down to rest and to eat some *biltong* or sun-dried flesh which they had with them. They finished their meal, and were preparing to return to the camp, when one of the four Zulus who were with them went to drink at a little stream that ran at a distance of not more than ten paces away. Half a minute later they heard a hideous grunting noise and a splashing of water, and saw the Zulu fly into the air. All the while that they were eating, the wounded buffalo had been lying in wait for them under a thick bush on the banks of the streamlet, knowing—cunning brute that he was—that sooner or later his turn would come. With a shout of consternation they rushed forward to see the bull vanish over the rise before Hadden could get a chance of firing at him, and to find their companion dying, for the great horn had pierced his lung.

"It is not a buffalo, it is a devil," the poor fellow gasped, and expired.

"Devil or not, I mean to kill it," exclaimed Hadden. So leaving the others to carry the body of their comrade to camp, he started on accompanied by Nahoon only. Now the ground was more open and the chase easier, for they sighted their quarry frequently, though they could not come near enough to fire. Presently they travelled down a steep cliff.

"Do you know where we are?" asked Nahoon, pointing to a belt of forest opposite. "That is *Emagudu,* the Home of the Dead—and look, the bull heads thither."

Hadden glanced round him. It was true; yonder to the left were the Fall, the Pool of Doom, and the hut of the Bee.

"Very well," he answered; "then we must head for it too."

Nahoon halted. "Surely you would not enter there," he exclaimed.

"Surely I will," replied Hadden, "but there is no need for you to do so if you are afraid."

"I am afraid—of ghosts," said the Zulu, "but I will come."

So they crossed the strip of turf, and entered the haunted wood. It was a gloomy place indeed; the great wide-topped trees grew thick there shutting out the sight of the sky; moreover, the air in it which no breeze stirred, was heavy with the exhalations of rotting foliage. There seemed to be no life here and no sound—only now and again a loathsome spotted snake would uncoil itself and glide away, and now and again a heavy rotten bough fell with a crash.

Hadden was too intent upon the buffalo, however, to be much impressed by his surroundings. He only remarked that the light would be bad for shooting, and went on.

They must have penetrated a mile or more into the forest when the sudden increase of blood upon the spoor told them that the bull's wound was proving fatal to him.

"Run now," said Hadden cheerfully.

"Nay, *hamba gachle*—go softly—" answered Nahoon, "the devil is dying, but he will try to play us another trick before he dies." And he went on peering ahead of him cautiously.

"It is all right here, anyway," said Hadden, pointing to the spoor that ran straight forward printed deep in the marshy ground.

Nahoon did not answer, but stared steadily at the trunks of

two trees a few paces in front of them and to their right. "Look," he whispered.

Hadden did so, and at length made out the outline of something brown that was crouched behind the trees.

"He is dead," he exclaimed.

"No," answered Nahoon, "he has come back on his own path and is waiting for us. He knows that we are following his spoor. Now if you stand there, I think that you can shoot him through the back between the tree trunks."

Hadden knelt down, and aiming very carefully at a point just below the bull's spine, he fired. There was an awful bellow, and the next instant the brute was up and at them. Nahoon flung his broad spear, which sank deep into its chest, then they fled this way and that. The buffalo stood still for a moment, its fore legs straddled wide and its head down, looking first after the one and then the other, till of a sudden it uttered a low moaning sound and rolled over dead, smashing Nahoon's assegai to fragments as it fell.

"There! he's finished," said Hadden, "and I believe it was your assegai that killed him. Hullo! what's that noise?"

Nahoon listened. In several quarters of the forest, but from how far away it was impossible to tell, there rose a curious sound, as of people calling to each other in fear but in no articulate language. Nahoon shivered.

"It is the *Esemkofu,*" he said, "the ghosts who have no tongue, and who can only wail like infants. Let us be going; this place is bad for mortals."

"And worse for buffaloes," said Hadden, giving the dead bull a kick, "but I suppose that we must leave him here for your friends, the *Esemkofu,* as we have got meat enough, and can't carry his head."

So they started back towards the open country. As they threaded their way slowly through the tree trunks, a new idea came into Hadden's head. Once out of this forest, he was within an hour's run of the Zulu border, and once over the Zulu border, he would feel a happier man than he did at that moment. As has been said, he had intended to attempt to escape in the darkness, but the plan was risky. All the Zulus might not over-eat themselves and go to sleep, especially after the death of their comrade; Nahoon, who watched him day and night, certainly would not. This was his opportunity—there remained the question of Nahoon.

Well, if it came to the worst, Nahoon must die: it would be easy—he had a loaded rifle, and now that his assegai was gone, Nahoon had only a kerry. He did not wish to kill the man, though it was clear to him, seeing that his own safety was at stake, that he would be amply justified in so doing. Why should he not put it to him—and then be guided by circumstances?

Nahoon was walking across a little open space about ten spaces ahead of him where Hadden could see him very well, whilst he himself was under the shadow of a large tree with low horizontal branches running out from the trunk.

"Nahoon," he said.

The Zulu turned round, and took a step towards him.

"No, do not move, I pray. Stand where you are, or I shall be obliged to shoot you. Listen now: do not be afraid for I shall not fire without warning. I am your prisoner, and you are charged to take me back to the king to be his servant. But I believe that a war is going to break out between your people and mine; and this being so, you will understand that I do not wish to go to Cetywayo's kraal, because I should either come to a violent death there, or my own brothers will believe that I am a traitor and treat me accordingly. The Zulu border is not much more than an hour's journey away—let us say an hour and a half's: I mean to be across it before the moon is up. Now, Nahoon, will you lose me in the forest and give me this hour and a half's start—or will you stop here with that ghost people of whom you talk? Do you understand? No, please do not move."

"I understand you," answered the Zulu, in a perfectly composed voice, "and I think that was a good name which we gave you this morning, though, Black Heart, there is some justice in your words and more wisdom. Your opportunity is good, and one which a man named as you are should not let fall."

"I am glad to find that you take this view of the matter, Nahoon. And now will you be so kind as to lose me, and to promise not to look for me till the moon is up?"

"What do you mean, Black Heart?"

"What I say. Come, I have no time to spare."

"You are a strange man," said the Zulu reflectively. "You heard the king's order to me: would you have me disobey the order of the king?"

"Certainly, I would. You have no reason to love Cetywayo, and it does not matter to you whether or no I return to his kraal to mend guns there. If you think that he will be angry because I am missing, you had better cross the border also; we can go together."

"And leave my father and all my brethren to his vengeance? Black Heart, you do not understand. How can you, being so named? I am a soldier, and the king's word is the king's word. I hoped to have died fighting, but I am the bird in your noose. Come, shoot, or you will not reach the border before moonrise," and he opened his arms and smiled.

"If it must be, so let it be. Farewell, Nahoon, at least you are a brave man, but every one of us must cherish his own life," answered Hadden calmly.

Then with much deliberation he raised his rifle and covered the Zulu's breast.

Already—whilst his victim stood there still smiling, although a twitching of his lips betrayed the natural terrors that no bravery can banish—already his finger was contracting on the trigger, when of a sudden, as instantly as though he had been struck by lightning, Hadden went down backwards, and behold! there stood upon him a great spotted

beast that waved its long tail to and fro and glared down into
his eyes.

It was a leopard—a tiger as they call it in Africa—which,
crouched upon a bough of the tree above, had been unable to
resist the temptation of satisfying its savage appetite on the
man below. For a second or two there was silence, broken
only by the purring, or rather the snoring sound made by the
leopard. In those seconds, strangely enough, there sprang
up before Hadden's mental vision a picture of the *inyanga*
called *Inyosi* or the Bee, her death-like head resting against
the thatch of the hut, and her death-like lips muttering "think
of my word when the great cat purrs above your face."

Then the brute put out its strength. The claws of one paw
it drove deep into the muscles of his left thigh, while with
another it scratched at his breast, tearing the clothes from it
and furrowing the flesh beneath. The sight of the white skin
seemed to madden it, and in its fierce desire for blood it
drooped its square muzzle and buried its fangs in its victim's
shoulder. Next moment there was a sound of running feet
and of a club falling heavily. Up reared the leopard with an
angry snarl, up till it stood as high as the attacking Zulu. At
him it came, striking out savagely and tearing the black man
as it had torn the white. Again the kerry fell full on its jaws,
and down it went backwards. Before it could rise again, or
rather as it was in the act of rising, the heavy knob-stick
struck it once more, and with fearful force, this time as it
chanced, full on the nape of the neck, and paralysing the
brute. It writhed and bit and twisted, throwing up the earth
and leaves, while blow after blow was rained upon it, till at
length with a convulsive struggle and a stifled roar it lay
still—the brains oozing from its shattered skull.

Hadden sat up, the blood running from his wounds.

"You have saved my life, Nahoon," he said faintly, "and I
thank you."

"Do not thank me, Black Heart," answered the Zulu, "it
was the king's word that I should keep you safely. Still this

tiger has been hardly dealt with, for certainly *he* has saved *my* life," and lifting the Martini he unloaded the rifle.

At this juncture Hadden swooned away.

Twenty-four hours had gone by when, after what seemed to him to be but a little time of troubled and dreamful sleep, through which he could hear voices without understanding what they said, and feel himself borne he knew not whither, Hadden awoke to find himself lying upon a kaross in a large and beautifully clean Kaffir hut with a bundle of furs for a pillow. There was a bowl of milk at his side and tortured as he was by thirst, he tried to stretch out his arm to lift it to his lips, only to find to his astonishment that his hand fell back to his side like that of a dead man. Looking round the hut impatiently, he found that there was nobody in it to assist him, so he did the only thing which remained for him to do—he lay still. He did not fall asleep, but his eyes closed, and a kind of gentle torpor crept over him, half obscuring his recovered senses. Presently he heard a soft voice speaking; it seemed far away, but he could clearly distinguish the words.

"Black Heart still sleeps," the voice said, "but there is colour in his face; I think that he will wake soon, and find his thoughts again."

"Have no fear, Nanea, he will surely wake, his hurts are not dangerous," answered another voice, that of Nahoon. "He fell heavily with the weight of the tiger on top of him, and that is why his senses have been shaken for so long. He went near to death, but certainly he will not die."

"It would have been a pity if he had died," answered the soft voice, "he is so beautiful; never have I seen a white man who was so beautiful."

"I did not think him beautiful when he stood with his rifle pointed at my heart," answered Nahoon sulkily.

"Well, there is this to be said," she replied, "he wished to escape from Cetywayo, and that is not to be wondered at," and she sighed. "Moreover he asked you to come with him, and it might have been well if you had done so, that is, if you would have taken me with you!"

"How could I have done it, girl?" he asked angrily. "Would you have me set at nothing the order of the king?"

"The king!" she replied raising her voice. "What do you owe to this king? You have served him faithfully, and your reward is that within a few days he will take me from you—me, who should have been your wife, and I must—I must——" And she began to weep softly, adding between her sobs, "if you loved me truly, you would think more of me and of yourself, and less of the Black One and his orders. Oh! let us fly, Nahoon, let us fly to Natal before this spear pierces me."

"Weep not, Nanea," he said; "why do you tear my heart in two between my duty and my love? You know that I am a soldier, and that I must walk the path whereon the king has set my feet. Soon I think I shall be dead, for I seek death, and then it will matter nothing."

"Nothing to you, Nahoon, who are at peace, but to me? Yet, you are right, and I know it, therefore forgive me, who am no warrior, but a woman who must also obey—the will of the king." And she cast her arms about his neck, sobbing her fill upon his breast.

CHAPTER IV
Nanea

Presently, muttering something that the listener could not catch, Nahoon left Nanea, and crept out of the hut by its bee-hole entrance. Then Hadden opened his eyes and looked round him. The sun was sinking and a ray of its red light streaming through the little opening filled the place with a soft and crimson glow. In the centre of the hut—supporting it—stood a thorn-wood roof-tree coloured black by the smoke of the fire; and against this, the rich light falling full upon her, leaned the girl Nanea—a very picture of gentle despair.

As is occasionally the case among Zulu women, she was beautiful—so beautiful that the sight of her went straight to the white man's heart, for a moment causing the breath to catch in his throat. Her dress was very simple. On her shoulders, hanging open in front, lay a mantle of soft white stuff edged with blue beads, about her middle was a buck-skin moocha, also embroidered with blue beads, while round her forehead and left knee were strips of grey fur, and on her right wrist a shining bangle of copper. Her naked bronze-hued figure was tall and perfect in its proportions; while her face had little in common with that of the ordinary native girl, showing as it did strong traces of the ancestral Arabian or Semitic blood. It was oval in shape, with delicate aquiline features, arched eyebrows, a full mouth, that drooped a little at the corners, tiny ears, behind which the wavy coal-black hair hung down to the shoulders, and the very loveliest pair of dark and liquid eyes that it is possible to imagine.

For a minute or more Nanea stood thus, her sweet face bathed in the sunbeam, while Hadden feasted his eyes upon its beauty. Then sighing heavily, she turned, and seeing that he was awake, started, drew her mantle over her breast and came, or rather glided, towards him.

"The chief is awake," she said in her soft Zulu accents. "Does he need aught?"

"Yes, Lady," he answered; "I need to drink, but alas! I am too weak."

She knelt down beside him, and supporting him with her left arm, with her right held the gourd to his lips.

How it came about Hadden never knew, but before that draught was finished a change passed over him. Whether it was the savage girl's touch, or her strange and fawn-like loveliness, or the tender pity in her eyes, matters not—the issue was the same. She struck some cord in his turbulent uncurbed nature, and of a sudden it was filled full with passion for her—a passion which if, not elevated, at least was real. He did not for a moment mistake the significance of the flood of feeling that surged through his veins. Hadden never shirked facts.

"By Heaven!" he said to himself, "I have fallen in love with a black beauty at first sight—more in love than I have ever been before. It's awkward, but there will be compensations. So much the worse for Nahoon, or for Cetywayo, or for both of them. After all, I can always get rid of her if she becomes a nuisance."

Then, in a fit of renewed weakness, brought about by the turmoil of his blood, he lay back upon the pillow of furs, watching Nanea's face while with a native salve of pounded leaves she busied herself dressing the wounds that the leopard had made.

It almost seemed as though something of what was passing in his mind communicated itself to that of the girl. At least, her hand shook a little at her task, and getting done with it as quickly as she could, she rose from her knees with a courteous "It is finished, *Inkoos,*" and once more took up her position by the roof-tree.

"I thank you, Lady," he said; "your hand is kind."

"You must not call me lady, *Inkoos,*" she answered, "I am no chieftainess, but only the daughter of a headman, Umgona."

"And named Nanea," he said. "Nay, do not be surprised, I have heard of you. Well, Nanea, perhaps you will soon become a chieftainess—up at the king's kraal yonder."

"Alas! and alas!" she said, covering her face with her hands.

"Do not grieve, Nanea, a hedge is never so tall and thick but that it cannot be climbed or crept through."

She let fall her hands and looked at him eagerly, but he did not pursue the subject.

"Tell me, how did I come here, Nanea?"

"Nahoon and his companions carried you, *Inkoos.*"

"Indeed, I begin to be thankful to the leopard that struck me down. Well, Nahoon is a brave man, and he has done me a great service. I trust that I may be able to repay it—to you, Nanea."

This was the first meeting of Nanea and Hadden; but, although she did not seek them, the necessities of his sickness and of the situation brought about many another. Never for a moment did the white man waver in his determination to get into his keeping the native girl who had captivated him, and to attain his end he brought to bear all his powers and charm to detach her from Nahoon, and win her affections for himself. He was no rough wooer, however, but proceeded warily, weaving her about with a web of flattery and attention that must, he thought, produce the desired effect upon her mind. Without a doubt, indeed, it would have done so—for she was but a woman, and an untutored one—had it not been for a simple fact which dominated her whole nature. She loved Nahoon, and there was no room in her heart for any other man, white or black. To Hadden she was courteous and kindly but no more, nor did she appear to notice any of the subtle advances by which he attempted to win a foothold in her heart. For a while this puzzled him, but he remembered that the Zulu women do not usually permit themselves to show feeling towards an undeclared suitor. Therefore it became necessary that he should speak out.

His mind once made up, he had not to wait long for an opportunity. He was now quite recovered from his hurts, and accustomed to walk in the neighbourhood of the kraal. About two hundred yards from Umgona's huts rose a spring, and thither it was Nanea's habit to resort in the evening to bring back drinking-water for the use of her father's household. The path between this spring and the kraal ran through a patch of bush, where on a certain afternoon towards sundown Hadden took his seat under a tree, having first seen Nanea go down to the little stream as was her custom. A quarter of an hour later she reappeared carrying a large gourd upon her head. She wore no garment now except her moocha, for she had but one mantle and was afraid lest the water should splash it. He watched her advancing along the path, her hands resting on her hips, her splendid naked figure outlined against the westering sun, and wondered what excuse he could make to talk with her. As it chanced fortune favoured him, for when she was near him a snake glided across the path in front of the girl's feet, causing her to spring backwards in alarm and overset the gourd of water. He came forward, and picked it up.

"Wait here," he said laughing; "I will bring it to you full."

"Nay, *Inkoos*," she remonstrated, "that is a woman's work."

"Among my people," he said, "the men love to work for the women," and he started for the spring, leaving her wondering.

Before he reached her again, he regretted his gallantry, for it was necessary to carry the handleless gourd upon his shoulder, and the contents of it spilling over the edge soaked him. Of this, however, he said nothing to Nanea.

"There is your water, Nanea, shall I carry it for you to the kraal?"

"Nay, *Inkoos*, I thank you, but give it to me, you are weary with its weight."

"Stay awhile, and I will accompany you. Ah! Nanea, I am still weak, and had it not been for you I think that I should be dead."

"It was Nahoon who saved you—not I, *Inkoos*."

"Nahoon saved my body, but you, Nanea, you alone can save my heart."

"You talk darkly, *Inkoos*."

"Then I must make my meaning clear, Nanea. I love you."

She opened her brown eyes wide.

"You, a white lord, love me, a Zulu girl? How can that be?"

"I do not know, Nanea, but it is so, and were you not blind you would have seen it. I love you, and I wish to take you to wife."

"Nay, *Inkoos,* it is impossible. I am already betrothed."

"Ay," he answered, "betrothed to the king."

"No, betrothed to Nahoon."

"But it is the king who will take you within a week; is it not so? And would you not rather that I should take you than the king?"

"It seems to be so, *Inkoos,* and I would rather go with you than with the king, but most of all I desire to marry Nahoon. It may be that I shall not be able to marry him, but if that is so, at least I will never become one of the king's women."

"How will you prevent it, Nanea?"

"There are waters in which a maid may drown, and trees upon which she can hang," she answered with a quick setting of the mouth.

"That were a pity, Nanea, you are too fair to die."

"Fair or foul, yet I die, *Inkoos.*"

"No, no, come with me—I will find a way—and be my wife," and he put his arm about her waist, and strove to draw her to him.

Without any violence of movement, and with the most perfect dignity, the girl disengaged herself from his embrace.

"You have honoured me, and I thank you, *Inkoos,*" she said quietly, "but you do not understand. I am the wife of Nahoon—I belong to Nahoon; therefore, I cannot look on any other man while Nahoon lives. It is not our custom, *Inkoos,* for we are not as the white women, but ignorant and simple, and when we vow ourselves to a man, we abide by that vow till death."

"Indeed," said Hadden; "and so now you go to tell Nahoon that I have offered to make you my wife."

"No, *Inkoos,* why should I tell Nahoon your secrets? I

have said 'nay' to you, not 'yea,' therefore he has no right to know," and she stooped to lift the gourd of water.

Hadden considered the situation rapidly, for his repulse only made him the more determined to succeed. Of a sudden under the emergency he conceived a scheme, or rather its rough outline. It was not a nice scheme, and some men might have shrunk from it, but as he had no intention of suffering himself to be defeated by a Zulu girl, he decided—with regret, it is true—that having failed to attain his ends by means which he considered fair, he must resort to others of more doubtful character.

"Nanea," he said, "you are a good and honest woman, and I respect you. As I have told you, I love you also, but if you refuse to listen to me there is nothing more to be said, and after all, perhaps it would be better that you should marry one of your own people. But, Nanea, you will never marry him, for the king will take you; and, if he does not give you to some other man, either you will become one of his 'sisters,' or to be free of him, as you say, you will die. Now hear me, for it is because I love you and wish your welfare that I speak thus. Why do you not escape into Natal, taking Nahoon with you, for there as you know you may live in peace out of reach of the arm of Cetywayo?"

"That is my desire, *Inkoos,* but Nahoon will not consent. He says that there is to be war between us and you white men, and he will not break the command of the king and desert from his army."

"Then he cannot love you much, Nahoon, and at least you have to think of yourself. Whisper into the ear of your father and fly together, for be sure that Nahoon will soon follow you. Ay! and I myself will fly with you, for I too believe that there must be war, and then a white man in this country will be as a lamb among the eagles."

"If Nahoon will come, I will go, *Inkoos,* but I cannot fly without Nahoon; it is better I should stay here and kill myself."

"Surely then being so fair and loving him so well, you can teach him to forget his folly and to escape with you. In four days' time we must start for the king's kraal, and if you win over Nahoon, it will be easy for us to turn our faces southwards and across the river that lies between the land of the Amazulu and Natal. For the sake of all of us, but most of all for your own sake, try to do this, Nanea, whom I have loved and whom I now would save. See him and plead with him as you know how, but as yet do not tell him that I dream of flight, for then I should be watched."

"In truth, I will, *Inkoos,*" she answered earnestly, "and oh! I thank you for your goodness. Fear not that I will betray you—first would I die. Farewell."

"Farewell, Nanea," and taking her hand he raised it to his lips.

Late that night, just as Hadden was beginning to prepare himself for sleep, he heard a gentle tapping at the board which closed the entrance to his hut.

"Enter," he said, unfastening the door, and presently by the light of the little lantern that he had with him, he saw Nanea creep into the hut, followed by the great form of Nahoon.

"Inkoos," she said in a whisper when the door was closed again, "I have pleaded with Nahoon, and he has consented to fly; moreover, my father will come also."

"Is it so, Nahoon?" asked Hadden.

"It is so," answered the Zulu, looking down shamefacedly; "to save this girl from the king, and because the love of her eats out my heart, I have bartered away my honour. But I tell you, Nanea, and you, White Man, as I told Umgona just now, that I think no good will come of this flight, and if we are caught or betrayed, we shall be killed every one of us."

"Caught we can scarcely be," broke in Nanea anxiously, "for who could betray us, except the *Inkoos* here——"

"Which he is not likely to do," said Hadden quietly, "seeing that he desires to escape with you, and that his life is also at stake."

"That is so, Black Heart," said Nahoon, "otherwise I tell you that I should not have trusted you."

Hadden took no notice of this outspoken saying, but until very late that night they sat there together making their plans.

On the following morning Hadden was awakened by sounds of violent altercation. Going out of his hut he found that the disputants were Umgona and a fat and evil-looking Kaffir chief who had arrived at the kraal on a pony. This chief, he soon discovered, was named Maputa, being none other than the man who had sought Nanea in marriage and brought about Nahoon's and Umgona's unfortunate appeal to the king. At present he was engaged in abusing Umgona furiously, charging him with having stolen certain of his oxen and bewitched his cows so that they would not give milk. The alleged theft it was comparatively easy to disprove, but the wizardry remained a matter of argument.

"You are a dog, and a son of a dog," shouted Maputa, shaking his fat fist in the face of the trembling but indignant Umgona. "You promised me your daughter in marriage, then having vowed her to that *umfagozan*—that low lout of a soldier, Nahoon, the son of Zomba—you went, the two of you, and poisoned the king's ear against me, bringing me into trouble with the king, and now you have bewitched my cattle. Well, wait, I will be even with you, Wizard; wait till you wake up in the cold morning to find your fence red with fire, and the slayers standing outside your gates to eat up you and yours with spears——"

At this juncture Nahoon, who till now had been listening in silence, intervened with effect.

"Good," he said, "we will wait, but not in your company, Chief Maputa. *Hamba!* (go)——" and seizing the fat old ruffian by the scruff of his neck, he flung him backwards with such violence that he rolled over and over down the little slope.

Hadden laughed, and passed on towards the stream where he proposed to bathe. Just as he reached it, he caught sight of Maputa riding along the footpath, his head-ring covered with mud, his lips purple and his black face livid with rage.

"There goes an angry man," he said to himself. "Now, how would it be——" and he looked upwards like one seeking an inspiration. It seemed to come; perhaps the devil finding it open whispered in his ear, at any rate—in a few seconds his plan was formed, and he was walking through the bush to meet Maputa.

"Go in peace, Chief," he said; "they seem to have treated you roughly up yonder. Having no power to interfere, I came away for I could not bear the sight. It is indeed shameful that an old and venerable man of rank should be struck into the dirt, and beaten by a soldier drunk with beer."

"Shameful, White Man!" gasped Maputa; "your words are true indeed. But wait a while. I, Maputa, will roll that stone over, I will throw that bull upon its back. When next the harvest ripens, this I promise, that neither Nahoon nor Umgona, nor any of his kraal shall be left to gather it."

"And how will you manage that, Maputa?"

"I do not know, but I will find a way. Oh! I tell you, a way shall be found."

Hadden patted the pony's neck meditatively, then leaning forward, he looked the chief in the eyes and said:—

"What will you give me, Maputa, if I show you that way, a sure and certain one, whereby you may be avenged to the death upon Nahoon, whose violence I also have seen, and upon Umgona, whose witchcraft brought sore sickness upon me?"

"What reward do you seek, White Man?" asked Maputa eagerly.

"A little thing, Chief, a thing of no account, only the girl Nanea, to whom as it chances I have taken a fancy."

"I wanted her for myself, White Man, but he who sits at Ulundi has laid his hand upon her."

"That is nothing, Chief; I can arrange with him who 'sits at Ulundi.' It is with you who are great here that I wish to come to terms. Listen: if you grant my desire, not only will I fulfil yours upon your foes, but when the girl is delivered into my hands I will give you this rifle and a hundred rounds of cartridges."

Maputa looked at the sporting Martini, and his eyes glistened.

"It is good," he said; "it is very good. Often have I wished for such a gun that will enable me to shoot game, and to talk with my enemies from far away. Promise it to me, White Man, and you shall take the girl if I can give her to you."

"You swear it, Maputa?"

"I swear it by the head of Chaka, and the spirits of my fathers."

"Good. At dawn on the fourth day from now it is the purpose of Umgona, his daughter Nanea, and Nahoon, to cross the river into Natal by the drift that is called Crocodile Drift, taking their cattle with them and flying from the king. I also shall be of their company, for they know that I have learned their secret, and would murder me if I tried to leave them. Now you who are chief of the border and guardian of that drift, must hide at night with some men among the rocks in the shallows of the drift and await our coming. First Nanea will cross driving the cows and calves, for so it is arranged, and I shall help her; then will follow Umgona and Nahoon with the oxen and heifers. On these two you must fall, killing them and capturing the cattle, and afterwards I will give you the rifle."

"What if the king should ask for the girl, White Man?"

"Then you shall answer that in the uncertain light you did not recognise her and so she slipped away from you; moreover, that at first you feared to seize the girl lest her cries should alarm the men and they should escape you."

"Good, but how can I be sure that you will give me the gun once you are across the river?"

"Thus: before I enter the ford I will lay the rifle and cartridges upon a stone by the bank, telling Nanea that I shall return to fetch them when I have driven over the cattle."

"It is well, White Man; I will not fail you."

So the plot was made, and after some further conversation upon points of detail, the two conspirators shook hands and parted.

"That ought to come off all right," reflected Hadden to himself as he plunged and floated in the waters of the stream, "but somehow I don't quite trust our friend Maputa. It would have been better if I could have relied upon myself to get rid of Nahoon and his respected uncle—a couple of shots would do it in the water. But then that would be murder and murder is unpleasant; whereas the other thing is only the delivery to justice of two base deserters, a laudable action in a military country. Also personal interference upon my part might turn the girl against me; while after Umgona and Nahoon have been wiped out by Maputa, she *must* accept my escort. Of course there is a risk, but in every walk of life the most cautious have to take risks at times."

As it chanced, Philip Hadden was correct in his suspicions of his coadjutor, Maputa. Even before that worthy chief reached his own kraal, he had come to the conclusion that the white man's plan, though attractive in some ways, was too dangerous, since it was certain that if the girl Nanea escaped, the king would be indignant. Moreover, the men he took with him to do the killing in the drift would suspect something and talk. On the other hand he would earn much credit with his majesty by revealing the plot, saying that he had learned it from the lips of the white hunter, whom Umgona and Nahoon had forced to participate in it, and of whose coveted rifle he must trust to chance to possess himself.

*   *   *

An hour later two discreet messengers were bounding across the plains, bearing words from the Chief Maputa, the Warden of the Border, to the "great Black Elephant" at Ulundi.

CHAPTER V

The Doom Pool

Fortune showed itself strangely favourable to the plans of Nahoon and Nanea. One of the Zulu captain's perplexities was as to how he should lull the suspicions and evade the vigilance of his own companions, who together with himself had been detailed by the king to assist Hadden in his hunting and to guard against his escape. As it chanced, however, on the day after the incident of the visit of Maputa, a messenger arrived from no less a person than the great military Induna, Tvingwayo ka Marolo, who afterwards commanded the Zulu army at Isandhlwana, ordering these men to return to their regiment, the Umcityu Corps, which was to be placed upon full war footing. Accordingly Nahoon sent them, saying that he himself would follow with Black Heart in the course of a few days, as at present the white man was not sufficiently recovered from his hurts to allow of his travelling fast and far. So the soldiers went, doubting nothing.

Then Umgona gave it out that in obedience to the command of the king he was about to start for Ulundi, taking with him his daughter Nanea to be delivered over into the *Sigodhla,* and also those fifteen head of cattle that had been *lobola'd* by Nahoon in consideration of his forthcoming marriage, whereof he had been fined by Cetywayo. Under pretence that they required a change of veldt, the rest of his cattle he sent away in charge of a Basuto herd who knew nothing of their plans, telling him to keep them by the Crocodile Drift, as there the grass was good and sweet.

All preparations being completed, on the third day the party started, heading straight for Ulundi. After they had

travelled some miles, however, they left the road and turning
sharp to the right, passed unobserved of any through a great
stretch of uninhabited bush. Their path now lay not far from
the Pool of Doom, which, indeed, was close to Umgona's
kraal, and the forest that was called Home of the Dead, but
out of sight of these. It was their plan to travel by night,
reaching the broken country near the Crocodile Drift on the
following morning. Here they proposed to lie hid that day
and through the night; then, having first collected the cattle
which had preceded them, to cross the river at the break of
dawn and escape into Natal. At least this was the plan of his
companions; but, as we know, Hadden had another programme, whereon after one last appearance two of the party
would play no part.

During that long afternoon's journey Umgona, who knew
every inch of the country, walked ahead driving the fifteen
cattle and carrying in his hand a long travelling stick of
black and white *umzimbeet* wood, for in truth the old man
was in a hurry to reach his journey's end. Next came Nahoon, armed with a broad assegai, but naked except for his
moocha and necklet of baboon's teeth, and with him Nanea
in her white bead-bordered mantle. Hadden, who brought up
the rear, noticed that the girl seemed to be under the spell of
an imminent apprehension, for from time to time she clasped
her lover's arm, and looking up into his face, addressed him
with vehemence, almost with passion.

Curiously enough, the sight touched Hadden, and once or
twice he was shaken by so sharp a pang of remorse at the
thought of his share in this tragedy, that he cast about in his
mind seeking a means to unravel the web of death which he
himself had woven. But ever that evil voice was whispering
at his ear. It reminded him that he, the white *Inkoos,* had
been refused by this dusky beauty, and that if he found a way
to save him, within some few hours she would be the wife of
the savage gentleman at her side, the man who had named
him Black Heart and who despised him, the man whom he

had meant to murder and who immediately repaid his treachery by rescuing him from the jaws of the leopard at the risk of his own life. Moreover, it was a law of Hadden's existence never to deny himself of anything that he desired if it lay within his power to take it—a law which had led him always deeper into sin. In other respects, indeed, it had not carried him far, for in the past he had not desired much, and he had won little; but this particular flower was to his hand, and he would pluck it. If Nahoon stood between him and the flower, so much the worse for Nahoon, and if it should wither in his grasp, so much the worse for the flower; it could always be thrown away. Thus it came about that, not for the first time in his life, Philip Hadden discarded the somewhat spasmodic prickings of conscience and listened to that evil whispering at his ear.

About half-past five o'clock in the afternoon the four refugees passed the stream that a mile or so down fell over the little precipice into the Doom Pool; and, entering a patch of thorn trees on the further side, walked straight into the midst of two-and-twenty soldiers, who were beguiling the tedium of expectancy by the taking of snuff and the smoking of *dakka* or native hemp. With these soldiers, seated on his pony, for he was too fat to walk, waited the Chief Maputa.

Observing that their expected guests had arrived, the men knocked out the *dakka* pipe, replaced the snuff boxes in the slits made in the lobes of their ears, and secured the four of them.

"What is the meaning of this, O King's soldiers?" asked Umgona in a quavering voice. "We journey to the kraal of U'Cetywayo; why do you molest us?"

"Indeed. Wherefore then are your faces set towards the south. Does the Black One live in the south? Well, you will journey to another kraal presently," answered the jovial-looking captain of the party with a callous laugh.

"I do not understand," stammered Umgona.

"Then I will explain while you rest," said the captain. "The Chief Maputa yonder sent word to the Black One at Ulundi that he had learned of your intended flight to Natal from the lips of this white man, who had warned him of it. The Black One was angry, and despatched us to catch you and make an end of you. That is all. Come on now, quietly, and let us finish the matter. As the Doom Pool is near, your deaths will be easy."

Nahoon heard the words, and sprang straight at the throat of Hadden; but he did not reach it, for the soldiers pulled him down. Nanea heard them also, and turning, looked the traitor in the eyes; she said nothing, she only looked, but he could never forget that look. The white man for his part was filled with a fiery indignation against Maputa.

"You wicked villain," he gasped, whereat the chief smiled in a sickly fashion, and turned away.

Then they were marched along the banks of the stream till they reached the waterfall that fell into the Pool of Doom.

Hadden was a brave man after his fashion, but his heart quailed as he gazed into that abyss.

"Are you going to throw me in there?" he asked of the Zulu captain in a thick voice.

"You, White Man?" replied the soldier unconcernedly. "No, our orders are to take you to the king, but what he will do with you I do not know. There is to be war between your people and ours, so perhaps he means to pound you into medicine for the use of the witch-doctors, or to peg you over an ant-heap as a warning to other white men."

Hadden received this information in silence, but its effect upon his brain was bracing, for instantly he began to search out some means of escape.

By now the party had halted near the two thorn trees that hung over the waters of the pool.

"Who dives first," asked the captain of the Chief Maputa.

"The old wizard," he replied, nodding at Umgona; "then

his daughter after him, and last of all this fellow," and he struck Nahoon in the face with his open hand.

"Come on, Wizard," said the captain, grasping Umgona by the arm, "and let us see how you can swim."

At the words of doom Umgona seemed to recover his self-command, after the fashion of his race.

"No need to lead me, soldier," he said, shaking himself loose, "who am old and ready to die." Then he kissed his daughter at his side, wrung Nahoon by the hand, and turning from Hadden with a gesture of contempt walked out upon the platform that joined the two thorn trunks. Here he stood for a moment looking at the setting sun, then suddenly, and without a sound, he hurled himself into the abyss below and vanished.

"That was a brave one," said the captain with admiration. "Can you spring too, girl, or must we throw you?"

"I can walk my father's path," Nanea answered faintly, "but first I crave leave to say one word. It is true that we were escaping from the king, and therefore by the law we must die; but it was Black Heart here who made the plot, and he who has betrayed us. Would you know why he has betrayed us? Because he sought my favour, and I refused him, and this is the vengeance that he takes—a white man's vengeance."

"Wow!" broke in the chief Maputa, "this pretty one speaks truth, for the white man would have made a bargain with me under which Umgona, the wizard, and Nahoon, the soldier, were to be killed at the Crocodile Drift, and he himself suffered to escape with the girl. I spoke him softly and said 'yes,' and then like a loyal man I reported to the king."

"You hear," sighed Nanea. "Nahoon, fare you well, though presently perhaps we shall be together again. It was I who tempted you from your duty. For my sake you forgot your honour, and I am repaid. Farewell, my husband, it is better to die with you than to enter the house of the king's women," and Nanea stepped on to the platform.

Here, holding to a bough of one of the thorn trees, she turned and addressed Hadden, saying:—

"Black Heart, you seem to have won the day, but me at least you lose and—the sun is not yet set. After sunset comes the night, Black Heart, and in that night I pray that you may wander eternally, and be given to drink of my blood and the blood of Umgona my father, and the blood of Nahoon my husband, who saved your life, and whom you have murdered. Perchance, Black Heart, we may yet meet yonder—in the House of the Dead."

Then uttering a low cry Nanea clasped her hands and sprang upwards and outwards from the platform. The watchers bent their heads forward to look. They saw her rush headlong down the face of the fall to strike the water fifty feet below. A few seconds, and for the last time, they caught sight of her white garment glimmering on the surface of the gloomy pool. Then the shadows and mist-wreaths hid it, and she was gone.

"Now, husband," cried the cheerful voice of the captain, "yonder is your marriage bed, so be swift to follow a bride who is so ready to lead the way. *Wow!* but you are good people to kill; never have I had to do with any who gave less trouble. You——" and he stopped, for mental agony had done its work, and suddenly Nahoon went mad before his eyes.

With a roar like that of a lion the great man cast off those who held him and seizing one of them round the waist and thigh, he put out all his terrible strength. Lifting him as though he had been an infant, he hurled him over the edge of the cliff to find his death on the rocks of the Pool of Doom. Then crying:—

"Black Heart! your turn, Black Heart the traitor!" he rushed at Hadden, his eyes rolling and foam flying from his lips, as he passed striking the chief Maputa from his horse with a backward blow of his hand. Ill would it have gone with the white man if Nahoon had caught him. But he could not come at him, for the soldiers sprang upon him and notwithstanding his fearful struggles they pulled him to the ground, as at certain festivals the Zulu regiments with their naked hands pull down a bull in the presence of the king.

"Cast him over before he can work more mischief," said a voice. But the captain cried out, "Nay, nay, he is sacred; the fire from Heaven has fallen on his brain, and we may not harm him, else evil would overtake us all. Bind him hand and foot, and bear him tenderly to where he can be cared for. Surely I thought that these evil-doers were giving us too little trouble, and thus it has proved."

So they set themselves to make fast Nahoon's hands and wrists, using as much gentleness as they might, for among the Zulus a lunatic is accounted holy. It was no easy task, and it took time.

Hadden glanced around him, and saw his opportunity. On the ground close beside him lay his rifle, where one of the soldiers had placed it, and about a dozen yards away Maputa's pony was grazing. With a swift movement, he seized the Martini and five seconds later he was on the back of the pony, heading for the Crocodile Drift at a gallop. So quickly indeed did he execute this masterly retreat, that occupied as they all were in binding Nahoon, for half a minute or more none of the soldiers noticed what had happened. Then Maputa chanced to see, and waddled after him to the top of the rise, screaming:—

"The white thief, he has stolen my horse, and the gun too, the gun that he promised to give me."

Hadden, who by this time was a hundred yards away, heard him clearly, and a rage filled his heart. This man had made an open murderer of him; more, he had been the means of robbing him of the girl for whose sake he had dipped his hands in these iniquities. He glanced over his shoulder; Maputa was still running, and alone. Yes, there was time; at any rate he would risk it.

Pulling up the pony with a jerk, he leapt from its back,

slipping his arm through the rein with an almost simultaneous movement. As it chanced, and as he had hoped would be the case, the animal was a trained shooting horse, and stood still. Hadden planted his feet firmly on the ground and drawing a deep breath, he cocked the rifle and covered the advancing chief. Now Maputa saw his purpose and with a yell of terror turned to fly. Hadden waited a second to get the sight fair on his broad back, then just as the soldiers appeared above the rise he pressed the trigger. He was a noted shot, and in this instance his skill did not fail him; for, before he heard the bullet tell, Maputa flung his arms wide and plunged to the ground dead.

Three seconds more, and with a savage curse, Hadden had remounted the pony and was riding for his life towards the river, which a while later he crossed in safety.

CHAPTER VI

The Ghost of the Dead

When Nanea leapt from the dizzy platform that overhung the Pool of Doom, a strange fortune befell her. Close in to the precipice were many jagged rocks, and on these the waters of the fall fell and thundered, bounding from them in spouts of spray into the troubled depths of the foss beyond. It was on these stones that the life was dashed out from the bodies of the wretched victims who were hurled from above. But Nanea, it will be remembered, had not waited to be treated thus, and as it chanced the strong spring with which she had leapt to death carried her clear of the rocks. By a very little she missed the edge of them and striking the deep water head first like some practised diver, she sank down and down till she thought that she would never rise again. Yet she did rise, at the end of the pool in the mouth of the rapid, along which she sped swiftly, carried down by the rush of the water. Fortunately there were no rocks here; and, since she was a skilful swimmer, she escaped the danger of being thrown against the banks.

For a long distance she was borne thus till at length she saw that she was in a forest, for trees cut off the light from the water, and their drooping branches swept its surface. One of these Nanea caught with her hand, and by the help of it she dragged herself from the River of Death whence none had escaped before. Now she stood upon the bank gasping but quite unharmed; there was not a scratch on her body; even her white garment was still fast about her neck.

But though she had suffered no hurt in her terrible voyage, so exhausted was Nanea that she could scarcely stand. Here the gloom was that of night, and shivering with cold she looked helplessly to find some refuge. Close to the water's edge grew an enormous yellow-wood tree, and to this she staggered—thinking to climb it, and seek shelter in its boughs where, as she hoped, she would be safe from wild beasts. Again fortune befriended her, for at a distance of a few feet from the ground there was a great hole in the tree which, she discovered, was hollow. Into this hole she crept, taking her chance of its being the home of snakes or other evil creatures, to find that the interior was wide and warm. It was dry also, for at the bottom of the cavity lay a foot or more of rotten tinder and moss brought there by rats or birds. Upon this tinder she lay down, and covering herself with the moss and leaves soon sank into sleep or stupor.

How long Nanea slept she did not know, but at length she was awakened by a sound as of guttural human voices talking in a language that she could not understand. Rising to her knees she peered out of the hole in the tree. It was night, but the stars shone brilliantly, and their light fell upon an open circle of ground close by the edge of the river. In this circle there burned a great fire, and at a little distance from the fire were gathered eight or ten horrible-looking beings, who appeared to be rejoicing over something that lay upon the ground. They were small in stature, men and women together, but no children, and all of them were nearly naked. Their hair was long and thin, growing down almost to the eyes, their jaws and teeth protruded and the girth of their black bodies was out of all proportion to their height. In their hands they held sticks with sharp stones lashed on to them, or rude hatchet-like knives of the same material.

Now Nanea's heart shrank within her, and she nearly fainted with fear, for she knew that she was in the haunted forest, and without a doubt these were the *Esemkofu,* the evil ghosts that dwelt therein. Yes, that was what they were, and yet she could not take her eyes off them—the sight of them held her with a horrible fascination. But if they were ghosts, why did they sing and dance like men? Why did they wave those sharp stones aloft, and quarrel and strike each other? And why did they make a fire as men do when they wish to cook food? More, what was it that they rejoiced over, that long dark thing which lay so quiet upon the ground? It did not look like a head of game, and it could scarcely be a crocodile, yet clearly it was food of some sort, for they were sharpening the stone knives in order to cut it up.

While she wondered thus, one of the dreadful-looking little creatures advanced to the fire, and taking from it a burning bough, held it over the thing that lay upon the ground, to give light to a companion who was about to do something to it with the stone knife. Next instant Nanea drew back her head from the hole, a stifled shriek upon her lips. She saw what it was now—it was the body of a man. Yes, and these were no ghosts; they were cannibals of whom when she was little, her mother had told her tales to keep her from wandering away from home.

But who was the man they were about to eat? It could not be one of themselves, for his stature was much greater. Oh! now she knew; it must be Nahoon, who had been killed up yonder, and whose dead body the waters had brought down to the haunted forest as they had brought her alive. Yes, it must be Nahoon, and she would be forced to see her husband

devoured before her eyes. The thought of it overwhelmed
her. That he should die by order of the king was natural, but
that he should be buried thus! Yet what could she do to prevent it? Well, if it cost her her life, it should be prevented. At
the worst they could only kill and eat her also, and now that
Nahoon and her father were gone, being untroubled by any
religious or spiritual hopes and fears, she was not greatly
concerned to keep her own breath in her.

Slipping through the hole in the tree, Nanea walked quietly towards the cannibals—not knowing in the least what
she should do when she reached them. As she arrived in line
with the fire this lack of programme came home to her mind
forcibly, and she paused to reflect. Just then one of the cannibals looked up to see a tall and stately figure wrapped in a
white garment which, as the flame-light flickered on it, seemed
now to advance from the dense background of shadow,
and now to recede into it. The poor savage wretch was holding a stone knife in his teeth when he beheld her, but it did
not remain there long, for opening his great jaws he uttered
the most terrified and piercing yell that Nanea had ever
heard. Then the others saw her also, and presently the forest
was ringing with shrieks of fear. For a few seconds the out-
casts stood and gazed, then they were gone this way and that,
bursting their path through the undergrowth like startled
jackals. The *Esemkofu* of Zulu tradition had been routed in
their own haunted home by what they took to be a spirit.

Poor *Esemkofu!* they were but miserable and starving
bushmen who, driven into that place of ill omen many years
ago, had adopted this means, the only one open to them, to
keep the life in their wretched bodies. Here at least they were
unmolested, and as there was little other food to be found
amid that wilderness of trees, they took what the river brought
them. When executions were few in the Pool of Doom, times
were hard for them indeed—for then they were driven to eat
each other. That is why there were no children.

As their inarticulate outcry died away in the distance,

Nanea ran forward to look at the body that lay on the ground, and staggered back with a sigh of relief. It was not Nahoon, but she recognised the face for that of one of the party of executioners. How did he come here? Had Nahoon killed him? Had Nahoon escaped? She could not tell, and at the best it was improbable, but still the sight of this dead soldier lit her heart with a faint ray of hope, for how did he come to be dead if Nahoon had no hand in his death? She could not bear to leave him lying so near her hiding-place, however; therefore, with no small toil, she rolled the corpse back into the water, which carried it swiftly away. Then she returned to the tree, having first replenished the fire, and awaited the light.

At last it came—so much of it as ever penetrated this darksome den—and Nanea, becoming aware that she was hungry, descended from the tree to search for food. All day long she searched, finding nothing, till towards sunset she remembered that on the outskirts of the forest there was a flat rock where it was the custom of those who had been in any way afflicted, or who considered themselves or their belongings to be bewitched, to place propitiatory offerings of food wherewith the *Esemkofu* and *Amalhosi* were supposed to satisfy their spiritual cravings. Urged by the pinch of starvation, to this spot Nanea journeyed rapidly, and found to her joy that some neighbouring kraal had evidently been in recent trouble, for the Rock of Offering was laden with cobs of corn, gourds of milk, porridge and even meat. Helping herself to as much as she could carry, she returned to her lair, where she drank of the milk and cooked meat and mealies at the fire. Then she crept back into the tree, and slept.

For nearly two months Nanea lived thus in the forest, since she could not venture out of it—fearing lest she should be seized, and for a second time taste of the judgment of the king. In the forest at least she was safe, for none dared enter there, nor did the *Esemkofu* give her further trouble. Once or twice she saw them, but on each occasion they fled from her presence—seeking some distant retreat, where they hid them-selves or perished. Nor did food fail her, for finding that it was taken, the pious givers brought it in plenty to the Rock of Offering.

But, oh! the life was dreadful, and the gloom and loneli-ness coupled with her sorrows at times drove her almost to insanity. Still she lived on, though often she desired to die, for if her father was dead, the corpse she had found was not the corpse of Nahoon, and in her heart there still shone that spark of hope. Yet what she hoped for she could not tell.

When Philip Hadden reached civilised regions, he found that war was about to be declared between the Queen and Cety-wayo, King of the Amazulu; also that in the prevailing ex-citement his little adventure with the Utrecht store-keeper had been overlooked or forgotten. He was the owner of two good buck-waggons with spans of salted oxen, and at that time vehicles were much in request to carry military stores for the columns which were to advance into Zululand; in-deed the transport authorities were glad to pay £90 a month for the hire of each waggon and to guarantee the owners against all loss of cattle. Although he was not desirous of returning to Zululand, this bait proved too much for Had-den, who accordingly leased out his waggons to the Com-missariat, together with his own services as conductor and interpreter.

He was attached to No. 3 column of the invading force, which it may be remembered was under the immediate command of Lord Chelmsford, and on the 20th of January, 1879, he marched with it by the road that runs from Rorke's Drift to the Indeni forest, and encamped that night beneath the shadow of the steep and desolate mountain known as Isandhlwana.

That day also a great army of King Cetywayo's, number-ing twenty thousand men and more, moved down from the Upindo Hill and camped upon the stony plain that lies a mile and a half to the east of Isandhlwana. No fires were lit, and it lay there in utter silence, for the warriors were "sleeping on their spears."

With that *impi* was the Umcityu regiment, three thousand five hundred strong. At the first break of dawn the Induna in command of the Umcityu looked up from beneath the shelter of the black shield with which he had covered his body, and through the thick mist he saw a great man standing before him, clothed only in a moocha, a gaunt wild-eyed man who held a rough club in his hand. When he was spoken to, the man made no answer; he only leaned upon his club looking from left to right along the dense array of innumerable shields.

"Who is this *Silwana* (wild creature)?" asked the Induna of his captains, wondering.

The captains stared at the wanderer, and one of them replied, "This is Nahoon-ka-Zomba, it is the son of Zomba who not long ago held rank in this regiment of the Umcityu. His betrothed, Nanea, daughter of Umgona, was killed together with her father by order of the Black One, and Nahoon went mad with grief at the sight of it, for the fire of Heaven entered his brain, and mad he has wandered ever since."

"What would you here, Nahoon-ka-Zomba?" asked the Induna.

Then Nahoon spoke slowly. "My regiment goes down to war against the white men; give me a shield and a spear, O Captain of the king, that I may fight with my regiment, for I seek a face in the battle."

So they gave him a shield and a spear, for they dared not turn away one whose brain was alight with the fire of Heaven.

When the sun was high that day, bullets began to fall among the ranks of the Umcityu. Then the black-shielded, black-plumed Umcityu arose, company by company, and after them arose the whole vast Zulu army, breast and horns together, and swept down in silence upon the doomed British camp, a moving sheen of spears. The bullets pattered on the shields, the shells tore long lines through their array, but they never halted or wavered. Forward on either side shot out the horns of armed men, clasping the camp in an embrace of steel. Then as these began to close, out burst the war cry of the Zulus, and with the roar of a torrent and the rush of a storm, with a sound like the humming of a billion bees, wave after wave the deep breast of the *impi* rolled down upon the white men. With it went the black-shielded Umcityu and with them went Nahoon, the son of Zomba. A bullet struck him in the side, glancing from his ribs, he did not heed; a white man fell from his horse before him, he did not stab, for he sought but one face in the battle.

He sought—and at last he found. There, among the waggons where the spears were busiest, there standing by his horse and firing rapidly was Black Heart, he who had given Nanea his betrothed to death. Three soldiers stood between them, one of them Nahoon stabbed, and two he brushed aside; then he rushed straight at Hadden.

But the white man saw him come, and even through the mask of his madness he knew Nahoon again, and terror took hold of him. Throwing away his empty rifle, for his ammunition was spent, he leaped upon his horse and drove his spurs into its flanks. Away it went among the carnage, springing over the dead and bursting through the lines of shields, and after it came Nahoon, running long and low with head stretched forward and trailing spear, running as a hound runs when the buck is at view.

Hadden's first plan was to head for Rorke's Drift, but a glance to the left showed him that the masses of the Undi barred that way, so he fled straight on, leaving his path to fortune. In five minutes he was over a ridge, and there was nothing of the battle to be seen, in ten all sounds of it had died away, for few guns were fired in the dread race to Fugitive's

Drift, and the assegai makes no noise. In some strange fashion, even at this moment, the contrast between the dreadful scene of blood and turmoil that he had left, and the peaceful face of Nature over which he was passing, came home to his brain vividly. Here birds sang and cattle grazed; here the sun shone undimmed by the smoke of cannon, only high up in the blue and silent air long streams of vultures could be seen winging their way to the Plain of Isandhlwana.

The ground was very rough, and Hadden's horse began to tire. He looked over his shoulder—there some two hundred yards behind came the Zulu, grim as Death, unswerving as Fate. He examined the pistol in his belt; there was but one undischarged cartridge left, all the rest had been fired and the pouch was empty. Well, one bullet should be enough for one savage: the question was should he stop and use it now? No, he might miss or fail to kill the man; he was on horseback and his foe on foot, surely he could tire him out.

A while passed, and they dashed through a little stream. It seemed familiar to Hadden. Yes, that was the pool where he used to bathe when he was the guest of Umgona, the father of Nanea; and there on the knoll to his right were the huts, or rather the remains of them, for they had been burnt with fire. What chance had brought him to this place, he wondered; then again he looked behind him at Nahoon, who seemed to read his thoughts, for he shook his spear and pointed to the ruined kraal.

On he went at speed for here the land was level, and to his joy he lost sight of his pursuer. But presently there came a mile of rocky ground, and when it was past, glancing back he saw that Nahoon was once more in his old place. His horse's strength was almost spent, but Hadden spurred it forward blindly, whither he knew not. Now he was travelling along a strip of turf and ahead of him he heard the music of a river, while to his left rose a high bank. Presently the turf bent inwards and there, not twenty yards away from him, was a Kaffir hut standing on the brink of a river. He looked at it, yes, it was the hut of that accursed *inyanga,* the Bee, and standing by the fence of it was none other than the Bee herself. At the sight of her the exhausted horse swerved violently, stumbled and came to the ground, where it lay panting. Hadden was thrown from the saddle but sprang to his feet unhurt.

"Ah! Black Heart, is it you? What news of the battle, Black Heart?" cried the Bee in a mocking voice.

"Help me, mother, I am pursued," he gasped.

"What of it, Black Heart, it is but by one tired man. Stand then and face him, for now Black Heart and White Heart are together again. You will not? Then away to the forest and seek shelter among the dead who await you there. Tell me, tell me, was it the face of Nanea that I saw beneath the waters a while ago? Good! bear my greetings to her when you two meet in the House of the Dead."

Hadden looked at the stream; it was in flood. He could not swim it, so followed by the evil laugh of the prophetess, he sped towards the forest. After him came Nahoon, his tongue hanging from his jaws like the tongue of a wolf.

Now he was in the shadow of the forest, but still he sped on following the course of the river, till at length his breath failed, and he halted on the further side of a little glade, beyond which a great tree grew. Nahoon was more than a spear's throw behind him; therefore he had time to draw his pistol and make ready.

"Halt, Nahoon," he cried, as once before he had cried; "I would speak with you."

The Zulu heard his voice, and obeyed.

"Listen," said Hadden. "We have run a long race and fought a long fight, you and I, and we are still alive both of us. Very soon, if you come on, one of us must be dead, and it will be you, Nahoon, for I am armed and as you know I can shoot straight. What do you say?"

Nahoon made no answer, but stood still at the edge of the

glade, his wild and glowering eyes fixed on the white man's face and his breath coming in short gasps.

"Will you let me go, if *I* let *you* go?" Hadden asked once more. "I know why you hate me, but the past cannot be undone, nor can the dead be brought to earth again."

Still Nahoon made no answer, and his silence seemed more fateful and more crushing than any speech; no spoken accusation would have been so terrible in Hadden's ear. He made no answer, but lifting his assegai he stalked grimly towards his foe.

When he was within five paces Hadden covered him and fired. Nahoon sprang aside, but the bullet struck him somewhere, for his right arm dropped, and the stabbing spear that he held was jerked from it harmlessly over the white man's head. But still making no sound, the Zulu came on and gripped him by the throat with his left hand. For a space they struggled terribly, swaying to and fro, but Hadden was unhurt and fought with the fury of despair, while Nahoon had been twice wounded, and there remained to him but one sound arm wherewith to strike. Presently forced to earth by the white man's iron strength, the soldier was down, nor could he rise again.

"Now we will make an end," muttered Hadden savagely, and he turned to seek the assegai, then staggered slowly back with starting eyes and reeling gait. For there before him, still clad in her white robe, a spear in her hand, stood the spirit of Nanea!

"Think of it," he said to himself, dimly remembering the words of the *inyanga,* "when you stand face to face with the ghost of the dead in the Home of the Dead."

There was a cry and a flash of steel; the broad spear leapt towards him to bury itself in his breast. He swayed, he fell, and presently Black Heart clasped that great reward which the word of the Bee had promised him.

*   *   *

"Nahoon! Nahoon!" murmured a soft voice, "awake, it is no ghost, but I—Nanea—I, your living wife, to whom my *Ehlose** has given it me to save you."

Nahoon heard and opened his eyes to look and his madness left him.

"Welcome, wife," he said faintly, "now I will live since Death has brought you back to me in the House of the Dead."

To-day Nahoon is one of the Indunas of the English Government in Zululand, and there are children about his kraal. It was from the lips of none other than Nanea his wife that the teller of this tale heard its substance.

The Bee also lives and practises as much magic as she dares under the white man's rule. On her black hand shines a golden ring shaped like a snake with ruby eyes, and of this trinket the Bee is very proud.

* Guardian Spirit.

The Dragon Tamers

by E. Nesbit

When Tolkien was around the age of seven (his own accounts vary), he began to write a story about a dragon. In 1955 he recalled in a letter to W. H. Auden: "I remember nothing about it except a philological fact. My mother said nothing about the dragon, but pointed out that one could not say 'a green great dragon,' but had to say 'a great green dragon.' I wondered why, and still do."

It is perhaps a coincidence that when Tolkien was seven, the most popular magazine of the day, the *Strand Magazine*, published a series of stories on dragons by E. Nesbit. The series was titled *The Seven Dragons* and ran from March through September 1899, with an eighth dragon story appearing in December. In the third story, "The Deliverers of Their Country," a "whole flight of green dragons" rises up out of a field and a dragon with yellow wings is seen lying "on his great green scaly side." In the sixth story, "The Dragon Tamers," we find a dragon with strong similarities of temperament with Chrysophylax Dives, the dragon in Tolkien's wry tale *Farmer Giles of Ham*.

"The Dragon Tamers" originally appeared in the *Strand Magazine* for August 1899. It was collected in *The Book of Dragons* (1900).

THERE was once an old, old castle—it was so old that its walls and towers and turrets and gateways and arches had crumbled to ruins, and of all its old splendour there were only two little rooms left; and it was here that John the black-smith had set up his forge. He was too poor to live in a proper house, and no one asked any rent for the rooms in the ruin, because all the lords of the castle were dead and gone this many a year. So there John blew his bellows, and hammered his iron, and did all the work which came his way. This was not much, because most of the trade went to the mayor of the town, who was also a blacksmith in quite a large way of business, and had his huge forge facing the square of the town, and had twelve apprentices, all hammering like a nest of woodpeckers, and twelve journeymen to order the ap-prentices about, and a patent forge and a self-acting hammer and electric bellows, and all things handsome about him. So that of course the townspeople, whenever they wanted a horse shod or a shaft mended, went to the mayor. And John the blacksmith struggled on as best he could, with a few odd jobs from travellers and strangers who did not know what a superior forge the mayor's was. The two rooms were warm and weather-tight, but not very large; so the blacksmith got into the way of keeping his old iron, and his odds and ends, and his fagots, and his twopenn'orth of coal, in the great dungeon down under the castle. It was a very fine dungeon indeed, with a handsome vaulted roof and big iron rings, whose staples were built into the wall, very strong and con-venient for tying captives up to, and at one end was a broken flight of wide steps leading down no one knew where. Even the lords of the castle in the good old times had never known where those steps led to, but every now and then they would kick a prisoner down the steps in their light-hearted, hopeful way, and, sure enough, the prisoners never came back. The blacksmith had never dared to go beyond the seventh step, and no more have I—so I know no more than he did what was at the bottom of those stairs.

John the blacksmith had a wife and a little baby. When his wife was not doing the housework she used to nurse the baby and cry, remembering the happy days when she lived with her father, who kept seventeen cows and lived quite in the country, and when John used to come courting her in the summer evenings, as smart as smart, with a posy in his button-hole. And now John's hair was getting grey, and there was hardly ever enough to eat.

As for the baby, it cried a good deal at odd times; but at night, when its mother had settled down to sleep, it would always begin to cry, quite as a matter of course, so that she hardly got any rest at all. This made her very tired. The baby could make up for its bad nights during the day, if it liked, but the poor mother couldn't. So whenever she had nothing to do she used to sit and cry, because she was tired out with work and worry.

One evening the blacksmith was busy with his forge. He was making a goat-shoe for the goat of a very rich lady, who wished to see how the goat liked being shod, and also whether the shoe would come to fivepence or sevenpence before she ordered the whole set. This was the only order John had had that week. And as he worked his wife sat and nursed the baby, who, for a wonder, was not crying.

Presently, over the noise of the bellows, and over the clank of the iron, there came another sound. The blacksmith and his wife looked at each other.

"I heard nothing," said he.

"Neither did I," said she.

But the noise grew louder—and the two were so anxious not to hear it that he hammered away at the goat-shoe harder than he had ever hammered in his life, and she began to sing to the baby—a thing she had not had the heart to do for weeks.

But through the blowing and hammering and singing the noise came louder and louder, and the more they tried not to hear it, the more they had to. It was like the noise of some great creature purring, purring, purring—and the reason they did not want to believe they really heard it was that it came from the great dungeon down below, where the old iron was, and the firewood and the twopenn'orth of coal, and the broken steps that went down into the dark and ended no one knew where.

"It *can't* be anything in the dungeon," said the blacksmith, wiping his face. "Why, I shall have to go down there after more coals in a minute."

"There isn't anything there, of course. How could there be?" said his wife. And they tried so hard to believe that there could be nothing there that presently they very nearly did believe it.

Then the blacksmith took his shovel in one hand and his riveting hammer in the other, and hung the old stable lantern on his little finger, and went down to get the coals.

"I am not taking the hammer because I think there is anything there," said he, "but it is handy for breaking the large lumps of coal."

"I quite understand," said his wife, who had brought the coal home in her apron that very afternoon, and knew that it was all coal-dust.

So he went down the winding stairs to the dungeon, and stood at the bottom of the steps holding the lantern above his head just to see that the dungeon really *was* empty as usual. Half of it was empty as usual, except for the old iron and odds and ends, and the firewood and the coals. But the other side was not empty. It was quite full, and what it was full of was *Dragon*.

"It must have come up those nasty broken steps from goodness knows where," said the blacksmith to himself, trembling all over, as he tried to creep back up the winding stairs.

But the dragon was too quick for him—it put out a great claw and caught him by the leg, and as it moved it rattled like a great bunch of keys, or like the sheet-iron they make thunder out of in pantomimes.

"No you don't," said the dragon, in a spluttering voice, like a damp squib.

"Deary, deary me," said poor John, trembling more than ever in the claw of the dragon; "here's a nice end for a respectable blacksmith!"

The dragon seemed very much struck by this remark.

"Do you mind saying that again?" said he, quite politely.

So John said again, very distinctly: "Here—Is—A—Nice—End—For—A—Respectable—Blacksmith."

"I didn't know," said the dragon. "Fancy now! You're the very man I wanted."

"So I understood you to say before," said John, his teeth chattering.

"Oh, I don't mean what you mean," said the dragon; "but I should like you to do a job for me. One of my wings has got some of the rivets out of it just above the joint. Could you put that to rights?"

"I might, sir," said John, politely, for you must always be polite to a possible customer, even if he be a dragon.

"A master craftsman—you *are* a master, of course?—can see in a minute what's wrong," the dragon went on. "Just come round here and feel my plates, will you?"

John timidly went round when the dragon took his claw away; and, sure enough, the dragon's off wing was hanging loose and all anyhow, and several of the plates near the joint certainly wanted riveting.

The dragon seemed to be made almost entirely of iron armour—a sort of tawny, red-rust colour it was; from damp, no doubt—and under it he seemed to be covered with something furry.

All the blacksmith welled up in John's heart, and he felt more at ease.

"You could certainly do with a rivet or two, sir," said he; "in fact, you want a good many."

"Well, get to work, then," said the dragon. "You mend my wing, and then I'll go out and eat up all the town, and if you make a really smart job of it I'll eat you last. There!"

"I don't want to be eaten last, sir," said John.

"Well, then, I'll eat you *first,*" said the dragon.

"I don't want that, sir, either," said John.

"Go on with you, you silly man," said the dragon; "you don't know your own silly mind. Come, set to work."

"I don't like the job, sir," said John, "and that's the truth. I know how easily accidents happen. It's all fair and smooth, and 'Please rivet me, and I'll eat you last'—and then you get to work and you give a gentleman a bit of a nip or a dig under his rivets—and then it's fire and smoke, and no apologies will meet the case."

"Upon my word of honour as a dragon," said the other.

"I know you wouldn't do it on purpose, sir," said John; "but any gentleman will give a jump and a sniff if he's nipped, and one of your sniffs would be enough for me. Now, if you'd just let me fasten you up?"

"It would be so undignified," objected the dragon.

"We always fasten a horse up," said John, "and he's the 'noble animal.' "

"It's all very well," said the dragon, "but how do I know you'd untie me again when you'd riveted me? Give me something in pledge. What do you value most?"

"My hammer," said John. "A blacksmith is nothing without a hammer."

"But you'd want that for riveting me. You must think of something else, and at once, or I'll eat you first."

At this moment the baby in the room above began to scream. Its mother had been so quiet that it thought she had settled down for the night, and that it was time to begin.

"Whatever's that?" said the dragon, starting so that every plate on his body rattled.

"It's only the baby," said John.

"What's that?" asked the dragon—"something you value?"

"Well, yes, sir, rather," said the blacksmith.

"Then bring it here," said the dragon; "and I'll take care of it till you've done riveting me, and you shall tie me up."

"All right, sir," said John; "but I ought to warn you. Babies are poison to dragons, so I don't deceive you. It's all right to touch—but don't you go putting it into your mouth. I shouldn't like to see any harm come to a nice-looking gentleman like you."

The dragon purred at this compliment and said: "All right, I'll be careful. Now go and fetch the thing, whatever it is."

So John ran up the steps as quickly as he could, for he knew that if the dragon got impatient before it was fastened up, it could heave up the roof of the dungeon with one heave of its back, and kill them all in the ruins. His wife was asleep, in spite of the baby's cries; and John picked up the baby and took it down and put it between the dragon's front paws.

"You just purr to it, sir," he said, "and it'll be as good as gold."

So the dragon purred, and his purring pleased the baby so much that it left off crying.

Then John rummaged among the heap of old iron and found there some heavy chains and a great collar that had been made in the days when men sang over their work and put their hearts into it, so that the things they made were strong enough to bear the weight of a thousand years, let alone a dragon.

John fastened the dragon up with the collar and the chains, and when he had padlocked them all on safely he set to work to find out how many rivets would be needed.

"Six, eight, ten—twenty, forty," said he; "I haven't half enough rivets in the shop. If you'll excuse me, sir, I'll step round to another forge and get a few dozen. I won't be a minute."

And off he went, leaving the baby between the dragon's fore-paws, laughing and crowing with pleasure at the very large purr of it.

John ran as hard as he could into the town, and found the mayor and corporation.

"There's a dragon in my dungeon," he said; "I've chained him up. Now come and help to get my baby away."

And he told them all about it.

But they all happened to have engagements for that evening; so they praised John's cleverness, and said they were quite content to leave the matter in his hands.

"But what about my baby?" said John.

"Oh, well," said the mayor, "if anything should happen, you will always be able to remember that your baby perished in a good cause."

So John went home again, and told his wife some of the tale.

"You've given the baby to the dragon!" she cried. "Oh, you unnatural parent!"

"Hush," said John, and he told her some more.

"Now," he said, "I'm going down. After I've been down you can go, and if you keep your head the boy will be all right."

So down went the blacksmith, and there was the dragon purring away with all his might to keep the baby quiet.

"Hurry up, can't you?" he said. "I can't keep up this noise all night."

"I'm very sorry, sir," said the blacksmith, "but all the shops are shut. The job must wait till the morning. And don't forget you've promised to take care of that baby. You'll find it a little wearing, I'm afraid. Good-night, sir."

The dragon had purred till he was quite out of breath—so now he stopped, and as soon as everything was quiet the baby thought everyone must have settled for the night, and that it was time to begin to scream. So it began.

"Oh dear," said the dragon, "this is awful."

He patted the baby with his claw, but it screamed more than ever.

"And I am so tired, too," said the dragon. "I did so hope I should have had a good night."

The baby went on screaming.

"There'll be no peace for me after this," said the dragon; "it's enough to ruin one's nerves. Hush, then—did 'ums, then." And he tried to quiet the baby as if it had been a young dragon. But when he began to sing "Hush-a-by, dragon," the baby screamed more and more and more. "I can't keep it quiet," said the dragon; and then suddenly he saw a woman sitting on the steps. "Here, I say," said he, "do you know anything about babies?"

"I do, a little," said the mother.

"Then I wish you'd take this one, and let me get some sleep," said the dragon, yawning. "You can bring it back in the morning before the blacksmith comes."

So the mother picked up the baby and took it upstairs and told her husband, and they went to bed happy, for they had caught the dragon and saved the baby.

The next day John went down and explained carefully to the dragon exactly how matters stood, and he got an iron gate with a grating to it, and set it up at the foot of the steps, and the dragon mewed furiously for days and days, but when he found it was no good he was quiet.

So now John went to the mayor, and said: "I've got the dragon and I've saved the town."

"Noble preserver," cried the mayor, "we will get up a subscription for you, and crown you in public with a laurel wreath."

So the mayor put his name down for five pounds, and the corporation each gave three, and other people gave their guineas, and half-guineas, and half-crowns and crowns, and while the subscription was being made the mayor ordered three poems at his own expense from the town poet to celebrate the occasion. The poems were very much admired, especially by the mayor and corporation.

The first poem dealt with the noble conduct of the mayor in arranging to have the dragon tied up. The second described the splendid assistance rendered by the corporation. And the third expressed the pride and joy of the poet in being

permitted to sing such deeds, beside which the actions of
Saint George must appear quite commonplace to all with a
feeling heart or a well-balanced brain.

When the subscription was finished there was a thousand
pounds, and a committee was formed to settle what should
be done with it. A third of it went to pay for a banquet to the
mayor and corporation; another third was spent in buying a
gold collar with a dragon on it for the mayor, and gold
medals with dragons on them for the corporation; and what
was left went in committee expenses.

So there was nothing for the blacksmith except the laurel
wreath, and the knowledge that it really *was* he who had
saved the town. But after this things went a little better with
the blacksmith. To begin with, the baby did not cry so much
as it had before. Then the rich lady who owned the goat was
so touched by John's noble action that she ordered a complete set of shoes at 2s. 4d., and even made it up to 2s. 6d. in
grateful recognition of his public-spirited conduct. Then
tourists used to come in breaks from quite a long way off,
and pay twopence each to go down the steps and peep
through the iron grating at the rusty dragon in the dungeon—
and it was threepence extra for each party if the blacksmith
let off coloured fire to see it by, which, as the fire was extremely short, was twopence-halfpenny clear profit every
time. And the blacksmith's wife used to provide teas at
ninepence a head, and altogether things grew brighter week
by week.

The baby—named John, after his father, and called Johnnie for short—began presently to grow up. He was great
friends with Tina, the daughter of the whitesmith, who lived
nearly opposite. She was a dear little girl, with yellow pig-
tails and blue eyes, and she was never tired of hearing the
story of how Johnnie, when he was a baby, had been minded
by a real dragon.

The two children used to go together to peep through the
iron grating at the dragon, and sometimes they would hear

him mew piteously. And they would light a halfpennyworth of coloured fire to look at him by. And they grew older and wiser.

Now, at last one day the mayor and corporation, hunting the hare in their gold gowns, came screaming back to the town gates with the news that a lame, humpy giant, as big as a tin church, was coming over the marshes towards the town.

"We're lost," said the mayor. "I'd give a thousand pounds to anyone who could keep that giant out of the town. *I* know what he eats—by his teeth."

No one seemed to know what to do. But Johnnie and Tina were listening, and they looked at each other, and ran off as fast as their boots would carry them.

They ran through the forge, and down the dungeon steps, and knocked at the iron door.

"Who's there?" said the dragon.

"It's only us," said the children.

And the dragon was so dull from having been alone for ten years that he said: "Come in, dears."

"You won't hurt us, or breathe fire at us or anything?" asked Tina.

And the dragon said, "Not for worlds."

So they went in and talked to him, and told him what the weather was like outside, and what there was in the papers, and at last Johnnie said: "There's a lame giant in the town. He wants you."

"Does he?" said the dragon, showing his teeth. "If only I were out of this!"

"If we let you loose you might manage to run away before he could catch you."

"Yes, I *might*," answered the dragon, "but then again I mightn't."

"Why—you'd never fight him?" said Tina.

"No," said the dragon; "I'm all for peace, I am. You let me out, and you'll see."

So the children loosed the dragon from the chains and the

collar, and he broke down one end of the dungeon and went out—only pausing at the forge door to get the blacksmith to rivet his wing.

He met the lame giant at the gate of the town, and the giant banged on the dragon with his club as if he were banging an iron foundry, and the dragon behaved like a smelting works—all fire and smoke. It was a fearful sight, and people watched it from a distance, falling off their legs with the shock of every bang, but always getting up to look again.

At last the dragon won, and the giant sneaked away across the marshes, and the dragon, who was very tired, went home to sleep, announcing his intention of eating the town in the morning. He went back into his old dungeon because he was a stranger in the town, and he did not know of any other respectable lodging. Then Tina and Johnnie went to the mayor and corporation and said, "The giant is settled. Please give us the thousand pounds reward."

But the mayor said, "No, no, my boy. It is not you who have settled the giant, it is the dragon. I suppose you have chained him up again? When *he* comes to claim the reward he shall have it."

"He isn't chained up yet," said Johnnie. "Shall I send him to claim the reward?"

But the mayor said he need not trouble; and now he offered a thousand pounds to anyone who would get the dragon chained up again.

"I don't trust you," said Johnnie. "Look how you treated my father when he chained up the dragon."

But the people who were listening at the door interrupted, and said that if Johnnie could fasten up the dragon again they would turn out the mayor and let Johnnie be mayor in his place. For they had been dissatisfied with the mayor for some time, and thought they would like a change.

So Johnnie said, "Done," and off he went, hand-in-hand with Tina, and they called on all their little friends and said: "Will you help us to save the town?"

And all the children said, "Yes, of course we will. What fun!"

"Well, then," said Tina, "you must all bring your basins of bread and milk to the forge tomorrow at breakfast-time."

"And if ever I am mayor," said Johnnie, "I will give a banquet, and you shall be invited. And we'll have nothing but sweet things from beginning to end."

All the children promised, and next morning Tina and Johnnie rolled the big washing-tub down the winding stair.

"What's that noise?" asked the dragon.

"It's only a big giant breathing," said Tina; "he's gone by, now."

Then, when all the town children brought their bread and milk, Tina emptied it into the wash-tub, and when the tub was full Tina knocked at the iron door with the grating in it, and said: "May we come in?"

"Oh, yes," said the dragon; "it's very dull here."

So they went in, and with the help of nine other children they lifted the washing-tub in and set it down by the dragon. Then all the other children went away, and Tina and Johnnie sat down and cried.

"What's this?" asked the dragon, "and what's the matter?"

"*This* is bread and milk," said Johnnie; "it's our breakfast all of it."

"Well," said the dragon, "I don't see what you want with breakfast. I'm going to eat everyone in the town as soon as I've rested a little."

"Dear Mr. Dragon," said Tina, "I wish you wouldn't eat us. How would you like to be eaten yourself?"

"Not at all," the dragon confessed, "but nobody will eat me."

"I don't know," said Johnnie, "there's a giant—"

"I know. I fought with him, and licked him—"

"Yes, but there's another come now—the one you fought was only this one's little boy. This one is half as big again."

"He's seven times as big," said Tina.

"No, nine times," said Johnnie. "He's bigger than the steeple."

"Oh dear," said the dragon. "I never expected this."

"And the mayor has told him where you are," Tina went on, "and he is coming to eat you as soon as he has sharpened his big knife. The mayor told him you were a wild dragon—but he didn't mind. He said he only ate wild dragons—with bread sauce."

"That's tiresome," said the dragon, "and I suppose this sloppy stuff in the tub is the bread sauce?"

The children said it was. "Of course," they added, "bread sauce is only served with wild dragons. Tame ones are served with apple sauce and onion stuffing. What a pity you're not a tame one: he'd never look at you then," they said. "Good-bye, poor dragon, we shall never see you again, and now you'll know what it's like to be eaten." And they began to cry again.

"Well, but look here," said the dragon, "couldn't you pretend I was a tame dragon? Tell the giant that I'm just a poor little, timid tame dragon that you kept for a pet."

"He'd never believe it," said Johnnie. "If you were our tame dragon we should keep you tied up, you know. We shouldn't like to risk losing such a dear, pretty pet."

Then the dragon begged them to fasten him up at once, and they did so: with the collar and chains that were made years ago—in the days when men sang over their work and made it strong enough to bear any strain.

And then they went away and told the people what they had done, and Johnnie was made mayor, and had a glorious feast exactly as he had said he would—with nothing in it but sweet things. It began with Turkish delight and halfpenny buns, and went on with oranges, toffee, cocoanut-ice, peppermints, jam-puffs, raspberry-noyeau, ice-creams, and meringues, and ended with bull's-eyes and ginger-bread and acid-drops.

This was all very well for Johnnie and Tina; but if you are

kind children with feeling hearts you will perhaps feel sorry for the poor deceived, deluded dragon—chained up in the dull dungeon, with nothing to do but to think over the shocking untruths that Johnnie had told him.

When he thought how he had been tricked the poor captive dragon began to weep—and the large tears fell down over his rusty plates. And presently he began to feel faint, as people sometimes do when they have been crying, especially if they have not had anything to eat for ten years or so.

And then the poor creature dried his eyes and looked about him, and there he saw the tub of bread and milk. So he thought, "If giants like this damp, white stuff, perhaps *I* should like it too," and he tasted a little, and liked it so much that he ate it all up.

And the next time the tourists came, and Johnnie let off the coloured fire, the dragon said, shyly: "Excuse my troubling you, but could you bring me a little more bread and milk?"

So Johnnie arranged that people should go round with cars every day to collect the children's bread and milk for the dragon. The children were fed at the town's expense—on whatever they liked; and they ate nothing but cake and buns and sweet things, and they said the poor dragon was very welcome to their bread and milk.

Now, when Johnnie had been mayor ten years or so he married Tina, and on their wedding morning they went to see the dragon. He had grown quite tame, and his rusty plates had fallen off in places, and underneath he was soft and furry to stroke. So now they stroked him.

And he said, "I don't know how I could ever have liked eating anything but bread and milk. I am a tame dragon, now, aren't I?" And when they said "Yes, he was," the dragon said: "I *am* so tame, won't you undo me?" And some people would have been afraid to trust him, but Johnnie and Tina were so happy on their wedding-day that they could not believe any harm of anyone in the world. So they loosed the chains, and the dragon said, "Excuse me a moment, there are one or two little things I should like to fetch," and he moved off to those mysterious steps and went down them, out of sight into the darkness. And as he moved more and more of his rusty plates fell off.

In a few minutes they heard him clanking up the steps. He brought something in his mouth—it was a bag of gold.

"It's no good to me," he said; "perhaps you might find it come in useful." So they thanked him very kindly.

"More where that came from," said he, and fetched more and more and more, till they told him to stop. So now they were rich, and so were their fathers and mothers. Indeed, everyone was rich, and there were no more poor people in the town. And they all got rich without working, which is very wrong; but the dragon had never been to school, as you have, so he knew no better.

And as the dragon came out of the dungeon, following Johnnie and Tina into the bright gold and blue of their wedding-day, he blinked his eyes as a cat does in the sunshine, and he shook himself, and the last of his plates dropped off, and his wings with them, and he was just like a very, very extra-sized cat. And from that day he grew furrier and furrier, and he was the beginning of all cats. Nothing of the dragon remained except the claws, which all cats have still, as you can easily ascertain.

And I hope you see now how important it is to feed your cat with bread and milk. If you were to let it have nothing to eat but mice and birds it might grow larger and fiercer, and scalier and tailier, and get wings and turn into the beginning of dragons. And then there would be all the bother over again.

The Far Islands

by John Buchan

In his biography of Tolkien, Humphrey Carpenter wrote that Tolkien "liked the stories of John Buchan." Buchan was a prolific writer, and unfortunately there is no further guidance to Tolkien's opinions of Buchan's writings. However, some of Buchan's stories have some striking Tolkienian resonances. "The Far Islands" is one such tale—its theme of a man's hereditary haunting by the sea recurs in Tolkien's writings, from the mariner figure of Aelfwine/Eriol of the early "Silmarillion" legends (published as *The Book of Lost Tales*) who traveled to islands in the west, on to Alwin Arundel Lowdham, the philologist whose father was haunted by the sea in Tolkien's unfinished "Notion Club Papers" (published in *Sauron Defeated*). The Celtic notion of islands in the west, and the striving to reach them, is central to Tolkien's mythology.

"The Far Islands" was first published in the November 1899 issue of *Blackwood's Magazine*, and was collected in *The Watcher by the Threshold and Other Tales* (1902).

"Lady Alice, Lady Louise,
Between the wash of the tumbling seas—"

I.

WHEN Bran the Blessed, as the story goes, followed the white bird on the Last Questing, knowing that return was not for him, he gave gifts to his followers. To Heliodorus he gave the gift of winning speech, and straightway the man went south to the Italian seas, and, becoming a scholar, left many descendants who sat in the high places of the Church. To Raymond he gave his steel battle-axe, and bade him go out to the warrior's path and hew his way to a throne; which the man forthwith accomplished, and became an ancestor in the fourth degree of the first king of Scots. But to Colin, the youngest and the dearest, he gave no gift, whispering only a word in his ear and laying a finger on his eyelids. Yet Colin was satisfied, and he alone of the three, after their master's going, remained on that coast of rock and heather.

In the third generation from Colin, as our elders counted years, came one Colin the Red, who built his keep on the cliffs of Acharra and was a mighty sea-rover in his day. Five times he sailed to the rich parts of France, and a good score of times he carried his flag of three stars against the easterly vikings. A mere name in story, but a sounding piece of nomenclature well garnished with tales. A master-mind by all accounts, but cursed with a habit of fantasy; for, hearing in his old age of a land to the westward, he forthwith sailed into the sunset, and three days later was washed up, a twisted body, on one of the outer isles.

So far it is but legend, but with his grandson, Colin the Red, we fall into the safer hands of the chroniclers. To him God gave the unnumbered sorrows of story-telling, for he was a bard, cursed with a bard's fervours, and none the less a mighty warrior among his own folk. He it was who wrote the lament called "The White Waters of Usna," and the exquisite chain of romances, "Glede-red Gold and Grey Silver." His tales were told by many fires, down to our grandfathers' time, and you will find them still pounded at by the folklorists. But his airs—they are eternal. On harp and pipe they have lived through the centuries; twisted and tortured, they survive in many songbooks; and I declare that the other day I heard the most beautiful of them all murdered by a band at a German watering-place. This Colin led the wanderer's life, for he disappeared at middle-age, no one knew whither, and his return was long looked for by his people. Some thought that he became a Christian monk, the holy man living in the sea-girt isle of Cuna, who was found dead in extreme old age, kneeling on the beach, with his arms, contrary to the fashion of the Church, stretched to the westward.

As history narrowed into bonds and forms the descendants of Colin took Raden for their surname, and settled more firmly on their lands in the long peninsula of crag and inlets which runs west to the Atlantic. Under Donald of the Isles they harried the Kings of Scots, or, on their own authority, made war on Macleans and Macranalds, till their flag of the three stars, their badge of the grey-goose feather, and their on-cry of "Cuna" were feared from Lochalsh to Cantire. Later they made a truce with the King, and entered into the royal councils. For years they warded the western coast, and as king's lieutenants smoked out the inferior pirates of Eigg and Toronsay. A Raden was made a Lord of Sleat, another was given lands in the low country and the name Baron of Strathyre, but their honours were transitory and short as their lives. Rarely one of the house saw middle age. A bold, handsome, and stirring race, it was their fate to be cut off in the rude warfare of the times, or, if peace had them in its clutches, to man vessel and set off once more on those mad western voyages which were the weird of the family. Three of the name were found drowned on the far shore of Cuna; more than one sailed straight out of the ken of mortals. One rode with the Good Lord James on the pilgrimage of the Heart of Bruce, and died by his leader's side in the Saracen battle. Long afterwards a Raden led the western men against the Cheshire archers at Flodden, and was slain himself in the steel circle around the king.

But the years brought peace and a greater wealth, and soon the cold stone tower was left solitary on the headland, and the new house of Kinlochuna rose by the green links of the stream. The family changed its faith, and an Episcopal chaplain took the place of the old mass-priest in the tutoring of the sons. Radens were in the '15 and the '45. They rose with Bute to power, and they long disputed the pride of Dundas in the northern capital. They intermarried with great English houses till the sons of the family were Scots only in name, living much abroad or in London, many of them English landowners by virtue of a mother's blood. Soon the race was of the common over-civilised type, graceful, well-mannered, with abundant good looks, but only once in a generation reverting to the rugged northern strength. Eton and Oxford had in turn displaced the family chaplain, and the house by the windy headland grew emptier and emptier save when grouse and deer brought home its fickle masters.

II.

A childish illness brought Colin to Kinlochuna when he had reached the mature age of five, and delicate health kept him there for the greater part of the next six years. During the winter he lived in London, but from the late northern spring through all the long bright summers he lived in the great tenantless place without company—for he was an only child. A French nurse had the charge of his doings, and when he had passed through the formality of lessons there were the long pinewoods at his disposal, the rough moor, the wonderful black holes with the rich black mud in them, and best of all the bay of Acharra, below the headland, with Cuna lying in the waves a mile to the west. At such times his father was busy elsewhere; his mother was dead; the family had few near relatives; so he passed a solitary childhood in the company of seagulls and the birds of the moor.

His time for the beach was the afternoon. On the left as you go down through the woods from the house there runs out the great headland of Acharra, red and grey with mosses, and with a nimbus always of screaming sea-fowl. To the right runs a low beach of sand, passing into rough limestone boulders and then into the heather of the wood. This in turn is bounded by a reef of low rocks falling by gentle breaks to the water's edge. It is crowned with a tangle of heath and fern, bright at most seasons with flowers, and dwarf pine-trees straggle on its crest till one sees the meaning of its Gaelic name, "The Ragged Cock's-Comb." This place was Colin's playground in fine weather. When it blew rain or snow from the north he dwelt indoors among dogs and books, puzzling his way through great volumes from his father's shelves. But when the mild west-wind weather fell on the sea, then he would lie on the hot sand—Amèlie the nurse reading a novel on the nearest rock—and kick his small heels as he followed his fancy. He built great sand castles to the shape of Acharra old tower, and peopled them with preposterous knights and ladies; he drew great moats and rivers for the tide to fill; he fought battles innumerable with crackling seaweed, till Amèlie, with her sharp cry of "Colín, Colín," would carry him houseward for tea.

Two fancies remained in his mind through those boyish years. One was about the mysterious shining sea before him. In certain weathers it seemed to him a solid pathway. Cuna, the little ragged isle, ceased to block the horizon, and his own white road ran away down into the west, till suddenly it stopped and he saw no farther. He knew he ought to see more, but always at one place, just when his thoughts were pacing the white road most gallantly, there came a baffling mist to his sight, and he found himself looking at a commonplace sea with Cuna lying very real and palpable in the offing. It was a vexatious limitation, for all his dreams were about this pathway. One day in June, when the waters slept in a deep heat, he came down the sands barefoot, and lo! there was his pathway. For one moment things seemed clear, the mist had not gathered on the road, and with a cry he ran down to the tide's edge and waded in. The touch of water dispelled the illusion, and almost in tears he saw the cruel back of Cuna blotting out his own magic way.

The other fancy was about the low ridge of rocks which bounded the bay on the right. His walks had never extended beyond it, either on the sands or inland, for that way lay a steep hillside and a perilous bog. But often on the sands he had come to its foot and wondered what country lay beyond. He made many efforts to explore it, difficult efforts, for the vigilant Amèlie had first to be avoided. Once he was almost at the top when some seaweed to which he clung gave way, and he rolled back again to the soft warm sand. By-and-by he found that he knew what was beyond. A clear picture had built itself up in his brain of a mile of reefs, with sand in bars between them, and beyond all a sea-wood of alders slipping from the hill's skirts to the water's edge. This was not what he wanted in his explorations, so he stopped till one day it struck him that the westward view might reveal something beyond the hog-backed Cuna. One day, pioneering alone, he scaled the steepest heights of the seaweed and pulled his chin over the crest of the ridge. There, sure enough, was his picture—a mile of reefs and the tattered sea-wood. He turned eagerly seawards. Cuna still lay humped on the waters, but beyond it he seemed to see his shining pathway running far to a speck which might be an island. Crazy with pleasure he stared at the vision, till slowly it melted into the waves, and Cuna the inexorable once more blocked the sky-line. He climbed down, his heart in a doubt between despondency and hope.

It was the last day of such fancies, for on the morrow he had to face the new world of school.

*   *   *

At Cecil's Colin found a new life and a thousand new interests. His early delicacy had been driven away by the sea-winds of Acharra, and he was rapidly growing up a tall, strong child, straight of limb like all his house, but sinewy and alert beyond his years. He learned new games with astonishing facility, became a fast bowler with a genius for twists, and a Rugby three-quarters full of pluck and cunning. He soon attained to the modified popularity of a private school, and, being essentially clean, strong, and healthy, found himself a mark for his juniors' worship and a favourite with masters. The homage did not spoil him, for no boy was ever less self-possessed. On the cricket-ground and the football-field he was a leader, but in private he had the nervous, sensitive manners of the would-be recluse. No one ever accused him of "side"—his polite, halting address was the same to junior and senior; and the result was that wild affection which simplicity in the great is wont to inspire. He spoke with a pure accent, in which lurked no northern trace; in a little he had forgotten all about his birthplace and his origin. His name had at first acquired for him the sobriquet of "Scottie," but the title was soon dropped from its manifest inaptness.

In his second year at Cecil's he caught a prevalent fever, and for days lay very near the brink of death. At his worst he was wildly delirious, crying ceaselessly for Acharra and the beach at Kinlochuna. But as he grew convalescent the absorption remained, and for the moment he seemed to have forgotten his southern life. He found himself playing on the sands, always with the boundary ridge before him, and the hump of Cuna rising in the sea. When dragged back to his environment by the inquiries of Bellew, his special friend, who came to sit with him, he was so abstracted and forgetful that the good Bellew was seriously grieved. "The chap's a bit cracked, you know," he announced in hall. "Didn't know me. Asked me what 'footer' meant when I told him about the

Bayswick match, and talked about nothing but a lot of hea-
then Scotch names."

One dream haunted Colin throughout the days of his
recovery. He was tormented with a furious thirst, poorly
assuaged at long intervals by watered milk. So when he
crossed the borders of dreamland his first search was always
for a well. He tried the brushwood inland from the beach, but
it was dry as stone. Then he climbed with difficulty the
boundary ridge, and found little pools of salt water, while far
on the other side gleamed the dark black bog-holes. Here
was not what he sought, and he was in deep despair, till suddenly over the sea he caught a glimpse of his old path running beyond Cuna to a bank of mist. He rushed down to the
tide's edge, and to his amazement found solid ground. Now
was the chance for which he had long looked, and he ran
happily westwards, till of a sudden the solid earth seemed to
sink with him, and he was in the waters struggling. But two
curious things he noted. One was that the far bank of mist
seemed to open for a pinpoint of time, and he had a gleam of
land. He saw nothing distinctly, only a line which was not
mist and was not water. The second was that the water was
fresh, and as he was drinking from this curious new fresh sea
he awoke. The dream was repeated three times before he left
the sick-room. Always he wakened at the same place, always
he quenched his thirst in the fresh sea, but never again did
the mist open for him and show him the strange country.

From Cecil's he went to the famous school which was the
tradition in his family. The Head spoke to his house-master
of his coming. "We are to have another Raden here," he said,
"and I am glad of it, if the young one turns out to be anything like the others. There's a good deal of dry-rot among
the boys just now. They are all too old for their years and too
wise in the wrong way. They haven't anything like the enthusiasm in sports they had twenty years ago when I first came
here. I hope this young Raden will stir them up." The house-

master agreed, and when he first caught sight of Colin's slim, well-knit figure, looked into the handsome kindly eyes, and heard his curiously diffident speech, his doubts vanished. "We have got the right stuff now," he told himself, and the senior for whom the new boy fagged made the same comment.

From the anomalous insignificance of fagdom Colin climbed up the School, leaving everywhere a record of honest good-nature. He was allowed to forget his cricket and football, but in return he was initiated into the mysteries of the river. Water had always been his delight, so he went through the dreary preliminaries of being coached in a tub-pair till he learned to swing steadily and get his arms quickly forward. Then came the stages of scratch fours and scratch eights, till after a long apprenticeship he was promoted to the dignity of a thwart in the Eight itself. In his last year he was Captain of Boats, a position which joins the responsibility of a Cabinet Minister to the rapturous popular applause of a successful warrior. Nor was he the least distinguished of a great band. With Colin at seven the School won the Ladies' after the closest race on record.

The Head's prophecy fell true, for Colin was a born leader. For all his good-humour and diffidence of speech, he had a trick of shutting his teeth which all respected. As captain he was the idol of the school, and he ruled it well and justly. For the rest, he was a curious boy with none of the ordinary young enthusiasms, reserved for all his kindliness. At house "shouters" his was not the voice which led the stirring strains of "Stroke it all you know," though his position demanded it. He cared little about work, and the School-house scholar, who fancied him from his manner a devotee of things intellectual, found in Colin but an affected interest. He read a certain amount of modern poetry with considerable boredom; fiction he never opened. The truth was that he had a romance in his own brain which, willy nilly, would play itself out, and which left him small relish for the pale second-hand inanities

of art. Often, when with others he would lie in the deep
meadows by the river on some hot summer's day, his fancies
would take a curious colour. He adored the soft English landscape, the lush grasses, the slow streams, the ancient secular
trees. But as he looked into the hazy green distance a colder
air would blow on his cheek, a pungent smell of salt and
pines would be for a moment in his nostrils, and he would be
gazing at a line of waves on a beach, a ridge of low rocks,
and a shining sea-path running out to—ah, that he could not
tell! The envious Cuna would suddenly block all the vistas.
He had constantly the vision before his eyes, and he strove to
strain into the distance before Cuna should intervene. Once
or twice he seemed almost to achieve it. He found that by
keeping on the top of the low rock-ridge he could cheat Cuna
by a second or two, and get a glimpse of a misty something
out in the west. The vision took odd times for recurring,—
once or twice in lecture, once on the cricket-ground, many
times in the fields of a Sunday, and once while he paddled
down to the start in a Trials race. It gave him a keen pleasure:
it was his private domain, where at any moment he might
make some enchanting discovery.

At this time he began to spend his vacations at Kinlochuna. His father, an elderly ex-diplomat, had permanently
taken up his abode there, and was rapidly settling into the
easy life of the Scotch laird. Colin returned to his native
place without enthusiasm. His childhood there had been full
of lonely hours, and he had come to like the warm south
country. He found the house full of people, for his father en-
tertained hugely, and the talk was of sport and sport alone.
As a rule, your very great athlete is bored by Scotch shooting. Long hours of tramping and crouching among heather
cramp without fully exercising the body; and unless he has
the love of the thing ingrained in him, the odds are that he
will wish himself home. The father, in his new-found admiration for his lot, was content to face all weathers; the son
found it an effort to keep pace with such vigour. He thought

upon the sunlit fields and reedy watercourses with regret, and saw little in the hills but a rough waste scarred with rock and sour with mosses.

He read widely throughout these days, for his father had a taste for modern letters, and new books lay littered about the rooms. He read queer Celtic tales which he thought "sickening rot," and mild Celtic poetry which he failed to understand. Among the guests was a noted manufacturer of fiction, whom the elder Raden had met somewhere and bidden to Kinlochuna. He had heard the tale of Colin's ancestors and the sea headland of Acharra, and one day he asked the boy to show him the place, as he wished to make a story of it. Colin assented unwillingly, for he had been slow to visit this place of memories, and he did not care to make his first experiment in such company. But the gentleman would not be gainsaid, so the two scrambled through the sea-wood and climbed the low ridge which looked over the bay. The weather was mist and drizzle; Cuna had wholly hidden herself, and the bluff Acharra loomed hazy and far. Colin was oddly disappointed: this reality was a poor place compared with his fancies. His companion stroked his peaked beard, talked nonsense about Colin the Red and rhetoric about "the spirit of the misty grey weather having entered into the old tale." "Think," he cried; "to those old warriors beyond that bank of mist was the whole desire of life, the Golden City, the Far Islands, whatever you care to call it." Colin shivered, as if his holy places had been profaned, set down the man in his mind most unjustly as an "awful little cad," and hurried him back to the house.

Oxford received the boy with open arms, for his reputation had long preceded him. To the majority of men he was the one freshman of his year, and gossip was busy with his prospects. Nor was gossip disappointed. In his first year he rowed seven in the Eight. The next year he was captain of his college boats, and a year later the O.U.B.C. made him its president. For three years he rowed in the winning Eight, and old coaches agreed that in him the perfect seven had been found. It was he who in the famous race of 18— caught up in the last three hundred yards the quickened stroke which gave Oxford victory. As he grew to his full strength he became a splendid figure of a man—tall, supple, deep-chested for all his elegance. His quick dark eyes and his kindly hesitating manners made people think his face extraordinarily handsome, when really it was in no way above the common. But his whole figure, as he stood in his shorts and sweater on the raft at Putney, was so full of youth and strength that people involuntarily smiled when they saw him—a smile of pleasure in so proper a piece of manhood.

Colin enjoyed life hugely at Oxford, for to one so frank and well equipped the place gave of its best. He was the most distinguished personage of his day there, but, save to school friends and the men he met officially on the river, he was little known. His diffidence and his very real exclusiveness kept him from being the centre of a host of friends. His own countrymen in the place were utterly non-plussed by him. They claimed him eagerly as a fellow, but he had none of the ordinary characteristics of the race. There were Scots of every description around him—pale-faced Scots who worked incessantly, metaphysical Scots who talked in the Union, robustious Scots who played football. They were all men of hearty manners and many enthusiasms,—who quoted Burns and dined to the immortal bard's honour every 25th of January; who told interminable Scotch stories, and fell into fervours over national sports, dishes, drinks, and religions. To the poor Colin it was all inexplicable. At the remote house of Kinlochuna he had never heard of a Free Kirk or a haggis. He had never read a line of Burns, Scott bored him exceedingly, and in all honesty he thought Scots games inferior to southern sports. He had no great love for the bleak country, he cared nothing for the traditions of his house, so he was promptly set down by his compatriots as "denationalised and degenerate."

He was idle, too, during these years as far as his "schools" were concerned, but he was always very intent upon his own private business. Whenever he sat down to read, when he sprawled on the grass at river picnics, in chapel, in lecture—in short, at any moment when his body was at rest and his mind at leisure—his fancies were off on the same old path. Things had changed, however, in that country. The boyish device of a hard road running over the waters had gone, and now it was invariably a boat which he saw beached on the shingle. It differed in shape. At first it was an ugly salmon-coble, such as the fishermen used for the nets at Kinlochuna. Then it passed, by rapid transitions, through a canvas skiff which it took good watermanship to sit, a whiff, an ordinary dinghey, till at last it settled itself into a long rough boat, pointed at both ends, with oar-holes in the sides instead of row-locks. It was the devil's own business to launch it, and launch it anew he was compelled to for every journey; for though he left it bound in a little rock hollow below the ridge after landing, yet when he returned, lo! there was the clumsy thing high and dry upon the beach.

The odd point about the new venture was that Cuna had ceased to trouble him. As soon as he had pulled his first stroke the island disappeared, and nothing lay before him but the sea-fog. Yet, try as he might, he could come little nearer. The shores behind him might sink and lessen, but the impenetrable mist was still miles to the westward. Sometimes he rowed so far that the shore was a thin line upon the horizon, but when he turned the boat it seemed to ground in a second on the beach. The long laboured journey out and the instantaneous return puzzled him at first, but soon he became used to them. His one grief was the mist, which seemed to grow denser as he neared it. The sudden glimpse of land which he had got from the ridge of rock in the old boyish days was now denied him, and with the denial came a keener exultation in the quest. Somewhere in the west, he knew, must be land, and in this land a well of sweet water—for so he had interpreted his feverish dream. Sometimes, when the wind blew against him, he caught scents from it—generally the scent of pines, as on the little ridge on the shore behind him.

One day on his college barge, while he was waiting for a picnic party to start, he seemed to get nearer than before. Out on that western sea, as he saw it, it was fresh, blowing weather, with a clear hot sky above. It was hard work rowing, for the wind was against him, and the sun scorched his forehead. The air seemed full of scents—and sounds, too, sounds of far-away surf and wind in trees. He rested for a moment on his oars and turned his head. His heart beat quickly, for there was a rift in the mist, and far through a line of sand ringed with snow-white foam.

Somebody shook him roughly,—"Come on, Colin, old man. They're all waiting for you. Do you know you've been half asleep?"

Colin rose and followed silently, with drowsy eyes. His mind was curiously excited. He had looked inside the veil of mist. Now he knew what was the land he sought.

He made the voyage often, now that the spell was broken. It was short work to launch the boat, and, whereas it had been a long pull formerly, now it needed only a few strokes to bring him to the Rim of the Mist. There was no chance of getting farther, and he scarcely tried. He was content to rest there, in a world of curious scents and sounds, till the mist drew down and he was driven back to shore.

The change in his environment troubled him little. For a man who has been an idol at the University to fall suddenly into the comparative insignificance of town is often a bitter experience; but Colin, whose thoughts were not ambitious, scarcely noticed it. He found that he was less his own master than before, but he humbled himself to his new duties without complaint. Many of his old friends were about him; he had plenty of acquaintances; and, being "sufficient unto himself," he was unaccustomed to ennui. Invitations showered upon him thick and fast. Match-making mothers, knowing his birth and his father's income, and reflecting that he was the only child of his house, desired him as a son-in-law. He was bidden welcome everywhere, and the young girls, for whose sake he was thus courted, found in him an attractive mystery. The tall good-looking athlete, with the kind eyes and the preposterously nervous manner, wakened their maidenly sympathies. As they danced with him or sat next to him at dinner, they talked fervently of Oxford, of the north, of the army, of his friends. "Stupid, but nice, my dear," was Lady Afflint's comment; and Miss Clarissa Herapath, the beauty of the year, declared to her friends that he was a "dear boy, but so awkward." He was always forgetful, and ever apologetic; and when he forgot the Shandwicks' theatre-party, the Herapaths' dance, and at least a dozen minor matters, he began to acquire the reputation of a cynic and a recluse.

"You're a queer chap, Col," Lieutenant Bellew said in expostulation.

Colin shrugged his shoulders; he was used to the description.

"Do you know that Clara Herapath was trying all she knew to please you this afternoon, and you looked as if you weren't listening? Most men would have given their ears to be in your place."

"I'm awfully sorry, but I thought I was very polite to her."

"And why weren't you at the Marshams' garden-party?"

"Oh, I went to polo with Collinson and another man. And, I say, old chap, I'm not coming to the Logans tomorrow. I've got a fence on with Adair at the school."

Little Bellew, who was a tremendous mirror of fashion and chevalier in general, looked up curiously at his tall friend.

"Why don't you like the women, Col, when they're so fond of you?"

"They aren't," said Colin, hotly, "and I don't dislike 'em. But, Lord! they bore me. I might be doing twenty things when I talk nonsense to one of 'em for an hour. I come back as stupid as an owl, and besides there's heaps of things better sport."

The truth was that, while among men he was a leader and at his ease, among women his psychic balance was so oddly upset that he grew nervous and returned unhappy. The boat on the beach, ready in general to appear at the slightest call, would delay long after such experiences, and its place would be taken by some woman's face for which he cared not a straw. For the boat, on the other hand, he cared a very great deal. In all his frank wholesome existence there was this enchanting background, this pleasure-garden which he cherished more than anything in life. He had come of late to look at it with somewhat different eyes. The eager desire to search behind the mist was ever with him, but now he had also some curiosity about the details of the picture. As he pulled out to the Rim of the Mist sounds seemed to shape themselves on his lips, which by-and-by grew into actual words in his memory. He wrote them down in scraps, and after some sorting they seemed to him a kind of Latin. He remembered a college friend of his, one Medway, now reading for the Bar, who had been the foremost scholar of his acquaintance; so with the scrap of paper in his pocket he climbed one evening to Medway's rooms in the Temple.

The man read the words curiously, and puzzled for a bit. "What's made you take to Latin comps so late in life, Colin? It's baddish, you know, even for you. I thought they'd have licked more into you at Eton."

Colin grinned with amusement. "I'll tell you about it later," he said. "Can you make out what it means?"

"It seems to be a kind of dog-Latin or monkish Latin or something of the sort," said Medway. "It reads like this:

'*Soles occidere solent*' (that's cribbed from Catullus, and besides it's the regular monkish pun) . . . *qua* . . . then *blandula* something. Then there's a lot of Choctaw, and then *illæ insulæ dilectæ in quas festinant somnia animulæ gaudia.* That's pretty fair rot. Hullo, by George! here's something better—*Insula pomorum insula vitæ.* That's Geoffrey of Monmouth."

He made a dive to a bookcase and pulled out a battered little calf-bound duodecimo. "Here's all about your Isle of Apple-trees. Listen. 'Situate far out in the Western ocean, beyond the Utmost Islands, beyond even the little Isle of Sheep where the cairns of dead men are, lies the Island of Apple-trees where the heroes and princes of the nations live their second life.' " He closed the book and put it back. "It's the old ancient story, the Greek Hesperides, the British Avilion, and this Apple-tree Island is the northern equivalent."

Colin sat entranced, his memory busy with a problem. Could he distinguish the scents of apple-trees among the perfumes of the Rim of the Mist. For the moment he thought he could. He was roused by Medway's voice asking the story of the writing.

"Oh, it's just some nonsense that was running in my head, so I wrote it down to see what it was."

"But you must have been reading. A new exercise for you, Colin?"

"No, I wasn't reading. Look here. You know the sort of pictures you make for yourself of places you like."

"Rather! Mine is a Devon moor with a little red shooting-box in the heart of it."

"Well, mine is different. Mine is a sort of beach with a sea and a lot of islands somewhere far out. It is a jolly place, fresh, you know, and blowing, and smells good. 'Pon my word, now I think of it, there's always been a scent of apples."

"Sort of cider-press? Well, I must be off. You'd better

come round to the club and see the telegrams about the war. *You* should be keen about it."

One evening, a week later, Medway met a friend called Tillotson at the club, and, being lonely, they dined together. Tillotson was a man of some note in science, a dabbler in psychology, an amateur historian, a ripe genealogist. They talked of politics and the war, of a new book, of Mrs. Runnymede, and finally of their hobbies.

"I am writing an article," said Tillotson. "Craikes asked me to do it for the 'Monthly.' It's on a nice point in psychics. I call it 'The Transmission of Fallacies,' but I do not mean the logical kind. The question is, Can a particular form of hallucination run in a family for generations. The proof must, of course, come from my genealogical studies. I maintain it can. I instance the Douglas-Ernotts, not one of whom can see straight with the left eye. That is one side. In another class of examples I take the Drapiers, who hate salt water and never go on board ship if they can help it. Then you remember the Durwards? Old Lady Balcrynie used to tell me that no one of the lot could ever stand the sight of a green frock. There's a chance for the romancer. The Manorwaters have the same madness, only their colour is red."

A vague remembrance haunted Medway's brain.

"I know a man who might give you points from his own case. Did you ever meet a chap Raden—Colin Raden?"

Tillotson nodded. "Long chap—in the Guards? 'Varsity oar, and used to be a crack bowler? No, I don't know him. I know him well by sight, and I should like to meet him tremendously—as a genealogist, of course."

"Why?" asked Medway.

"Why? Because the man's family is unique. You never hear much about them nowadays, but away up in that northwest corner of Scotland they have ruled since the days of Noah. Why, man, they were aristocrats when our Howards and Nevilles were green-grocers. I wish you would get this Raden to meet me some night."

"I am afraid there's no chance of it just at present," said Medway, taking up an evening paper. "I see that his regiment has been ordered to the front. But remind me when he comes back, and I'll be delighted."

III.

And now there began for Colin a curious divided life,—without, a constant shifting of scene, days of heat and bustle and toil,—within, a slow, tantalising, yet exquisite adventure. The Rim of the Mist was now no more the goal of his journeys, but the starting-point. Lying there, amid cool, fragrant sea-winds, his fanciful ear was subtly alert for the sounds of the dim land before him. Sleeping and waking the quest haunted him. As he flung himself on his bed the kerosene-filled air would change to an ocean freshness, the old boat would rock beneath him, and with clear eye and a boyish hope he would be waiting and watching. And then suddenly he would be back on shore, Cuna and the Acharra headland shining grey in the morning light, and with gritty mouth and sand-filled eyes he would awaken to the heat of the desert camp.

He was kept busy, for his good-humour and energy made him a willing slave, and he was ready enough for volunteer work when others were weak with heat and despair. A thirty-mile ride left him untired; more, he followed the campaign with a sharp intelligence and found a new enthusiasm for his profession. Discomforts there might be, but the days were happy; and then—the cool land, the bright land, which was his for the thinking of it.

Soon they gave him reconnoitring work to do, and his wits were put to the trial. He came well out of the thing, and earned golden praise from the silent colonel in command. He enjoyed it as he had enjoyed a hard race on the river or a good cricket match, and when his worried companions marvelled at his zeal he stammered and grew uncomfortable.

"How the deuce do you keep it up, Colin?" the major asked him. "I'm an old hand at the job, and yet I've got a temper like devilled bones. You seem as chirpy as if you were going out to fish a chalk-stream on a June morning."

"Well, the fact is——" and Colin pulled himself up short, knowing that he could never explain. He felt miserably that he had an unfair advantage of the others. Poor Bellew, who groaned and swore in the heat at his side, knew nothing of the Rim of the Mist. It was really rough luck on the poor beggars, and who but himself was the fortunate man?

As the days passed a curious thing happened. He found fragments of the Other world straying into his common life. The barriers of the two domains were falling, and more than once he caught himself looking at a steel-blue sea when his eyes should have found a mustard-coloured desert. One day, on a reconnoitring expedition, they stopped for a little on a hillock above a jungle of scrub, and, being hot and tired, scanned listlessly the endless yellow distances.

"I suppose yon hill is about ten miles off," said Bellew with dry lips.

Colin looked vaguely. "I should say five."

"And what's that below it—the black patch? Stones or scrub?"

Colin was in a day-dream. "Why do you call it black? It's blue, quite blue."

"Rot," said the other. "It's grey-black."

"No, it's water with the sun shining on it. It's blue, but just at the edges it's very near sea-green."

Bellew rose excitedly. "Hullo, Col, you're seeing the mirage! And you the fittest of the lot of us! You've got the sun in your head, old man!"

"Mirage!" Colin cried in contempt. He was awake now, but the thought of confusing his own bright western sea with a mirage gave him a curious pain. For a moment he felt the gulf of separation between his two worlds, but only for a moment. As the party remounted he gave his fancies the rein, and ere he reached camp he had felt the oars in his hand and sniffed the apple-tree blossom from the distant beaches.

The major came to him after supper.

"Bellew told me you saw the mirage to-day, Colin," he said. "I expect your eyes are getting a bit bad. Better get your sand-spectacles out."

Colin laughed. "Thanks. It's awfully good of you to bother, but I think Bellew took me up wrong. I never was fitter in my life."

By-and-by the turn came for pride to be humbled. A low desert fever took him, and though he went through the day as usual, it was with dreary lassitude; and at night, with hot hands clasped above his damp hair, he found sleep a hard goddess to conquer.

It was the normal condition of the others, so he had small cause to complain, but it worked havoc with his fancies. He had never been ill since his childish days, and this little fever meant much to one whose nature was poised on a needle-point. He found himself confronted with a hard bare world, with the gilt rubbed from its corners. The Rim of the Mist seemed a place of vague horrors; when he reached it his soul was consumed with terror; he struggled impotently to advance; behind him Cuna and the Acharra coast seemed a place of evil dreams. Again, as in his old fever, he was tormented with a devouring thirst, but the sea beside him was not fresh, but brackish as a rock-pool. He yearned for the apple-tree beaches in front; there, he knew, were cold springs of water; the fresh smell of it was blown towards him in his nightmare.

But as the days passed and the misery for all grew more intense, an odd hope began to rise in his mind. It could not last, coolness and health were waiting near, and his reason for the hope came from the odd events at the Rim of the

Mist. The haze was clearing from the foreground, the surf-lined coast seemed nearer, and though all was obscure save the milk-white sand and the foam, yet here was earnest enough for him. Once more he became cheerful; weak and light-headed he rode out again; and the major, who was recovering from sunstroke, found envy take the place of pity in his soul.

The hope was near fulfilment. One evening when the heat was changing into the cooler twilight, Colin and Bellew were sent with a small picked body to scour the foothills above the river in case of a flank attack during the night-march. It was work they had done regularly for weeks, and it is possible that precautions were relaxed. At any rate, as they turned a corner of a hill, in a sandy pass where barren rocks looked down on more barren thorn thickets, a couple of rifle shots rang out from the scarp, and above them appeared a line of dark faces and white steel. A mere handful, taken at a disadvantage, they could not hope to disperse numbers, so Colin gave the word to wheel about and return. Again shots rang out, and little Bellew had only time to catch at his friend's arm to save him from falling from the saddle.

The word of command had scarcely left Colin's mouth when a sharp pain went through his chest, and his breath seemed to catch and stop. He felt as in a condensed moment of time the heat, the desert smell, the dust in his eyes and throat, while he leaned helplessly forward on his horse's mane. Then the world vanished for him. . . . The boat was rocking under him, the oars in his hand. He pulled and it moved, straight, arrow-like towards the forbidden shore. As if under a great wind the mist furled up and fled. Scents of pines, of apple-trees, of great fields of thyme and heather, hung about him; the sound of wind in a forest, of cool waters falling in showers, of old moorland music, came thin and faint with an exquisite clearness. A second and the boat was among the surf, its gunwale ringed with white foam, as it leaped to the still waters beyond. Clear and deep and still the water lay, and then the white beaches shelved downward, and the boat grated on the sand. He turned, every limb alert with a strange new life, crying out words which had shaped themselves on his lips and which an echo seemed to catch and answer. There was the green forest before him, the hills of peace, the cold white waters. With a passionate joy he leaped on the beach, his arms outstretched to this new earth, this light of the world, this old desire of the heart—youth, rapture, immortality.

Bellew brought the body back to camp, himself half-dead with fatigue and whimpering like a child. He almost fell from his horse, and when others took his burden from him and laid it reverently in his tent, he stood beside it, rubbing sand and sweat from his poor purblind eyes, his teeth chattering with fever. He was given something to drink, but he swallowed barely a mouthful.

"It was some d-d-damned sharpshooter," he said. "Right through the breast, and he never spoke to me again. My poor old Col! He was the best chap God ever created, and I do-don't care a dash what becomes of me now. I was at school with him, you know, you men."

"Was he killed outright?" asked the Major hoarsely.

"N-no. He lived for about five minutes. But I think the sun had got into his head or he was mad with pain, for he d-d-didn't know where he was. He kept crying out about the smell of pine-trees and heather and a lot of pure non-sense about water."

"Et dulces reminiscitur Argos," somebody quoted mournfully, as they went out to the desert evening.

The Drawn Arrow

by Clemence Housman

Clemence Housman published little fiction but had a greater renown for her wood engravings, some of which adorned the books of fairy tales by her brother Laurence Housman. Her writings somewhat resemble those of George MacDonald, blending myth, fantasy, and allegory with a slow, contemplative prose style. "The Drawn Arrow" concerns extremes of heroism, and personal salvation. It was probably, like the rest of Housman's fiction, written around the turn of the century, though it was first published years later in the anthology *Thirty and One Stories by Thirty and One Authors* (1923), edited by Ernest Rhys and C. A. Dawson Scott.

THE king lay hid in a hollow of the red sandhills. He watched the poisonous grey asp flicking through the burnt crouch-thorn, and the little long-legged rat nimble at the fray, and the tawny flatwing that is never still; and no other life showed astir within the round horizon. Red sand was all the world, overhung by a yellow sky; the sun swung up the dome to his highest pitch.

"The half of my kingdom would I give for one draught of water."

Not many days ago he had been on his throne, a great king, with peace at home and conquering armies abroad. Then rose the tribes ripened to revolt by a traitor half-brother; and treason had opened his gates, and fired his palace over his head; and treason had broken his ranks in the field, so that of his first army none outlived the day save himself and his armour-bearer. Now was he cut off from all relief, for his foes warded the river and held the desert wells, knowing that a few more hours must deliver him to death if not to them.

The king waited his armour-bearer and waited in vain. "He has found no water. He is dead by thirst. He is slain. He is taken." The face of his armour-bearer rose to mind, such a face as grows over a true brave heart. "No," thought the king, "he is not taken: he himself would take his knowledge of me out of reach of the tormentors: he is dead."

He drew out a wavy dagger, and tested it again on his sleeve that gave way like mist, on his palm that gave way like water. The studs of emerald gave a good grip; though he were weak as a child he could yet baulk his half-brother's hate of a promised satisfaction. "Me alive he shall not have to flay. No."

The anguish of thirst was terrible. It ached through every exhausted vein like fever, and like fever waxed and waned, stinging the brain into acute recognition of its scope, blanking it till the whole surrounding universe was impregnated with thirst, and a symbol.

Scents strangely strong took possession of his brain: the scent of a melon, the gold-laced melon that overhung the water-tank where as a boy he bathed; the scent of a woman, one bronze-dark woman: from a cup tinkling with mountain ice they drank together, and she struck him, the king, in lovely intoxication when the wine spilled into her bosom; the scent of sodden corn in the floods; the scent of camels by the summer wells; the scent of date-buds in the cool of dusk, when as a youth he stood at the ford, and saw across the water great manes stooped to lap. One draught bit keen from memory, quaffed on a day's chase, rank with bruised fennel; and another quaffed but late in the press of disastrous battle, tingeing red as he drank: it was the reek of his own blood he drew. And between all these and others came wafts of a far remembrance, a scent unrecognisable so long forgotten; it pervaded all others, it dominated all others, blossoming late from the remotest corner of the brain: it was the scent of his mother's milk.

The signal call of the restless flatwings gave a warning, and down in the trough of the sandhills he spied a figure coming. The king lay close in his lair, and pulled forward his screen of crouch-thorn. No faithful armour-bearer came here: this, by his fillet of yellow, was a man of the river hills, from a tribe of doubtful fidelity with claims to independence against him. Tough and spare he was, hairy, red as the sand; a goatskin was all his clothing, and his only weapon a staff headed with stone; a wallet and a gourd swung at his back.

At sight of the gourd the king's hand sought his dagger, and his thirst became a torment quite intolerable. Lo! the man halted not far off, sat him down on the red hillside, and loosed the thong of wallet and gourd. At that the king thrust away his screen; his sword he left, for his dagger was enough; he turned inwards the bezel of his signet-ring, as he stepped out on the crumbling, shelving sand.

Little rat and grey asp ceased fight and scudded, and the flatwing shrilled away. The hillman turned, looking up, and sprang to his feet; he held up his right hand in token of peace, but the king came on. Then he caught up his staff, poised and swung it, but dropped it again, and once more offered the sign of peace. And then the king stood and held up his right hand, for he was dizzy and weak, and he saw that the man was wary, hardy, agile, more than his match.

So the hillman said, "Come on in peace"; and as the king came close he read in him the extremes of drought, and took the gourd and offered it instantly. And the king drank, blessed him by all his gods, and gave it back to him half-drained. Also food the hillman offered; and there they sat down together and shared like brothers of dates and a morsel of bread, and passed the gourd to and fro; but from the hill-man's hand hardly did it pass any lighter, for he saw how great was the thirst of the other.

Naught knew the red man of the shaking of a kingdom. He shaded his eyes, and looked.

"Yonder ride horsemen."

Not a sign of them could the eyes of the king descry. "Be-like a troop of wild ass," he said.

"Three days," said the hillman, "did I follow the wild ass southward, seeking a lost pair of mine who shun the bit and disown the slayer of the night lion."

"Even so would the hillmen by their king."

"Lions are the hillmen and not asses; let the king know!" And he added the loyal formula: "As the sun's be the king's reign."

Still he looked. "Northward go these. They are fighting men, and many. They head for the passage of the river."

He caught up wallet and gourd. "Do they think to take the pass of our hills?" he muttered. "Not with arms in their hands, though they should be of the royal army!"

"Stay!" said the king; and the man turned and looked sharply at him who spoke with authority in the desert of the red sandhills.

"Water and food have you given for no asking; add thereto a third boon, the sound of your name."

"I have not asked yours," said the hillman sullenly.

"Harken! Go you to the hillmen, and warn them that till the king's army come they keep the pass of the hills against his enemies. In the presence of the king only shall you know my name; and ask you him then whatsoever boon you will and for my sake will he grant it."

"Give then a token."

"No token to bear lest you fall in with the king's enemies; for you the token of my hand and eye."

The king held up his right hand, took the other's held up likewise, and gripped it hard, and their eyes met and held till the hillman was satisfied. Released he said: "My name is Speed."

He glanced down at his palm: a rayed disk was faintly indented from the signet. One more keen look he cast. "As the sun's be the king's reign!" he said, caught up his staff, and swung away along the trough of the red hills.

Soon he was out of sight, and the king could see no living thing but the asp and the rat and the flatwing. Northward hung a blur on the horizon, dust raised of the horse he could not discern.

Long hours trailed down the sky, and the king lay close, waiting for cover of night to amend his chances.

With the edge of dark came his faithful armour-bearer, burnt with thirst and despairing. Past speech, he gave to the king one poor plant of the water-cactus, his only gain. But the king bade him slake his own thirst with this, and live and listen. Then he told all that had passed between himself and the hillman.

The armour-bearer got his voice, and said, "O my lord, was this a hairy man, all red, hair and skin, small headed, long in the thigh?"

"Even so."

The armour-bearer smote his hands together.

"Oh, my lord, rise, haste and flee! the enemy have that man. He passed me, I hiding, though quick were his eyes; a nimble man and light in build, but going heavy and hard like a dog that runs mad. A misgiving I had then. And later, edging above the plain, I saw far off a chase, and my man running and doubling to win the farther side, and in the end ridden down and taken. Oh, my lord, he was taken alive!"

The king, without a word, took his sword and set forward. He pointed. "Yonder is the star of my birth; be that our guide, since reason can prefer no road."

On through the weary night they went as destiny led; slower and slower, for the armour-bearer flagged, then dropped, and the king sat and waited for light to show him his fate.

With one breath of dawn rose broad day.

"My star!" cried the king. "Look and live."

But the armour-bearer said hoarsely, "My lord, I cannot see."

"Yonder, in sight, is the river," said the king, "and my horse hold the bank, and the foot cross thick as locusts, and the battle joins on this side. From all quarters the foe gathers, with pickets streaming in, keeping the wells no longer."

"Water!" muttered the armour-bearer, and got on his feet, but reeled and could not see.

Yet, in the end, both he and the king got down from the hills to the next well, and laying their sleeves over the mud of it, drew in delicious moisture of life. Also the water-cactus grew there.

While battle raged on the river bank, and the fortune of the day hung, a cry rose up, "The king, the king!" and with it the thrill that foretells victory ran through the royal army. And the enemy broke and fled, smitten without swords by the cry.

Now when the fight was ended and the slaughter, the king, riding by the river through the camping ground of the vanquished, spied among the herd of prisoners fillets of yellow, and bethought him of Speed the hillman. At his bidding his armour-bearer went, and presently came again with a man under his hand.

"My lord, two women there bound wear the yellow. Too dazed are they for speech or for knowing friend from foe. But this man of the prisoners knows of a foul thing to tell."

Then the prisoner told over how the hillman had been taken and brought before the traitor brother; when though he denied stoutly all knowledge of the fugitive king, his goings were held against him, and torture was ordained to make him speak. Yet still he denied stoutly, spite of all persuasion by steel and cord and fire. Then the traitor, knowing that an army drew near, and most eager for his brother's person, sent swift horsemen to the river hills, who by guile got from the tribe the mother and the sister; and he purposed to torture them also before the eyes of the hillman. But the day coming, and the battle, they were left bound in the camp.

"Where now is the hillman?" said the king.

"Yonder he lies in the river caves."

Awhile the king stood in thought; then he ordered that the mother and sister should be kept bound, and that none should speak with them, and he took his armour-bearer with him to the river caves.

"Go in," he said, "and see."

And the armour-bearer went, and came out the paler.

"It is the man. Go not in my lord. Yes, my lord, he lives: his eyes are shut, but he surely lives."

The king stood saying nought.

"My lord," said the armour-bearer, "the title of Most Faithful, ordained by you this day for my reward, I cannot hold. This poor hillman has the better claim."

"It is truth," said the king. "Great shall be his reward."

Then he turned to his guards and bade fetch the women.

"I have a mind," he said, "to try the man, and the greater shall be his reward."

And while his tent was pitching hard by he told his armour-bearer all that was to be done, and when the women came, put them in his hand for the doing, while he turned himself to the gathering of the captains.

So soon as the armour-bearer came again in at the tent the king bade for silence that he might speak.

"My lord, at the voices of the women he opened his eyes and sat, strong-alive yet. Oh, my lord, I got another with a stiffer throat than I to speak further. They, no less than he, doubted not the dead earnest of all; and they used all the power of woman-speech beseeching him for pity on himself and on them, and still he shook his head and denied that he had any knowledge of the king to deliver. Then that young woman, his sister, caught me by the knees beseeching pity of me, protesting that he knew nothing, for he would withhold nothing for the life of his mother and her, his sister, his twin sister. And yet when the order was given for her to be led away as to death, the hillman muttered something at her ear: 'As the sun's be the king's reign,' I thought it to be. And the young woman looked him in the eyes, and kissed him, and with no word more, went out straight. Then was brought in a human heart fresh killed, and put into his hand as his sister's heart, with the heat and the beat of it still there. And he holds the heart and looks at his mother, and still he shakes his head."

"Great shall be his reward," said the king. "And the mother?"

"Oh, my lord, pardon!" said the armour-bearer, kneeling. "I have carried your command no further. Had you witnessed you could desire no further trial. Oh, my lord, spare him more."

"Go," said the king in anger, "and obey." And the armour-bearer went.

When he came again tears were running down to his beard.

"Oh, my lord, I was born of woman. She uncovered the breast to her son; she was taken out struggling and crying to him to save her. And a second heart was brought in and put hot into his hand. And he sits there, holding in his blistered hands those two hearts that he takes to be his sister's and his mother's, and now one and now the other he holds against his breast to keep it warm, and he mutters over them, and all he says is: 'As the sun's be the king's reign.' "

"It is enough," said the king. "Great shall be his reward."

Then by order Speed the hillman was cleansed and dressed with wine and oil; and a costly ointment the king gave, fit for the healing of blood royal.

Then on the next day the king had the hillman brought and set down in the tent where he lay. And he entered alone and closed the entrance, having on him the royal boss and the purple, and all the gear of the throne.

On the red man had been put a linen tunic to cover most of him, but with the aroma of the royal balm the smell of the torture came off him yet, and the look of torture lay dead on his face; and though the king in his splendour stood before him, the eyes of Speed the hillman stayed wide and blank without speculation, and when the king spoke to him by name they never moved.

Then the king, for a token, took what was left of the right hand of Speed in his own, and lifted it up, and fixed his eyes straight upon his and held so. And in a while the flesh he grasped quivered as the man's eyes wavered with sense; recognition swam into them; his hand answered feebly; a great straight grin came out; he drew a thirsty breath and laughed low in his throat. At the dreadful noise the king, loosing, stepped back, when Speed reached to the hem of his sleeve and touched it at his brow. "As the sun's be the king's reign," he muttered; and his head sank on his breast and his eyes settled.

Outside sounded the ringing of silver bells and the king uncovered the door of the tent, took Speed and set him there, and bade him look out.

Before the hillman's eyeballs came, at slow pace upon white asses housed with silver and blue, two women with fillets of yellow, and the gowns of the tribe under long veils of gold; and they held up their hands and called him by name, and brother and son. With a sound little and shrill like the voice of a bat Speed the hillman spun round twice, beat the air and fell flat.

Now the women were come and had bowed at the king's feet, and had taken up Speed upon their knees, and the king was fain with his own mouth to discover the circuits of his grace. But when a glimmer of recognition came with a shape of their names, yet the wells of joy lay all untouched, viewless and dark, the heart of the king so swelled with compassion that he had no voice to speak. He went out hastily, and calling his armour-bearer bade him go in and do the telling. "And when all things are made clear to Speed the hillman, bring him out hither, in the midst of all to me hither." And the armour-bearer was pale and shook as he went at the king's bidding.

Under a wide tented canopy of gold sat the king to deal out justice without mercy, and honours and rewards without stint. And many and many came before him, but not the armour-bearer with the man Speed, whose reward was to exceed all others; till the king, impatient, sent for the armour-bearer and questioned.

"My lord, all has been told, and his mother and his sister have told it after me, and he says nothing at all but their names. His eyes never leave them, and now to one and now to the other he thrusts his hand, and beneath the closing of the gown feels at the warm beating of the heart."

"Send home the women," cried the king, "and make straight his understanding."

So the armour-bearer went, and again the king waited in vain, and again sent.

"What of the man Speed? What says he?"

"My lord," said the armour-bearer, "he says nothing at all." The king stamped for anger.

"Is this your duty? Have you not made him to know yet?"

"He knows! he does know. Oh, my lord, my lord."

"Bring him here then," cried the king. And the armour-bearer lifted his arms and cried: "Oh, my lord, my lord!" and went.

Every eye turned for the coming of the man above all others proved loyal and true by transcendent trial. In the midst sat the king on a throne, his nobles and his captains standing thick on either hand, backed by the glittering line of his guard. Six chosen men stood by him, three and three on either side; two swordsmen with blade drawn and up; two bowmen with strung bow and the arrow notched ready on the string; two spearmen with stooped spear. Brought in by the armour-bearer before all these, the red man in the linen tunic, with the smell of torture and the face of dead torture, stood on his feet and lifted a patient inanimate gaze.

Then, smiling, the king rose up from his throne to honour the man. "Oh, faithful and true," he said, "great shall be your reward. No service of these the greatest in all my land has equalled yours. Turn your eyes and behold."

And Speed turned his head this way and that, and saw all heads bowed to the earth honouring him. Only the king and his six guards stood upright, and the armour-bearer who forgot to worship with his body.

"Hear first the recompense that a king gives unasked; then ask your boon, and by the word of one who drank with you in the desert, is it granted.

"Hear all ye the recompense that a king gives unasked.

"It is my will that henceforth and for ever the tribe of the hillmen be free of tribute and toll; and that they have beyond the river of the water-lands as far as their flocks can in a day travel.

"It is my will that the sister of Speed the hillman be taken to wife of what man he shall choose in all my land, barring only the blood royal.

"It is my will that the mother of Speed the hillman be entitled Honourable, and that he make choice of a city for her maintenance.

"Also I will that the yellow fillet be worn of the royal brides.

"And for you, oh, Speed, shall be herds of white asses, and lordship, and trumpets shall be blown for your entrance of a city, and no man, not of my house, shall have place before you. Also the fair virgins of my land shall be sought out for your choice. Also my half-brother who is taken shall be given alive into your hand, that you may strip off his skin to serve you with covering till yours be whole. And the title of Brother to the King shall be yours; and the name you shall bear shall be my name, so only you yield me the gift of your name in exchange."

Then the king took off the boss of gold and set it on the head of Speed, and on his neck a collar of gold, and on his finger the signet-ring; and he took off his mantle stiff with gold and with it clothed Speed the hillman, whose eyes had sunk and whose head had bent while these honours were laid upon him. And the majesty of grace was all the adornment left to the king's person, therefore the more did all heads worship towards him.

Then the hillman lifted his head and looked into the eyes of the gracious king a while: with full understanding he looked: with mild eyes and weary he looked: with eyes that never shifted he held the king as he took the boss from his head and laid it on the throne, and likewise the collar of gold from his neck, and the signet-ring from his finger, and loosed the mantle and let it fall. And he turned, and from the presence of the king and his great ones went out softly upon the hot sand, and turned his face towards the river hills.

All men there looking on the king held breath; his breathing only, in the silence, was heard rattling.

"Shoot!" said the king. Quick, quick the bow-strings rang; an arrow sang out across the sand, stopped mute at the heart of Speed.

Quick, quick and frantic high tore out recall: too late. The voice of the king's agony never reached the heart of Speed. He clutched the sand once and died.

No man but the armour-bearer dared look in the king's face when he stood by the dead man. The arrow stood upright in his back quite still. His hands had all they could hold.

But it was the voice of a king's displeasure that said: "One arrow!"

The armour-bearer with his left hand held up another; held up his right hand: it was stricken through.

"Most Faithful," said the King low, "bury you him—where he lies; you and none other."

He turned away with the face of a king, and the day went down on the last of the army winding away, and the armour-bearer alone smoothing the vacant sand half-way between the caves and the river.

But the king beheld the face of his most faithful armour-bearer never again.

Now when the king died, being of very great age and honours, and entered his chamber of silence for the last time, the new king, his son's son, according to custom entered also for the first time. And there for his reading on the walls with strong lines and fair colours was set out the record of the dead king's life from the star of his birth. And very long and splendid was the tale of his deeds and his conquests; and the woes that fell when his foes flourished because of the sleep of the gods were also set there and not diminished.

To the high-priest the young king said: "What means this arrow that stands in the heart of the king: with his foot on the neck of his half-brother he stands, and an arrow is in his heart; and never after find I him without it sticking there."

But the high-priest could not tell him, nor could any man; and the craftsmen who wrought the walls had not marked in those arrows.

In dull red were the arrows drawn, and in the last of them the line wavered. And the first arrow of all was lined beneath the feet of the king, and a red man giving him drink from a gourd in the desert.

Above the rest of the hillman and above the rest of the king the wind of centuries with equal wing has smoothed the vacant sand.

The Enchanted Buffalo

by L. Frank Baum

L. Frank Baum, developing a trend initiated by Frank R. Stockton, created what can truly be called the first American-styled fairy tales, stories written in particular to please modern American children. Such stories would not take place in a historical past but in the present (in Baum's own time) and in an American (rather than a European) setting. His novel *The Wonderful Wizard of Oz* (1900), is unquestionably his most successful American fairy tale. It spawned a series of thirteen sequels by Baum and many further Oz books by other hands, as well as the famous 1939 film *The Wizard of Oz*.

"The Enchanted Buffalo" was one of a series of nine "Animal Fairy Tales" by Baum that appeared in the *Delineator* between January and September 1905. "The Enchanted Buffalo" presents a mythological background for the bison of the Great Plains of the Midwest. It was the fifth in the series and appeared in the issue for May 1905.

THIS is a tale of the Royal Tribe of Okolom—those mighty buffaloes that once dominated all the Western prairies. Seven hundred strong were the Okolom—great, shaggy creatures herding together and defying all enemies. Their range was well known to the Indians, to lesser herds of bisons and to all the wild animals that roamed in the open; but none cared to molest or interfere with the Royal Tribe.

Dakt was the first King of the Okolom. By odds the

fiercest and most intelligent of his race, he founded the Tribe, made the Laws that directed their actions and led his subjects through wars and dangers until they were acknowledged masters of the prairie.

Dakt had enemies, of course; even in the Royal Tribe. As he grew old it was whispered he was in league with Pagshat, the Evil Genius of the Prairies; yet few really believed the lying tale, and those who did but feared King Dakt the more.

The days of this monarch were prosperous days for the Okolom. In Summer their feeding grounds were ever rich in succulent grasses; in Winter Dakt led them to fertile valleys in the shelter of the mountains.

But in time the great leader grew old and gray. He ceased quarreling and fighting and began to love peace—a sure sign that his days were numbered. Sometimes he would stand motionless for hours, apparently in deep thought. His dignity relaxed; he became peevish; his eye, once shrewd and compelling, grew dim and glazed.

Many of the younger bulls, who coveted his Kingship, waited for Dakt to die; some patiently, and some impatiently. Throughout the herd there was an undercurrent of excitement. Then, one bright Spring morning, as the Tribe wandered in single file toward new feeding grounds, the old King lagged behind. They missed him, presently, and sent Barrag the Bull back over the hills to look for him. It was an hour before this messenger returned, coming into view above the swell of the prairie.

"The King is dead," said Barrag the Bull, as he walked calmly into the midst of the tribe. "Old age has at last overtaken him."

The members of the Okolom looked upon him curiously. Then one said: "There is blood upon your horns, Barrag. You did not wipe them well upon the grass."

Barrag turned fiercely. "The old King is dead," he repeated. "Hereafter, I am the King!"

No one answered in words; but, as the Tribe pressed backward into a dense mass, four young bulls remained standing before Barrag, quietly facing the would-be King. He looked upon them sternly. He had expected to contend for his royal office. It was the Law that any of the Tribe might fight for the right to rule the Okolom. But it surprised him to find there were four who dared dispute his assertion that he was King.

Barrag the Bull had doubtless been guilty of a cowardly act in goring the feeble old King to his death. But he could fight; and fight he did. One after another the powerful young bulls were overthrown, while every member of the Tribe watched the great tournament with eager interest. Barrag was not popular with them, but they could not fail to marvel at his prowess. To the onlookers he seemed inspired by unseen powers that lent him a strength fairly miraculous. They murmured together in awed tones, and the name of the dread Pagshat was whispered more than once.

As the last of the four bulls—the pride of half the Tribe—lay at the feet of the triumphant Barrag, the victor turned and cried aloud: "I am King of the Okolom! Who dares dispute my right to rule?"

For a moment there was silence. Then a fresh young voice exclaimed: "I dare!" and a handsome bull calf marched slowly into the space before Barrag and proudly faced him. A muttered protest swelled from the assemblage until it became a roar. Before it had subsided the young one's mother rushed to his side with a wail of mingled love and fear.

"No, no, Oknu!" she pleaded, desperately. "Do not fight, my child. It is death! See—Barrag is twice thy size. Let him rule the Okolom!"

"But I myself am the son of Dakt the King, and fit to rule in his place," answered Oknu, tossing his head with pride. "This Barrag is an interloper! There is no drop of royal blood in his veins."

"But he is nearly twice thy size!" moaned the mother, nearly frantic with terror. "He is leagued with the Evil Genius. To fight him means defeat and death!"

"He is a murderer!" returned the young bull, glaring upon Barrag. "He has killed his King, my father!"

"Enough!" roared the accused. "I am ready to silence this King's cub. Let us fight."

"No!" said an old bull, advancing from the herd. "Oknu shall not fight to-day. He is too young to face the mighty Barrag. But he will grow, both in size and strength; and then, when he is equal to the contest, he may fight for his father's place among the Okolom. In the meantime we acknowledge Barrag our King!"

A shout of approval went up from all the Tribe, and in the confusion that followed the old Queen thrust her bold son out of sight amidst the throng.

Barrag was King. Proudly he accepted the acclaims of the Okolom—the most powerful Tribe of his race. His ambition was at last fulfilled; his plotting had met with success. The unnatural strength he had displayed had vanquished every opponent. Barrag was King.

Yet as the new ruler led his followers away from the field of conflict and into fresh pastures, his heart was heavy within him. He had not thought of Prince Oknu, the son of the terrible old King he had assisted to meet death. Oknu was a mere youth, half-grown and untried. Yet the look in his dark eyes as he had faced his father's murderer filled Barrag with a vague uneasiness. The youth would grow, and bade fair to become as powerful in time as old Dakt himself. And when he was grown he would fight for the leadership of the Okolom.

Barrag had not reckoned upon that.

When the moon came up, and the prairie was dotted with the reclining forms of the hosts of the Royal Tribe, the new King rose softly to his feet and moved away with silent tread. His pace was slow and stealthy until he had crossed the first rolling swell of the prairie; then he set off at a brisk trot that covered many leagues within the next two hours.

At length Barrag reached a huge rock that towered above the plain. It was jagged and full of rents and fissures, and after a moment's hesitation the King selected an opening and stalked fearlessly into the black shadows. Presently the rift became a tunnel; but Barrag kept on, feeling his way in the darkness with his fore feet. Then a tiny light glimmered ahead, guiding him, and soon after he came into a vast cave hollowed in the centre of the rock. The rough walls were black as ink, yet glistened with an unseen light that shed its mellow but awesome rays throughout the cavern.

Here Barrag paused, saying in a loud voice:

"To thee, O Pagshat, Evil Genius of the Prairies, I give greeting! All has occurred as thou didst predict. The great Dakt is dead, and I, Barrag the Bull, am ruler of the Tribe of Okolom."

For a moment after he ceased the stillness was intense. Then a Voice, grave and deep, answered in the language of the buffaloes: "It is well!"

"But all difficulties are not yet swept aside," continued Barrag. "The old King left a son, an audacious young bull not half grown, who wished to fight me. But the patriarchs of the Tribe bade him wait until he had size and strength. Tell me, can the young Prince Oknu defeat me then?"

"He can," responded the Voice.

"Then what shall I do?" demanded the King. "Thou hast promised to make me secure in my power."

"I promised only to make you King of the Tribe—and you are King. Farther than that, you must protect yourself," the Voice of the Evil Genius made answer. "But, since you are hereafter my slave, I will grant you one more favor—the power to remove your enemy by enchantment."

"And how may I do that?" asked Barrag, eagerly.

"I will give you the means," was the reply. "Bow low thine head, and between the horns I will sprinkle a magical powder."

Barrag obeyed. "And now?" said he, inquiringly.

"Now," responded the unseen Voice, "mark well my injunctions. You must enchant the young Prince and transform him from a buffalo into some small and insignificant animal. Therefore, to-morrow you must choose a spring, and before any of the Tribe has drunk therein, shake well your head above the water, that the powder may sift down into the spring. At the same time centre your thoughts intently upon the animal into which you wish the Prince transformed. Then let him drink of the water in the spring, and the transformation on the instant will be accomplished."

"That is very simple," said Barrag. "Is the powder now between my horns?"

"It is," answered the Voice.

"Then, farewell, O Pagshat!"

From the cavern of the Evil Genius the King felt his way through the passages until he emerged upon the prairie. Then, softly—that he might not disturb the powder of enchantment—he trotted back to the sleeping herd.

Just before he reached it a panther, slender, lithe and black as coal, bounded across his path, and with a quick blow of his hoof Barrag crushed in the animal's skull. "Panthers are miserable creatures," mused the King, as he sought his place among the slumbering buffaloes. "I think I shall transform young Oknu into a black panther."

Secure in his great strength, he forgot that a full-grown panther is the most terrible foe known to his race.

At sunrise the King led the Royal Tribe of Okolom to a tiny spring that welled clear and refreshing from the centre of a fertile valley.

It is the King's right to drink first, but after bending his head above the spring and shaking it vigorously Barrag drew back and turned to the others.

"Come! I will prove that I bear no ill will," said he, treacherously. "Prince Oknu is the eldest son of our dead but venerated King Dakt. It is not for me to usurp his rights. Prince Oknu shall drink first."

Hearing this, the patriarchs looked upon one another in surprise. It was not like Barrag the Bull to give way to another. But the Queen-mother was delighted at the favor shown her son, and eagerly pushed him forward. So Oknu advanced proudly to the spring and drank, while Barrag bent his thoughts intently upon the black panther.

An instant later a roar of horror and consternation came from the Royal Tribe; for the form of Prince Oknu had vanished, and in its place crouched the dark form of a trembling, terrified panther.

Barrag sprang forward. "Death to the vermin!" he cried, and raised his cloven hoof to crush in the panther's skull.

A sudden spring, a flash through the air, and the black panther alighted upon Barrag's shoulders. Then its powerful jaws closed over the buffalo's neck, pressing the sharp teeth far into the flesh.

With a cry of pain and terror the King reared upright, striving to shake off his tormentor; but the panther held fast. Again Barrag reared, whirling this way and that, his eyes staring, his breath quick and short, his great body trembling convulsively.

The others looked on fearfully. They saw the King kneel and roll upon the grass; they saw him arise with his foe still clinging to his back with claw and tooth; they heard the moan of despair that burst from their stricken leader, and the next instant Barrag was speeding away across the prairie like an arrow fresh from a bow, and his bellows of terror grew gradually fainter as he passed from their sight.

The prairie is vast. It is lonely, as well. A vulture, resting on outstretched wings, watched anxiously the flight of Barrag the Bull as hour by hour he sped away to the southward—the one moving thing on all that great expanse.

The sun sank low and buried itself in the prairie's edge. Twilight succeeded, and faded into night. And still a black shadow, leap by leap, sprang madly through the gloom. The jackals paused, listening to the short, quick pants of breath— the irregular hoof-beats of the galloping bull. But while they hesitated the buffalo passed on, with the silent panther still crouched upon its shoulders.

In the black night Barrag suddenly lifted up his voice.

"Come to me, O Pagshat—Evil Genius that thou art— come to my rescue!" he cried.

And presently it seemed that another dark form rushed along beside his own.

"Save me, Pagshat!" he moaned. "Crush thou mine enemy, and set me free!"

A cold whisper reached him in reply: "I cannot!"

"Change him again into his own form," panted Barrag; "hark ye, Pagshat: 'tis the King's son—the cub—the weakling! Disenchant him, ere he proves my death!"

Again came the calm reply, like a breath of Winter sending a chill to his very bones: "I cannot."

Barrag groaned, dashing onward—ever onward.

"When you are dead," continued the Voice, "Prince Oknu will resume his own form. But not before."

"Did we not make a compact?" questioned Barrag, in despairing tone.

"We did," said the Evil Genius, "and I have kept my pact. But you have still to fulfil a pledge to me."

"At my death—only at my death, Pagshat!" cried the bull, trembling violently.

A cruel laugh was the only response. The moon broke through a rift in the clouds, flooding the prairie with silver light. The Evil Genius had disappeared, and the form of the solitary buffalo, with its clinging, silent foe, stumbled blindly across the endless plains.

Barrag had bargained with the Evil One for strength, and the strength of ten bulls was his. The legends do not say how many days and nights the great buffalo fled across the prairies with the black panther upon his shoulders. We know that the Utes saw him, and the Apaches, for their legends tell of it. Far to the south, hundreds of miles away, lived the tribe of the Comanches; and those Indians for many years told their children of Barrag the Bull, and how the Evil Genius of the Prairies, having tempted him to sin, betrayed the self-made King and abandoned him to the vengeance of the Black Panther, who was the enchanted son of the murdered King Dakt.

The strength of ten bulls was in Barrag; but even that could not endure forever. The end of the wild run came at last, and as Barrag fell lifeless upon the prairie the black panther relaxed its hold and was transformed into its original shape. For the enchantment of the Evil Genius was broken, and, restored to his own proper form, Prince Oknu cast one last glance upon his fallen enemy and then turned his head to the north.

It would be many moons before he could rejoin the Royal Tribe of the Okolom.

Since King Barrag had left them in his mad dash to the southward the Royal Tribe had wandered without a leader. They knew Oknu, as the black panther, would never relax his hold on his father's murderer; but how the strange adventure might end all were unable to guess.

So they remained in their well-known feeding grounds and patiently awaited news of the absent ones.

A full year had passed when a buffalo bull was discovered one day crossing the prairie in the direction of the Okolom. Dignity and pride was in his step; his glance was fearless, but full of wisdom. As he stalked majestically to the very centre of the herd his gigantic form towered far above that of any buffalo among them.

A stillness fraught with awe settled upon the Royal Tribe.

"It is old King Dakt, come to life again!" finally exclaimed one of the patriarchs.

"Not so," answered the newcomer, in a clear voice; "but it

is the son of Dakt—who has avenged his father's death. Look upon me! I am Oknu, King of the Royal Tribe of Okolom. Dares any dispute my right to rule?"

No voice answered the challenge. Instead, every head of the seven hundred was bowed in silent homage to Oknu the son of Dakt, the first King of the Okolom.

Chu-bu and Sheemish

by Lord Dunsany

Lord Dunsany was *the* master of the fantasy short story. His tales have the true feel of fables, with a modern wit and a truly mellifluent style, which makes them endlessly rereadable. Equally attractive is how Dunsany playfully overturns fairy-tale conventions. The one Dunsany collection that we know Tolkien certainly read, *The Book of Wonder*, is also one of Dunsany's best. Tolkien retained a clear memory of this collection and of the tale from it called "Chu-bu and Sheemish." In a letter from 1972, Tolkien admitted that being a cult figure in one's own lifetime was not at all pleasant, but he felt that "even the nose of a very modest idol (younger than Chu-bu and not much older than Sheemish) cannot remain entirely untickled by the sweet smell of incense!" In 1967, two interviewers quoted Tolkien as saying, "When you invent a language you more or less catch it out of the air. You say *boo-hoo* and that means something." Tolkien responded to this quotation by writing: "If I attributed meaning to *boo-hoo* I should not in this case be influenced by the words containing *bū* in many other European languages, but by a story by Lord Dunsany (read many years ago) about two idols enshrined in the same temple: Chu-bu and Sheemish. If I used *boo-hoo* at all it would be as the name of some ridiculous, fat, self-important character, mythological or human."

"Chu-bu and Sheemish" first appeared in the 30 December 1911 issue of the *Saturday Review* and was included in *The Book of Wonder* (1912).

IT was the custom on Tuesdays in the temple of Chu-bu for the priests to enter at evening and chant, "There is none but Chu-bu."

And all the people rejoiced and cried out, "There is none but Chu-bu." And honey was offered to Chu-bu, and maize and fat. Thus was he magnified.

Chu-bu was an idol of some antiquity, as may be seen from the colour of the wood. He had been carved out of mahogany, and after he was carved he had been polished. Then they had set him up on the diorite pedestal with the brazier in front of it for burning spices and the flat gold plates for fat. Thus they worshipped Chu-bu.

He must have been there for over a hundred years when one day the priests came in with another idol into the temple of Chu-bu, and set it up on a pedestal near Chu-bu's and sang, "There is also Sheemish."

And all the people rejoiced and cried out, "There is also Sheemish."

Sheemish was palpably a modern idol, and although the wood was stained with a dark-red dye, you could see that he had only just been carved. And honey was offered to Sheemish as well as Chu-bu, and also maize and fat.

The fury of Chu-bu knew no time-limit; he was furious all that night, and next day he was furious still. The situation called for immediate miracles. To devastate the city with a pestilence and kill all his priests was scarcely within his power, therefore he wisely concentrated such divine powers as he had in commanding a little earthquake. "Thus," thought Chu-bu, "will I reassert myself as the only god, and men shall spit upon Sheemish."

Chu-bu willed it and willed it and still no earthquake came, when suddenly he was aware that the hated Sheemish was daring to attempt a miracle too. He ceased to busy himself about the earthquake and listened, or shall I say felt, for what Sheemish was thinking; for gods are aware of what passes in the mind by a sense that is other than any of our five. Sheemish was trying to make an earthquake too.

The new god's motive was probably to assert himself. I doubt if Chu-bu understood or cared for his motive, it was sufficient for an idol already aflame with jealousy that his detestable rival was on the verge of a miracle. All the power of Chu-bu veered round at once and set dead against an earthquake, even a little one. It was thus in the temple of Chu-bu for some time, and then no earthquake came.

To be a god and to fail to achieve a miracle is a despairing sensation; it is as though among men one should determine upon a hearty sneeze and as though no sneeze should come; it is as though one should try to swim in heavy boots or re-member a name that is utterly forgotten: all these pains were Sheemish's.

And upon Tuesday the priests came in, and the people, and they did worship Chu-bu and offered fat to him, saying, "O Chu-bu who made everything," and then the priests sang, "There is also Sheemish"; and Chu-bu was put to shame and spake not for three days.

Now there were holy birds in the temple of Chu-bu, and when the third day was come and the night thereof, it was as it were revealed to the mind of Chu-bu, that there was dirt upon the head of Sheemish.

And Chu-bu spake unto Sheemish as speak the gods, mov-ing no lips nor yet disturbing the silence, saying, "There is dirt upon thy head, O Sheemish." All night long he muttered again and again, "There is dirt upon Sheemish's head." And when it was dawn and voices were heard far off, Chu-bu became exultant with Earth's awakening things, and cried out till the sun was high, "Dirt, dirt, dirt, upon the head of Sheemish," and at noon he said, "So Sheemish would be a god." Thus was Sheemish confounded.

And with Tuesday one came and washed his head with rose-water, and he was worshipped again when they sang "There is also Sheemish." And yet was Chu-bu content, for he said, "The head of Sheemish has been defiled," and again, "His head was defiled, it is enough." And one evening lo! there was dirt on the head of Chu-bu also, and the thing was perceived of Sheemish.

It is not with the gods as it is with men. We are angry one with another and turn from our anger again, but the wrath of the gods is enduring. Chu-bu remembered and Sheemish did not forget. They spake as we do not speak, in silence yet heard of each other, nor were their thoughts as our thoughts. We should not judge them merely by human standards. All night long they spake and all night said these words only: "Dirty Chu-bu," "Dirty Sheemish." "Dirty Chu-bu," "Dirty Sheemish," all night long. Their wrath had not tired at dawn, and neither had wearied of his accusation. And gradually Chu-bu came to realize that he was nothing more than the equal of Sheemish. All gods are jealous, but this equality with the upstart Sheemish, a thing of painted wood a hundred years newer than Chu-bu, and this worship given to Sheemish in Chu-bu's own temple, were particularly bitter. Chu-bu was jealous even for a god; and when Tuesday came again, the third day of Sheemish's worship, Chu-bu could bear it no longer. He felt that his anger must be revealed at all costs, and he returned with all the vehemence of his will to achieving a little earthquake. The worshippers had just gone from his temple when Chu-bu settled his will to attain this miracle, now and then his meditations were disturbed by that now familiar dictum, "Dirty Chu-bu," but Chu-bu willed ferociously, not even stopping to say what he longed to say and had already said nine hundred times, and presently even these interruptions ceased.

They ceased because Sheemish had returned to a project that he had never definitely abandoned, the desire to assert himself and exalt himself over Chu-bu by performing a miracle, and the district being volcanic he had chosen a little earthquake as the miracle most easily accomplished by a small god.

Now an earthquake that is commanded by two gods has double the chance of fulfilment than when it is willed by one, and an incalculably greater chance than when two gods are pulling different ways; as, to take the case of older and greater gods, when the sun and the moon pull in the same direction we have the biggest tides.

Chu-bu knew nothing of the theory of tides, and was too much occupied with his miracle to notice what Sheemish was doing. And suddenly the miracle was an accomplished thing.

It was a very local earthquake, for there are other gods than Chu-bu or even Sheemish, and it was only a little one as the gods had willed, but it loosened some monoliths in a colonnade that supported one side of the temple and the whole of one wall fell in, and the low huts of the people of that city were shaken a little and some of their doors were jammed so that they would not open; it was enough, and for a moment it seemed that it was all; neither Chu-bu nor Sheemish commanded there should be more, but they had set in motion an old law older than Chu-bu, the law of gravity that that colonnade had held back for a hundred years, and the temple of Chu-bu quivered and then stood still, swayed once and was overthrown, on the heads of Chu-bu and Sheemish.

No one rebuilt it, for nobody dared go near such terrible gods. Some said that Chu-bu wrought the miracle, but some said Sheemish, and thereof schism was born; the weakly amiable, alarmed by the bitterness of rival sects, sought compromise and said that both had wrought it, but no one guessed the truth that the thing was done in rivalry.

And a saying arose, and both sects held this belief in common, that whoso toucheth Chu-bu shall die or whoso looketh upon Sheemish.

That is how Chu-bu came into my possession when I travelled once beyond the hills of Ting. I found him in the fallen temple of Chu-bu with his hands and toes sticking up out of the rubbish, lying upon his back, and in that attitude just as I found him I keep him to this day on my mantelpiece, as he is less liable to be upset that way. Sheemish was broken, so I left him where he was.

And there is something so helpless about Chu-bu with his fat hands stuck up in the air that sometimes I am moved out of compassion to bow down to him and pray, saying, "O Chu-bu, thou that made everything, help thy servant."

Chu-bu cannot do much, though once I am sure that at a game of bridge he sent me the ace of trumps after I had not held a card worth having for the whole of the evening. And chance alone could have done as much as that for me. But I do not tell this to Chu-bu.

The Baumoff Explosive

by William Hope Hodgson

C. S. Lewis described William Hope Hodgson's *The Night Land* (1912) as having an "unforgettable sombre splendour" in the images it presents, but he also complained about the sentimental romantic interest in it and the flatness and philological imprecision of its pseudoarchaic prose. Lewis is correct on its defects, but *The Night Land* is still a kind of masterpiece. It has both a tremendous scope and an awesome vision, telling of a far-future world under a dead sun with malevolent but dimly manifest powers inhabiting the endless darkness. Lewis and Tolkien probably read the book in the late 1930s. In the Moria chapters of *The Lord of the Rings* Tolkien evokes the powers of darkness in a manner reminiscent of Hodgson.

"The Baumoff Explosive" is another of Hodgson's tales that manages to convey his obsession with darkness. Here it has additional religious overtones, but few writers are as capable as Hodgson in bringing darkness to life. "The Baumoff Explosive" was written in January 1912 and published in the 20 September 1919 issue of *Nash's Illustrated Weekly*.

DALLY, Whitlaw and I were discussing the recent stupendous explosion which had occurred in the vicinity of Berlin. We were marvelling concerning the extraordinary period of darkness that had followed, and which had aroused so much newspaper comment, with theories galore.

The papers had got hold of the fact that the War Authorities had been experimenting with a new explosive, invented by a certain chemist, named Baumoff, and they referred to it constantly as "The New Baumoff Explosive."

We were in the Club, and the fourth man at our table was John Stafford, who was professionally a medical man, but privately in the Intelligence Department. Once or twice, as we talked, I had glanced at Stafford, wishing to fire a question at him; for he had been acquainted with Baumoff. But I managed to hold my tongue; for I knew that if I asked out pointblank, Stafford (who's a good sort, but a bit of an ass as regards his almost ponderous code-of-silence) would be just as like as not to say that it was a subject upon which he felt he was not entitled to speak.

Oh, I know the old donkey's way; and when he had once said that, we might just make up our minds never to get another word out of him on the matter as long as we lived. Yet, I was satisfied to notice that he seemed a bit restless, as if he were on the itch to shove in his oar; by which I guessed that the papers we were quoting had got things very badly muddled indeed, in some way or other, at least as regarded his friend Baumoff. Suddenly, he spoke:

"What unmitigated, wicked piffle!" said Stafford, quite warm. "I tell you it *is* wicked, this associating of Baumoff's name with war inventions and such horrors. He was the most intensely poetical and earnest follower of the Christ that I have ever met; and it is just the brutal Irony of Circumstance that has attempted to use one of the products of his genius for a purpose of Destruction. But you'll find they won't be able to use it, in spite of their having got hold of Baumoff's formula. As an explosive it is not practicable. It is, shall I say, too impartial; there is no way of controlling it.

"I know more about it, perhaps, than any man alive; for I was Baumoff's greatest friend, and when he died, I lost the best comrade a man ever had. I need make no secret about it to you chaps. I was 'on duty' in Berlin, and I was deputed to get in touch with Baumoff. The government had long had an eye on him; he was an Experimental Chemist, you know, and altogether too jolly clever to ignore. But there was no need to worry about him. I got to know him, and we became enormous friends; for I soon found that *he* would never turn his abilities towards any new war-contrivance; and so, you see, I was able to enjoy my friendship with him, with a comfy conscience—a thing our chaps are not always able to do in their friendships. Oh, I tell you, it's a mean, sneaking, treacherous sort of business, ours; though it's necessary; just as some odd man, or other, has to be a hangsman. There's a number of unclean jobs to be done to keep the Social Machine running!

"I think Baumoff was the most enthusiastic *intelligent* believer in Christ that it will be ever possible to produce. I learned that he was compiling and evolving a treatise of most extraordinary and convincing proofs in support of the more inexplicable things concerning the life and death of Christ. He was, when I became acquainted with him, concentrating his attention particularly upon endeavouring to show that the Darkness of the Cross, between the sixth and the ninth hours, was a very real thing, possessing a tremendous significance. He intended at one sweep to smash utterly all talk of a timely thunderstorm or any of the other more or less inefficient theories which have been brought forward from time to time to explain the occurrence away as being a thing of no particular significance.

"Baumoff had a pet aversion, an atheistic Professor of Physics, named Hautch, who—using the 'marvellous' element of the life and death of Christ, as a fulcrum from which to attack Baumoff's theories—smashed at him constantly, both in his lectures and in print. Particularly did he pour bitter unbelief upon Baumoff's upholding that the Darkness of the Cross was anything more than a gloomy hour or two, magnified into blackness by the emotional inaccuracy of the Eastern mind and tongue.

"One evening, some time after our friendship had become

very real, I called on Baumoff, and found him in a state of tremendous indignation over some article of the Professor's which attacked him brutally; using his theory of the *Significance* of the 'Darkness', as a target. Poor Baumoff! It was certainly a marvellously clever attack; the attack of a thoroughly trained, well-balanced Logician. But Baumoff was something more; he was Genius. It is a title few have any rights to; but it was his!

"He talked to me about his theory, telling me that he wanted to show me a small experiment, presently, bearing out his opinions. In his talk, he told me several things that interested me extremely. Having first reminded me of the fundamental fact that light is conveyed to the eye through the means of that indefinable medium, named the Aether, he went a step further, and pointed out to me that, from an aspect which more approached the primary, Light was a vibration of the Aether, of a certain definite number of waves per second, which possessed the power of producing upon our retina the sensation which we term Light.

"To this, I nodded; being, as of course is everyone, acquainted with so well-known a statement. From this, he took a quick, mental stride, and told me that an ineffably vague, but measurable, darkening of the atmosphere (greater or smaller according to the personality-force of the individual) was always evoked in the immediate vicinity of the human, during any period of great emotional stress.

"Step by step, Baumoff showed me how his research had led him to the conclusion that this queer darkening (a million times too subtle to be apparent to the eye) could be produced only through something which had power to disturb or temporally interrupt or break up the Vibration of Light. In other words, there was, at any time of unusual emotional activity, some disturbance of the Aether in the immediate vicinity of the person suffering, which had some effect upon the Vibration of Light, interrupting it, and producing the aforementioned infinitely vague darkening.

" 'Yes?' I said, as he paused, and looked at me, as if expecting me to have arrived at a certain definite deduction through his remarks. 'Go on.'

" 'Well,' he said, 'don't you see, the subtle darkening around the person suffering, is greater or less, according to the personality of the suffering human. Don't you?'

" 'Oh!' I said, with a little gasp of astounded comprehension, 'I see what you mean. You—you mean that if the agony of a person of ordinary personality can produce a faint disturbance of the Aether, with a consequent faint darkening, then the Agony of Christ, possessed of the Enormous Personality of the Christ, would produce a terrific disturbance of the Aether, and therefore, it might chance, of the Vibration of Light, and that this is the true explanation of the Darkness of the Cross; and that the fact of such an extraordinary and apparently unnatural and improbable Darkness having been recorded is not a thing to weaken the Marvel of Christ. But one more unutterably wonderful, infallible proof of His God-like power? Is that it? Is it? Tell me?'

"Baumoff just rocked on his chair with delight, beating one fist into the palm of his other hand, and nodding all the time to my summary. How he *loved* to be understood; as the Searcher always craves to be understood.

" 'And now,' he said, 'I'm going to show you something.'

"He took a tiny, corked test-tube out of his waistcoat pocket, and emptied its contents (which consisted of a single, grey-white grain, about twice the size of an ordinary pin's head) on to his dessert plate. He crushed it gently to powder with the ivory handle of a knife, then damped it gently, with a single minim of what I supposed to be water, and worked it up into a tiny patch of grey-white paste. He then took out his gold tooth-pick, and thrust it into the flame of a small chemist's spirit lamp, which had been lit since dinner as a pipe-lighter. He held the gold tooth-pick in the flame, until the narrow, gold blade glowed white hot.

" 'Now look!' he said, and touched the end of the tooth-pick against the infinitesimal patch upon the dessert plate. There came a swift little violet flash, and suddenly I found that I was staring at Baumoff through a sort of transparent darkness, which faded swiftly into a black opaqueness. I thought at first this must be the complementary effect of the flash upon the retina. But a minute passed, and we were still in that extraordinary darkness.

" 'My Gracious! Man! What is it?' I asked, at last.

"His voice explained then, that he had produced, through the medium of chemistry, an exaggerated effect which simulated, to some extent, the disturbance in the Aether produced by waves thrown off by any person during an emotional crisis or agony. The waves, or vibrations, sent out by his experiment produced only a partial simulation of the effect he wished to show me—merely the temporary interruption of the Vibration of Light, with the resulting darkness in which we both now sat.

" 'That stuff,' said Baumoff, 'would be a tremendous explosive, under certain conditions.'

"I heard him puffing at his pipe, as he spoke, but instead of the glow of the pipe shining out visible and red, there was only a faint glare that wavered and disappeared in the most extraordinary fashion.

" 'My Goodness!' I said, 'when's this going away?' And I stared across the room to where the big kerosene lamp showed only as a faintly glimmering patch in the gloom; a vague light that shivered and flashed oddly, as though I saw it through an immense gloomy depth of dark and disturbed water.

" 'It's all right,' Baumoff's voice said from out of the darkness. 'It's going now; in five minutes the disturbance will have quieted, and the waves of light will flow off evenly from the lamp in their normal fashion. But, whilst we're waiting, isn't it immense, eh?'

" 'Yes,' I said. 'It's wonderful; but it's rather unearthly, you know.'

" 'Oh, but I've something much finer to show you,' he said. 'The real thing. Wait another minute. The darkness is going. See! You can see the light from the lamp now quite plainly. It looks as if it were submerged in a boil of waters, doesn't it? that are growing clearer and clearer and quieter and quieter all the time.'

"It was as he said; and we watched the lamp, silently, until all signs of the disturbance of the light-carrying medium had ceased. Then Baumoff faced me once more.

" 'Now,' he said. 'You've seen the somewhat casual effects of just crude combustion of that stuff of mine. I'm going to show you the effects of combusting it in the human furnace, that is, in my own body; and then, you'll see one of the great wonders of Christ's death reproduced on a miniature scale.'

"He went across to the mantelpiece, and returned with a small, 120 minim glass and another of the tiny, corked test-tubes, containing a single grey-white grain of his chemical substance. He uncorked the test-tube, and shook the grain of substance into the minim glass, and then, with a glass stirring-rod, crushed it up in the bottom of the glass, adding water, drop by drop as he did so, until there were sixty minims in the glass.

" 'Now!' he said, and lifting it, he drank the stuff. 'We will give it thirty-five minutes,' he continued; 'then, as carbonization proceeds, you will find my pulse will increase, as also the respiration, and presently there will come the darkness again, in the subtlest, strangest fashion; but accompanied now by certain physical and psychic phenomena, which will be owing to the fact that the vibrations it will throw off, will be blent into what I might call the emotional-vibrations, which I shall give off in my distress. These will be enormously intensified, and you will possibly experience an extraordinarily interesting demonstration of the soundness of my more theoretical reasonings. I tested it by myself last week' (He waved a bandaged finger at me), 'and I read a paper to the Club on the results. They are very enthusiastic, and have promised their co-operation in the big demonstration I intend to give on next Good Friday—that's seven weeks off, to-day.'

"He had ceased smoking; but continued to talk quietly in this fashion for the next thirty-five minutes. The Club to which he had referred was a peculiar association of men, banded together under the presidentship of Baumoff himself, and having for their appellation the title of—so well as I can translate it—'The Believers And Provers Of Christ'. If I may say so, without any thought of irreverence, they were, many of them, men fanatically crazed to uphold the Christ. You will agree later, I think, that I have not used an incorrect term, in describing the bulk of the members of this extraordinary club, which was, in its way, well worthy of one of the religio-maniacal extrudences which have been forced into temporary being by certain of the more religiously-emotional minded of our cousins across the water.

"Baumoff looked at the clock; then held out his wrist to me. 'Take my pulse,' he said, 'it's rising fast. Interesting data, you know.'

"I nodded, and drew out my watch. I had noticed that his respirations were increasing; and I found his pulse running evenly and strongly at 105. Three minutes later, it had risen to 175, and his respirations to 41. In a further three minutes, I took his pulse again, and found it running at 203, but with the rhythm regular. His respirations were then 49. He had, as I knew, excellent lungs, and his heart was sound. His lungs, I may say, were of exceptional capacity, and there was at this stage no marked dyspnoea. Three minutes later I found the pulse to be 227, and the respiration 54.

" 'You've plenty of red corpuscles, Baumoff!' I said. 'But I hope you're not going to overdo things.'

"He nodded at me, and smiled; but said nothing. Three minutes later, when I took the last pulse, it was 233, and the two sides of the heart were sending out unequal quantities of blood, with an irregular rhythm. The respiration had risen to

67 and was becoming shallow and ineffectual, and dyspnoea was becoming very marked. The small amount of arterial blood leaving the left side of the heart betrayed itself in the curious bluish and white tinge of the face.

" 'Baumoff!' I said, and began to remonstrate; but he checked me, with a queerly invincible gesture.

" 'It's all right!' he said, breathlessly, with a little note of impatience. 'I know what I'm doing all the time. You must remember I took the same degree as you in medicine.'

"It was quite true. I remembered then that he had taken his M.D. in London; and this in addition to half a dozen other degrees in different branches of the sciences in his own country. And then, even as the memory reassured me that he was not acting in ignorance of the possible danger, he called out in a curious, breathless voice:

" 'The Darkness! It's beginning. Take note of every single thing. Don't bother about me. I'm all right!'

"I glanced swiftly round the room. It was as he had said. I perceived it now. There appeared to be an extraordinary quality of gloom growing in the atmosphere of the room. A kind of bluish gloom, vague, and scarcely, as yet, affecting the transparency of the atmosphere to light.

"Suddenly, Baumoff did something that rather sickened me. He drew his wrist away from me, and reached out to a small metal box, such as one sterilizes a hypodermic in. He opened the box, and took out four rather curious looking drawing-pins, I might call them, only they had spikes of steel fully an inch long, whilst all around the rim of the heads (which were also of steel) there projected downward, parallel with the central spike, a number of shorter spikes, maybe an eighth of an inch long.

"He kicked off his pumps; then stooped and slipped his socks off, and I saw that he was wearing a pair of linen inner-socks.

" 'Antiseptic!' he said, glancing at me. 'Got my feet ready before you came. No use running unnecessary risks.' He gasped as he spoke. Then he took one of the curious little steel spikes.

" 'I've sterilized them,' he said; and therewith, with deliberation, he pressed it in up to the head into his foot between the second and third branches of the dorsal artery.

" 'For God's sake, what are you doing!' I said, half rising from my chair.

" 'Sit down!' he said, in a grim sort of voice. 'I can't have any interference. I want you simply to observe; keep note of *everything*. You ought to thank me for the chance, instead of worrying me, when you know I shall go my own way all the time.'

"As he spoke, he had pressed in the second of the steel spikes up to the hilt in his left instep, taking the same precaution to avoid the arteries. Not a groan had come from him; only his face betrayed the effect of this additional distress.

" 'My dear chap!' he said, observing my upsetness. 'Do be sensible. I know exactly what I'm doing. There simply *must be distress,* and the readiest way to reach that condition is through physical pain.' His speech had become a series of spasmodic words, between gasps, and sweat lay in great clear drops upon his lip and forehead. He slipped off his belt and proceeded to buckle it round both the back of his chair and his waist; as if he expected to need some support from falling.

" 'It's wicked!' I said. Baumoff made an attempt to shrug his heaving shoulders, that was, in its way, one of the most piteous things that I have seen, in its sudden laying bare of the agony that the man was making so little of.

"He was now cleaning the palms of his hands with a little sponge, which he dipped from time to time in a cup of solution. I knew what he was going to do, and suddenly he jerked out, with a painful attempt to grin, an explanation of his bandaged finger. He had held his finger in the flame of the spirit lamp, during his previous experiment; but now, as he made clear in gaspingly uttered words, he wished to simulate as far as possible the actual conditions of the great scene that he had so much in mind. He made it so clear to me that we might expect to experience something very extraordinary, that I was conscious of a sense of almost superstitious nervousness.

" 'I wish you wouldn't, Baumoff!' I said.

" 'Don't—be—silly!' he managed to say. But the two latter words were more groans than words; for between each, he had thrust home right to the heads in the palms of his hands the two remaining steel spikes. He gripped his hands shut, with a sort of spasm of savage determination, and I saw the point of one of the spikes break through the back of his hand, between the extensor tendons of the second and third fingers. A drop of blood beaded the point of the spike. I looked at Baumoff's face; and he looked back steadily at me.

" 'No interference,' he managed to ejaculate. 'I've not gone through all this for nothing. I know—what—I'm doing. Look—it's coming. Take note—everything!'

"He relapsed into silence, except for his painful gasping. I realised that I must give way, and I stared round the room, with a peculiar commingling of an almost nervous discomfort and a stirring of very real and sober curiosity.

" 'Oh,' said Baumoff, after a moment's silence, 'something's going to happen. I can tell. Oh, wait—till I—I have my—big demonstration. I'll show that brute Hautch.'

"I nodded; but I doubt that he saw me; for his eyes had a distinctly in-turned look, the iris was rather relaxed. I glanced away round the room again; there was a distinct occasional breaking up of the light-rays from the lamp, giving a coming-and-going effect.

"The atmosphere of the room was also quite plainly darker—heavy, with an extraordinary *sense* of gloom. The bluish tint was unmistakably more in evidence; but there was, as yet, none of that opacity which we had experienced before, upon simple combustion, except for the occasional, vague coming-and-going of the lamp-light.

"Baumoff began to speak again, getting his words out between gasps. 'Th'—this dodge of mine gets the—pain into the—the—right place. Right association of—of ideas—emotions—for—best—results. You follow me? Parallelising things—as—much as—possible. Fixing whole attention—on the—the death scene—'

"He gasped painfully for a few moments. 'We demonstrate truth of—of The Darkening; but—but there's psychic effect to be—looked for, through—results of parallelisation of—conditions. May have extraordinary simulation of—the *actual thing*. Keep note. Keep note.' Then, suddenly, with a clear, spasmodic burst: 'My God, Stafford, keep note of everything. Something's going to happen. Something—wonderful—Promise not—to bother me. I know—what I'm doing.'

"Baumoff ceased speaking, with a gasp, and there was only the labour of his breathing in the quietness of the room. As I stared at him, halting from a dozen things I needed to say, I realised suddenly that I could no longer see him quite plainly; a sort of wavering in the atmosphere, between us, made him seem momentarily unreal. The whole room had darkened perceptibly in the last thirty seconds; and as I stared around, I realised that there was a constant invisible swirl in the fast-deepening, extraordinary blue gloom that seemed now to permeate everything. When I looked at the lamp, alternate flashings of light and blue—darkness followed each other with an amazing swiftness.

" 'My God!' I heard Baumoff whispering in the half-darkness, as if to himself, 'how did Christ bear the nails!'

"I stared across at him, with an infinite discomfort, and an irritated pity troubling me; but I knew it was no use to remonstrate now. I saw him vaguely distorted through the wavering tremble of the atmosphere. It was somewhat as if I looked at him through convolutions of heated air; only there were marvellous waves of blue-blackness making gaps in my sight. Once I saw his face clearly, full of an infinite pain, that was somehow, seemingly, more spiritual than physical, and dominating everything was an expression of enormous resolution and concentration, making the livid, sweat-damp, agonized face somehow heroic and splendid.

"And then, drenching the room with waves and splashes of opaqueness, the vibration of his abnormally stimulated agony finally broke up the vibration of Light. My last, swift glance round, showed me, as it seemed, the invisible Aether boiling and eddying in a tremendous fashion; and, abruptly, the flame of the lamp was lost in an extraordinary swirling patch of light, that marked its position for several moments, shimmering and deadening, shimmering and deadening; until, abruptly, I saw neither that glimmering patch of light, nor anything else. I was suddenly lost in a black opaqueness of night, through which came the fierce, painful breathing of Baumoff.

"A full minute passed; but so slowly that, if I had not been counting Baumoff's respirations, I should have said that it was five. Then Baumoff spoke suddenly, in a voice that was, somehow, curiously changed—a certain toneless note in it:

" 'My God!' he said, from out of the darkness, 'what must Christ have suffered!'

"It was in the succeeding silence, that I had the first realisation that I was vaguely afraid; but the feeling was too indefinite and unfounded, and I might say subconscious, for me to face it out. Three minutes passed, whilst I counted the almost desperate respirations that came to me through the darkness. Then Baumoff began to speak again, and still in that peculiarly altering voice:

" 'By Thy Agony and Bloody Sweat,' he muttered. Twice he repeated this. It was plain indeed that he had fixed his whole attention with tremendous intensity, in his abnormal state, upon the death scene.

"The effect upon me of his intensity was interesting and in some ways extraordinary. As well as I could, I analysed my sensations and emotions and general state of mind, and realised that Baumoff was producing an effect upon me that was almost hypnotic.

"Once, partly because I wished to get my level by the aid of a normal remark, and also because I was suddenly newly anxious by a change in the breathsounds, I asked Baumoff how he was. My voice going with a peculiar and really uncomfortable blankness through that impenetrable blackness of opacity.

"He said: 'Hush! I'm carrying the Cross.' And, do you know, the effect of those simple words, spoken in that new, toneless voice, in that atmosphere of almost unbearable tenseness, was so powerful that, suddenly, with eyes wide open, I saw Baumoff clear and vivid against that unnatural darkness, carrying a Cross. Not, as the picture is usually shown of the Christ, with it crooked over the shoulder; but with the Cross gripped just under the cross-piece in his arms, and the end trailing behind, along rocky ground. I saw even the pattern of the grain of the rough wood, where some of the bark had been ripped away; and under the trailing end there was a tussock of tough wire-grass, that had been uprooted by the lowing end, and dragged and ground along upon the rocks, between the end of the Cross and the rocky ground. I can see the thing now, as I speak. Its vividness was extraordinary; but it had come and gone like a flash, and I was sitting there in the darkness, mechanically counting the respirations; yet unaware that I counted.

"As I sat there, it came to me suddenly—the whole entire marvel of the thing that Baumoff had achieved. I was sitting there in a darkness which was an actual reproduction of the miracle of the Darkness of the Cross. In short, Baumoff had, by producing in himself an abnormal condition, developed an Energy of Emotion that must have almost, in its effects, paralleled the Agony of the Cross. And in so doing, he had shown from an entirely new and wonderful point, the indisputable truth of the stupendous personality and the enormous spiritual force of the Christ. He had evolved and made practical to the average understanding a proof that would make to live again the *reality* of that wonder of the world— *CHRIST.* And for all this, I had nothing but admiration of an almost stupefied kind.

"But, at this point, I felt that the experiment should stop. I had a strangely nervous craving for Baumoff to end it right there and then, and not to try to parallel the psychic conditions. I had, even then, by some queer aid of subconscious suggestion, a vague reaching-out-towards the danger of 'monstrosity' being induced, instead of any actual knowledge gained.

" 'Baumoff!' I said. 'Stop it.'

"But he made no reply, and for some minutes there followed a silence, that was unbroken, save by his gasping breathing. Abruptly, Baumoff said, between his gasps: 'Woman— behold—thy—son.' He muttered this several times, in the same uncomfortably toneless voice in which he had spoken since the darkness became complete.

" 'Baumoff,' I said again. 'Baumoff! *Stop it!*' And as I listened for his answer, I was relieved to think that his breathing was less shallow. The abnormal demand for oxygen was evidently being met, and the extravagant call upon the heart's efficiency was being relaxed.

" 'Baumoff!' I said, once more. 'Baumoff! Stop it!'

"And, as I spoke, abruptly, I thought the room was shaken a little.

"Now, I had already as you will have realised, been vaguely conscious of a peculiar and growing nervousness. I think that is the word that best describes it, up to this moment. At this curious little shake that seemed to stir through the utterly dark room, I was suddenly more than nervous. I felt a thrill of actual and literal fear; yet with no sufficient cause of reason to justify me; so that, after sitting very tense for some long minutes, and feeling nothing further, I decided that I needed to take myself in hand, and keep a firmer grip upon my nerves. And then, just as I had arrived at this more

comfortable state of mind, the room was shaken again, with
the most curious and sickening oscillatory movement, that
was beyond all comfort of denial.

" 'My God!' I whispered. And then, with a sudden effort
of courage, I called: 'Baumoff! *For God's sake stop it!*'

"You've no idea of the effort it took to speak aloud into
that darkness; and when I did speak, the sound of my voice
set me afresh on edge. It went so empty and *raw* across the
room; and somehow, the room seemed to be incredibly big.
Oh, I wonder whether you realise how beastly I felt, without
my having to make any further effort to tell you.

"And Baumoff never answered a word; but I could hear
him breathing, a little fuller; though still heaving his thorax
painfully, in his need for air. The incredible shaking of the
room eased away; and there succeeded a spasm of quiet, in
which I felt that it was my duty to get up and step across to
Baumoff's chair. But I could not do it. Somehow, I would not
have touched Baumoff then for any cause whatever. Yet,
even in that moment, as now I know, I was not aware that I
was *afraid* to touch Baumoff.

"And then the oscillations commenced again. I felt the
seat of my trousers slide against the seat of my chair, and I
thrust out my legs, spreading my feet against the carpet, to
keep me from sliding off one way or the other on to the floor.
To say I was afraid, was not to describe my state at all. I was
terrified. And suddenly, I had comfort, in the most extraordinary fashion; for a single idea literally glazed into my brain,
and gave me a reason to which to cling. It was a single line:

" 'Aether, the soul of iron and sundry stuffs' which Baumoff had once taken as a text for an extraordinary lecture on
vibrations, in the earlier days of our friendship. He had for-
mulated the suggestion that, in embryo, Matter was, from a
primary aspect, a localised vibration, traversing a closed
orbit. These primary localised vibrations were inconceivably
minute. But were capable, under certain conditions, of combining under the action of keynote-vibrations into secondary

vibrations of a size and shape to be determined by a multitude of only guessable factors. These would sustain their new form, so long as nothing occurred to disorganise their combination or depreciate or divert their energy—their unity being partially determined by the inertia of the still Aether outside of the closed path which their area of activities covered. And such combination of the primary localised vibrations was neither more nor less than matter. Men and worlds, aye! and universes.

"And then he had said the thing that struck me most. He had said, that if it were possible to produce a vibration of the Aether of a sufficient energy, it would be possible to disorganise or confuse the vibration of matter. That, given a machine capable of creating a vibration of the Aether of a sufficient energy, he would engage to destroy not merely the world, but the whole universe itself, including heaven and hell themselves, if such places existed, and had such existence in a material form.

"I remember how I looked at him, bewildered by the pregnancy and scope of his imagination. And now his lecture had come back to me to help my courage with the sanity of reason. Was it not possible that the Aether disturbance which he had produced, had sufficient energy to cause some disorganisation of the vibration of matter, in the immediate vicinity, and had thus created a miniature quaking of the ground all about the house, and so set the house gently a-shake?

"And then, as this thought came to me, another and a greater, flashed into my mind. 'My God!' I said out loud into the darkness of the room. It explains one more mystery of the Cross, the disturbance of the Aether caused by Christ's Agony, disorganised the vibration of matter in the vicinity of the Cross, and there was then a small local earthquake, which opened the graves, and rent the veil, possibly by disturbing its supports. And, of course, the earthquake was an effect, and *not* a cause, as belittlers of the Christ have always insisted.

" 'Baumoff!' I called. 'Baumoff, you've proved another thing. Baumoff! Baumoff! Answer me. Are you all right?'

"Baumoff answered, sharp and sudden out of the darkness; but not to me:

" 'My God!' he said. 'My God!' His voice came out at me, a cry of veritable mental agony. He was suffering, in some hypnotic, induced fashion, something of the very agony of the Christ Himself.

" 'Baumoff!' I shouted, and forced myself to my feet. I heard his chair clattering, as he sat there and shook. 'Baumoff!'

"An extraordinary quake went across the floor of the room, and I heard a creaking of the woodwork, and something fell and smashed in the darkness. Baumoff's gasps hurt me; but I stood there. I dared not go to him. I knew *then* that I was afraid of him—of his condition, or something I don't know what. But, oh, I was horribly afraid of him.

" 'Bau—' I began, but suddenly I was afraid even to speak to him. And I could not move. Abruptly, he cried out in a tone of incredible anguish:

" 'Eloi, Eloi, lama sabach*thani!*'* But the last word changed in his mouth, from his dreadful hypnotic grief and pain, to a scream of simply infernal terror.

"And, suddenly, a horrible mocking voice roared out in the room, from Baumoff's chair: 'Eloi, Eloi, lama sabach-thani!'

"Do you understand, the voice was not Baumoff's at all. It was not a voice of despair; but a voice sneering in an incredible, bestial, monstrous fashion. In the succeeding silence, as I stood in an ice of fear, I knew that Baumoff no longer gasped. The room was absolutely silent, the most dreadful and silent place in all this world. Then I bolted; caught my foot, probably in the invisible edge of the hearth-rug, and pitched headlong into a blaze of internal brain-

---

* Hebrew, "My God! My God! Why hast Thou forsaken me?"

stars. After which, for a very long time, certainly some hours, I knew nothing of any kind.

"I came back into this Present, with a dreadful headache oppressing me, to the exclusion of all else. But the Darkness had dissipated. I rolled over on to my side, and saw Baumoff and forgot even the pain in my head. He was leaning forward towards me: his eyes wide open, but dull. His face was enormously swollen, and there was, somehow, something *beastly* about him. He was dead, and the belt about him and the chair-back, alone prevented him from falling forward on to me. His tongue was thrust out of one corner of his mouth. I shall always remember how he looked. He was leering, like a human-beast, more than a man.

"I edged away from him, across the floor; but I never stopped looking at him, until I had got to the other side of the door, and closed between us. Of course, I got my balance in a bit, and went back to him; but there was nothing I could do.

"Baumoff died of heart-failure, of course, obviously! I should never be so foolish as to suggest to any sane jury that, in his extraordinary, self-hypnotised, defenseless condition, he was 'entered' by some Christ-apeing Monster of the Void. I've too much respect for my own claim to be a common-sensible man, to put forward such an idea with seriousness! Oh, I know I may seem to speak with a jeer; but what can I do but jeer at myself and all the world, when I dare not acknowledge, even secretly to myself, what my own thoughts are. Baumoff did, undoubtedly die of heart-failure; and, for the rest, how much was I hypnotised into believing. Only, there was over by the far wall, where it had been shaken down to the floor from a solidly fastened-up bracket, a little pile of glass that had once formed a piece of beautiful Venetian glassware. You remember that I heard something fall, when the room shook. Surely the room *did* shake? Oh, I must stop thinking. My head goes round.

"The explosive the papers are talking about. Yes, that's Baumoff's; that makes it all seem true, doesn't it? They had the darkness at Berlin, after the explosion. There is no getting away from *that*. The Government know only that Baumoff's formula is capable of producing the largest quantity of gas, in the shortest possible time. That, in short, it is ideally *explosive*. So it is; but I imagine it will prove an explosive, as I have already said, and as experience has proved, a little too impartial in its action for it to create enthusiasm on either side of a battlefield. Perhaps this is but a mercy, in disguise; certainly a mercy, if Baumoff's theories as to the possibility of disorganising matter, be anywhere near to the truth.

"I have thought sometimes that there might be a more normal explanation of the dreadful thing that happened at the end. Baumoff *may* have ruptured a blood-vessel in the brain, owing to the enormous arterial pressure that his experiment induced; and the voice I heard and the mockery and the horrible expression and leer may have been nothing more than the immediate outburst and expression of the natural 'obliqueness' of a deranged mind, which so often turns up a side of a man's nature and produces an inversion of character, that is the very complement of his normal state. And certainly, poor Baumoff's normal religious attitude was one of marvellous reverence and loyalty towards the Christ.

"Also, in support of this line of explanation, I have frequently observed that the voice of a person suffering from mental derangement is frequently wonderfully changed, and has in it often a very repellant and inhuman quality. I try to think that this explanation fits the case. But I can never forget that room. Never."

The Regent of the North

by Kenneth Morris

Kenneth Morris's tales span the world's mythologies, ranging from Celtic to Toltec, Greek to Taoist, and Buddhist to Roman. Each of his tales reflects a deep understanding of the underlying mythology or religious system, yet they are not retellings of familiar tales but new stories. There is no evidence that Tolkien knew of Morris, a Welshman who lived for many years in California before returning to his native Wales, but it seems that he would have appreciated Morris's deft evoking of the religion of the Vikings as is found in the following story. "The Regent of the North" was first published in the August 1915 issue of the *Theosophical Path*.

THE northern winter is altogether ghostly and elemental; there is no friendliness to man to be found in it. There, the snow has its proper habitation; there, in the gaunt valleys of Lapland, in the terrible, lonely desolations, the Frost Giants abide. They are servants of the Regent of the North: smiths, that have the awful mountains for their anvils; and, with cold for flame tempering water into hardness, fashion spears and swords of piercing ice, or raise glittering ramparts about the Pole. All for the dreadful pleasure of doing it! They go about their work silently in the gray darkness; heaven knows what dreams may be haunting them—dreams that no mind could imagine, unless death had already frozen its brain. When the wind wolves come howling down from the Pole, innumerous, unflagging, and insatiable: when the snow drives down, a horde of ghosts wandering senseless, hurrying and hurrying through the night: the giants do their work. They make no sound: they fashion terror, and illimitable terror, and terror. . . . Or—is it indeed only terror that they fashion? . . .

And then spring comes, and the sun rises at last on the world of the North. The snow melts in the valleys; white wisps of cloud float over skies blue as the gentian; over a thousand lakes all turquoise and forget-me-not: waters infinitely calm and clear, infinitely lovely. Then the snow on the mountain dreams dazzling whiteness by day, defiantly glittering against the sun; dreams tenderness, all faint rose and heliotrope and amber, in the evening; blue solemn mystery in the night. Quick with this last mysterious dreaming!—for the nights are hurrying away; they grow shorter always; they slink Poleward, immersed in ghostly preoccupations; by midsummer they have vanished altogether. Then the sun peers incessantly wizardlike over the horizon; the dumb rocks and the waters are invincibly awake, alert, and radiant with some magic instilled into them by the Regent of the North. . . . It is in this spring- and summer-time that you shall see bloom the flowers of Lapland: great pure blossoms in blue and purple and rose and citron, such as are not found elsewhere in the world. The valleys are a dreaming, silent wonder with the myriads there are of them—silent, for the Lapps have followed the reindeer, and the reindeer have followed the snows.

Into this region it was that Halfdan the Aged came, when he was tired of the new ways and faith that had come into the south. The viking days were over forever, one could see that. Meek, crozier-bearing men had invaded the realms of Odin and Balder; laying terrible axes of soft words, of chanted prayers and hymns, to the roots of—? All the ancient virtue of the race, said Halfdan the Aged; all the mighty and mystic dreams that had been surging through the Northlands these hundreds of years; sending the brave forth to wonderful deeds and wonderful visions about the seas and coasts of the world. And Inge the king at Upsala, forgetting all things noble and generous, had foresworn Odin and battle-breaking Thor; had foresworn Balder the Beautiful; had welcomed these chanting, canting foreigners, and decreed their faith for his people. So that now nothing remained but a fat, slothful life and the straw-death at the end of it: there should be no more Viking expeditions, no more Valhalla; no more Asgard and the Gods. "Faugh!" thought Halfdan Halfdansson, old hero of a hundred raids in the west and south; "this small-souled life for them that can abide it; it is worse than death for a *Man's Son.*"

Not but that his own days of action were over: had been these ten years; had passed with the age of the Vikings. Also his seven sons were in Valhalla long since, and beyond being troubled; they had fallen like men in battle before there was any talk of this Christian heaven and hell; as for his wife, she, royal-hearted woman, had died when the youngest of them was born. So that it would have been easy for him to cut himself adrift from the world and voyage down through pleasant dreams towards death, after the fashion of clean old age. He had already put by, somewhat sadly, the prospect of future expeditions, and was reconciling himself to old age and its illumination, when King Inge went besotted over the foreign faith. From his house, Bravik on the hillside, through whose door the sea-winds blew in salt and excellent, he could watch the changes of the Swan-way, and nourish peace upon the music of the sea. Below at the foot of the hill, was the harbor from which his ships used to sail; drawn up on the beach, sheer hulks, still they lay there, the *Wild Swan* and the *Dragon,* accustomed to Mediterranean voyagings of old. For his own life, he found no action to regret in it; it had all been heroic doing, clean and honorable and vigorous; and the Gods had had their proper place in it, lighting it mysteriously from within.

But what room was there for dreaming, when the cry *The glory is departed!* rang so insistent? The new order liked him so little, that in place of peace and its accompanying wisdom, the years brought him unease increasingly. With his old skalds about him, to sing to him in the hall in the evenings; with his old and pagan servants, faithful all of them to the past as to himself, he watched the change coming on Sweden with disquietude and disgust; and for the first time in his life, experienced a kind of fear. But it was a pagan and great-hearted fear, and had nought to do with his own fate or future.

He knew the kind of tales these becroziered men from the south were telling, and that were becoming increasingly a substitute for the old valiant stories of the skalds. A man had come to Bravik once, and was welcomed there, who, when the feast was over, and the poets were relating their sagas, had risen in his turn with a story to tell—of a white-faced, agonizing God, who died a felon's death amongst ignoble and unwarlike people. Halfdan had listened to it with growing anger: where was the joy, where the mighty and beautiful forms, the splendid life, of the Divine Ones in this? At the end of it he had called to the stranger:

"Thy tale is a vile one, O foreign skald! Fraught with lies it is, and unwholesome to the hearing."

"Lies it is not, but the truth of truths, O chieftain, and except thou believest, thou shalt suffer the vengeance of God throughout eternity."

"Go!" cried the Viking; and in the one word rang all the outraged ideals that had stood him in stead for sixty years. One does not defend his standpoint, but merely states it. He saw none of the virtues of Christianity; while its crude presentation shocked his religious feelings as profoundly as the blatant negations of atheism shock those of the pious of our own day. And his aspirations had a core of real spirituality in them. The Gods, for these high-souled Pagans, were the fountain of right, the assurance and stability of virtue. Thor,

probably, stood for courage, spiritual as well as physical;
Odin for a secret and internal wisdom; Balder for a peace
that passeth understanding. Things did not end in Berserker
fury: the paths of the spirit were open, or had been of old;
beyond the hero stood the God; beyond strife, a golden peace
founded on the perfection of life. Wars, adventure, and
strenuous living were to fashion something divinely calm
and grand in the lives of men; that once established, and no
possibility of evil left lurking in any human soul, Balder's
reign would come, something like the glow and afterglow of
sunset, or a vast and perfect music enveloping the world—
there should be a love as of comrades, as of dear brothers,
between all men. But that Peace of Balder and of Odin was
separated by all Berserkerism from the peace that is fear or
greed. It was a high, perpetual exultation: a heaven into
which the meek and weak could not slide passively, but the
strong man armed (spiritually) should take it by storm.—
And here was negation of the doctrine of the strong man
armed; here was proclaiming godhood a thing not robust,
joyless, unbeautiful. . . . Old Halfdan went moody and depressed for a week after the priest's visit. The serene Balder-
mood, into the fulness of which now, in the evening of his
life, he had the right to grow naturally had been attacked, and
could not be induced to return. A God crucified! . . . his soul
cried out for Gods triumphant.

Inge might launch his decrees at Upsala; at Bravik, not the
least intention existed of obeying them. With dogged and de-
fiant faith Halfdan performed the rites of the religion of
Odin, having dismissed from his house all who hankered
after the newly proclaimed orthodoxy. With it all, he was ill
at ease; as seeing that Sweden would not long hold a man
faithful to her ancient ideals. Tales were brought in, how
such and such a pagan chief had suffered the king's vengeance,
or had been compelled to profess and call himself Christian.
Heaven knew when his own turn might come; Inge would
not overlook him forever. Well, there would be no giving

in for him, no lip profession—a thing not in him to understand. He could swing a battle-ax yet, at the head of his retainers; he could die in his burning house like a Viking's son.
That would be something: a blow struck for olden virtue: a
beacon of remembrance for Sweden, in the dark days he
feared and foresaw. His religious broodings deepened; he
strove incessantly to come nearer to the Gods; for although
he held it a coward's creed to think They exist to help men,
and a brave man's, that men exist to help Them; yet at such a
time, he deemed, They might find it worth Their while to
turn from vaster wars for a moment, and concern themselves
with the fate of Sweden. So he prayed, but his prayer was no
petition nor whining after gains; it was a silencing of the
mind, a stedfast driving it upward towards heights it had not
attained before: eagle altitudes, and sunlight in the windless
blue, where no passion comes, and the eternal voices may be
heard.

The tide of trouble drew nearer. Presently a messenger
came from Inge, with a priest. Halfdan was to install the latter in his house, and learn from him the faith of the Naza-
rene; was to forgo the Gods, or expect the king's armies.
Halfdan sent them back; to say that Inge would be welcome
at Bravik: as a friend, as of old; or still more as a foe. Then
he dismissed the few women there were in his house, called
in his men, and prepared for a siege: thoroughly if fiercely
happy at last. But there was no bottom to the king's degen-
eration, it seemed. After three weeks this came from Upsala:
"Halfdan Halfdansson, you are senile; you will die soon, and
your false religion will all but die with you. The faith of
Christ commands forbearance and forgiveness. You shall die
in peace, and suffer hell-flame thereafter; I will not trouble
with you." *I will not trouble with you.* . . . For a week the old
man raged inwardly. Inge should not thus triumphantly insult
him; he would not die in peace, but lead his fifty against Upsala, and go out fighting. . . . Then the Balder-mood came

once more; and with it, light and direction vouchsafed him. He would go a-viking.

He summoned his fifty, and proclaimed his intention in the hall. Let who would, stay behind—in a Sweden that at least would let them be. For himself, he would take the Swan-way: he would have delight again of the crisping of blue waves against his prow: he would go under purple sails into the evening, into the mystery, into the aloneness where grandeur is, and it is profitable for souls to be, and there are none to tell heart-sickening tales. . . . There, what should befall him, who could say? Perhaps there would be sweet battle on the Christian coasts; perhaps he would burn and break a church or two, and silence the jangling of the bells that called ignoble races to ignoble prayer. Perhaps there would be battling only with the storm: going out into that vast unstable region the Aesir loved, perhaps they would expend their manhood nobly in war with the shrieking wind, the sweet wild tempest of heaven. At such times the Gods come near, they come very near; they buffet and slay in their love, and out of a wild and viking death, the Valkyrie ride, the Valkyrie ride! . . . There were fifty men in the hall that heard him; there were fifty men that rose and shouted their acclamation; fifty that would take the Swan-way with their lord.

So there came to be noise of ax and hammer in the haven under Bravik: the *Wild Swan* and the *Dragon* being refurbished and made all taut for voyaging. Within a month they set sail. But not southward, and then through Skagerack and Cattegat, out into the waters of Britain and France, as Halfdan had intended. On the first day, a sudden storm overtook them, and singing they plunged into black seas, beneath blind and battling skies. Singing they combatted the wave of the north; they went on, plunging blindly, driven for three days whither they knew not; then, with a certain triumph in their souls, they succumbed singing, to the gale. They saw the Valkyrie ride through heaven, they gave their bodies to the foam about the rocks and rose upon the howling winds, clean and joyous of soul at the last.

Halfdan had forgotten Christianity: all thought and memory of it deserted him utterly before the storm had been beating them an hour. In the end it was all pagan, all Viking, exultant lover and fighter of the Gods, that he leaped from his sinking ship in the night, fully armed, into the driving froth and blackness; struggled as long as might be with the overwhelming waters, as befitted his manhood; then lost consciousness, and was buffeted and tossed where the grand elements listed; and thrown at last, unconscious, on the shore.

Certainly he had seen the Valkyrie riding, had heard their warsong above the winds and waves: like the lightning of heaven they had ridden, beautiful and awful beyond any of his old dreaming; why then had they not taken him? This was no Valhalla into which he had come: this dark place smokily lamp-lit; this close air, heavy, it must be said, with stench. And were these the dwarfs, these little figures that moved and chattered unintelligibly in the gloom? . . . Slowly he took in the uncouth surroundings; raising himself, rather painfully, on his elbow from the bed of dry heather on which he was lying. There, on the tent-pole, hung his armor: his helmet with the raven wings; his shield, sword, and battle-ax; these were skins with which he was covered, and of which the walls of the tent were made. He was not dead then? No; it appeared that it was still mortal flesh that he was wearing. He had been thrown on some shore by the waves, and rescued by these quaint, squat people. Ah! he had been driven into the far north, and was among Lapps in the unknown north of the world.

He lay back, exhausted by his bodily and mental effort; and the sigh that broke from him brought the Lapp woman to his side, and the Lapp man after her. They brought him hot broth, and spoke to him, their unknown and liquid tongue, in

which no sound unmusical intrudes, was full of gentle kindliness; their words were almost caressing, and full of encour-
agement and cheer. He had no strength to sit up; the Lapp
woman squatted at his head and lifted him in her arms; and
while he so leaned and rested the Lapp man fed him, sup by
sup; the two of them crooning and chuckling their good will
the while. In three days he was on his feet; and convinced
that he could not outwear the kindly hospitality of his hosts.

The weeks of the northern spring went by; the flowers of
Lapland were abloom in the valley, and old Halfdan wandered daily and brooded amidst the flowers. His mood now
had become very inward. He hungered no more after action,
nor dwelt in pictures of the past; rather an interiority of
the present haunted him: a sweetness, as of dear and near
deities, in the crag-reflecting waters, in the fleet cloud-
fleeces, in the heather on the hills, and in the white and yellow poppies on the valley-floor. As the summer passed this
mood grew deeper: from a prevalent serene peace, it became
filled with divine voices almost audibly calling. As for the
Lapps, they behaved to him at all times with such tenderness
as might be given to a father growing helpless in old age, but
loved beyond ordinary standards.

The first frosts were withering the heather; in the valley
the flowers had died; the twilight of early winter, a wan iris
withering, drooped mournful petals over the world. On the
hills all was ghostly whiteness: the Lapps had come south
with the winter, and there was a great encampment of them
in the valley; it never occurred to Halfdan to wonder why the
couple that had saved him had remained during the summer
so far from the snows. One day he wandered down to the
shore: the sea had already frozen, and the icy leagues of it
shone tinted with rose and faint violet and beryl where light
from the sun, far and low in the horizon, caught them. Wonderful and beautiful seemed to him the world of the North.
There was no taint in the cold, electric air; no memory to

make his soul ashamed for his fellow men. The wind blew
keen over the ice, blowing back his hair and his beard; it was
intense and joyful for him with that Divine life of the Gods
that loves and opposes us. He walked out on the ice; something at his feet caught his attention, and he stooped to examine it; it was a spar, belike from the *Wild Swan* or the *Dragon,*
the ships he had loved. Then came memory in a flood. All his
life had gone from him; the faces familiar of old had vanished; down there, in the south, in the Gothland, all the glory
had departed; and there was nothing left for him on earth,
but the queer, evil-smelling life in the Lapp tent. . . . Yes,
there were still the Gods. . . . A strange unrest came upon
him; he must away and find the Aesir. . . . He had no plan;
only he must find the Bright Ones: must stand in their visible
presence, who had been the secret illumination of the best of
his life. In mingled longing and exultation he made his way
back to the camp.

He found his Lapp friends standing before their tent, and
their best reindeer harnessed to an *akja**; they knew, it appeared, that he was to go; and mournfully and unbidden, had
made preparation. They brought out his armor, and fondled
his hands as they armed him; a crowd gathered about him, all
crooning and chuckling their good will, and their sorrow to
lose the old man in whose shining eyes, it seemed to them,
was much unearthly wisdom. On all sides, evidently, there
was full understanding of his purpose, and sad acquies-
cence; and this did not seem to him strange at all: the Gods
were near and real enough to control and arrange all things.
He sat down in the *akja,* and took the rein; the Lapps heaped
skins about him for warmth; then, waving farewells, amidst
an outburst of sorrowful crooning and chuckling, he started.
Whither the reindeer might list; whither the mighty Undying
Ones might direct.

* The Lapp sledge of wicker and skin, capable of holding one man sitting
with legs stretched out, and guiding the reindeer with a single thong of rein.

On, and on, and on. Through ghostly valleys and through the snowstorm, right into the heart of the northern night, the reindeer, never uncertain of the way, drew him. The Balder-mood came to him in the weird darkness; in the cold desolation the bright Gods seemed nearer than ever. Through ghostly passes where the north wind, driving ice particles that stung, came shrieking, boisterous and dismal, down from the Pole to oppose him, on sped the reindeer while the mind of the old Viking was gathered into dreams. —Waiting for him, somewhere beyond, were Those whose presence was a growing glory on the horizon of his soul. . . . The snow-ghosts, wan, innumerable, and silent, came hurrying by; on sped the reindeer, a beautiful beast, heeding never the snow-ghosts over frozen rivers and frozen mountains, through ghostly cold valleys and the snow. Under vast precipices that towered up, iron and mournful into the night; or along the brink of awful cliffs, with the snowstorm howling below . . . on and on. Who was to measure time on that weird journey? There were no changes of day and night; and Halfdan, wrapped in the warmth of his dreams, hardly would have heeded them if there had been. Now and again the reindeer halted to feed, scraping in the snow for his familiar moss-diet; then on again, and on. It was the beast, or some invisible presence, not the man, who chose the way.

A valley stretched out endlessly before; and afar, afar, a mountain caught on its whiteness some light from heaven, so that amid all the ghostly darkness it shone and shot up, a little dazzling beacon of purity on the rim of the world. The snow had ceased to fall, and no longer the north wind came shrieking to oppose; there was quiet in the valley broken only by the tinkling of the reindeer bells and the scrunch of the falling hoofs on the snow. The white mountain caught the eyes, and at last the mind of the long dreaming Viking; so that he began to note the tinkling of the bells, the sound of the hoofs falling, the desolation before and around. And at last another sound also: long howling out of the mountains on this side and that; long, dreary howling behind, like the cry of ghosts in a nightmare, or the lamentation of demons driven forever through darkness beyond the margin of space. For some time he listened, before waking to knowledge that it was actual sound he listened to; and then for some time longer before it came to him to know whence the sound was. It had drawn nearer by then, much nearer; and peering forth through the glint and gloom, he saw the shadows that were wolves streaming up after him through the valley, and coming down from the mountains; singly, in twos and threes, in multitudes. The reindeer snuffed, tossed its head, and speeded on prodigiously, yet with what gathered on the hillsides, it would be a marvel if he escaped. On came the shadows, until one could see the green fire-sparks of their eyes, behind, to the right and to the left, almost before; and on sped the reindeer, and the white mountain drew nearer.

Then Halfdan the Viking scented war: he remembered his youth and its prowess; he made ready his shield and battle-ax; and thanked the Gods fervently that after all he should go out fighting. The brave reindeer should have what chance it might to escape by its own untrammeled fleetness: so he drew his sword and cut the harness. The beast was away over the snow at twice its former speed; and Halfdan in the *akja* shot forward thirty paces, fell out, and was on his feet in a moment to wait what should come.

A black, shag shadow, the foremost of them, hurled itself howling at his throat—eyes green fire and bared teeth gleaming; the ax swept down, clave its head in midair, and the howl went out in a rattling groan and sob. No question of failing strength now; old age was a memory—forgotten. The joy of battle came to him, and as the first wolf fell he broke into song:

In the bleak of the night and the ghost-held region,
By frozen valley and frozen lake,

A son of the Vikings, breaking his battle,
Doth lovely deeds for Asgard's sake.

Odin All-Father, for thee I slew him!
For thee I slew him, bolt-wielding Thor!
Joy to ye now, ye Aesir, Brothers!
That drive the demons forevermore!

While he sang, another wolf was upon him, and then another and another; and the war-ax that had made play under Mediterranean suns of old, God, how it turned and swept and drove and clave things in the northern night! While they came up one by one, or even in twos, the fight was all in his favor, so he slew as many as a dozen at his singing; then the end began to draw near. They were in a ring about him now; rather fearful of the whirling ax, but closing in. Old age began to tell upon his limbs; he fought on wearying; and the delight of war ebbed from him; his thigh had been snapped at and torn, and he had lost much blood with the wound. Then the ax fell, and he leaned on it for support for a moment, his head bent down over his breast. The war-mood had gone altogether; his mind sped out to the Gods. Of inward time there had been enough, since the ax fell, for the change of mood, for the coming of calm wonder and exaltation; of the time we measure in minutes, enough for the leaping of a wolf. He saw it, and lifted the ax; knowing that nothing could be done. At his left it leaped up; he saw the teeth snap a hand's-breadth from his face. . . . An ax that he knew not, brighter than the lightning, swung; the jaws snapped; the head and the body apart fell to the ground. . . . And there was a wolf leaping on his right, and no chance in the world of his slaying it; and a spear all-glorious suddenly hurtling out of the night, and taking the wolf through the throat, and pinning it dead to the ground. And here was a man, a Viking, gray-bearded, one-eyed, glorious, fighting upon his left; and here was a man, a Viking, young and surpassing beautiful of form and face and mien, doing battle at his right. And he himself was young again, and strong; and knew that against the three of them all the wolves in the world, and all the demons in hell, would have little chance. They fled yelping into the dark; and Halfdan turned to hail those that had fought for him.

And behold, the shining mountain that had seemed so far, shone now near at hand, and for a mountain, it was a palace, exceedingly well-built, lovely with towers and pinnacles and all the fair appurtenances of a king's house. No night nor winter was near it; amidst gardens of eternal sunlight it shone; its portals flung wide, and blithe all things for his entering. And he greeted Odin All-Father, as one might who had done nothing in his life to mar the pleasant friendliness of that greeting. And in like manner he greeted Balder the Beautiful. They linked their arms in his, and in cheerful conversation he passed in with them into the Valhalla.

The Coming of the Terror

by Arthur Machen

The initial stories of Tolkien's invented mythology were devised during World War I, and in fact war is a central theme in Tolkien's works, from the legends of the First Age of Middle-earth and the war with the first dark lord, Morgoth, to the Third Age, as told in *The Lord of the Rings*, which relates the war against Sauron, who was formerly one of Morgoth's chief servants.

It is interesting to see how easily war gives rise to fantasy. During World War I, Arthur Machen was a journalist on the staff of the London newspaper the *Evening News*. On 29 September 1914, Machen published in the paper a short story titled "The Bowmen: The Angels of Mons." It tells of a small band of Englishmen fighting against an overwhelming German force and how, following a soldier's invocation, Saint George's bowmen appear as shining figures and put rout to the Germans. The story quickly spread, becoming a popular war legend. Witnesses stepped forward to elaborate on the story, despite Machen's firm statement that he had made up the whole thing.

Machen used the war as a basis for some other of his fantasies, including a short novel called *The Terror*. It also appeared serially (under the title "The Great Terror") in the *Evening News*, from 16 to 31 October 1916, and in book form early the next year. The first American serial rights were sold to the *Century Magazine*, who trimmed the story considerably (as Machen himself noted "with a skill that was really remarkable"), publishing it in October 1917 as "The Coming of the Terror." This skillful condensation of Machen's story is here republished for the first time.

AFTER two years we are turning once more to the morning's news with a sense of appetite and glad expectation. There were thrills at the beginning of the war, the thrill of horror and of a doom that seemed at once incredible and certain. This was when Namur fell, and the German host swelled like a flood over the French fields, and drew very near to the walls of Paris. Then we felt the thrill of exultation when the good news came that the awful tide had been turned back, that Paris and the world were safe, for a while, at all events.

Then for days we hoped for more news as good as this or better. Has Kluck been surrounded? Not to-day, but perhaps he will be surrounded to-morrow. But the days became weeks, the weeks drew out to months; the battle in the West seemed frozen. People speculated as to the reason of this in-action: the hopeful said that Joffre had a plan, that he was "nibbling"; others declared that we were short of munitions, others again that the new levies were not yet ripe for battle. So the months went by, and almost two years of war had been completed before the motionless English line began to stir and quiver as if it awoke from a long sleep, and began to roll onward, overwhelming the enemy.

The secret of the long inaction of the British armies has been well kept. On the one hand it was rigorously protected by the censorship, which, severe, and sometimes severe to the point of absurdity, became in this particular matter fero-cious. As soon as the real significance of that which was happening was perceived by the authorities, an underlined circular was issued to the newspaper proprietors of Great Britain and Ireland. It warned each proprietor that he might impart the contents of this circular to one other person only, such person being the responsible editor of his paper, who was to keep the communication secret under the severest penalties. The circular forbade any mention of certain events that had taken place, that might take place; it forbade any kind of reference to these events or any hint of their existence. The subject was not to be referred to in conversation, it was not to be hinted at, however obscurely, in letters; the very existence of the circular, its subject apart, was to be a dead secret.

Now, a censorship that is sufficiently minute and utterly remorseless can do amazing things in the way of hiding what it wants to hide. Once one would have thought otherwise; one would have said that, censor or no censor, the fact of the murder at X—— would certainly become known, if not through the press, at all events through rumor and the passage of the news from mouth to mouth. And this would be true of England three hundred years ago. But we have grown of late to such a reverence for the printed word and such a reliance on it that the old faculty of disseminating news by word of mouth has become atrophied. Forbid the press to mention the fact that Jones has been murdered, and it is marvelous how few people will hear of it, and of those who hear how few will credit the story that they have heard.

And, then, again, the very fact of these vain rumors and fantastic tales having been so widely believed for a time was fatal to the credit of any stray mutterings that may have got abroad.

Before the secret circular had been issued my curiosity had somehow been aroused by certain paragraphs concerning a "Fatal Accident to Well-known Airman." The propeller of the airplane had been shattered, apparently by a collision with a flight of pigeons; the blades had been broken, and the machine had fallen like lead to the earth. And soon after I had seen this account, I heard of some very odd circumstances relating to an explosion in a great munition factory in the Midlands. I thought I saw the possibility of a connection between two very different events.

It has been pointed out to me by friends who have been good enough to read this record that certain phrases I have used may give the impression that I ascribe all the delays of the war on the Western front to the extraordinary circumstances which occasioned the issue of the secret circular. Of course this is not the case; there were many reasons for the immobility of our lines from October, 1914, to July, 1916. We could undertake to supply the defects of our army both in men and munitions *if* the new and incredible danger could be overcome. It has been overcome,—rather, perhaps, it has ceased to exist,—and the secret may now be told.

I have said my attention was attracted by an account of the death of a well-known airman. I have not the habit of preserving cuttings, I am sorry to say, so that I cannot be precise as to the date of this event. To the best of my belief it was either toward the end of May or the beginning of June, 1915. The manner in which Western-Reynolds met his death struck me as extraordinary. He was brought down by a flight of pigeons, as appeared by what was found on the blood-stained and shattered blades of the propeller. An eyewitness of the accident, a fellow-officer, described how Western-Reynolds set out from the aërodrome on a fine afternoon, there being hardly any wind. He was going to France.

" 'Wester' rose to a great height at once, and we could scarcely see the machine. I was turning to go when one of the fellows called out: 'I say! What's this?' He pointed up, and we saw what looked like a black cloud coming from the south at a tremendous rate. I saw at once it wasn't a cloud; it came with a swirl and a rush quite different from any cloud I've ever seen. It turned into a great crescent, and wheeled and veered about as if it was looking for something. The man who had called out had got his glasses, and was staring for all he was worth. Then he shouted that it was a tremendous flight of birds, 'thousands of them.' They went on wheeling and beating about high up in the air, and we were watching them, thinking it was interesting, but not supposing that they would make any difference to 'Wester,' who was just about out of sight. Then the two arms of the crescent drew in as quick as lightning, and these thousands of birds shot in a solid mass right up there across the sky, and flew away. Then Henley, the man with the glasses, called out, 'He's down!' and started running, and I went after him. We got a car, and as we were going along Henley told me that he'd seen the machine drop dead, as if it came out of that cloud of birds. We found the propeller-blades all broken and covered with blood and pigeon-feathers, and carcasses of the birds had got wedged in between the blades, and were sticking to them."

It was, I think, about a week or ten days after the airman's death that my business called me to a Northern town, the name of which, perhaps, had better remain unknown. My mission was to inquire into certain charges of extravagance which had been laid against the munition-workers of this special town. I found, as usual, that there was a mixture of truth and exaggeration in the stories that I had heard.

"And how can you be surprised if people will have a bit of a fling?" a worker said to me. "We're seeing money for the first time in our lives, and it's bright. And we work hard for it, and we risk our lives to get it. You've heard of explosion yonder?"

He mentioned certain works on the outskirts of the town. Of course neither the name of the works nor that of the town had been printed; there had been a brief notice of "Explosion at Munition Works in the Northern District: Many Fatalities." The working-man told me about it, and added some dreadful details.

"They wouldn't let their folks see bodies; screwed them up in coffins as they found them in shop. The gas had done it."

"Turned their faces black, you mean?"

"Nay. They were all as if they had been bitten to pieces."

This was a strange gas.

I asked the man in the Northern town all sorts of questions about the extraordinary explosion of which he had spoken to me, but he had very little more to say. As I have noted already, secrets that may not be printed are often deeply kept;

last summer there were very few people outside high official circles who knew anything about the "tanks," of which we have all been talking lately, though these strange instruments of war were being exercised and tested in a park not far from London.

I gave him up, and took a tram to the district of the disaster, a sort of industrial suburb, five miles from the center of the town. When I asked for the factory, I was told that it was no good my going to it, as there was nobody there. But I found it, a raw and hideous shed, with a walled yard about it, and a shut gate. I looked for signs of destruction, but there was nothing. The roof was quite undamaged; and again it struck me that this had been a strange accident. There had been an explosion of sufficient violence to kill people in the building, but the building itself showed no wounds or scars.

A man came out of the gate and locked it behind him. I began to ask him some sort of question, or, rather, I began to "open" for a question with "A terrible business here, they tell me," or some such phrase of convention. I got no further. The man asked me if I saw a policeman walking down the street. I said I did, and I was given the choice of getting about my business forthwith or of being instantly given in charge as a spy. "Th' 'ast better be gone, and quick about it," was, I think, his final advice, and I took it.

It was a day or two later that the accident to the airman Western-Reynolds came into my mind. For one of those instants which are far shorter than any measure of time there flashed out the possibility of a link between the two disasters. But here was a wild impossibility, and I drove it away. And yet I think that the thought, mad as it seemed, never left me; it was the secret light that at last guided me through a somber grove of enigmas.

It was about this time, so far as the date can be fixed, that a whole district, one might say a whole county, was visited by a series of extraordinary and terrible calamities, which were the more terrible inasmuch as they continued for some time to be inscrutable mysteries. It is indeed doubtful whether these awful events do not still remain mysteries to many of those concerned; for before the inhabitants of this part of the country had time to join one link of evidence to another the circular was issued, and thenceforth no one knew how to distinguish undoubted fact from wild and extravagant surmise.

The district in question is in the far west of Wales; I shall call it, for convenience, Meirion. Here, then, one sees a wild and divided and scattered region, a land of outland hills and secret and hidden valleys.

Such, then, in the main is Meirion, and on this land in the early summer of last year terror descended—a terror without shape, such as no man there had ever known.

It began with the tale of a little child who wandered out into the lanes to pick flowers one sunny afternoon, and never came back to the cottage on the hill. It was supposed that she must have crossed the road and gone to the cliff's edge, possibly in order to pick the sea-pinks that were then in full blossom. She must have slipped, they said, and fallen into the sea, two hundred feet below. It may be said at once that there was no doubt some truth in this conjecture, though it stopped far short of the whole truth. The child's body must have been carried out by the tide, for it was never found.

The conjecture of a false step or of a fatal slide on the slippery turf that slopes down to the rocks was accepted as being the only explanation possible. People thought the accident a strange one, because, as a rule, country children living by the cliffs and the sea become wary at an early age, and the little girl was almost ten years old. Still, as the neighbors said, "That's how it must have happened; and it's a great pity, to be sure." But this would not do when in a week's time a strong young laborer failed to come to his cottage after the day's work. His body was found on the rocks six or seven miles from the cliffs where the child was supposed to have fallen; he was going home by a path that he had used every night of his life for eight or nine years, that he used on dark nights in perfect security, knowing every inch of it. The police asked if he drank, but he was a teetotaler; if he was subject to fits, but he wasn't. And he was not murdered for his wealth, since agricultural laborers are not wealthy. It was only possible again to talk of slippery turf and a false step; but people began to be frightened. Then a woman was found with her neck broken at the bottom of a disused quarry near Llanfihangel, in the middle of the county. The false-step theory was eliminated here, for the quarry was guarded by a natural hedge of gorse. One would have to struggle and fight through sharp thorns to destruction in such a place as this; and indeed the gorse was broken, as if some one had rushed furiously through it, just above the place where the woman's body was found. And this also was strange: there was a dead sheep lying beside her in the pit, as if the woman and the sheep together had been chased over the brim of the quarry. But chased by whom or by what? And then there was a new form of terror.

This was in the region of the marshes under the mountain. A man and his son, a lad of fourteen or fifteen, set out early one morning to work, and never reached the farm whence they were bound. Their way skirted the marsh, but it was broad, firm, and well metalled, and it had been raised about two feet above the bog. But when search was made in the evening of the same day, Phillips and his son were found dead in the marsh, covered with black slime and pond-weed. And they lay some ten yards from the path, which, it would seem, they must have left deliberately. It was useless, of course, to look for tracks in the black ooze, for if one threw a big stone into it, a few seconds removed all marks of the disturbance. The men who found the two bodies beat about the verges and purlieus of the marsh in hope of finding some trace of the murderers; they went to and fro over the rising ground where the black cattle were grazing, they searched the alder-thickets by the brook: but they discovered nothing.

Most horrible of all these horrors, perhaps, was the affair of the Highway, a lonely and unfrequented by-road that winds for many miles on high and lonely land. Here, a mile from any other dwelling, stands a cottage on the edge of a dark wood. It was inhabited by a laborer named Williams, his wife, and their three children. One hot summer's evening a man who had been doing a day's gardening at a rectory three or four miles away passed the cottage, and stopped for a few minutes to chat with Williams, who was pottering about his garden, while the children were playing on the path by the door. The two talked of their neighbors and of the potatoes till Mrs. Williams appeared at the doorway and said supper was ready, and Williams turned to go into the house. This was about eight o'clock, and in the ordinary course the family would have had their supper and be in bed by nine, or by half-past nine at the latest. At ten o'clock that night the local doctor was driving home along the Highway. His horse shied violently and then stopped dead just opposite the gate to the cottage. The doctor got down, and there on the roadway lay Williams, his wife, and the three children, stone-dead. Their skulls were battered in as if by some heavy iron instrument; their faces were beaten into a pulp.

It is not easy to make any picture of the horror that lay dark on the hearts of the people of Meirion. It was no longer possible to believe or to pretend to believe that these men and women and children had met their deaths through strange accidents. For a time people said that there must be a madman at large, a sort of country variant of Jack the Ripper, some horrible pervert who was possessed by the passion of death, who prowled darkling about that lonely land, hiding in woods and in wild places, always watching and seeking for the victims of his desire.

Indeed, Dr. Lewis, who found poor Williams, his wife, and children, was convinced at first that the presence of a

concealed madman in the country-side offered the only possible solution to the difficulty.

"I felt sure," he said to me afterward, "that the Williamses
had been killed by a homicidal maniac. It was the nature of
the poor creatures' injuries that convinced me that this was
the case. Those poor people had their heads smashed to
pieces by what must have been a storm of blows. Any one of
them would have been fatal, but the murderer must have
gone on raining blows with his iron hammer on people who
were already stone-dead. And *that* sort of thing is the work
of a madman, and nothing but a madman. That's how I argued
the matter out to myself just after the event. I was utterly
wrong, monstrously wrong; but who could have suspected
the truth?"

I quote Dr. Lewis, or the substance of him, as representative of most of the educated opinion of the district at the be-
ginnings of the terror. People seized on this theory largely
because it offered at least the comfort of an explanation, and
any explanation, even the poorest, is better than an intolerable and terrible mystery. Besides, Dr. Lewis's theory was
plausible; it explained the lack of purpose that seemed to
characterize the murders.

And yet there were difficulties even from the first. It was
hardly possible that a strange madman would be able to keep
hidden in a country-side where any stranger is instantly
noted and noticed; sooner or later he would be seen as he
prowled along the lanes or across the wild places.

Then another theory, or, rather, a variant of Dr. Lewis's
theory, was started. This was to the effect that the person responsible for the outrages was indeed a madman, but a madman only at intervals. It was one of the members of the Porth
Club, a certain Mr. Remnant, who was supposed to have
originated this more subtle explanation. Mr. Remnant was
a middle-aged man who, having nothing particular to do, read
a great many books by way of conquering the hours. He
talked to the club—doctors, retired colonels, parsons,

lawyers—about "personality," quoted various psychological text-books in support of his contention that personality was sometimes fluid and unstable, went back to "Dr. Jekyll and Mr. Hyde" as good evidence of this proposition, and laid stress on *Dr. Jekyll*'s speculation that the human soul, so far from being one and indivisible, might possibly turn out to be a mere polity, a state in which dwelt many strange and incongruous citizens, whose characters were not merely unknown, but altogether unsurmised by that form of consciousness which rashly assumed that it was not only the president of the republic, but also its sole citizen.

However, Mr. Remnant's somewhat crazy theory became untenable when two more victims of an awful and mysterious death were offered up in sacrifice, for a man was found dead in the Llanfihangel quarry where the woman had been discovered, and on the same day a girl of fifteen was found broken on the jagged rocks under the cliffs near Porth. Now, it appeared that these two deaths must have occurred at about the same time, within an hour of one another, certainly, and the distance between the quarry and the cliffs by Black Rock is certainly twenty miles.

And now a fresh circumstance or set of circumstances became manifest to confound judgment and to awaken new and wild surmises; for at about this time people realized that none of the dreadful events that were happening all about them was so much as mentioned in the press. Horror followed on horror, but no word was printed in any of the local journals. The curious went to the newspaper offices,—there were two left in the county,—but found nothing save a firm refusal to discuss the matter. Then the Cardiff papers were drawn and found blank, and the London press was apparently ignorant of the fact that crimes that had no parallel were terrorizing a whole country-side. Everybody wondered what could have happened, what was happening; and then it was whispered that the coroner would allow no inquiry to be made as to these deaths of darkness.

Clearly, people reasoned, these government restrictions and prohibitions could only refer to the war, to some great danger in connection with the war. And that being so, it followed that the outrages which must be kept so secret were the work of the enemy; that is, of concealed German agents.

It is time, I think, for me to make one point clear. I began this history with certain references to an extraordinary accident to an airman whose machine fell to the ground after collision with a huge flock of pigeons, and then to an explosion in a Northern munition factory of a very singular kind. Then I deserted the neighborhood of London and the Northern district, and dwelt on a mysterious and terrible series of events which occurred in the summer of 1915 in a Welsh county, which I have named for convenience Meirion.

Well, let it be understood at once that all this detail that I have given about the occurrences in Meirion does not imply that the county in Wales was alone or specially afflicted by the terror that was over the land. They tell me that in the villages about Dartmoor the stout Devonshire hearts sank as men's hearts used to sink in the time of plague and pestilence. There was horror, too, about the Norfolk Broads, and far up by Perth no one would venture on the path that leads by Scone to the wooded heights above the Tay. And in the industrial districts. I met a man by chance one day in an odd London corner who spoke with horror of what a friend had told him.

" 'Ask no questions, Ned,' he says to me, 'but I tell yow a was in Bairnigan t' other day, and a met a pal who'd seen three hundred coffins going out of a works not far from there.' "

Then there was the vessel that hovered outside the mouth of the Thames with all sails set, and beat to and fro in the wind, and never answered any signals and showed no light. The forts shot at her, and brought down one of the masts; but she went suddenly about, stood down channel, and drove ashore at last on the sand-banks and pine-woods of Arcachon, and not a man alive on her, but only rattling heaps of bones! That last voyage of the *Semiramis* would be something horribly worth telling; but I heard it only at a distance as a yarn, and believed it only because it squared with other things that I knew for certain.

This, then, is my point: I have written of the terror as it fell on Meirion simply because I have had opportunities of getting close there to what really happened.

Well, I have said that the people of that far Western county realized not only that death was abroad in their quiet lanes and on their peaceful hills, but that for some reason it was to be kept secret. And so they concluded that this veil of secrecy must somehow be connected with the war; and from this position it was not a long way to a further inference that the murderers of innocent men and women and children were either Germans or agents of Germany. It would be just like the Huns, everybody agreed, to think out such a devilish scheme as this; and they always thought out their schemes beforehand.

It all seemed plausible enough; Germany had by this time perpetrated so many horrors and had so excelled in devilish ingenuities that no abomination seemed too abominable to be probable or too ingeniously wicked to be beyond her tortuous malice. But then came the questions as to who the agents of this terrible design were, as to where they lived, as to how they contrived to move unseen from field to field, from lane to lane. All sorts of fantastic attempts were made to answer these questions, but it was felt that they remained unanswered. Some suggested that the murderers landed from submarines, or flew from hiding-places on the west coast of Ireland, coming and going by night; but there were seen to be flagrant impossibilities in both these suggestions. Everybody agreed that the evil work was no doubt the work of Germany; but nobody could begin to guess how it was done.

It was, I suppose, at about this time when the people were puzzling their heads as to the secret methods used by the

Germans or their agents to accomplish their crimes that a very singular circumstance became known to a few of the Porth people. It related to the murder of the Williams family on the Highway in front of their cottage door. I do not know that I have made it plain that the old Roman road called the Highway follows the course of a long, steep hill that goes steadily westward till it slants down toward the sea. On each side of the road the ground falls away, here into deep shadowy woods, here into high pastures, but for the most part into the wild and broken land that is characteristic of Arfon.

Now, on the lower slopes of it, beneath the Williams cottage, some three or four fields down the hill, there is a military camp. The place has been used as a camp for many years, and lately the site has been extended and huts have been erected; but a considerable number of the men were under canvas here in the summer of 1915.

On the night of the Highway murder this camp, as it appeared afterward, was the scene of the extraordinary panic of horses.

A good many men in the camp were asleep in their tents soon after 9:30. They woke up in panic. There was a thundering sound on the steep hillside above them, and down upon the tents came half a dozen horses, mad with fright, trampling the canvas, trampling the men, bruising dozens of them, and killing two.

Everything was in wild confusion, men groaning and screaming in the darkness, struggling with the canvas and the twisted ropes, and some of them, raw lads enough, shouting out that the Germans had at last landed.

Some of the men had seen the horses galloping down the hill as if terror itself was driving them. They scattered off into the darkness, and somehow or other found their way back in the night to their pasture above the camp. They were grazing there peacefully in the morning, and the only sign of the panic of the night before was the mud they had scattered all over themselves as they pelted through a patch of wet

ground. The farmer said they were as quiet a lot as any in
Meirion; he could make nothing of it.

Then two or three other incidents, quite as odd and incom-
prehensible, came to be known, borne on chance trickles of
gossip that came into the towns from outland farms. And in
such ways it came out that up at Plas Newydd there had been
a terrible business over swarming the bees; they had turned
as wild as wasps and much more savage. They had come
about the people who were taking the swarms like a cloud.
They settled on one man's face so that you could not see the
flesh for the bees crawling over it, and they had stung him so
badly that the doctor did not know whether he would get
well; they had chased a girl who had come out to see the
swarming, and settled on her and stung her to death. Then
they had gone off to a brake below the farm and got into a
hollow tree, and it was not safe to go near it, for they would
come out at you by day or by night.

And much the same thing had happened, it seemed, at
three or four farms and cottages where bees were kept. And
there were stories, hardly so clear or so credible, of sheep-
dogs, mild and trusted beasts, turning as savage as wolves
and injuring the farm boys in a horrible manner, in one case,
it was said, with fatal results. It was certainly true that old
Mrs. Owens's favorite Dorking cock had gone mad. She
came into Porth one Saturday morning with her face and her
neck all bound up and plastered. She had gone out to her bit
of field to feed the poultry the night before, and the bird had
flown at her and attacked her most savagely, inflicting some
very nasty wounds before she could beat it off.

"There was a stake handy, lucky for me," she said, "and I
did beat him and beat him till the life was out of him. But
what is come to the world, whatever?"

Now Remnant, the man of theories, was also a man of extreme leisure. He was no more brutal than the general public,
which revels in the details of mysterious crime; but it must

be said that the terror, black though it was, was a boon to him. He peered and investigated and poked about with the relish of a man to whose life a new zest has been added. He listened attentively to the strange tales of bees and dogs and poultry that came into Porth with the country baskets of butter, rabbits, and green peas, and he evolved at last a most extraordinary theory. He went one night to see Dr. Lewis.

"I want to talk to you," he said to the doctor, "about what I have called provisionally the Z-ray."

Dr. Lewis, smiling indulgently, and quite prepared for some monstrous piece of theorizing, led Remnant into the room that overlooked the terraced garden and the sea.

"I suppose, Lewis, you've heard these extraordinary stories of bees and dogs and things that have been going about lately?"

"Certainly I have heard them. I was called in at Plas Newydd, and treated Thomas Trevor, who's only just out of danger, by the way. I certified for the poor child, Mary Trevor. She was dying when I got to the place."

"Well, then there are the stories of good-tempered old sheep-dogs turning wicked and 'savaging' children."

"Quite so. I haven't seen any of these cases professionally; but I believe the stories are accurate enough."

"And the old woman assaulted by her own poultry?"

"That's perfectly true."

"Very good," said Mr. Remnant. He spoke now with an italic impressiveness. *"Don't you see the link between all this and the horrible things that have been happening about here for the last month?"*

Lewis stared at Remnant in amazement. He lifted his red eyebrows and lowered them in a kind of scowl. His speech showed traces of his native accent.

"Great burning!" he exclaimed, "what on earth are you getting at now? It is madness. Do you mean to tell me that you think there is some connection between a swarm or two of bees that have turned nasty, a cross dog, and a wicked old barn-door cock, and these poor people that have been pitched over the cliffs and hammered to death on the road? There's no sense in it, you know."

"I am strongly inclined to believe that there is a great deal of sense in it," replied Remnant, with extreme calmness. "Look here, Lewis. I saw you grinning the other day at the club when I was telling the fellows that in my opinion all these outrages had been committed, certainly by the Germans, but by some method of which we have no conception. Do you see my point?"

"Well, in a sort of way. You mean there's an absolute originality in the method? I suppose that is so. But what next?"

Remnant seemed to hesitate, partly from a sense of the portentous nature of what he was about to say, partly from a sort of half-unwillingness to part with so profound a secret.

"Well," he said, "you will allow that we have two sets of phenomena of a very extraordinary kind occurring at the same time. Don't you think that it's only reasonable to connect the two sets with one another?"

"So the philosopher of Tenterden steeple and the Goodwin Sands thought, certainly," said Lewis. "But what is the connection? Those poor folks on the Highway weren't stung by bees or worried by a dog. And horses don't throw people over cliffs or stifle them in marshes."

"No; I never meant to suggest anything so absurd. It is evident to me that in all these cases of animals turning suddenly savage the cause has been terror, panic, fear. The horses that went charging into the camp were mad with fright, we know. And I say that in the other instances we have been discussing the cause was the same. The creatures were exposed to an infection of fear, and a frightened beast or bird or insect uses its weapons, whatever they may be. If, for example, there had been anybody with those horses when they took their panic, they would have lashed out at him with their heels."

"Yes. I dare say that that is so. Well?" demanded the doctor.

"Well, my belief is that the Germans have made an extraordinary discovery. I have called it the Z-ray. You know that the ether is merely an hypothesis; we have to suppose that it's there to account for the passage of the Marconi current from one place to another. Now, suppose that there is a psychic ether as well as a material ether, suppose that it is possible to direct irresistible impulses across this medium, suppose that these impulses are toward murder or suicide; then I think that you have an explanation of the terrible series of events that have been happening in Meirion for the last few weeks. And it is quite clear to my mind that the horses and the other creatures have been exposed to this Z-ray, and that it has produced on them the effect of terror, with ferocity as the result of terror. Now, what do you say to that? Telepathy, you know, is well established; so is hypnotic suggestion. Now don't you feel that putting telepathy and suggestion together, as it were, you have more than the elements of what I call the Z-ray? I feel that I have more to go on in making my hypothesis than the inventor of the steam-engine had in making his hypothesis when he saw the lid of the kettle bobbing up and down. What do you say?"

Dr. Lewis made no answer. He was watching the growth of a new, unknown tree in his garden.

It was a dark summer night. The moon was old and faint above the Dragon's Head, on the opposite side of the bay, and the air was very still. It was so still that Lewis had noted that not a leaf stirred on the very tip of a high tree that stood out against the sky; and yet he knew that he was listening to some sound that he could not determine or define. It was not the wind in the leaves, it was not the gentle wash of the water of the sea against the rocks; that latter sound he could distinguish easily. But there was something else. It was scarcely a sound; it was as if the air itself trembled and fluttered, as the air trembles in a church when they open the great pedal pipes of the organ.

The doctor listened intently. It was not an illusion, the

sound was not in his own head, as he had suspected for a moment; but for the life of him he could not make out whence it came or what it was. He gazed down into the night, over the terraces of his garden, now sweet with the scent of the flowers of the night; tried to peer over the tree-tops across the sea toward the Dragon's Head. It struck him suddenly that this strange, fluttering vibration of the air might be the noise of a distant aëroplane or airship; there was not the usual droning hum, but this sound might be caused by a new type of engine. A new type of engine? Possibly it was an enemy airship; their range, it had been said, was getting longer, and Lewis was just going to call Remnant's attention to the sound, to its possible cause, and to the possible danger that might be hovering over them, when he saw something that caught his breath and his heart with wild amazement and a touch of terror.

He had been staring upward into the sky, and, about to speak to Remnant, he had let his eyes drop for an instant. He looked down toward the trees in the garden, and saw with utter astonishment that one had changed its shape in the few hours that had passed since the setting of the sun. There was a thick grove of ilexes bordering the lowest terrace, and above them rose one tall pine, spreading its head of sparse branches dark against the sky.

As Lewis glanced down over the terraces he saw that the tall pine-tree was no longer there. In its place there rose above the ilexes what might have been a greater ilex; there was the blackness of a dense growth of foliage rising like a broad, far-spreading, and rounded cloud over the lesser trees.

Dr. Lewis glared into the dimness of the night, at the great, spreading tree that he knew could not be there. And as he gazed he saw that what at first appeared the dense blackness of foliage was fretted and starred with wonderful appearances of lights and colors.

The night had gloomed over; clouds obscured the faint

moon and the misty stars. Lewis rose, with some kind of warning and inhibiting gesture to Remnant, who, he was aware, was gaping at him in astonishment. He walked to the open French window, took a pace forward on the path outside, and looked very intently at the dark shape of the tree. He shaded the light of the lamp behind him by holding his hands on each side of his eyes.

The mass of the tree—the tree that couldn't be there—stood out against the sky, but not so clearly now that the clouds had rolled up. Its edges, the limits of its leafage, were not so distinct. Lewis thought that he could detect some sort of quivering movement in it, though the air was at a dead calm. It was a night on which one might hold up a lighted match and watch it burn without any wavering or inclination of the flame.

"You know," said Lewis, "how a bit of burned paper will sometimes hang over the coals before it goes up the chimney, and little worms of fire will shoot through it. It was like that, if you should be standing some distance away. Just threads and hairs of yellow light I saw, and specks and sparks of fire, and then a twinkling of a ruby no bigger than a pinpoint, and a green wandering in the black, as if an emerald were crawling, and then little veins of deep blue. 'Woe is me!' I said to myself in Welsh. 'What is all this color and burning?'

"At that very moment there came a thundering rap at the door of the room inside, and there was my man telling me that I was wanted directly up at the Garth, as old Mr. Trevor Williams had been taken very bad. I knew his heart was not worth much, so I had to go off directly, and leave Remnant alone to make what he could of it all."

Dr. Lewis was kept some time at the Garth. It was past twelve when he got back to his house. He went quickly to the room that overlooked the garden and the sea, threw open the French window, and peered into the darkness. There, dim indeed against the dim sky, but unmistakable, was the tall pine, with its sparse branches, high above the dense growth of the ilex-trees. The strange boughs which had amazed him had vanished; there was no appearance of colors or of fires.

The doctor did not say anything about the strange tree to Remnant. When they next met, he said that he had thought there was a man hiding among the bushes. This was in explanation of that warning gesture he had used, and of his going out into the garden and staring into the night. He concealed the truth because he dreaded the Remnant doctrine that would undoubtedly be produced; indeed, he hoped that he had heard the last of the theory of the Z-ray. But Remnant firmly reopened this subject.

"We were interrupted just as I was putting my case to you," he said. "And to sum it all up, it amounts to this: the Huns have made one of the great leaps of science. They are sending 'suggestions' (which amount to irresistible commands) over here, and the persons affected are seized with suicidal or homicidal mania. In my opinion Evans was the murderer of the Williams family. You know he said he stopped to talk to Williams. It seems to me simple. And as for the animals,—the horses, dogs, and so forth,—they, as I say, were no doubt panic-stricken by the ray, and hence driven to frenzy."

"Why should Evans have murdered Williams instead of Williams murdering Evans? Why should the impact of the ray affect one and not the other?"

"Why does one man react violently to a certain drug, while it makes no impression on another man? Why is A able to drink a bottle of whisky and remain sober, while B is turned into something very like a lunatic after he has drunk three glasses?"

"It is a question of idiosyncrasy," said the doctor.

Lewis escaped from the club and from Remnant. He did not want to hear any more about that dreadful ray, because he felt sure that the ray was all nonsense. But asking himself why he felt this certitude in the matter, he had to confess that he didn't know. An aëroplane, he reflected, was all nonsense before it was made.

But he thought with fervor of the extraordinary thing he had seen in his own garden with his own eyes. How could one fail to be afraid with great amazement at the thought of such a mystery?

Dr. Lewis's thoughts were distracted from the incredible adventure of the tree by the visit of his sister and her husband. Mr. and Mrs. Merritt lived in a well-known manufacturing town of the Midlands, which was now, of course, a center of munition work. On the day of their arrival at Porth, Mrs. Merritt, who was tired after the long, hot journey, went to bed early, and Merritt and Lewis went into the room by the garden for their talk and tobacco. They spoke of the year that had passed since their last meeting, of the weary dragging of the war, of friends that had perished in it, of the hopelessness of an early ending of all this misery. Lewis said nothing of the terror that was on the land. One does not greet with a tale of horror a tired man who is come to a quiet, sunny place for relief from black smoke and work and worry. Indeed, the doctor saw that his brother-in-law looked far from well. He seemed "jumpy"; there was an occasional twitch of his mouth that Lewis did not like at all.

"Well," said the doctor, after an interval of silence and port wine, "I am glad to see you here again. Porth always suits you. I don't think you're looking quite up to your usual form; but three weeks of Meirion air will do wonders."

"Well, I hope it will," said the other. "I am not up to the mark. Things are not going well at Midlingham."

"Business is all right, isn't it?"

"Yes; but there are other things that are all wrong. We are living under a reign of terror. It comes to that."

"What on earth do you mean?"

"It's not much. I didn't dare write it. But do you know that at every one of the munition-works in Midlingham and all about it there's a guard of soldiers with drawn bayonets and loaded rifles day and night? Men with bombs, too. And machine-guns at the big factories."

"German spies?"

"You don't want machine-guns and bombs to fight spies with."

"But what against?"

"Nobody knows. Nobody knows what is happening," Merritt repeated, and he went on to describe the bewilderment and terror that hung like a cloud over the great industrial city in the Midlands; how the feeling of concealment, or some intolerable secret danger that must not be named, was worst of all.

Merritt made a sort of picture of the great town cowering in its fear of an unknown danger.

"There's a queer story going about," he said, "as to a place right out in the country, over the other side of Midlingham. They've built one of the new factories out there, a great red brick town of sheds. About two hundred yards from this place there's an old footpath through a pretty large wood, most of it thick undergrowth. It's a black place of nights.

"A man had to go this way one night. He got along all right till he came to the wood, and then he said his heart dropped out of his body. It was awful to hear the noises in that wood. Thousands of men were in it, he swears. It was full of rustling, and pattering of feet trying to go dainty, and the crack of dead boughs lying on the ground as some one trod on them, and swishing of the grass, and some sort of chattering speech going on that sounded, so he said, as if the dead sat in their bones and talked! He ran for his life, anyhow, across fields, over hedges, through brooks. He must have run, by his tale, ten miles out of his way before he got home to his wife, beat at the door, broke in, and bolted it behind him."

"There is something rather alarming about any wood at night," said Dr. Lewis.

Merritt shrugged his shoulders.

"People say that the Germans have landed, and that they are hiding in underground places all over the country."

Lewis gasped for a moment, silent in contemplation of the magnificence of rumor. The Germans already landed, hiding underground, striking by night, secretly, terribly, at the power of England!-It was monstrous, and yet—

"People say they've got a new kind of poison-gas," continued Merritt. "Some think that they dig underground places and make the gas there, and lead it by secret pipes into the shops; others say that they throw gas bombs into the factories. It must be worse than anything they've used in France, from what the authorities say."

"The authorities? Do *they* admit that there are Germans in hiding about Midlingham?"

"No. They call it 'explosions.' But we know it isn't explosions. We know in the Midlands what an explosion sounds like and looks like. And we know that the people killed in these 'explosions' are put into their coffins in the works. Their own relations are not allowed to see them."

"And do you believe in the German theory?"

"If I do, it's because one must believe in something. Some say they've seen the gas. I heard that a man living in Dunwich saw it one night like a black cloud, with sparks of fire in it, floating over the tops of the trees by Dunwich Common."

The light of an ineffable amazement came into Lewis's eyes. The night of Remnant's visit, the trembling vibration of the air, the dark tree that had grown in his garden since the setting of the sun, the strange leafage that was starred with burning, and all vanished away when he returned from his visit to the Garth; and such a leafage had appeared as a burning cloud far in the heart of England. What intolerable mystery, what tremendous doom was signified in this? But one thing was clear and certain: the terror of Meirion was also the terror of the Midlands.

Merritt told the story of how a Swedish professor, Hu-

velius, had sold to the Germans a plan for filling England
with German soldiers. Land was to be bought in certain suit-
able and well-considered places. Englishmen were to be
bought as the apparent owners of such land, and secret exca-
vations were to be made, till the country was literally under-
mined. A subterranean Germany, in fact, was to be dug under
selected districts of England; there were to be great caverns,
underground cities, well drained, well ventilated, supplied
with water, and in these places vast stores both of food and
of munitions were to be accumulated year after year till "the
Day" dawned. And then, warned in time, the secret garrison
would leave shops, hotels, offices, villas, and vanish underground, ready to begin their work of bleeding England at the
heart.

"Well," said Lewis, "of course, it may be so. If it is so, it
is terrible beyond words."

Indeed, he found something horribly plausible in the
story. It was an extraordinary plan, of course, an unheard-of
scheme; but it did not seem impossible. It was the Trojan
Horse on a gigantic scale. And this theory certainly squared
with what one had heard of German preparations in Belgium
and in France.

And it seemed from that wonder of the burning tree that
the enemy mysteriously and terribly present at Midlingham
was present also in Meirion. Yet, he thought again, there was
but little harm to be done in Meirion to the armies of England or to their munitionment. They were working for panic
terror. Possibly that might be so; but the camp under the
Highway? That should be their first object, and no harm had
been done there.

Lewis did not know that since the panic of the horses men
had died terribly in that camp; that it was now a fortified
place, with a deep, broad trench, a thick tangle of savage
barbed wire about it, and a machine-gun planted at each
corner.

One evening the doctor was summoned to a little hamlet

on the outskirts of Porth. In one of the cottages the doctor found a father and mother weeping and crying out to "Doctor Bach, Doctor Bach," two frightened children, and one little body, still and dead.

The doctor found that the child had been asphyxiated. His clothes were dry; it was not a case of drowning. There was no mark of strangling. He asked the father how it had happened, and father and mother, weeping most lamentably, declared they had no knowledge of how their child had been killed, "unless it was the People that had done it." The Celtic fairies are still malignant. Lewis asked what had happened that evening; where had the child been?

"Was he with his brother and sister?" asked the doctor. "Don't they know anything about it?"

The children had been playing in the road at dusk, and just as their mother called them in one child had heard Johnnie cry out:

"Oh, what is that beautiful, shiny thing over the stile?"

They found the little body, under the ash-grove in the middle of the field. He was quite still and dead, so still that a great moth had settled on his forehead, fluttering away when they lifted him up.

Dr. Lewis heard this story. There was nothing to be done, little to be said to these most unhappy people.

"Take care of the two that you have left to you," said the doctor as he went away. "Don't let them out of your sight if you can help it. It is dreadful times that we are living in."

About ten days later a young farmer had been found by his wife lying in the grass close to the castle, with no scar on him or any mark of violence, but stone-dead.

Lewis was sent for, and knew at once, when he saw the dead man, that he had perished in the way that the little boy had perished, whatever that awful way might be.

It seemed that he had gone out at about half-past nine to look after some beasts. He told his wife he would be back in a quarter of an hour or twenty minutes. He did not return, and when he had been gone for three quarters of an hour Mrs. Cradock went out to look for him. She went into the field where the beasts were, and everything seemed all right; but there was no trace of Cradock. She called out: there was no answer.

She told the doctor:

"There was something that I could not make out at all. It seemed to me that the hedge did look different from usual. To be sure, things do look different at night, and there was a bit of sea mist about; but somehow it did look odd to me, and I said to myself, 'Have I lost my way, then?' "

. She declared that the shape of the trees in the hedge appeared to have changed, and besides, it had a look "as if it was lighted up, somehow," and so she went on toward the stile to see what all this could be; and when she came near, everything was as usual. She looked over the stile and called, hoping to see her husband coming toward her or to hear his voice; but there was no answer, and glancing down the path, she saw, or thought she saw, some sort of brightness on the ground, "a dim sort of light, like a bunch of glow-worms in a hedge-bank.

"And so I climbed over the stile and went down the path, and the light seemed to melt away; and there was my poor husband lying on his back, saying not a word to me when I spoke to him and touched him."

So for Lewis the terror blackened and became altogether intolerable, and others, he perceived, felt as he did. He did not know, he never asked, whether the men at the club had heard of these deaths of the child and the young farmer; but no one spoke of them. Indeed, the change was evident; at the beginning of the terror men spoke of nothing else; now it had become all too awful for ingenious chatter or labored and grotesque theories. And Lewis had received a letter from his brother-in-law, who had gone back to Midlingham; it contained the sentence, "I am afraid Fanny's health has not greatly benefited by her visit to Porth; there are still several symptoms I don't at all like." This told him, in a phraseology that the doctor and Merritt had agreed upon, that the terror remained heavy in the Midland town.

It was soon after the death of Cradock that people began to tell strange tales of a sound that was to be heard of nights about the hills and valleys to the northward of Porth. A man who had missed the last train from Meiros and had been forced to tramp the ten miles between Meiros and Porth seems to have been the first to hear it. He said he had got to the top of the hill by Tredonoc, somewhere between half-past ten and eleven, when he first noticed an odd noise that he could not make out at all; it was like a shout, a long-drawn-out, dismal wail coming from a great way off. He stopped to listen, thinking at first that it might be owls hooting in the woods; but it was different, he said, from that. He could make nothing of it, and feeling frightened, he did not quite know of what, he walked on briskly, and was glad to see the lights of Porth station. Then others heard it.

Let it be remembered again and again that all the while that the terror lasted there was no common stock of information as to the dreadful things that were being done. The press had not said one word upon it, there was no criterion by which the mass of the people could separate fact from mere vague rumor, no test by which ordinary misadventure or disaster could be distinguished from the achievements of the secret and awful force that was at work. And since the real nature of all this mystery of death was unknown, it followed easily that the signs and warnings and omens of it were all the more unknown. Here was horror, there was horror; but there were no links to join one horror with another, no common basis of knowledge from which the connection between this horror and that horror might be inferred.

The sound had been heard for three or perhaps four nights, when the people coming out of Tredonoc church after morn-

ing service on Sunday noticed that there was a big yellow
sheep-dog in the churchyard. The dog, it appeared, had been
waiting for the congregation; for it at once attached itself to
them, at first to the whole body, and then to a group of half a
dozen who took the turning to the right till they came to a
gate in the hedge, whence a roughly made farm-road went
through the fields, and dipped down into the woods and to
Treff Loyne farm.

Then the dog became like a possessed creature. He barked
furiously. He ran up to one of the men and looked up at him,
"as if he were begging for his life," as the man said, and then
rushed to the gate and stood by it, wagging his tail and barking at intervals. The men stared.

"Whose dog will that be?" said one of them.

"It will be Thomas Griffith's. Treff Loyne," said another.

"Well, then, why doesn't he go home? Go home, then!"
He went through the gesture of picking up a stone from the
road and throwing it at the dog. "Go home, then! Over the
gate with you!"

But the dog never stirred. He barked and whined and ran
up to the men and then back to the gate. The farmer shook
the dog off, and the four went on their way, and the dog stood
in the road and watched them, and then put up its head and
uttered a long and dismal howl that was despair.

Then it occurred to somebody, so far as I can make out
with no particular reference to the odd conduct of the Treff
Loyne sheep-dog, that Thomas Griffith had not been seen for
some time past.

One September afternoon, therefore, a party went up to
discover what had happened to Griffith and his family. There
were half a dozen farmers, a couple of policemen, and four
soldiers, carrying their arms; those last had been lent by the
officer commanding at the camp. Lewis, too, was of the
party; he had heard by chance that no one knew what had become of Griffith and his family, and he was anxious about a

young fellow, a painter, of his acquaintance who had been lodging at Treff Loyne all the summer.

They came to the gate in the hedge where the farm-road led down to Treff Loyne. Here was the farm inclosure, the outlying walls of the yard and the barns and sheds and out-houses. One of the farmers threw open the gate and walked into the yard, and forthwith began bellowing at the top of his voice:

"Thomas Griffith! Thomas Griffith! Where be you, Thomas Griffith?"

The rest followed him. The corporal snapped out an order over his shoulder, and there was a rattling metallic noise as the men fixed their bayonets.

There was no answer to this summons; but they found poor Griffith lying on his face at the edge of the pond in the middle of the yard. There was a ghastly wound in his side, as if a sharp stake had been driven into his body.

It was a still September afternoon. No wind stirred in the hanging woods that were dark all about the ancient house of Treff Loyne; the only sound in the dim air was the lowing of the cattle. They had wandered, it seemed, from the fields and had come in by the gate of the farm-yard and stood there melancholy, as if they mourned for their dead master. And the horses, four great, heavy, patient-looking beasts, were there, too, and in the lower field the sheep were standing, as if they waited to be fed.

Lewis knelt down by the dead man and looked closely at the gaping wound in his side.

"He's been dead a long time," he said. "How about the family? How many are there of them? I never attended them."

"There was Griffith, and his wife, his son Thomas, and Mary Griffith, his daughter. And I do think there was a gentleman lodging with them this summer."

That was from one of the farmers. They all looked at one another, this party of rescue, who knew nothing of the danger that had smitten this house of quiet people, nothing of the peril which had brought them to this pass of a farm-yard, with a dead man in it, and his beasts standing patiently about him as if they waited for the farmer to rise up and give them their food. Then the party turned to the house. The windows were shut tight. There was no sign of any life or movement about the place. The party of men looked at one another.

They did not know what the danger was or where it might strike them or whether it was from without or from within. They stared at the murdered man, and gazed dismally at one another.

"Come," said Lewis, "we must do something. We must get into the house and see what is wrong."

"Yes, but suppose they are at us while we are getting in?" said the sergeant, "Where shall we be then, Doctor Lewis?"

The corporal put one of his men by the gate at the top of the farm-yard, another at the gate by the bottom, and told them to challenge and shoot. The doctor and the rest opened the little gate of the front garden and went up to the porch and stood listening by the door. It was all dead silence. Lewis took an ash stick from one of the farmers and beat heavily three times on the old, black, oaken door studded with antique nails.

There was no answer from within. He beat again, and still silence. He shouted to the people within, but there was no answer. They all turned and looked at one another. There was an iron ring on the door. Lewis turned it, but the door stood fast; it was evidently barred and bolted. The sergeant of police called out to open, but again there was no answer.

They consulted together. There was nothing for it but to blow the door open, and some one of them called in a loud voice to those that might be within to stand away from the door or they would be killed. And at this very moment the yellow sheep-dog came bounding up the yard from the woods and licked their hands and fawned on them and barked joyfully.

"Indeed, now," said one of the farmers, "he did know that there was something amiss. A pity it was, Thomas Williams, that we did not follow him when he implored us last Sunday."

The corporal disengaged his bayonet and shot into the keyhole, calling out once more before he fired. He shot and shot again, so heavy and firm was the ancient door, so stout its bolts and fastenings. At last he had to fire at the massive hinges, and then they all pushed together, and at that the door lurched open suddenly and fell forward.

Young Griffith was lying dead before the hearth. They went on toward the parlor, and in the doorway of the room was the body of the artist Secretan, as if he had fallen in trying to get to the kitchen. Up-stairs the two women, Mrs. Griffith and her daughter, a girl of eighteen, were lying together on the bed in the big bedroom, clasped in each other's arms.

They went about the house, searched the pantries, the back kitchen, and the cellars; there was no life in it. There was no bread in the place, no milk, no water.

The group of men stood in the big kitchen and stared at one another, a dreadful perplexity in their eyes. The old man had been killed with the piercing thrust of some sharp weapon; the rest had perished, it seemed probable, of thirst; but what possible enemy was this that besieged the farm and shut in its inhabitants? There was no answer.

The sergeant of police spoke of getting a cart and taking the bodies into Porth, and Dr. Lewis went into the parlor that Secretan had used as a sitting-room, intending to gather any possessions or effects of the dead artist that he might possibly find there. Half a dozen portfolios were piled up in one corner, there were some books on a side-table, a fishing-rod and basket behind the door; that seemed all. Lewis was about to rejoin the rest of the party in the kitchen, when he looked down at some scattered papers lying with the books on the side-table. On one of the sheets he read, to his astonishment, the words, "Dr. James Lewis, Porth." This was written in a staggering, trembling scrawl.

The table stood in a dark corner of the room, and Lewis gathered up the sheets of paper and took them to the window and began to read this:

I do not think that I can last much longer. We shared out the last drops of water a long time ago. I do not know how many days ago. We fall asleep and dream and walk about the house in our dreams, and I am often not sure whether I am awake or still dreaming, and so the days and nights are confused in my mind. I awoke not long ago, at least I suppose I awoke, and found I was lying in the passage.

There seems no hope for any of us. We are in the dream of death.

Here the manuscript became unintelligible for half a dozen lines. There was a fresh start, as it were, and the writer began again, in ordinary letter-form:

Dear Lewis:

I hope you will excuse all this confusion and wandering. I intended to begin a proper letter to you, and now I find all that stuff that you have been reading, if this ever gets into your hands. I have not the energy even to tear it up. If you read it you will know to what a sad pass I had come when it was written.

I have said of what I am writing, "if this ever gets into your hands," and I am not at all sure that it ever will. If what is happening here is happening everywhere else, then, I suppose, the world is coming to an end. I cannot understand it; even now I can hardly believe it.

And then there's another thing that bothers me. Now and then I wonder whether we are not all mad together in this house. Despite what I see and know, or, perhaps, I should say, because what I see and know is so impossible, I wonder whether we are not all suffering from a delusion. Perhaps we are our own jailers, and we are really free to go out and live.

Perhaps what we think we see is not there at all. I wonder now and then whether we are all like this in Treff Loyne; yet in my heart I feel sure that it is not so.

Still, I do not want to leave a madman's letter behind me, and so I will not tell you the full story of what I have seen or believe I have seen. If I am a sane man, you will be able to fill in the blanks for yourself from your own knowledge. If I am mad, burn the letter and say nothing about it.

I think that it was on a Tuesday that we first noticed that there was something queer about. I came home about five or six o'clock and found the family at Treff Loyne laughing at old Tiger, the sheep-dog. He was making short runs from the farm-yard to the door of the house, barking, with quick, short yelps. Mrs. Griffith and Miss Griffith were standing by the porch, and the dog would go to them, look into their faces, and then run up the farm-yard to the gate, and then look back with that eager, yelping bark, as if he were waiting for the women to follow him. Then, again and again he ran up to them and tugged at their skirts, as if he would pull them by main force away from the house.

The dog barked and yelped and whined and scratched at the door all through the evening. They let him in once, but he seemed to have become quite frantic. He ran up to one member of the family after another; his eyes were bloodshot, and his mouth was foaming, and he tore at their clothes till they drove him out again into the darkness. Then he broke into a long, lamentable howl of anguish, and we heard no more of him.

It was soon after dawn when I finally roused myself. The people in the house were talking to each other in high voices, arguing about something that I did not understand.

"It is those damned Gipsies, I tell you," said old Griffith.

"What would they do a thing like that for?" asked Mrs. Griffith. "If it was stealing, now—"

They seemed puzzled and angry, so far as I could make out, but not at all frightened. I got up and began to dress. I don't think I looked out of the window. The glass on my dressing-table is high and broad, and the window is small;

one would have to poke one's head round the glass to see anything.

The voices were still arguing down-stairs. I heard the old man say, "Well, here's for a beginning, anyhow," and then the door slammed.

A minute later the old man shouted, I think, to his son. Then there was a great noise which I will not describe more particularly, and a dreadful screaming and crying inside the house and a sound of rushing feet. They all cried out at once to each other. I heard the daughter crying: "It is no good, Mother; he is dead. Indeed they have killed him," and Mrs. Griffith screaming to the girl to let her go. And then one of them rushed out of the kitchen and shot the great bolts of oak across the door just as something beat against it with a thundering crash.

I ran down-stairs. I found them all in wild confusion, in an agony of grief and horror and amazement. They were like people who had seen something so awful that they had gone mad.

I went to the window looking out on the farm-yard. I won't tell you all that I saw, but I saw poor old Griffith lying by the pond, with the blood pouring out of his side.

I wanted to go out to him and bring him in. But they told me that he must be stone-dead, and such things also that it was quite plain that any one who went out of the house would not live more than a moment. We could not believe it even as we gazed at the body of the dead man; but it was there. I used to wonder sometimes what one would feel like if one saw an apple drop from the tree and shoot up into the air and disappear. I think I know now how one would feel.

Even then we couldn't believe that it would last. We were not seriously afraid for ourselves. We spoke of getting out in an hour or two, before dinner, anyhow. It couldn't last, because it was impossible. Indeed, at twelve o'clock young Griffith said he would go down to the well by the back way and draw another pail of water. I went to the door and stood by it. He had not gone a dozen yards before they were on him. He ran for his life, and we had all we could do to bar the door in time. And then I began to get frightened.

But day followed day, and it was still there. I went to Treff Loyne because it was buried in the narrow valley under the ash-trees, far away from any track. There was not so much as a footpath that was near it; no one ever came that way.

And now this thought came back without delight, with terror. Griffith thought that a shout might be heard on a still night up away on the Allt, "if a man was listening for it," he added doubtfully. My voice was clearer and stronger than his, and on the second night I said I would go up to my bedroom and call for help through the open window. I waited till it was all dark and still, and looked out through the window before opening it. And then I saw over the ridge of the long barn across the yard what looked like a tree, though I knew there was no tree there. It was a dark mass against the sky, with wide-spread boughs, a tree of thick, dense growth. I wondered what this could be, and I threw open the window not only because I was going to call for help, but because I wanted to see more clearly what the dark growth over the barn really was.

I saw in the depth of it points of fire, and colors in light, all glowing and moving, and the air trembled. I stared out into the night, and the dark tree lifted over the roof of the barn, rose up in the air, and floated toward me. I did not move till it was close to the house; and then I saw what it was, and banged the window down only just in time. I had to fight, and I saw the tree that was like a burning cloud rise up in the night and settle over the barn.

Another day went by, and at dusk I looked out, but the eyes of fire were watching me. I dared not open the window. And then I thought of another plan. There was the great old fireplace, with the round Flemish chimney going high above the house. If I stood beneath it and shouted, I thought perhaps the sound might be carried better than if I called out of the window; for all I knew the round chimney might act as a sort of megaphone. Night after night, then, I stood on the hearth and called for help from nine o'clock to eleven.

But we had drunk up the beer, and we would let ourselves have water only by little drops, and on the fourth night my throat was dry, and I began to feel strange and weak; I knew that all the voice I had in my lungs would hardly reach the length of the field by the farm.

It was then we began to dream of wells and fountains, and water coming very cold, in little drops, out of rocky places in the middle of a cool wood. We had given up all meals; now and then one would cut a lump from the sides of bacon on the kitchen wall and chew a bit of it, but the saltness was like fire.

And then we began to dream, as I say. And one day I dreamed that there was a bubbling well of cold, clear water in the cellar, and I had just hollowed my hand to drink it when I woke. I went into the kitchen and told young Griffith. I said I was sure there was water there. He shook his head, but he took up the great kitchen poker and we went down to the old cellar. I showed him the stone by the pillar, and he raised it up. But there was no well. Later I came upon young Griffith one evening evidently trying to make a subterranean passage under one of the walls of the house. I knew he was mad, as he knew I was mad when he saw me digging for a well in the cellar; but neither said anything to the other.

Now we are past all this. We are too weak. We dream when we are awake and when we dream we think we wake. Night and day come and go, and we mistake one for another.

Only a little while ago I heard a voice which sounded as if it were at my very ears, but rang and echoed and resounded as if it were rolling and reverberated from the vault of some cathedral, chanting in terrible modulations. I heard the words quite clearly, "Incipit liber iræ Domini Dei nostri" ("Here beginneth The Book of the Wrath of the Lord our God").

And then the voice sang the word *Aleph,* prolonging it, it seemed through ages, and a light was extinguished as it began the chapter:

"In that day, saith the Lord, there shall be a cloud over the land, and in the cloud a burning and a shape of fire, and out of the cloud shall issue forth my messengers; they shall run all together, they shall not turn aside; this shall be a day of exceeding bitterness, without salvation. And on every high hill, saith the Lord of Hosts, I will set my sentinels, and my armies shall encamp in the place of every valley; in the house

that is amongst rushes I will execute judgment, and in vain shall they fly for refuge to the munitions of the rocks. In the groves of the woods, in the places where the leaves are as a tent above them, they shall find the sword of the slayer; and they that put their trust in walled cities shall be confounded. Woe unto the armed man, woe unto him that taketh pleasure in the strength of his artillery, for a little thing shall smite him, and by one that hath no might shall he be brought down into the dust. That which is low shall be set on high; I will make the lamb and the young sheep to be as the lion from the swellings of Jordan; they shall not spare, saith the Lord, and the doves shall be as eagles on the hill Engedi; none shall be found that may abide the onset of their battle."

Here the manuscript lapsed again and finally into utter, lamentable confusion of thought.

Dr. Lewis maintained that we should never begin to understand the real significance of life until we began to study just those aspects of it which we now dismiss and overlook as utterly inexplicable and therefore unimportant.

We were discussing a few months ago the awful shadow of the terror which at length had passed away from the land. I had formed my opinion, partly from observation, partly from certain facts which had been communicated to me, and the passwords having been exchanged, I found that Lewis had come by very different ways to the same end.

"And yet," he said, "it is not a true end, or, rather, it is like all the ends of human inquiry—it leads one to a great mystery. We must confess that what has happened might have happened at any time in the history of the world. It did not happen till a year ago, as a matter of fact, and therefore we made up our minds that it never could happen; or, one would better say, it was outside the range even of imagination. But this is our way. Most people are quite sure that the Black Death—otherwise the Plague—will never invade Europe again. They have made up their complacent minds that it was due to dirt and bad drainage. As a matter of fact the Plague had nothing to do with dirt or with drains, and there is nothing to prevent its ravaging England to-morrow. But if you tell people so, they won't believe you."

I agreed with all this. I added that sometimes the world was incapable of seeing, much less believing, that which was before its own eyes.

"Look," I said, "at any eighteenth-century print of a Gothic cathedral. You will find that the trained artistic eye even could not behold in any true sense the building that was before it. I have seen an old print of Peterborough Cathedral that looks as if the artist had drawn it from a clumsy model, constructed of bent wire and children's bricks."

"Exactly; because Gothic was outside the esthetic theory, and therefore vision, of the time. You can't believe what you don't see; rather, you can't see what you don't believe.

"You must not suppose that my experiences of that afternoon at Treff Loyne had afforded me the slightest illumination. Indeed, if it had not been that I had seen poor old Griffith's body lying pierced in his own farm-yard, I think I should have been inclined to accept one of Secretan's hints, and to believe that the whole family had fallen a victim to a collective delusion or hallucination, and had shut themselves up and died of thirst through sheer madness. I think there have been such cases. But I had seen the body of the murdered man and the wound that had killed him.

"Did the manuscript left by Secretan give me no hint? Well, it seemed to me to make confusion worse confounded. You see, Secretan, in writing that extraordinary document, almost insisted on the fact that he was not in his proper senses; that for days he had been part asleep, part awake, part delirious. How was one to judge his statement, to separate delirium from fact? In one thing he stood confirmed; you remember he speaks of calling for help up the old chimney of Treff Loyne; that did seem to fit in with the tales of a hollow, moaning cry that had been heard upon the Allt. So far one could take him as a recorder of actual experiences. And I looked in the old cellars of the farm and found a frantic sort of rabbit-hole dug by one of the pillars; again he was confirmed. But what was one to make of that story of the chanting voice and the letters of the Hebrew alphabet and the chapter out of some unknown minor prophet? When one has the key it is easy enough to sort out the facts or the hints of facts from the delusions; but I hadn't the key on that September evening. I was forgetting the 'tree' with lights and fires in it; that, I think, impressed me more than anything with the feeling that Secretan's story was in the main a true story. I had seen a like appearance down there in my own garden: but what was it?

"Now, I was saying that, paradoxically, it is only by the inexplicable things that life can be explained. We are apt to say, you know, 'a very odd coincidence,' and pass the matter by, as if there were no more to be said or as if that were the end of it. Well, I believe that the only real path lies through the blind alleys."

"How do you mean?"

"Well, this is an instance of what I mean. I was talking with Merritt, my brother-in-law, about the strange things he had seen in a way that I thought all nonsense, and I was wondering how I was going to shut him up when a big moth flew into the room through that window, fluttered about, and succeeded in burning itself alive in the lamp. That gave me my cue. I asked Merritt if he knew why moths made for lamps or something of the kind; I thought it would be a hint to him that I was sick of his half-baked theories. So it was; he looked sulky and held his tongue.

"But a few minutes later I was called out by a man who had found his little boy dead in a field near his cottage about an hour before. The child was so still, they said, that a great moth had settled on his forehead and fluttered away only when they lifted up the body. It was absolutely illogical; but it was this odd 'coincidence' of the moth in my lamp and the moth on the dead boy's forehead that first set me on the track.

I can't say that it guided me in any real sense; it was more like a great flare of red paint on a wall.

"But, as you will remember, from having read my notes on the matter, I was called in about ten days later to see a man named Cradock who had been found in a field near his farm quite dead. This also was at night. His wife found him, and there were some very queer things in her story. She said that the hedge of the field looked as if it were changed; she began to be afraid that she had lost her way and got into the wrong field.

"Then came that extraordinary business of Treff Loyne. I took it all home, and sat down for the evening before it. It appalled me not only by its horror, but here again by the discrepancy between its terms.

"It was, I believe, a sudden leap of the mind that liberated me from the tangle. It was quite beyond logic. I went back to that evening when Merritt was boring me, to the moth in the candle, and to the moth on the forehead of poor Johnnie Roberts. There was no sense in it; but I suddenly determined that the child and Joseph Cradock the farmer, and that unnamed Stratfordshire man, all found at night, all asphyxiated, had been choked by vast swarms of moths. I don't pretend even now that this is demonstrated, but I'm sure it's true.

"Now suppose you encounter a swarm of these creatures in the dark. Suppose the smaller ones fly up your nostrils. You will gasp for breath and open your mouth. Then, suppose some hundreds of them fly into your mouth, into your gullet, into your windpipe, what will happen to you? You will be dead in a very short time, choked, asphyxiated."

"But the moths would be dead, too. They would be found in the bodies."

"The moths? Do you know that it is extremely difficult to kill a moth with cyanide of potassium? Take a frog, kill it, open its stomach. There you will find its dinner of moths and small beetles, and the 'dinner' will shake itself and walk off cheerily, to resume an entirely active existence. No; that is no difficulty.

"Well, now I came to this. I was shutting out all the other cases. I was confining myself to those that came under the one formula.

"Then the next step. Of course we know nothing really about moths; rather, we know nothing of moth reality. For all I know there may be hundreds of books which treat of moths and nothing but moths. But these are scientific books, and science deals only with surfaces. It has nothing to do with realities. To take a very minor matter: we don't even know why the moth desires the flame. But we do know what the moth does not do; it does not gather itself into swarms with the object of destroying human life. But here, by the hypothesis, were cases in which the moth had done this very thing; the moth race had entered, it seemed, into a malignant conspiracy against the human race. It was quite impossible, no doubt,—that is to say, it had never happened before,—but I could see no escape from this conclusion.

"These insects, then, were definitely hostile to man; and then I stopped, for I could not see the next step, obvious though it seems to me now. If the moths were infected with hatred of men, and possessed the design and the power of combining against him, why not suppose this hatred, this design, this power shared by other non-human creatures?

"The secret of the Terror might be condensed into a sentence: the animals had revolted against men.

"Now, the puzzle became easy enough; one had only to classify. Take the cases of the people who met their deaths by falling over cliffs or over the edge of quarries. We think of sheep as timid creatures, who always run away. But suppose sheep that don't run away; and, after all, in reason why should they run away? Quarry or no quarry, cliff or no cliff, what would happen to you if a hundred sheep ran after you instead of running from you? There would be no help for it; they would have you down and beat you to death or stifle you.

Then suppose man, woman, or child near a cliff's edge or a quarry-side, and a sudden rush of sheep. Clearly there is no help; there is nothing for it but to go over. There can be no doubt that that is what happened in all these cases.

"And again. You know the country and you know how a herd of cattle will sometimes pursue people through the fields in a solemn, stolid sort of way. They behave as if they wanted to close in on you. Townspeople sometimes get frightened and scream and run; you or I would take no notice, or, at the utmost, would wave our sticks at the herd, which would stop dead or lumber off. But suppose they don't lumber off? It was a quicker death for poor Griffith of Treff Loyne: one of his own beasts gored him to death with one sharp thrust of its horn into his heart. And from that morning those within the house were closely besieged by their own cattle and horses and sheep, and when those unhappy people within opened a window to call for help or to catch a few drops of rain-water to relieve their burning thirst, the cloud waited for them with its myriad eyes of fire. Can you wonder that Secretan's statement reads in places like mania? You perceive the horrible position of those people in Treff Loyne; not only did they see death advancing on them, but advancing with incredible steps, as if one were to die not only in nightmare, but by nightmare. But no one in his wildest, most fiery dreams had ever imagined such a fate. I am not astonished that Secretan at one moment suspected the evidence of his own senses, at another surmised that the world's end had come."

"And how about the Williamses who were murdered on the Highway near here?"

"The horses were the murderers, the horses that afterward stampeded the camp below. By some means which is still obscure to me they lured that family into the road and beat their brains out; their shod hoofs were the instruments of execution. The munition-works? Their enemy was rats. I believe that it has been calculated that in 'greater London' the number of rats is about equal to the number of human beings; that is, there are about seven millions of them. The proportion would be about the same in all the great centers of population; and the rat, moreover, is on occasion migratory in its habits. You can understand now that story of the *Semiramis* beating about the mouth of the Thames, and at last cast away by Arcachon, her only crew dry heaps of bones. The rat is an expert boarder of ships. And so one can understand the tale told by the frightened man who took the path by the wood that led up from the new munition-works. He thought he heard a thousand men treading softly through the wood and chattering to one another in some horrible tongue; what he did hear was the marshaling of an army of rats, their array before the battle.

"And conceive the terror of such an attack. Even one rat in a fury is said to be an ugly customer to meet; conceive, then, the irruption of these terrible, swarming myriads, rushing upon the helpless, unprepared, astonished workers in the munition-shops."

There can be no doubt, I think, that Dr. Lewis was entirely justified in these extraordinary conclusions. As I say, I had arrived at pretty much the same end, by different ways; but this rather as to the general situation, while Lewis had made his own particular study of those circumstances of the Terror that were within his immediate purview, as a physician in large practice in the southern part of Meirion. Of some of the cases which he reviewed he had, no doubt, no immediate or first-hand knowledge; but he judged these instances by their similarity to the facts which had come under his personal notice. He spoke of the affairs of the quarry at Llanfihangel on the analogy of the people who were found dead at the bottom of the cliffs near Porth, and he was no doubt justified in doing so. He told me that, thinking the whole matter over, he was hardly more astonished by the Terror in itself

than by the strange way in which he had arrived at his conclusions.

"You know," he said, "those certain evidences of animal
malevolence which we knew of, the bees that stung the child
to death, the trusted sheep-dog's turning savage, and so forth.
Well, I got no light whatever from all this; it suggested nothing to me. You do not believe; therefore you cannot see.

"And then, when the truth at last appeared, it was through
the whimsical 'coincidence,' as we call such signs, of the
moth in my lamp and the moth on the dead child's forehead.
This, I think, is very extraordinary."

"And there seems to have been one beast that remained
faithful—the dog at Treff Loyne. That is strange."

"That remains a mystery."

It would not be wise, even now, to describe too closely the
terrible scenes that were to be seen in the munition areas of
the North and the Midlands during the black months of the
Terror. Out of the factories issued at black midnight the
shrouded dead in their coffins, and their very kinsfolk did not
know how they had come by their deaths. All the towns were
full of houses of mourning, were full of dark and terrible rumors as incredible as the incredible reality. There were things
done and suffered that perhaps never will be brought to light,
memories and secret traditions of these things will be whispered in families, delivered from father to son, growing
wilder with the passage of the years, but never growing
wilder than the truth.

It is enough to say that the cause of the Allies was for a
while in deadly peril. The men at the front called in their
extremity for guns and shells. No one told them what was
happening in the places where these munitions were made.

But, after the first panic, measures were taken. The workers were armed with special weapons, guards were mounted,
machine-guns were placed in position, bombs and liquid
flame were ready against the obscene hordes of the enemy,

and the "burning clouds" found a fire fiercer than their own. Many deaths occurred among the airmen; but they, too, were given special guns, arms that scattered shot broadcast, and so drove away the dark flights that threatened the airplanes.

And then, in the winter of 1915–16, the Terror ended suddenly as it had begun. Once more a sheep was a frightened beast that ran instinctively from a little child; the cattle were again solemn, stupid creatures, void of harm; the spirit and the convention of malignant design passed out of the hearts of all the animals. The chains that they had cast off for a while were thrown again about them.

And finally there comes the inevitable "Why?" Why did the beasts who had been humbly and patiently subject to man, or affrighted by his presence, suddenly know their strength and learn how to league together and declare bitter war against their ancient master?

It is a most difficult and obscure question. I give what explanation I have to give with very great diffidence, and an eminent disposition to be corrected if a clearer light can be found.

Some friends of mine, for whose judgment I have very great respect, are inclined to think that there was a certain contagion of hate. They hold that the fury of the whole world at war, the great passion of death that seems driving all humanity to destruction, infected at last these lower creatures, and in place of their native instinct of submission gave them rage and wrath and ravening.

This may be the explanation. I cannot say that it is not so, because I do not profess to understand the working of the universe. But I confess that the theory strikes me as fanciful. There may be a contagion of hate as there is a contagion of smallpox; I do not know, but I hardly believe it.

In my opinion, and it is only an opinion, the source of the great revolt of the beasts is to be sought in a much subtler region of inquiry. I believe that the subjects revolted because the king abdicated. Man has dominated the beasts through-

out the ages, the spiritual has reigned over the rational
through the peculiar quality and grace of spirituality that
men possess, that makes a man to be that which he is. And
when he maintained this power and grace, I think it is pretty
clear that between him and the animals there was a certain
treaty and alliance. There was supremacy on the one hand
and submission on the other; but at the same time there was
between the two that cordiality which exists between lords
and subjects in a well-organized state. I know a socialist who
maintains that Chaucer's "Canterbury Tales" give a picture
of true democracy. I do not know about that, but I see that
knight and miller were able to get on quite pleasantly together, just because the knight knew that he was a knight and
the miller knew that he was a miller. If the knight had had
conscientious objections to his knightly grade, while the
miller saw no reason why he should not be a knight, I am
sure that their intercourse would have been difficult, unpleasant, and perhaps murderous.

So with man. I believe in the strength and truth of tradition. A learned man said to me a few weeks ago: "When I
have to choose between the evidence of tradition and the evidence of a document, I always believe the evidence of tradition. Documents may be falsified and often are falsified;
tradition is never falsified." This is true; and therefore, I
think, one may put trust in the vast body of folklore which
asserts that there was once a worthy and friendly alliance between man and the beasts. Our popular tale of Dick Whit-
tington and his cat no doubt represents the adaptation of a
very ancient legend to a comparatively modern personage,
but we may go back into the ages and find the popular tradition asserting that not only are the animals the subjects, but
also the friends of man.

All that was in virtue of that singular spiritual element in
man which the rational animals do not possess. Spiritual does
not mean respectable, it does not even mean moral, it
does not mean "good" in the ordinary acceptation of the

word. It signifies the royal prerogative of man, differentiating him from the beasts.

For long ages he has been putting off this royal robe, he has been wiping the balm of consecration from his own breast. He has declared again and again that he is not spiritual, but rational; that is, the equal of the beasts over whom he was once sovereign. He has vowed that he is not Orpheus, but Caliban.

But the beasts also have within them something which corresponds to the spiritual quality in men; we are content to call it instinct. They perceived that the throne was vacant; not even friendship was possible between them and the self-deposed monarch. If he was not king, he was a sham, an impostor, a thing to be destroyed.

Hence, I think, the Terror. They have risen once; they may rise again.

The Elf Trap

by Francis Stevens

Francis Stevens was the pseudonym of an American woman named Gertrude Barrows Bennett, and her stories were published exclusively in American magazines, all but one dating from the short span of 1917 through 1923, after which time she ceased writing. "The Elf Trap" is my favorite among her writings. It skillfully transplants the European traditions of the elves into the Appalachian Mountains in western North Carolina, transforming them in the process.

"The Elf Trap" was first published in the 5 July 1919 issue of *Argosy*.

I N this our well-advertised, modern world, crammed with engines, death-dealing shells, life-dealing serums, and science, he who listens to "old wives' tales" is counted idle. He who believes them, a superstitious fool. Yet there are some legends which have a strange, deathless habit of recrudescence in many languages and lands.

Of one such I have a story to tell. It was related to me by a well-known specialist in nervous diseases, not as an instance of the possible truth behind fable, but as a curious case in which—I quote his words—"the delusions of a diseased brain were reflected by a second and otherwise sound mentality."

No doubt his view was the right one. And yet, at the finish, I had the strangest flash of feeling. As if, somewhere, some time, I, like young Wharton, had stood and seen against blue sky—Elva, of the sky-hued scarf and the yellow honeysuckles.

But my part is neither to feel nor surmise. I will tell the story as I heard it, save for substitution of fictitious names for the real ones. My quotations from the red note-book are verbatim.

Theron Tademus, A. A. S., F. E. S., D. S., et cetera, occupied the chair of biology in a not-unfamed university. He was the author of a treatise on cytology, since widely used as a text-book, and of several important brochures on the more obscure infusoria. As a boy he had been—in appearance—a romantically charming person. The age of thirty-seven found him still handsome in a cold, fine-drawn manner, but almost inhumanly detached from any save scientific interests.

Then, at the height of his career, he died. Having entered his class-room with intent to deliver the first lecture of the fall term, he walked to his desk, laid down a small, red note-book, turned, opened his mouth, went ghastly white and subsided. His assistant, young Wharton, was first to reach him and first to discover the shocking truth.

Tademus was unmarried, and his will bequeathed all he possessed to the university.

The little red book was not at first regarded as important. Supposed to contain notes for his lecture, it was laid aside. On being at last read, however, by his assistant in course of arranging his papers, the book was found to contain not notes, but a diary covering the summer just passed.

Barring the circumstances of one peculiar incident, Wharton already knew the main facts of that summer.

Tademus, at the insistence of his physician—the specialist aforesaid—had spent July and August in the Carolina Mountains, not far north from the famous summer resort, Asheville. Dr. Locke was friend as well as medical adviser, and he lent his patient the use of a bungalow he owned there.

It was situated in a beautiful, but lonely spot, to which the nearest settlement was Carcassonne. In the valley below stood a tiny railroad-station, but Carcassonne was not built up around this, nor was it a town at all in the ordinary sense.

A certain landscape painter had once raised him a house on that mountainside, at a place chosen for its magnificent view. Later, he was wont to invite thither, for summer sketching, one or two of his more favored pupils. Later still, he increased this number. For their accommodation other structures were raised near his mountain studio, and the Blue Ridge summer class became an established fact, with a name of its own and a rather large membership.

Two roads led thither from the valley. One, that most in use by the artist colonists, was as good and broad as any Carolina mountain road could hope to be. The other, a winding, narrow, yellow track, passed the lonely bungalow of Dr. Locke, and at last split into two paths, one of which led on to further heights, the second to Carcassonne.

The distance between colony and bungalow was considerable, and neither was visible to the other. Tademus was not interested in art, and, as disclosed by the red book, he was not even aware of Carcassonne's existence until some days after his arrival at the bungalow.

Solitude, long walks, deep breathing, and abstinence from work or sustained thought had been Dr. Locke's prescription, accepted with seeming meekness by Tademus.

Nevertheless, but a short time passed till Wharton received a telegram from the professor ordering him to pack and send by express certain apparatus, including a microscope and dissecting stand. The assistant obeyed.

Another fortnight, and Dr. Locke in turn received an urgent wire. It was from Jake Higgins, the negro caretaker whom he had "lent" to Tademus along with the bungalow.

Leaving his practise to another man's care, Locke fled for the Carolina Blue Ridge.

He found his negro and his bungalow, but no Tademus.

By Jake's story, the professor had gone to walk one afternoon and had not returned. Having wired Locke, the negro
had otherwise done his best. He notified the county sheriff, and search-parties scoured the mountains. At his appeal,
also, the entire Carcassonnian colony, male and female,
turned out with enthusiasm to hunt for Tademus. Many of
them carried easel and sketch-box along, and for such it is to
be feared that their humane search ended with the discovery
of any tempting "bit" in the scenic line.

However, the colony's efforts were at least as successful as
the sheriff's, or indeed those of any one else.

Shortly before Tademus's vanishment, a band of gipsies
had settled themselves in a group of old, empty, half-ruined
negro shacks, about a mile from Locke's bungalow.

Suspicion fell upon them. A posse visited the encampment, searched it, and questioned every member of the mi-
grant band. They were a peculiarly ill-favored set, dirty and
villainous of feature. Nothing, however, could be found of
either the missing professor or anything belonging to him.

The posse left, after a quarrel that came near to actual
fighting. A dog—a wretched, starved yellow cur—had attacked one of the deputies and set its teeth in his boot. He
promptly shot it. In their resentment, the dog's owners drew
knives.

The posse were more efficiently armed, and under threat
of the latter's rifles and shotguns, the gipsies reconsidered.
They were warned to pack up and leave, and following a few
days' delay, they obeyed the mandate.

On the very morning of their departure, which was also
the eighth day after Tademus's disappearance, Dr. Locke sat
down gloomily to breakfast. The search, he thought, must be
further extended. Let it cover the whole Blue Ridge, if need
be. Somewhere in those mountains was a friend and patient
whom he did not propose to lose.

At one side of the breakfast-room was a door. It led into
the cleared-out bedroom which Locke had, with indignation,

discovered to have been converted into a laboratory by the patient he had sent here to "rest."

Suddenly this door opened. Out walked Theron Tademus.

He seemed greatly amazed to find Locke there, and said that he had come in shortly after midnight and been in his laboratory ever since.

Questioned as to his whereabouts before that, he replied surprisingly that throughout the week he had been visiting with friends in Carcassonne.

Dr. Locke doubted his statement, and reasonably.

Artists are not necessarily liars, and every artist and near-artist in the Carcassonne colony had not only denied knowledge of the professor, but spent a good part of the week helping hunt for him.

Later, after insisting that Locke accompany him to Carcassonne and meet his "friends" there, Tademus suddenly admitted that he had not previously been near the place. He declined, however, either to explain his untruthful first statement, or give any other account of his mysterious absence.

One week ago Tademus had left the bungalow, carrying nothing but a light cane, and wearing a white flannel suit, canvas shoes, and a Panama. That was his idea of a tramping costume. He had returned, dressed in the same suit, hat and shoes. Moreover, though white, they looked neat as when he started, save for a few grass-stains and the road's inevitable yellow clay about his shoe-soles.

If he had spent the week vagrant-wise, he had been remarkably successful in keeping his clothes clean.

"Asheville," thought the doctor. "He went by train, stopped at a hotel, and has returned without the faintest memory of his real doings. Lame, overtaxed nerves can play that sort of trick with a man's brain."

But he kept the opinion to himself. Like a good doctor, he soon dropped the whole subject, particularly because he saw that Tademus was deeply distressed and trying to conceal the fact.

On plea of taking a long-delayed vacation of his own, Locke remained some time at the bungalow, guarded his friend from the curiosity of those who had combed the hills for him, and did all in his power to restore him to health and a clear brain.

He was so far successful that Tademus returned to his classes in the fall, with Locke's consent.

To his classes—and death.

Wharton had known all this. He knew that Tademus's whereabouts during that mysterious week had never been learned. But the diary in the red book purported to cover the summer, *including that week.*

To Wharton, the record seemed so supremely curious that he took a liberty with what was now the university's property. He carried the red book to Dr. Locke.

It was evening, and the latter was about to retire after a day's work that began before dawn.

"Personal, you say?" Locke handled the book, frowning slightly.

"Personal. But I feel—when you've finished reading that, I have a rather queer thing to tell you in addition. You can't understand till you've read it. I am almost sure that what is described here has a secret bearing on Professor Tademus's death."

"His heart failed. Overwork. There was no mystery in that."

"Maybe not, doctor. And yet—won't you please read?"

"Run through it aloud for me," said the doctor. "I couldn't read one of my own prescriptions to-night, and you are more familiar with that microscopic writing of his."

Wharton complied.

Monday, July 3.

Arrived yesterday. Not worse than expected, but bad enough. If Locke were here, he should be satisfied. I have absolutely no occupation. Walked and climbed for two hours, as prescribed. Spent the rest of day pacing up and down indoors. Enough walking, at least. I can't sit idle. I can't stop thinking. Locke is a fool!

Thursday, July 6.

Telegraphed Wharton to-day. He will express me the Swift binocular, some slides, cover-glasses, and a very little other apparatus. Locke *is* a fool. I shall follow his advice, but within reason. There is a room here lighted by five windows. Old Jake has cleared the bedroom furniture out. It has qualities as a laboratory. Not, of course, that I intend doing any real work. An hour or so a day of micrological observation will only make "resting" tolerable.

Tuesday, July 11.

Jake hitched up his "ol' gray mule" and has brought my three cases from the station. I unpacked the old Stephenson-Swift and set it up. The mere touch of it brought tears to my eyes. Locke's "rest-cure" has done that to my nerves!

After unpacking, though, I resolutely let the microscope and other things be. Walked ten miles up-hill and down. Tried to admire the landscape, as Locke advised, but can't see much in it. Rocks, trees, lumpy hills, yellow roads, sky, clouds, buzzards. Beauty! What beauty is there in this vast, clumsy world that is the outer husk for nature's real and delicate triumphs?

I saw a man painting to-day. He was swabbing at a canvas with huge, clumsy brushes. He had his easel set up by the road, and I stopped to see what any human being could find hereabout worth picturing.

And what had this painter, this artist, this lover of beauty chosen for a subject? Why, about a mile from here there is a clump of ugly, dark trees. A stream runs between them and the road. It is yellow with clay, and too swift. The more interesting micro-organisms could not exist in it. A ramshackle, plank bridge crosses it, leading to the grove, and there, between the trees, stand and lean some dreary, half ruined huts.

That scene was the one which my "artist" had chosen for his subject!

For sheer curiosity I got into conversation with the fellow.

Unusual gibberish of chiaroscuro, flat tones, masses, *et cetera*. Not a definite thought in his head as to *why* he wished to paint those shacks. I learned one thing, though. He wasn't the isolated specimen of his kind I had thought him. Locke failed to tell me about Carcassonne. Think of it! Nearly a hundred of these insane pursuers of "beauty" are spending the summer within walking distance of the house I have promised to live in!

And the one who was painting the grove actually invited me to call on him! I smiled non-committally, and came home. On the way I passed the branch road that leads to the place. I had always avoided that road, but I didn't know why until to-day. Imagine it! Nearly a hundred. Some of them women, I suppose. No, I shall keep discreetly away from Carcassonne.

Saturday, July 15.

Jake informs me that a band of gipsies have settled themselves in the grove which my Carcassonnian acquaintance chose to paint. They are living in the ruined huts. Now I shall avoid that road, too. Talk of solitude! Why, the hills are fairly swarming with artists, gipsies, and Lord knows who else. One might as well try to rest in a beehive!

Found some interesting variations of the ciliata living in a near-by pond. Wonderful! Have recorded over a dozen specimens in which the macronucleus is unquestionably double. Not lobed, nor pulverate, as in Oxytricha, but *double!* My summer has not, after all, been wasted.

Felt singularly slack and tired this morning, and realized that I have hardly been out of the house in three days. Shall certainly take a long tramp to-morrow.

Monday, July 17.

Absent-mindedness betrayed me to-day. I had a very unpleasant experience. Resolutely keeping my promise to Locke,

I sallied forth this afternoon and walked briskly for some distance. I had, however, forgotten the gipsies and took my old route.

Soon I met a woman, or rather a girl. She was arrayed in the tattered, brilliantly colored garments which women of these wandering tribes affect. There was a scarf about her head. I noticed, because its blue was exactly the soft, brilliant hue of the sky over the mountains behind her. There was a stripe of yellow in it, too, and thrust in her sash she carried a great bunch of yellow flowers—wild honeysuckle, I think.

Her face was not dark, like the swart faces of most gipsies. On the contrary, the skin of it had a smooth, firm whiteness. Her features were fine and delicate.

Passing, we looked at one another, and I saw her eyes brighten in the strangest, most beautiful manner. I am sure that there was nothing bold or immodest in her glance. It was rather like the look of a person who recognizes an old acquaintance, and is glad of it. Yet we never met before. Had we met, I could not have forgotten her.

We passed without speaking, of course, and I walked on.

Meeting the girl, I had hardly thought of her as a gipsy, or indeed tried to classify her in any way. The impression she left was new in my experience. It was only on reaching the grove that I came to myself, as it were, and remembered Jake's story of the gipsies who are camping there.

Then I very quickly emerged from the vague, absurd happiness which sight of the girl had brought.

While talking with my Carcassonnian, I had observed that grove rather carefully. I had thought it perfect—that nothing added could increase the somber ugliness of its trees, nor the desolation of its gray, ruined, tumble-down old huts.

To-day I learned better. To be perfect, ugliness must include humanity.

The shacks, dreary in themselves, were hideous now. In their doorways lounged fat, unclean women nursing their filthy off-spring. Older children, clothed in rags, caked with dirt, sprawled and fought among themselves. Their voices were like the snarls of animals.

I realized that the girl with the sky-like scarf had come from here—out of this filth unspeakable!

A yellow cur, the mere, starved skeleton of a dog, came tearing down to the bridge. A rusty, jangling bell was tied about its neck with a string. The beast stopped on the far side and crouched there, yapping. Its anger seemed to surpass mere canine savagery. The lean jaws fairly writhed in maniacal but loathsomely feeble ferocity.

A few men, whiskered, dirty-faced, were gathered about a sort of forge erected in the grove. They were making something, beating it with hammers in the midst of showers of sparks. As the dog yapped, one of the men turned and saw me. He spoke to his mates, and to my dismay they stopped work and transferred their attention to me.

I was afraid that they would cross the bridge, and the idea of having to talk to them was for some reason inexpressibly revolting.

They stayed where they were, but one of them suddenly laughed out loudly, and held up to my view the thing upon which they had been hammering.

It was a great, clumsy, rough, *iron trap*. Even at that distance I could see the huge, jagged teeth, fit to maim a bear—or a man. It was the ugliest instrument I have ever seen.

I turned away and began walking toward home, and when I looked back they were at work again.

The sun shone brightly, but about the grove there seemed to be a queer darkness. It was like a place alone and aloof from the world. The trees, even, were different from the other mountain trees. Their heavy branches did not stir at all in the wind. They had a strange, dark, flat look against the sky, as though they had been cut from dark paper, or rather like the flat trees woven in a tapestry. That was it. The whole scene was like a flat, dark, unreal picture in tapestry.

I came straight home. My nerves are undoubtedly in bad shape, and I think I shall write Locke and ask him to prescribe medicine that will straighten me up. So far, his "rest-cure" has not been notably successful.

Wednesday, July 19.

I have met her again.

Last night I could not sleep at all. Round midnight I ceased trying, rose, dressed, and spent the rest of the night with the good old Stephenson-Swift. My light for night-work—a common oil lamp—is not very brilliant. This morning I suffered considerable pain behind the eyes, and determined to give Locke's "walking and open air" treatment another trial, though discouraged by previous results.

This time I remembered to turn my back on the road which leads to that hideous grove. The sunlight seemed to increase the pain I was already suffering. The air was hot, full of dust, and I had to walk slowly. At the slightest increase of pace my heart would set up a kind of fluttering, very unpleasant and giving me a sense of suffocation.

Then I came to the girl.

She was seated on a rock, her lap heaped with wild honeysuckle, and she was weaving the flower-stems together.

Seeing me, she smiled.

"I have your garland finished," she said, "and mine soon will be."

One would have thought the rock a trysting place at which we had for a long time been accustomed to meet! In her hand she was extending to me a wreath, made of the honeysuckle flowers.

I can't imagine what made me act as I did. Weariness and the pain behind my eyes may have robbed me of my usual good sense.

Anyway, rather to my own surprise, I took her absurd wreath and sat down where she made room for me on the boulder.

After that we talked.

At this moment, only a few hours later, I couldn't say whether or not the girl's English was correct, nor exactly what she said. But I can remember the very sound of her voice.

I recall, too, that she told me her name, Elva, and that when I asked for the rest of it, she informed me that one good name was enough for one good person.

That struck me as a charmingly humorous sally. I laughed like a boy—or a fool, God knows which!

Soon she had finished her second garland, and laughingly insisted that we each crown the other with flowers.

Imagine it! Had one of my students come by then, I am sure he would have been greatly startled. Professor Theron Tademus, seated on a rock with a gipsy girl, crowned with wild honeysuckle and adjusting a similar wreath to the girl's blue-scarfed head!

Luckily, neither the student nor any one else passed, and in a few minutes she said something that brought me to my senses. Due to that inexplicable dimness of memory, I quote the sense, not her words.

"My father is a ruler among our people. You must visit us. For my sake, the people and my father will make you welcome."

She spoke with the gracious air of a princess, but I rose hastily from beside her. A vision of the grove had returned—dark—oppressive—like an old, dark tapestry, woven with ugly forms and foliage. I remembered the horrible, filthy tribe from which this girl had sprung.

Without a word of farewell, I left her there on the rock. I did not look back, nor did she call after me. Not until reaching home, when I met old Jake at the door and saw him stare, did I remember the honeysuckle wreath. I was still wearing it, and carrying my hat.

Snatching at the flowers I flung them in the ditch and retreated with what dignity I might into the bungalow's seclusion.

It is night now, and a little while since I went out again. The wreath is here in the room with me. Its flowers were unsoiled by the ditch, and seem fresh as when she gave them to me. They are more fragrant than I had thought even wild honeysuckle could be.

Elva. Elva of the sky-blue scarf and the yellow honeysuckle!

My eyes are heavy, but the pain behind them is gone. I think I shall sleep to-night.

Friday, July 21.

Is there any man so gullible as he who prides himself on his accuracy of observation?

I ask this in humility, for I am that man.

Yesterday I rose, feeling fresher than for weeks past. After all, Locke's treatment seemed worthy of respect. With that in mind, I put in only a few hours staining some of my binucleate cilia and finishing the slides.

All the last part of the afternoon I faithfully tramped the roads. There is undoubtedly a sort of broad, coarse charm in mere landscape, with its reaches of green, its distant purples, and the sky like a blue scarf flung over it all. Had the pain of my eyes not returned, I could almost have enjoyed those vistas.

Having walked farther than usual, it was deep dusk when I reached home. As if from ambush, a little figure dashed out from behind some rhododendrons. It seemed to be a child, a boy, though I couldn't see him clearly, nor how he was dressed.

He thrust something into my hand. To my astonishment, the thing was a spray of wild honeysuckle.

"Elva—Elva—Elva!"

The strange youngster was fairly dancing up and down before me, repeating the girl's name and nothing else.

Recovering myself, I surmised that Elva must have sent this boy, and sure enough, at my insistence he managed to stop prancing long enough to deliver her message.

Elva's grandmother, he said, was very ill. She had been ailing for days, but to-night the sickness was worse—much worse. Elva feared that her grandmother would die, and, "of course," the boy said, "no doctor will come for our sending!" She had remembered me, as the only friend she knew among the "outside people." Wouldn't I come and look at her poor, sick grandmother? And if I had any of the outside people's medicine in my house, would I please bring that with me?

Well, yes, I did hesitate. Aside from practical and obvious suspicions, I was possessed with a senseless horror for not only the gipsy tribe, but the grove itself.

But there was the spray of honeysuckle. In her need, she had sent that for a token—and sent it to me! Elva, of the sky-like scarf and laughing mouth.

"Wait here," I said to the boy, rather bruskly, and entered the house. I had remembered a pocket-case of simple reme-dies, none of which I had ever used, but there was a direction pamphlet with them. If I must play amateur physician, that might help. I looked for Jake, meaning to inform him of my proposed expedition. Though he had left a chicken broiling on the kitchen range, the negro was not about. He might have gone to the spring for water.

Passing out again, I called the boy, but received no answer. It was very dark. Toward sunset, the sky had clouded over, so that now I had not even the benefit of starlight.

I was angry with the boy for not waiting, but the road was familiar enough, even in the dark. At least, I thought it was, till, colliding with a clump of holly, I realized that I must have strayed off and across a bare stretch of yellow clay which defaces the mountainside above Locke's bunga-low.

I looked back for the guiding lights of its windows, but the trees hid them. However, the road couldn't be far off. After some stumbling about, I was sure that my feet were in the right track again. Somewhat later I perceived a faint, ruddy point of light, to the left and ahead of me.

Walking toward it, the rapid rush and gurgle of water soon apprised me that I had reached the stream with the plank bridge across it.

There I stood for several minutes, staring toward the ruddy light. That was all I could see. It seemed, somehow, to cast no illumination about it.

There came a scamper of paws, the tinkle of a bell, and then a wild yapping broke out on the stream's far side. That vile, yellow cur, I thought. Elva, having imposed on my kind-ness to the extent of sending for me, might at least have arranged a better welcome than this.

Then I pictured her, crouched in her bright, summer-colored garments, tending the dreadful old hag that her grandmother must be. The rest of the tribe were probably indifferent. She could not desert her sick—and there stood I, hesitant as any other coward!

For the dog's sake I took a firm grip on my cane. Feeling about with it, I found the bridge and crossed over.

Instantly something flung itself against my legs and was gone before I could hit out. I heard the dog leaping and barking all around me. It suddenly struck me that the beast's voice was not like that of the yellow cur. There was nothing savage in it. This was the cheerful, excited bark of a well-bred dog that welcomes its master, or its master's friend. And the bell that tinkled to every leap had a sweet, silvery note, different from the cracked jangle of the cur's bell.

I had hated and loathed that yellow brute, and to think that I need not combat the creature was a relief. The huts, as I recalled them, weren't fifty yards beyond the stream. There was no sign of a campfire. Just that one ruddy point of light.

I advanced—

Wharton paused suddenly in his reading. "Here," he interpolated, "begins that part of the diary which passed from commonplace to amazing. And the queer part is that in writing it, Professor Tademus seems to have been unaware that he was describing anything but an unusually pleasant experience."

Dr. Locke's heavy brows knit in a frown.

"Pleasant!" he snapped. "The date of that entry?"

"July 21."

"The day he disappeared. I see. Pleasant! And that gipsy girl—faugh! What an adventure for such a man! No wonder he tried to lie out of it. I don't think I care to hear the rest, Wharton. Whatever it is, my friend is dead. Let him rest."

"Oh, but wait," cried the young man with startled earnestness. "Good Lord, doctor, do you believe I would bring this book even to you if it contained *that* kind of story—about Professor Tademus? No. Its amazing quality is along different lines than you can possibly suspect."

"Get on, then," grumbled Locke, and Wharton continued.

Suddenly, as though at a signal, not one, but a myriad of lights blazed into existence.

It was like walking out of a dark closet into broad day. The first dazzlement passing, I perceived that instead of the somber grove and ruined huts, I was facing a group of very beautiful houses.

It is curious how a previous and false assumption will rule a man. Having believed myself at the gipsy encampment, several minutes passed before I could overcome my bewilderment and realize that after losing my road I had not actually regained it.

That I had somehow wandered into the other branch road, and reached, not the grove, but Carcassonne!

I had no idea, either, that this artists' colony could be such a really beautiful place. It is cut by no streets. The houses are set here and there over the surface of such green lawns as I have never seen in these mountains of rock and yellow clay.

(Dr. Locke started slightly in his chair. Carcassonne, as he had himself seen it, flashed before his memory. He did not interrupt, but from that moment his attention was alertly set, like a man who listens for the keyword of a riddle.)

Everywhere were lights, hung in the flowering branches of trees, glowing upward from the grass, blazing from every door and window. Why they should have been turned on so abruptly, after that first darkness, I do not yet know.

Out of the nearest house a girl came walking. She was dressed charmingly, in thin, bright-colored silks. A bunch of wild honeysuckle was thrust in the girdle, and over her hair was flung a scarf of skylike blue. I knew her instantly, and began to see a glimmering of the joke that had been played on me.

The dog bounded toward the girl. He was a magnificent collie. A tiny silver bell was attached to his neck by a broad ribbon.

I take credit for considerable aplomb in my immediate behavior. The girl had stopped a little way off. She was laughing, but I had certainly allowed myself to be victimized.

On my accusation, she at once admitted to having deceived me. She explained that, perceiving me to be misled by her appearance into thinking her one of the gipsies, she could not resist carrying out the joke. She had sent her small brother with the token and message.

I replied that the boy deserted me, and that I had nearly invaded the camp of real gipsies while looking for her and the fictitious dying grandmother.

At this she appeared even more greatly amused. Elva's mirth has a peculiarly contagious quality. Instead of being angry, I found myself laughing with her.

By this time quite a throng of people had emerged on the lawns, and leading me to a dignified, fine-looking old man who she said was her father, she presented me. In the moment, I hardly noticed that she used my first name only, Theron, which I had told her when we sat on the roadside boulder. I have observed since that all these people use the single name only, in presentation and intercourse. Though lacking personal experience with artists, I have heard that they are inclined to peculiar "fads" of unconventionality. I had never, however, imagined that they could be attractive to a man like myself, or pleasant to know.

I am enlightened. These Carcassonnian "colonists" are the only charming, altogether delightful people whom I have ever met.

One and all, they seemed acquainted with Elva's amusing jest at my expense. They laughed with us, but in recompense have made me one of themselves in the pleasantest manner.

I dined in the house of Elva's father. The dining-room, or rather hall, is a wonderful place. Due to much microscopic work, I am inclined to see only clumsiness—*largeness*—in what other people characterize as beauty. Carcassonne is different. There is a minute perfection about the architecture of these artists' houses, the texture of their clothes, and even the delicate contour of their faces, which I find amazingly agreeable.

There is no conventionality of costume among them. Both

men and women dress as they please. Their individual taste is exquisite, and the result is an array of soft fabrics, and bright colors, flowerlike, rather than garish.

Till last night I never learned the charm of what is called "fancy dress," nor the genial effect it may exert on even a rather somber nature, such as I admit mine to be.

Elva, full of good-natured mischief, insisted that I must "dress for dinner." Her demand was instantly backed by the whole laughing throng. Carried off my feet in a way to which I am not at all used, I let them drape me in white robes, laced with silver embroideries like the delicate crystallization of hoar-frost. Dragged hilariously before a mirror, I was amazed at the change in my appearance.

Unlike the black, scarlet-hooded gown of my university, these glittering robes lent me not dignity, but a kind of—I can only call it a noble youthfulness. I looked younger, and at the same time *keener*—more alive. And either the contagious spirit of my companions, or some resurgence of boyishness filled me with a sudden desire to please; to be merry with the merry-makers, and—I must be frank—particularly to keep Elva's attention where it seemed temporarily fixed—on myself.

My success was unexpectedly brilliant. There is something in the very atmosphere of Carcassonne which, once yielded to, exhilarates like wine. I have never danced, nor desired to learn. Last night, after a banquet so perfect that I hardly recall its details, I danced. I danced with Elva—and with Elva—and always with Elva. She laughed aside all other partners. We danced on no polished floors, but out on the green lawns, under white, laughing stars. Our music was not orchestral. Wherever the light-footed couples chose to circle, there followed a young flutist, piping on his flute of white ivory.

Fluttering wings, driving clouds, wind-tossed leaves—all the light, swift things of the air were in that music. It lifted and carried one with it. One did not need to learn. One danced! It seems, as I write, that the flute's piping is still in my ears, and that its echoes will never cease. Elva's voice is like the ivory flute's. Last night I was mad with the music and her voice. We danced—I know not how long, nor when we ceased.

This morning I awakened in a gold-and-ivory room, with round windows that were full of blue sky and crossed by blossoming branches. Dimly I recalled that Elva's father had urged me to accept his hospitality for the night.

Too much of such new happiness may have gone to my head, I'm afraid. At least, it was nothing stronger. At dinner I drank only one glass of wine—sparkling, golden stuff, but mild and with a taste like the fragrance of Elva's wild honey-suckle blooms.

It is midmorning now, and I am writing this seated on a marble bench beside a pool in the central court of my host's house. I am waiting for Elva, who excused herself to attend to some duty or other. I found this book in my pocket, and thought best to make an immediate record of not only a good joke on myself, but the only really pleasant social experience I have ever enjoyed.

I must lay aside these fanciful white robes, bid Elva good-by, and return to my lonely bungalow and Jake. The poor old darky is probably tearing his wool over my unexplained absence. But I hope for another invitation to Carcassonne!

Saturday, July 22.

I seem to be "staying on" indefinitely. This won't do. I spoke to Elva of my extended visit, and she laughingly informed me that people who have drunk the wine and worn the woven robes of Carcassonne seldom wish to leave. She suggested that I give up trying to "escape" and spend my life here. Jest, of course; but I half wished her words were earnest. She and her people are spoiling me for the common, workaday world.

Not that they are idle, but their occupations as well as pleasures are of a delicate, fascinating beauty.

Whole families are stopping here, including the children. I don't care for children, as a rule, but these are harmless as butterflies. I met Elva's messenger, her brother. He is a funny, dear little elf. How even in the dark I fancied him one of those gipsy brats is hard to conceive. But then I took Elva herself for a gipsy!

My new friends engage in many pursuits besides painting. "Crafts," I believe they are called. This morning Elva took me around the "shops." Shops like architectural blossoms, carved out of the finest marble!

They make jewelry, weave fabrics, tool leather, and follow many other interesting occupations. Set in the midst of the lawns is a forge. Every part of it, even to the iron anvil, is embellished with a fernlike inlay of other metals. Several amateur silversmiths were at work there, but Elva hurried me away before I could see what they were about.

I have inquired for the young painter who first told me of Carcassonne and invited me to visit him here. I can't recall his name, but on describing him to Elva she replied vaguely that not every "outsider" was permanently welcome among her people.

I did not press the question. Remembering the ugliness which that same painter had been committing to canvas, I could understand that his welcome among these exquisite workers might be short-lived. He was probably banished, or banished himself, soon after our interview on the road.

I must be careful, lest I wear out my own welcome. Yet the very thought of that old, rough, husk of a world that I *must* return to, brings back the sickness, and the pain behind my eyes that I had almost forgotten.

Sunday, July 23.

Elva! Her presence alone is delight. The sky is not bluer than her scarf and eyes. Sunlight is a duller gold than the wild honeysuckle she weaves in garlands for our heads.

To-day, like child sweethearts, we carved our names on the smooth trunk of a tree. "Elva—Theron." And a wreath to shut them in. I am happy. Why—why, indeed should I leave Carcassonne?

Monday, July 24.

Still here, but this is the last night that I shall impose upon these regally hospitable people. An incident occurred to-day, pathetic from one view-point, outrageous from another. I was asleep when it happened, and only woke up at sound of the gunshot.

Some rough young mountaineers rode into Carcassonne and wantonly killed Elva's collie dog. They claimed, I believe, that the unlucky animal attacked one of their number. A lie! The dog was gentle as a kitten. He probably leaped and barked around their horses and annoyed the young brutes. They had ridden off before I reached the scene.

Elva was crying, and no wonder. They had blown her pet's head clean off with a shotgun. Don't know what will be done about it. I wanted to go straight to the county sheriff, but Elva wouldn't have that. I pretended to give in, but if her father doesn't see to the punishment of those men, I will. Murderous devils! Elva is too forgiving.

Wednesday, July 26.

I watched the silversmiths to-day. Elva was not with me. I had no idea that silver was worked like iron. They must use some peculiar amalgam, or it would melt in the furnace, instead of emerging white-hot, to be beaten with tiny, delicate hammers.

They were making a strange looking contraption. It was all silver, beaten into floral patterns, but the general shape was a riddle to me. Finally I asked one of the smiths what they were about. He is a tall fellow, with a merry, dark face.

"Guess!" he demanded.

"Can't. To my ignorance, it resembles a Chinese puzzle."

"Something more curious than that."

"What?"

"An—*elf-trap!*" He laughed mischievously.

"Please!"

"Well, it's a trap, anyway. See this?" The others had stepped back good naturedly. With his hammer he pressed on a lever. Instantly two slender, jawlike parts of the queer machine opened wide. They were set with needlelike points, or teeth. It was all red-hot, and when he removed his hammer the jaws clashed in a shower of sparks.

"It's a trap, of course." I was still puzzled.

"Yes, and a very remarkable one. This trap will not only catch, but it will *re*catch."

"I don't understand."

"If any creature—a man, say"—he was laughing again—"walks into this trap, he may escape it. But sooner or later—soon, I should think—it will catch him again. That is why we call it an elf-trap!"

I perceived suddenly that he was making pure game of me. His mates were all laughing at the nonsense. I moved off, not offended, but perturbed in another way.

He and his absurd, silver trap-toy had reminded me of the gipsies. What a horrible, rough iron thing that was which they had held up to me from their forge! Men capable of creating such an uncouthly cruel instrument as that jag-toothed trap would be terrible to meet in the night. And I had come near blundering in among them—at night!

This won't do. I have been happy. Don't let me drop back into the morbidly nervous condition which invested those gipsies with more than human horror. Elva is calling me. I have been too long alone.

Friday, July 28.

Home again. I am writing this in my bungalow-laboratory. Gray dawn is breaking, and I have been at work here since midnight. Feel strangely depressed. Need breakfast, probably.

Last night Elva and I were together in the court of her father's house. The pool in the center of it is lighted from below to a golden glow. We were watching the goldfish, with their wide, filmy tails of living lace.

Suddenly I gave a sharp cry. I had seen a thing in the water more important than goldfish. Snatching out the small collecting bottle, without which I never go abroad, I made a quick pass at the pool's glowing surface.

Elva had started back, rather frightened.

"What is it?"

I held the bottle up and peered closely. There was no mistake.

"Dysteria," I said triumphantly. "Dysteria ciliata. Dysteria giganticus, to give a unique specimen the separate name he deserves. Why, Elva, this enormous creature will give me a new insight on his entire species!"

"What enormous creature?"

For the first time I saw Elva nearly petulant. But I was filled with enthusiasm. I let her look in the bottle.

"There!" I ejaculated. "See him?"

"Where? I can't see anything but water—and a tiny speck in it."

"That," I explained proudly, "is dysterius giganticus! Large enough to be seen by the naked eye. Why, child, he's a monster of his kind. A fresh-water variety, too!"

I thrust the bottle in my pocket.

"Where are you going?"

"Home, of course. I can't get this fellow under the microscope any too quickly."

I had forgotten how wide apart are the scientific and artistic temperaments. No explanation I could make would persuade Elva that my remarkable capture was worth walking a mile to examine properly.

"You are all alike!" she cried. "All! You talk of love, but your love is for gold, or freedom, or some pitiful, foolish nothingness like that speck of life you call by a long name— and leave *me* for!"

"But," I protested, "only for a little while. I shall come back."

She shook her head. This was Elva in a new mood, dark brows drawn, laughing mouth drooped to a sullen curve. I felt sorry to leave her angry, but my visit had already been preposterously long. Besides, a rush of desire had swept me to get back to my natural surroundings. I wanted the feel of the micrometer adjuster in my fingers, and to see the round, speckled white field under the lens pass from blurred chaos to perfect definition.

She let me go at last. I promised solemnly to come to her whenever she should send or call. Foolish child! Why, I can walk over to Carcassonne every day, if she likes.

I hear Jake rattling about in the breakfast-room. Conscience informs me that I have treated that negro rather badly. Wonder where he thought I was? Couldn't have been much worried, or he would have hunted me up in Carcassonne.

August 30.

I shall not make any further entries in this book. My day for the making of records is over, I think. Any sort of records. I go back to my classes next month. God knows what I shall say to them! Elva!

I may as well finish the story here. Every day I find it harder to recall details. If I hadn't this book, with what I wrote in it when I was—when I was *there,* I should believe that my brain had failed in earnest.

Locke said I couldn't have been in Carcassonne. He stood in the breakfast-room, with the sunlight striking across him. I saw him clearly. I saw the huge, coarse, ugly creature that he was. And in that minute, *I knew.*

But I wouldn't admit it, even to myself. I made him go with me to Carcassonne. There was no stream. There was no bridge. The houses were wretched bungalows, set about on the bare, flat, yellow clay of the mountainside. The people— artists, save the mark!—were a common, carelessly dressed, painting-aproned crowd who fulfilled my original idea of an artists' colony.

Their coarse features and thick skins sickened me. Locke walked home beside me, very silent. I could hardly bear his company. He was gross—coarse—*human!*

Toward evening, managing to escape his company, I stole up the road to the gipsy's grove. The huts were empty. That queer look, as of a flat, dark tapestry, was gone from the grove.

I crossed the plank bridge. Among the trees I found ashes, and a depression where the forge had stood. Something else, too. A dog, or rather its unburied remains. The yellow cur. Its head had been blown off by a shot-gun. An ugly little bell lay in the mess, tied to a piece of string.

One of the trees—it had a smooth trunk—and carved in the bark—I can't write it. I went away and left those two names carved there.

The wild honeysuckle has almost ceased to bloom. I can leave now. Locke says I am well, and can return to my classes.

I have not entered my laboratory since that morning. Locke admires my "will-power" for dropping all that till physical health should have returned. Will-power! I shall never look into a microscope again.

Perhaps she will know that somehow, and send or call for me quickly.

I have drunk the wine and worn the woven robes of her people. They made me one of them. Is it right that they should cast me out, because I did not understand what I have since guessed so well?

I can't bear the *human* folk about me. They are clumsy, revolting. And I can't work. God knows what I shall say to my classes.

Here is the end of my last record—till she calls!

There was silence in Locke's private study. At last the doctor expelled his breath in a long sigh. He might have been holding it all that time.

"Great—Heavens!" he ejaculated. "Poor old Tademus! And I thought his trouble in the summer there was a temporary lapse. But he talked like a sane man. Acted like one, too, by Jove! With his mind in that condition! And in spite of the posse, he must have been with the gipsies all that week. You can see it. Even through his delusions, you catch occasional notes of reality.

"I heard of that dog-shooting, and he speaks of being asleep when it happened. Where was he concealed that the posse didn't find him? Drugged and hidden under some filthy heap of rags in one of the huts, do you think? And why hide him at all, and then let him go? He returned the very day they left."

At the volley of questions, Wharton shook his head.

"I can't even guess about that. He was certainly among the gipsies. But as for his delusions, to call them so, there is a kind of beauty and coherence about them which I—well, which I don't like!"

The doctor eyed him sharply.

"You can't mean that you—"

"Doctor," said Wharton softly, "do you recall what he wrote of the silversmiths and their work? They were making an elf-trap. Well, I think the elf-trap—caught him!"

"What?"

Locke's tired eyes opened wide. A look of alarm flashed into them. The alarm was for Wharton, not himself.

"Wait!" said the latter. "I haven't finished. You know that I was in the classroom when Professor Tademus died?"

"Yes."

"Yes! I was first to reach him. But before that, I stood near the desk. There are three windows at the foot of that room. Every other man there faced the desk. I faced the windows. The professor entered, laid down his book and turned to the class. As he did so, a head appeared in one of those windows. They are close to the ground, and a person standing outside could easily look in.

"The head was a woman's. No, I am not inventing this. I saw her head, draped in a blue scarf. I noticed, because the scarf's blueness gave me the strangest thrill of delight. It was the exact blue of the sky behind it. Then she had raised her hand. I saw it. In her fingers was a spray of yellow flowers—yellow as sunshine. She waved them in a beckoning motion. Like this. Then Tademus dropped.

"And there are legends, you know, of strange people, either more or less than human, who appear as gipsies, but are not the real gipsies, that possess queer powers. Their outer appearance is rough and vile, but behind that, as a veil, they live a wonderful hidden life of their own.

"And a man who has been with them once is caught—caught in the real elf-trap, which the smiths' work only symbolized. He may escape, but he can't forget nor be joined again with his own race, while to return among *them,* he must walk the dark road that Tademus went when she called.

"Oh, I've scoffed at 'old wives' tales with the rest of our overeducated, modern kind. I can't ever scoff again, because—

"What's that? A prescription? For me? Why, doctor, you don't yet understand. I *saw* her, I tell you. Elva! Elva, of the wild honeysuckle and the skylike scarf!"

The Thin Queen of Elfhame

by James Branch Cabell

James Branch Cabell was a prolific American writer, and much of his output centers on Dom Manuel, a swineherd in the imaginary medieval French province of Poictesme. Cabell represents a very different type of fantasy from Tolkien. Cabell's writings are at times heavily ironic, sometimes very subtly so, but also filled with wisdom and beauty. Frequently his protagonists seek some ideal, only to learn that what they find is not the same as what they thought they sought.

"The Thin Queen of Elfhame" was first published in the December 1922 issue of the *Century Magazine*. It was slightly revised to appear as chapter 4 in Cabell's *Straws and Prayer-Books* (1924). The magazine version is reprinted here.

How many silken ladies wept, well out of eyeshot of their husbands, when it was known that courteous Anavalt had left Count Emmerick's court, remains an indeterminable matter; but it is certain the number was large. There were, in addition, three women whose grieving for him was not ever to be ended: these did not weep. In the meanwhile, with all this furtive sorrowing some leagues behind him and with a dead horse at his feet, tall Anavalt stood at a sign-post and doubtfully considered a rather huge dragon.

"No," the dragon was saying comfortably; "no, for I have just had dinner, and exercise upon a full stomach is unwholesome. So I shall not fight you, and you are welcome, for all of me, to go your ways into the Woods of Elfhame."

"Yet what," says Anavalt, "if I were to be more observant than you of your duty and of your hellish origin? And what if I were to insist upon a fight to the death?"

When dragons shrug in sunlight, their bodies are one long, green, glittering ripple.

"I should be conquered. It is my business to be conquered in this world, where there are two sides to everything, and where one must look for reverses. I tell you frankly, tired man, that all we terrors who keep colorful the road to the Elle Maid are here for the purpose of being conquered. We make the way seem difficult, and that makes you who have souls in your bodies the more determined to travel on it. Our thin queen found out long ago that the most likely manner of alluring men to her striped windmill was to persuade men she is quite inaccessible."

Said Anavalt:

"That I can understand; but I need no such baits."

"Aha, so you have not been happy out yonder where people have souls? You probably are not eating enough; so long as one can keep on eating regularly, there is not much the matter. In fact, I see the hunger in your eyes, tired man."

Anavalt said:

"Let us not discuss anybody's eyes, for it is not hunger, or indigestion either, which drives me to the Wood of Elfhame. There is a woman yonder, dragon, a woman whom ten years ago I married. We loved each other then, we shared a noble dream. To-day we sleep together and have no dreams. To-day I go in flame-colored satin, with heralds before me, into bright, long halls where kings await my counsel, and my advising becomes the law of cities that I have not seen. The lords of this world accredit me with wisdom, and say that nobody is more shrewd than Anavalt. But when at home, as if by accident, I tell my wife about these things, she smiles not very merrily. For my wife knows more of the truth as to me and my powers and my achievements than I myself would care to know, and I can no longer endure the gaze of her forgiving eyes and the puzzled hurt which is behind that forgiveness. So let us not discuss anybody's eyes."

"Well, well," the dragon returned, "if you come to that, I think it would be more becoming for you not to discuss your married life with strangers, especially when I have just had dinner and am just going to have a nap."

With that the evil worm turned round three times, his whiskers drooped, and he coiled up snugly about the sign-post which said, "Keep Out Of These Woods." He was a time-worn and tarnished dragon, as you could see now, with no employment in the world since men had forgotten the myth in which he used to live appallingly; so he had come, in homeless decrepitude, to guard the Wood of Elfhame.

Anavalt thus left this inefficient and out-moded monster. Anavalt went into the wood. He did not think of the tilled meadows or the chests of new-minted coin or the high estate which belonged to Anavalt in the world where people have souls. He thought of quite other matters as he walked in a dubious place. Here to the right of Anavalt's pathway were seen twelve in red tunics; they had head-dresses of green, and upon their wrists were silver rings. These twelve were alike in shape and age and loveliness; there was no flaw in the appearance of any, there was no manner of telling one from another. All these made a lament with small, sweet voices that followed the course of a thin and tinkling melody. They sang of how much better were the old times than the new, and none could know more thoroughly than did Anavalt the reason of their grieving; but since they did not molest him, he had no need to meddle with these women's secrets any more. So he went on, and nothing as yet opposed him; at most, a grasshopper started from the path, sometimes a tiny frog made way for him.

He came to a blue bull that lay in the road, blocking it. This beast appeared more lusty and more terrible than other bulls; all his appurtenances were larger and seemed more prodigally ready to give life and death. Courteous Anavalt cried out:

"O Nandi, now be gracious and permit me to pass unhindered toward the striped windmill."

"To think," said the bull, "that you should mistake me for Nandi! No, tired man, the Bull of the Gods is white, and nothing of that serene color may ever come into these woods." And the bull nodded very gravely, shaking the blue curls that were between his cruel horns.

"Ah, then, sir, I must entreat your forgiveness for the not unnatural error into which I was betrayed by the majesty of your appearance."

While Anavalt was speaking, he wondered why he should be at pains to humor an illusion so trivial as he knew this bull to be. For this, of course, was just the ruler of the Kittle cattle which everywhere feed upon the dew pools. The Queen of Elfhame, in that low estate to which the world's redemption had brought her, could employ only the most inexpensive of retainers; the gods served her no longer.

"So you consider my appearance majestic! To think of that, now!" observed the flattered bull, and he luxuriously exhaled blue flames. "Well, certainly you have a mighty civil way with you, to be coming from that overbearing world of souls. Still, my duty is, as they say, my duty; fine words are less filling than moonbeams; and, in short, I do not know of any good reason why I should let you pass toward Queen Vae."

Anavalt answered:

"I must go to your thin mistress because among the women yonder whose bodies were not denied to me there is one woman whom I cannot forget. We loved each other once; we had, as I recall that radiant time, a quaint and callow faith in our shared insanity. Then somehow I stopped caring for these things; I turned to matters of more sensible worth. She took no second lover; she lives alone. Her beauty and her quick laughter are put away, she is old, and the home of no man is glad because of her, who should have been the tenderest of wives and the most merry of mothers. When I see her, there is no hatred in the brown eyes which once were bright and roguish, but only forgiveness and a puzzled griev-ing. Now there is in my mind no reason why I should think about this woman differently from some dozens of other women who were maids when I first knew them, but there is in my mind an unreason that will not put away the memory of this woman's notions about me."

"Well," said the bull, yawning, "for my part, I find one heifer as good as another; and I find, too, that in seeking Queen Vae one pretext is as good as another pretext, espe-cially from the mouth of such a civil gentleman. So do you climb over my back, and go your way to where there are no longer two sides to everything."

Thus Anavalt passed the king of the Kittle cattle. Anavalt journeyed deeper into the Wood of Elfhame. No trumpets sounded before him as they sounded when the Anavalt who was a great lord went about the world where people have souls; and the wonders which Anavalt saw to this side and to that side did not disturb him, nor he them. He came to a house of rough-hewn timber, where a black man, clothed in a goat-skin, barked like a dog and made old gestures. This, as Anavalt knew, was the Rago; within the house sat cross-legged at that very moment the Forest Mother, whose living is innocent of every normal vice, and whose food is the red she-goat and men. Yet upon the farther side of the home of perversity were to be seen a rusty nail in the pathway and bits of broken glass, prosaic relics which seemed to show that men had passed this place.

So Anavalt made no reply to the obscene enticements of the Rago. Anavalt went sturdily on to a tree which in the stead of leaves was overgrown with human hands; these hands had no longer any warmth in them as they caught at and tentatively fingered Anavalt, and presently released him.

Now the path descended amid undergrowth that bore small purple flowers with five petals. Anavalt came here upon wolves that went along with him a little way. Running, they could not be seen, but as each wolf leaped in his run-

ning, his gray body would show momentarily among the
green bushes that instantly swallowed it; and these wolves
cried hoarsely, "Abiron is dead!" But for none of these
things did Anavalt care any longer, and none of the peculiari-
ties of Elfhame stayed him until his path had led farther
downward and the roadway had become dark and moist.
Here were sentinels with draggled yellow plumes, a pair
of sentinels at whom Anavalt looked only once; then with
averted head he passed them, in what could not seem a merry
place to Anavalt, for in the world where people have souls he
was used to mirth and soft ease and to all such delights as
men clutch desperately in the shadow of death's clutching
hand. In this place Anavalt found also a naked boy whose
body was horrible with leprosy. This malady had eaten away
his fingers, so that they could retain nothing, but his face was
not much changed.

The leper stood knee-deep in a pile of ashes, and he demanded what Anavalt was called nowadays.

When courteous Anavalt had answered, the leper said then:

"You are not rightly called Anavalt. But my name is still
Owner of the World."

Said Anavalt, very sadly:

"Even though you bar my way, ruined boy, I must go forward to the Elle Maid."

"And for what reason must you be creeping to this last
woman? For she will be the last, as I forewarn you, tired
man, who still pretend to be Anavalt—she will be the last of
all, and of how many!"

Anavalt answered:

"I must go to this last love because of my first love. Once
I lay under her girdle, I was a part of the young body of my
first love. She bore me to her anguish, even then to her anguish. I cannot forget the love that was between us. But I out-
grew my childhood and all childishness; I became, they say,
the chief of Manuel's barons, and my living has got me fine
food and garments and tall servants and two castles and a

known name, and all which any reasonable mother could hope for her son. Yet I cannot forget the love that was between us or our shared faith in what was to be. To-day I visit this ancient woman now and then, and we make friendly talk together about everything except my wife, and our lips touch, and I go away. That is all. And it seems strange that I was once a part of this woman, I who have never won to or desired real intimacy with any one; and it seems strange to hear people applauding my wisdom and high deeds of state-craft and in all matters acclaiming the success of Anavalt. I think that this old woman also finds it strange. I do not know, for we can understand each other no longer. I only know that, viewing me, there is in this old woman's filmed eyes a sort of fondness even now, and a puzzled grieving. I only know that her eyes also I wish never to see any more."

"Still, still, you must be talking Oedipean riddles," the leper answered. "I prefer simplicity; I incline to the complex no longer. So, very frankly, I warn you, who were Anavalt, that you are going, spent and infatuate, toward your last illusion."

Anavalt replied:

"Rather do I flee from the illusions of others. Behind me I am leaving the bright swords of adversaries and the more deadly malice of outrivaled friends and the fury of some husbands, but not because I fear these things. Behind me I am leaving the puzzled eyes of women that put faith in me, because I fear these unendurably."

"You should have feared them earlier, tired man, in a sun-lit time when I, who am Owner of the World, would wonder-fully have helped you. Now you must go your way, as I go mine. There is one who may, perhaps, yet bring us together once again; but now we are parted, and you need look for no more reverses."

As he said this, the ruined boy sank slowly into the ash-heap and so disappeared, and Anavalt went on through tram-pled ashes into the quiet midst of the wood. Among the

bones about the striped windmill that is supported by four
pillars the witless Elle Maid was waiting.

She rose and cried:

"You are very welcome, Sir Anavalt. But what will you
give Maid Vae?"

Anavalt answered:

"All."

"Then we shall be happy together, dear Anavalt, and for
your sake I am well content to throw my bonnet over the
windmill."

She took the red bonnet from her head and turned. She
flung her bonnet fair and high. So was courteous Anavalt assured that the Queen of Elfhame was as he had hoped. For
when seen thus, from behind, the witless queen was hollow
and shadow-colored, because Maid Vae is just the bright,
thin mask of a woman, and, if looked at from behind, she is
like any other mask. So when she faced him now and smiled,
and, as if in embarrassment, looked down and pushed aside
a thigh-bone with her little foot, then Anavalt could see that
the Elle Maid was, when properly regarded, a lovely and
most dear illusion.

He kissed her. He was content. Here was the woman he
desired, the woman who did not exist in the world where
people have souls. The Elle Maid had no mortal body that
time would parody and ruin, she had no brain to fashion
dreams of which he would fall short, she had no heart that he
would hurt. There was an abiding peace in this quiet Wood of
Elfhame wherein no love could enter, and nobody could, in
consequence, hurt anybody else very deeply. At court the
silken ladies wept for Anavalt, and three women were not
ever to be healed of their memories; but in the Wood of
Elfhame, where all were soulless masks, there were no memories and no weeping, there were no longer two sides to
everything, and a man need look for no reverses.

"I think we shall do very well here," said courteous
Anavalt as yet again he kissed Maid Vae.

The Woman of the Wood

by A. Merritt

Tolkien is unlikely to have known of "The Woman of the Wood" by A. Merritt, an American writer, but would have sympathized with the impulse behind the story, which tells of how trees might defend themselves. In a letter published in the newspaper *Daily Telegraph* on 4 July 1972, Tolkien wrote that "in all my works I take the part of trees as against all their enemies." And Tolkien's Ents in *The Lord of the Rings* embody this same desire.

"The Woman of the Wood" was first published in the August 1926 issue of the American pulp magazine *Weird Tales*.

McKAY sat on the balcony of the little inn that squatted like a brown gnome among the pines that clothed the eastern shore of the lake.

It was a small and lonely lake high up on the Vosges; and yet the word "lonely" is not just the one to tag its spirit; rather was it aloof, withdrawn. The mountains came down on every side, making a vast tree-lined bowl that seemed filled, when McKay first saw it, with a still wine of peace.

McKay had worn the wings with honor in the World War. And as a bird loves the trees, so did McKay love them. They were to him not merely trunks and roots, branches and leaves; they were personalities. He was acutely aware of character differences even among the same species—that pine was jolly and benevolent; that one austere, monkish;

there stood a swaggering bravo and there a sage wrapped in green meditation; that birch was a wanton; the one beside her virginal, still adream.

The war had sapped McKay, nerve, brain, and soul. Through all the years that had passed the wound had kept open. But now, as he slid his car down the side of the great green bowl, he felt its peace reach out to him, caress and quiet him, promise him healing. He seemed to drift like a falling leaf through the cathedraled woods, to be cradled by the hands of the trees.

McKay had stopped at the little gnome of an inn, and there he had lingered, day after day, week after week.

The trees had nursed him; soft whisperings of the leaves, slow chant of the needled pines, had first deadened, then driven from him the re-echoing clamor of the war and its sorrow. The open wound of his spirit had closed under their healing, had closed and become scars; and then even the scars had been covered and buried, as the scars on Earth's breast are covered and buried beneath the falling leaves of autumn. The trees had laid healing hands upon his eyes. He had sucked strength from the green breasts of the hills.

As that strength flowed back to him, McKay grew aware that the place was—troubled, that there was ferment of fear within it.

It was as though the trees had waited until he himself had become whole before they made their own unrest known to him. But now they were trying to tell him something; there was a shrillness as of apprehension, of anger, in the whispering of the leaves, the needled chanting of the pines.

And it was this that had kept McKay at the inn—a definite consciousness of appeal. He strained his ears to catch words in the rustling branches, words that trembled on the brink of his human understanding. Never did they cross that brink.

Gradually he had focused himself, so he believed, to the point of the valley's unease.

On all the shores of the lake there were but two dwellings.

One was the inn, and around the inn the trees clustered protectively, confidingly, friendly. It was as though they had not only accepted it, but had made it part of themselves.

Not so was it of the other habitation. Once it had been the hunting lodge of long-dead lords; now it was half ruined, forlorn. It lay across the lake almost exactly opposite the inn and back upon the slope a half mile from the shore. Once there had been fat fields around it and a fair orchard.

The forest had marched down upon fields and lodge. Here and there scattered pines and poplars stood like soldiers guarding some outpost; scouting parties of saplings lurked among the gaunt, broken fruit trees. But the forest had not had its way unchecked; ragged stumps showed where those who dwelt in the old house had cut down the invaders; blackened patches showed where they had fired the woods.

Here was the center of the conflict. Here the green folk of the forest were both menaced and menacing, at war.

The lodge was a fortress beleaguered by the trees, a fortress whose garrison sallied forth with ax and torch to take their toll of their besiegers.

Yet McKay sensed a slow, inexorable pressing on of the forest; he saw it as an army ever filling the gaps in its enclosing ranks, shooting its seeds into the cleared places, sending its roots out to sap them, and armed always with a crushing patience. He had the impression of constant regard, of watchfulness, as though night and day the forest kept myriads of eyes upon the lodge, inexorably, not to be swerved from its purpose. He had spoken of this impression to the innkeeper and his wife, and they had looked at him, oddly.

"Old Polleau does not love the trees, no," the old man had said, "No, nor do his two sons. They do not love the trees— and very certainly the trees do not love them."

Between the lodge and the shore, marching down to the verge of the lake was a singularly beautiful little coppice of silver birches and firs. This coppice stretched for perhaps a quarter of a mile; it was not more than a hundred feet or two in depth, and not alone the beauty of its trees but also their curious grouping vividly aroused McKay's interest. At each end were a dozen or more of the glistening, needled firs, not clustered but spread out as though in open marching order; at widely spaced intervals along its other two sides paced single firs. The birches, slender and delicate, grew within the guard of these sturdier trees, yet not so thickly as to crowd one another.

To McKay the silver birches were for all the world like some gay caravan of lovely demoiselles under the protection of debonair knights. With that odd other sense of his he saw the birches as delectable damsels, merry and laughing—the pines as lovers, troubadours in green-needled mail. And when the winds blew and the crests of the trees bent under them, it was as though dainty demoiselles picked up fluttering, leafy skirts, bent leafy hoods, and danced while the knights of the firs drew closer round them, locked arms and danced with them to the roaring horns of the winds. At such times he almost heard sweet laughter from the birches, shoutings from the firs.

Of all the trees in that place McKay loved best this little wood. He had rowed across and rested in its shade, had dreamed there and, dreaming, had heard mysterious whisperings and the sound of dancing feet light as falling leaves, had taken dream draft of that gaiety which was the soul of the little wood.

Two days ago he had seen Polleau and his two sons. McKay had lain dreaming in the coppice all that afternoon. As dusk began to fall he had reluctantly arisen and begun to row back to the inn. When he had been a few hundred feet from shore three men had come out from the trees and had stood watching him—three grim, powerful men taller than the average French peasant.

He had called a friendly greeting to them, but they had not answered it; had stood there, scowling. Then as he bent again to his oars, one of the sons had raised a hatchet and driven it savagely into the trunk of a slim birch. McKay thought he heard a thin, wailing cry from the stricken tree, a sigh from all the little wood.

He had felt as though the keen edge had bitten into his own flesh.

"Stop that!" he had cried. "Stop it, damn you!"

For answer Polleau's son had struck again, and never had McKay seen hate etched so deep as on his face as he struck. Cursing, a killing rage in his heart, McKay had swung the boat around, raced back to shore. He had heard the hatchet strike again and again and, close now to shore, had heard a crackling and over it once more the thin, high wailing. He had turned to look.

The birch was tottering, was falling. Close beside it grew one of the firs, and, as the smaller tree crashed over, it dropped upon this fir like a fainting maid into the arms of her lover. And as it lay and trembled there, one of the branches of the other tree slipped from under it, whipped out, and smote the hatchet wielder a crushing blow upon the head, sending him to earth.

It had been, of course, only the chance blow of a bough, bent by pressure of the fallen trunk and then released as that had slipped down. Of course—yet there had been such suggestion of conscious action in the branch's recoil, so much of bitter anger in it, so much, in truth, had it been like a purposeful blow that McKay felt an eerie prickling of his scalp; his heart had missed its beat.

For a moment Polleau and the standing son had stared at the sturdy fir with the silvery birch lying upon its green breast, folded in and shielded by its needled boughs as though—again the swift impression came to McKay—as though it were a wounded maid stretched on breast, in arms, of knightly lover. For a long moment father and son had stared.

Then, still wordless but with that same bitter hatred in

both their faces, they had stooped and picked up the other and, with his arms around the neck of each, had borne him limply away.

McKay, sitting on the balcony of the inn that morning, went over and over that scene, realized more and more clearly the human aspect of fallen birch and clasping fir, and the conscious deliberateness of the latter's blow. During the two days that had elapsed since then, he had felt the unease of the trees increase, their whispering appeal become more urgent.

What were they trying to tell him? What did they want him to do?

Troubled, he stared across the lake, trying to pierce the mists that hung over it and hid the opposite shore. And suddenly it seemed that he heard the coppice calling him, felt it pull the point of his attention toward it irresistibly, as the lodestone swings and holds the compass needle.

The coppice called him; it bade him come.

McKay obeyed the command; he arose and walked down to the boat landing; he stepped into his skiff and began to row across the lake. As his oars touched the water his trouble fell from him. In its place flowed peace and a curious exaltation.

The mists were thick upon the lake. There was no breath of wind, yet the mists billowed and drifted, shook and curtained under the touch of unfelt airy hands.

They were alive—the mists; they formed themselves into fantastic palaces past whose opalescent façades he flew; they built themselves into hills and valleys and circled plains whose floors were rippling silk. Tiny rainbows gleamed out among them, and upon the water prismatic patches shone and spread like spilled wine of opals. He had the illusion of vast distances—the hillocks of mist were real mountains, the valleys between them were not illusory. He was a colossus cleaving through some elfin world. A trout broke, and it was like Leviathan leaping from the fathomless deep. Around the arc of the fish's body rainbows interlaced and then dissolved into rain of softly gleaming gems—diamonds in dance with sapphires, flame-hearted rubies, pearls with shimmering souls of rose. The fish vanished, diving cleanly without sound; the jeweled bows vanished with it; a tiny irised whirlpool swirled for an instant where trout and flashing arcs had been.

Nowhere was there sound. He let his oars drop and leaned forward, drifting. In the silence, before him and around him, he felt opening the gateways of an unknown world.

And suddenly he heard the sound of voices, many voices, faint at first and murmurous. Louder they became, swiftly; women's voices sweet and lilting, and mingled with them the deeper tones of men; voices that lifted and fell in a wild, gay chanting through whose *joyesse* ran undertones both of sorrow and of anger—as though faery weavers threaded through silk spun of sunbeams, somber strands dipped in the black of graves, and crimson strands stained in the red of wrathful sunsets.

He drifted on, scarce daring to breathe lest even that faint sound break the elfin song. Closer it rang and clearer, and now he became aware that the speed of his boat was increasing, that it was no longer drifting, as though the little waves on each side were pushing him ahead with soft and noiseless palms. His boat grounded, and as its keel rustled along over the smooth pebbles of the beach the song ceased.

McKay half arose and peered before him. The mists were thicker here, but he could see the outlines of the coppice. It was like looking at it through many curtains of fine gauze, and its trees seemed shifting, ethereal, unreal. And moving among the trees were figures that threaded among the boles and flitted round them in rhythmic measures, like the shadows of leafy boughs swaying to some cadenced wind.

He stepped ashore. The mists dropped behind him, shutting off all sight of the lake, and as they dropped, McKay lost all sense of strangeness, all feeling of having entered some unfamiliar world. Rather it was as though he had re-

turned to one he had once known well and that had been long
lost to him.

The rhythmic flitting had ceased; there was now no movement as there was no sound among the trees—yet he felt the
little wood full of watchful life. McKay tried to speak; there
was a spell of silence on his mouth.

"You called me. I have come to listen to you—to help you
if I can."

The words formed within his mind, but utter them he
could not. Over and over he tried, desperately; the words
seemed to die on his lips.

A pillar of mist whirled forward and halted, eddying half
an arm's length away. Suddenly out of it peered a woman's
face, eyes level with his own. A woman's face—yes; but
McKay, staring into those strange eyes probing his, knew
that, woman's though it seemed, it was that of no woman of
human breed. They were without pupils, the irises deer-large
and of the soft green of deep forest dells; within them
sparkled tiny star points of light like motes in a moonbeam.
The eyes were wide and set far apart beneath a broad, low
brow over which was piled braid upon braid of hair of palest
gold, braids that seemed spun of shining ashes of gold. The
nose was small and straight, the mouth scarlet and exquisite.
The face was oval, tapering to a delicately pointed chin.

Beautiful was that face, but its beauty was an alien one,
unearthly. For long moments the strange eyes thrust their
gaze deep into his. Then out of the mist were thrust two slender white arms, the hands long, the fingers tapering.

The tapering fingers touched his ears.

"He shall hear," whispered the red lips.

Immediately from all about him a cry arose; in it were the
whispering and rustling of the leaves beneath the breath of
the winds; the shrilling of the harp strings of the boughs; the
laughter of hidden brooks; the shoutings of waters flinging
themselves down into deep and rocky pools—the voices of
the forest made articulate.

"He shall hear!" they cried.

The long white fingers rested on his lips, and their touch was cool as bark of birch on cheek after some long upward climb through forest, cool and subtly sweet.

"He shall speak," whispered the scarlet lips of the wood woman.

"He shall speak!" answered the wood voices again, as though in litany.

"He shall see," whispered the woman, and the cold fingers touched his eyes.

"He shall see!" echoed the wood voices.

The mists that had hidden the coppice from McKay wavered, thinned, and were gone. In their place was a limpid, translucent, palely green *aether*, faintly luminous, as though he stood within some clear wan emerald. His feet pressed a golden moss spangled with tiny starry bluets. Fully revealed before him was the woman of the strange eyes and the face of unearthly beauty. He dwelt for a moment upon the slender shoulders, the firm, small, tip-tilted breasts, the willow litheness of her body. From neck to knees a smock covered her, sheer and silken and delicate as spun cobwebs; through it her body gleamed as though fire of the young spring moon ran in her veins.

He looked beyond her. There upon the golden moss were other women like her, many of them; they stared at him with the same wide-set green eyes in which danced the sparkling moonbeam motes; like her they were crowned with glistening, pallidly golden hair; like hers, too, were their oval faces with the pointed chins and perilous alien beauty. Only where she stared at him gravely, measuring him, weighing him, there were those of her sisters whose eyes were mocking; and those whose eyes called to him with a weirdly tingling allure, their mouths athirst; those whose eyes looked upon him with curiosity alone; those whose great eyes pleaded with him, prayed to him.

Within that pellucid, greenly luminous *aether* McKay was

abruptly aware that the trees of the coppice still had a place. Only now they were spectral indeed. They were like white shadows cast athwart a glaucous screen; trunk and bough, twig and leaf, they arose around him and they were as though etched in air by phantom craftsmen—thin and unsubstantial; they were ghost trees rooted in another space.

He was aware that there were men among the women; men whose eyes were set wide apart as were theirs, as strange and pupilless as were theirs, but with irises of brown and blue; men with pointed chins and oval faces, broad shouldered and clad in kirtles of darkest green; swarthy-skinned men, muscular and strong, with that same lithe grace of the women—and like them of a beauty that was alien and elfin.

McKay heard a little wailing cry. He turned. Close beside him lay a girl clasped in the arms of one of the swarthy, green-clad men. She lay upon his breast. His eyes were filled with a black flame of wrath, and hers were misted, anguished. For an instant McKay had a glimpse of the birch that old Polleau's son had sent crashing down into the boughs of the fir. He saw birch and fir as immaterial outlines around this man and this girl. For an instant girl and man and birch and fir seemed to be one and the same.

The scarlet-lipped woman touched his shoulder.

"She withers," sighed the woman, and in her voice McKay heard a faint rustling as of mournful leaves. "Now is it not pitiful that she withers—our sister who was so young, so slender, and so lovely?"

McKay looked again at the girl. The white skin seemed shrunken; the moon radiance that gleamed through the bodies of the others was still in hers, but dim and pallid; her slim arms hung listlessly; her body drooped. Her mouth was wan and parched, her long and misted green eyes dull. The palely golden hair was lusterless and dry. He looked on a slow death—a withering death.

"May the arm that struck her down wither!" said the green-clad man who held her, and in his voice McKay heard a savage strumming as of winter winds through bleak boughs: "May his heart wither and the sun blast him! May the rain and the waters deny him and the winds scourge him!"

"I thirst," whispered the girl.

There was a stirring among the watching women. One came forward holding a chalice that was like thin leaves turned to green crystal. She paused beside the trunk of one of the spectral trees, reached up, and drew down to her a branch. A slim girl with half-frightened, half-resentful eyes glided to her side and threw her arms around the ghostly bole. The woman cut the branch deep with what seemed an arrow-shaped flake of jade and held her chalice under it. From the cut a faintly opalescent liquid dripped into the cup. When it was filled, the woman beside McKay stepped forward and pressed her own long hands around the bleeding branch. She stepped away and McKay saw that the stream had ceased to flow. She touched the trembling girl and unclasped her arms.

"It is healed," said the woman gently. "And it was your turn, little sister. The wound is healed. Soon you will have forgotten."

The woman with the chalice knelt and set it to the wan, dry lips of her who was—withering. She drank of it, thirstily, to the last drop. The misty eyes cleared, they sparkled; the lips that had been so parched and pale grew red, the white body gleamed as though the waning light within it had been fed with new.

"Sing, sisters," the girl cried shrilly. "Dance for me, sisters!"

Again burst out that chant McKay had heard as he had floated through the mists upon the lake. Now, as then, despite his open ears, he could distinguish no words, but clearly he understood its mingled themes—the joy of spring's awakening, rebirth, with green life streaming, singing up through every bough, swelling the buds, burgeoning with tender leaves the branches; the dance of the trees in the scented winds of spring; the drums of the jubilant rain on leafy hoods; passion of summer sun pouring its golden flood down upon the trees; the moon passing with stately steps and slow, and green hands reaching up to her and drawing from her breast milk of silver fire; riot of wild gay winds with their mad pipings and strummings; soft interlacing of boughs; the kiss of amorous leaves—all these and more, much more that McKay could not understand since they dealt with hidden, secret things for which man has no images, were in that chanting.

And all these and more were in the rhythms of the dancing of those strange, green-eyed women and brown-skinned men; something incredibly ancient, yet young as the speeding moment; something of a world before and beyond man.

McKay listened; he watched, lost in wonder, his own world more than half forgotten.

The woman beside him touched his arm. She pointed to the girl.

"Yet she withers," she said. "And not all our life, if we poured it through her lips, could save her."

He saw that the red was draining slowly from the girl's lips, that the luminous life tides were waning. The eyes that had been so bright were misting and growing dull once more. Suddenly a great pity and a great rage shook him. He knelt beside her, took her hands in his.

"Take them away! Take away your hands! They burn me!" she moaned.

"He tries to help you," whispered the green-clad man, gently. But he reached over and drew McKay's hands away.

"Not so can you help her or us," said the woman.

"What can I do?" McKay arose, looked helplessly from one to the other. "What can I do to help you?"

The chanting died, the dance stopped. A silence fell, and he felt upon him the eyes of all these strange people. They were tense, waiting. The woman took his hands. Her touch was cool and sent a strange sweetness sweeping through his veins.

"There are three men yonder," she said. "They hate us. Soon we shall all be as she is there—withering! They have sworn it, and as they have sworn so will they do. Unless—"

She paused. The moonbeam-dancing motes in her eyes changed to tiny sparklings of red that terrified him.

"Three men?" In his clouded mind was dim memory of Polleau and his two strong sons. "Three men?" he repeated, stupidly. "But what are three men to you who are so many? What could three men do against those stalwart gallants of yours?"

"No," she shook her head. "No—there is nothing our—men—can do; nothing that we can do. Once, night and day, we were gay. Now we fear—night and day. They mean to destroy us. Our kin have warned us. And our kin cannot help us. Those three are masters of blade and flame. Against blade and flame we are helpless.

"Surely will they destroy us," murmured the woman. "We shall wither—all of us. Like her there, or burn—unless—"

Suddenly she threw white arms around McKay's neck. She pressed her body close to him. Her scarlet mouth sought and found his lips and clung to them. Through all McKay's body ran swift, sweet flames, green fire of desire. His own arms went around her, crushed her to him.

"You shall not die!" he cried. "No—by God, you shall not!"

She drew back her head, looked deep into his eyes.

"They have sworn to destroy us," she said, "and soon. With blade and flame they will destroy us—those three—unless—"

"Unless?" he asked, fiercely.

"Unless you—slay them first!" she answered.

A cold shock ran through McKay, chilling the fires of his

desire. He dropped his arm from around the woman, thrust her from him. For an instant she trembled before him.

"Slay!" he heard her whisper—and she was gone.

The spectral trees wavered; their outlines thickened out of immateriality into substance. The green translucence darkened. He had a swift vertiginous moment as though he swung between two worlds. He closed his eyes. The dizziness passed and he opened them, looked around him.

He stood on the lakeward skirts of the little coppice. There were no shadows flitting, no sign of white women nor of swarthy, green-clad men. His feet were on green moss. Gone was the soft golden carpet with its bluets. Birches and firs clustered solidly before him.

At his left was a sturdy fir in whose needled arms a broken birch tree lay withering. It was the birch that Polleau's son had so wantonly slashed down. For an instant he saw within the fir and birch the immaterial outlines of the green-clad man and the slim girl who withered. For that instant birch and fir and girl and man seemed one and the same. He stepped back, and his hands touched the smooth, cool bark of another birch that rose close at his right.

Upon his hands the touch of that bark was like—was like what? Curiously was it like the touch of the long slim hands of the woman of the scarlet lips!

McKay stood there, staring, wondering, like a man who has but half awakened from dream. And suddenly a little wind stirred the leaves of the rounded birch beside him. The leaves murmured, sighed. The wind grew stronger and the leaves whispered.

"Slay!" he heard them whisper—and again: "Slay! Help us! Slay!"

And the whisper was the voice of the woman of the scarlet lips!

Rage, swift and unreasoning, sprang up in McKay. He began to run up through the coppice, up to where he knew was the old lodge in which dwelt Polleau and his sons. And as he ran the wind blew stronger about him, and louder and louder grew the whispering of the trees.

"Slay!" they whispered. "Slay them! Save us! Slay!"

"I will slay! I will save you!" McKay, panting, hammer pulse beating in his ears, heard himself answering that ever more insistent command. And in his mind was but one desire—to clutch the throats of Polleau and his sons, to crack their necks, to stand by them then and watch them wither—wither like that slim girl in the arms of the green-clad man.

He came to the edge of the coppice and burst from it out into a flood of sunshine. For a hundred feet he ran, and then he was aware that the whispering command was stilled, that he heard no more that maddening rustling of wrathful leaves. A spell seemed to have been loosed from him; it was as though he had broken through some web of sorcery. McKay stopped, dropped upon the ground, buried his face in the grasses.

He lay there marshaling his thoughts into some order of sanity. What had he been about to do? To rush upon those three men who lived in the old lodge and—slay them! And for what? Because that unearthly, scarlet-lipped woman whose kisses he still could feel upon his mouth had bade him! Because the whispering trees of the little wood had maddened him with that same command! For this he had been about to kill three men!

What were that woman and her sister and the green-clad swarthy gallants of theirs? Illusions of some waking dream—phantoms born of the hypnosis of the swirling mists through which he had rowed and floated across the lake? Such things were not uncommon. McKay knew of those who by watching the shifting clouds could create and dwell for a time with wide-open eyes within some similar land of fantasy; knew others who needed but to stare at smoothly falling water to set themselves within a world of waking dreams; there were those who could summon dreams by gazing into a ball of crystal; others who found dream life in saucers of shining ink.

Might not the moving mists have laid those same fingers of hypnosis upon his own mind? And his love for the trees, the sense of appeal that he had felt so long, his memory of the wanton slaughter of the slim birch have all combined to paint upon his drugged consciousness the fantasms he had beheld?

McKay arose to his feet, shakily enough. He looked back at the coppice. There was no wind now; the leaves were silent, motionless. Reason with himself as he might, something deep within him stubbornly asserted the reality of his experience. At any rate, he told himself, the little wood was far too beautiful to be despoiled.

The old lodge was about a quarter of a mile away. A path led up to it through the ragged fields. McKay walked up the path, climbed rickety steps, and paused, listening. He heard voices and knocked. The door was flung open and old Polleau stood there, peering at him through half-shut, suspicious eyes. One of the sons stood close behind him. They stared at McKay with grim, hostile faces.

He thought he heard a faint, far-off despairing whisper from the distant wood. And it was as though the pair in the doorway heard it too, for their gaze shifted from him to the coppice, and he saw hatred flicker swiftly across their grim faces. Their gaze swept back to him.

"What do you want?" demanded Polleau, curtly.

"I am a neighbor of yours, stopping at the inn—" began McKay, courteously.

"I know who you are," Polleau interrupted, brusquely, "but what is it that you want?"

"I find the air of this place good for me." McKay stifled a rising anger. "I am thinking of staying for a year or more until my health is fully recovered. I would like to buy some of your land and build me a lodge upon it."

"Yes, *M'sieu?*" There was acid politeness now in the old man's voice. "But is it permitted to ask why you do not remain at the inn? Its fare is excellent and you are well-liked there."

"I have desire to be alone," replied McKay. "I do not like people too close to me. I would have my own land, and sleep under my own roof."

"But why come to me," asked Polleau. "There are many places upon the far side of the lake that you could secure. It is happy there, and this side is not happy, *M'sieu*. But tell me, what part of my land is it that you desire?"

"That little wood yonder," answered McKay, and pointed to the coppice.

"Ah! I thought so!" whispered Polleau, and between him and his son passed a look of somber understanding.

"That wood is not for sale, *M'sieu,*" he said.

"I can afford to pay well for what I want," said McKay. "Name your price."

"It is not for sale," repeated Polleau, stolidly, "at any price."

"Oh, come," urged McKay, although his heart sank at the finality in that answer. "You have many acres and what is it but a few trees? I can afford to gratify my fancies. I will give you all the worth of your other land for it."

"You have asked what that place that you so desire is, and you have answered that it is but a few trees," said Polleau, slowly, and the tall son behind him laughed, abruptly, maliciously. "But it is more than that, *M'sieu*—oh, much more than that. And you know it, else why should you pay such a price as you offer? Yes, you know it—since you know also that we are ready to destroy it, and you would save it. And who told you all that, *M'sieu?*" he snarled.

There was such malignance, such black hatred in the face

thrust suddenly close to McKay's, eyes blazing, teeth bared by uplifted lip, that involuntarily he recoiled.

"Only a few trees!" snarled old Polleau. "Then who told him what we mean to do—eh, Pierre?"

Again the son laughed. And at that laughter McKay felt within him resurgence of his own blind hatred as he had fled through the whispering wood. He mastered himself, turned away; there was nothing he could do—now. Polleau halted him.

"M'sieu," he said, "enter. There is something I would tell you; something, too, I would show you."

He stood aside, bowing with a rough courtesy. McKay walked through the doorway. Polleau with his son followed him. He entered a large, dim room whose ceiling was spanned with smoke-blackened beams. From these beams hung onion strings and herbs and smoke-cured meats. On one side was a wide fireplace. Huddled beside it sat Polleau's other son. He glanced up as they entered, and McKay saw that a bandage covered one side of his head, hiding his left eye. McKay recognized him as the one who had cut down the slim birch. The blow of the fir, he reflected with a certain satisfaction, had been no futile one.

Old Polleau strode over to that son.

"Look, M'sieu," he said, and lifted the bandage.

McKay saw, with a tremor of horror, a gaping blackened socket, red-rimmed and eyeless.

"Good God, Polleau!" he cried. "But this man needs medical attention. I know something of wounds. Let me go across the lake and bring back my kit. I will attend him."

Old Polleau shook his head, although his grim face for the first time softened. He drew the bandages back in place.

"It heals," he said. "We have some skill in such things. You saw what did it. You watched from your boat as the cursed tree struck him. The eye was crushed and lay upon his cheek. I cut it away. Now he heals. We do not need your aid, M'sieu."

"Yet he ought not have cut the birch," muttered McKay, more to himself than to be heard.

"Why not?" asked old Polleau, fiercely, "since it hated him."

McKay stared at him. What did this old peasant know? The words strengthened his stubborn conviction that what he had seen and heard in the coppice had been actuality—no dream. And still more did Polleau's next words strengthen that conviction.

"M'sieu," he said, "you come here as ambassador—of a sort. The wood has spoken to you. Well, as ambassador I shall speak to you. Four centuries my people have lived in this place. A century we have owned this land. *M'sieu,* in all those years there has been no moment that the trees have not hated us—nor we the trees.

"For all those hundred years there have been hatred and battle between us and the forest. My father, *M'sieu,* was crushed by a tree, my elder brother crippled by another. My father's father, woodsman that he was, was lost in the forest; he came back to us with mind gone, raving of wood women who had bewitched and mocked him, lured him into swamp and fen and tangled thicket, tormenting him. In every generation the trees have taken their toll of us—women as well as men—maiming or killing us."

"Accidents," interrupted McKay. "This is childish, Polleau. You cannot blame the trees."

"In your heart you do not believe so," said Polleau. "Listen, the feud is an ancient one. Centuries ago it began when we were serfs, slaves of the nobles. To cook, to keep us warm in winter, they let us pick up the fagots, the dead branches and twigs that dropped from the trees. But if we cut down a tree to keep us warm, to keep our women and our children warm, yes, if we but tore down a branch, they hanged us, or threw us into dungeons to rot, or whipped us till our backs were red lattices.

"They had their broad fields, the nobles, but we must raise

our food in the patches where the trees disdained to grow.
And if they did thrust themselves into our poor patches,
then, *M'sieu,* we must let them have their way—or be
flogged, or be thrown into the dungeons, or be hanged.

"They pressed us in—the trees," the old man's voice grew
sharp with fanatic hatred. "They stole our fields and they
took the food from the mouths of our children; they dropped
their fagots to us like dole to beggars; they tempted us to
warmth when the cold struck to our bones—and they bore us
as fruit aswing at the end of the foresters' ropes if we yielded
to their tempting.

"Yes, *M'sieu,* we died of cold that they might live! Our
children died of hunger that their young might find root
space! They despised us—the trees! We died that they might
live—and we were men!

"Then, *M'sieu,* came the Revolution and the freedom. Ah,
M'sieu, then we took our toll! Great logs roaring in the winter cold—no more huddling over the alms of fagots. Fields
where the trees had been—no more starving of our children
that theirs might live. Now the trees were the slaves and we
the masters.

"And the trees knew, and they hated us!

"But blow for blow, a hundred of their lives for each life
of ours—we have returned their hatred. With ax and torch
we have fought them—

"The trees!" shrieked Polleau suddenly, eyes blazing red
rage, face writhing, foam at the corners of his mouth, and
gray hair clutched in rigid hands. "The cursed trees! Armies
of the trees creeping—creeping—closer, ever closer—
crushing us in! Stealing our fields as they did of old! Building their dungeon round us as they built of old the dungeons
of stone! Creeping—creeping! Armies of trees! Legions of
trees! The trees! The cursed trees!"

McKay listened, appalled. Here was crimson heart of
hate. Madness! But what was at the root of it? Some deep
inherited instinct, coming down from forefathers who had

hated the forest as the symbol of their masters—forefathers whose tides of hatred had overflowed to the green life on which the nobles had laid their taboo, as one neglected child will hate the favorite on whom love and gifts are lavished? In such warped minds the crushing fall of a tree, the maiming sweep of a branch, might appear as deliberate; the natural growth of the forest seem the implacable advance of an enemy.

And yet—the blow of the fir as the cut birch fell *had* been deliberate! And there had been those women of the wood—

"Patience," the standing son touched the old man's shoulder. "Patience! Soon we strike our blow."

Some of the frenzy died out of Polleau's face.

"Though we cut down a hundred," he whispered, "by the hundred they return! But one of us, when they strike, he does not return, no! They have numbers and they have—time. We are now but three, and we have little time. They watch us as we go through the forest, alert to trip, to strike, to crush!

"But, *M'sieu,*" he turned bloodshot eyes to McKay, "we strike our blow, even as Pierre has said. We strike at that coppice that you so desire. We strike there because it is the very heart of the forest. There the secret life of the forest runs at full tide. We know—and you know! Something that, destroyed, will take the heart out of the forest—will make it know us for its masters."

"The women!" The standing son's eyes glittered, malignantly. "I have seen the women there! The fair women with the shining skins who invite—and mock and vanish before hands can seize them."

"The fair women who peer into our windows in the night—and mock us!" muttered the eyeless son.

"They shall mock no more!" shouted old Polleau. "Soon they shall lie, dying! All of them—all of them! They die!"

He caught McKay by the shoulders and shook him like a child.

"Go tell them that!" he shouted. "Say to them that this

very day we destroy them. Say to them it is *we* who will laugh when winter comes and we watch their bodies blaze in this hearth of ours and warm us! Go—tell them that!"

He spun McKay around, pushed him to the door, opened it, and flung him staggering down the steps. He heard the tall son laugh, the door close. Blind with rage he rushed up the steps and hurled himself against the door. Again the tall son laughed. McKay beat at the door with clenched fists, cursing. The three within paid no heed. Despair began to dull his rage. Could the trees help him—counsel him? He turned and walked slowly down the field path to the little wood.

Slowly and ever more slowly he went as he neared it. He had failed. He was a messenger bearing a warrant of death. The birches were motionless, their leaves hung listlessly. It was as though they knew he had failed. He paused at the edge of the coppice. He looked at his watch, noted with faint surprise that already it was high noon. Short shrift enough had the little wood. The work of destruction would not be long delayed.

McKay squared his shoulders and passed in between the trees. It was strangely silent in the coppice. And it was mournful. He had a sense of life brooding around him, withdrawn into itself, sorrowing. He passed through the silent, mournful wood until he reached the spot where the rounded, gleaming-barked tree stood close to the fir that held the withering birch. Still there was no sound, no movement. He laid his hands upon the cool bark of the rounded tree.

"Let me see again!" he whispered. "Let me hear! Speak to me!"

There was no answer. Again and again he called. The coppice was silent. He wandered through it, whispering, calling. The slim birches stood, passive, with limbs and leaves adroop like listless arms and hands of captive maids awaiting in dull woe the will of conquerors. The firs seemed to crouch like hopeless men with heads in hands. His heart ached to the woe that filled the little wood, this hopeless submission of the trees.

When, he wondered, would Polleau strike? He looked at his watch again; an hour had gone by. How long would Polleau wait? He dropped to the moss against a smooth bole.

And suddenly it seemed to McKay that he was a madman—as mad as Polleau and his sons. Calmly, he went over the old peasant's indictment of the forest, recalled the face and eyes filled with fanatic hate. They were all mad. After all, the trees were—only trees. Polleau and his sons—so he reasoned—had transferred to them the bitter hatred their forefathers had felt for those old lords who had enslaved them, had laid upon them too all the bitterness of their own struggle to exist in this high forest land. When they struck at the trees, it was the ghosts of those forefathers striking at the nobles who had oppressed them; it was themselves striking against their own destiny. The trees were but symbols. It was the warped minds of Polleau and his sons that clothed them in false semblance of conscious life, blindly striving to wreak vengeance against the ancient masters and the destiny that had made their lives one hard and unceasing battle against nature. The nobles were long dead, for destiny can be brought to grips by no man. But the trees were here and alive. Clothed in mirage, through them the driving lust for vengeance could be sated. So much for Polleau and his sons.

And he, McKay: was it not his own deep love and sympathy for the trees that similarly had clothed them in that false semblance of conscious life? Had he not built his own mirage? The trees did not really mourn, could not suffer, could not—know. It was his own sorrow that he had transferred to them, only his sorrow that he felt echoing back to him from them. The trees were—only trees.

Instantly, upon the heels of that thought, as though it were an answer, he was aware that the trunk against which he leaned was trembling; that the whole coppice was trembling; that all the little leaves were shaking, tremulously.

McKay, bewildered, leaped to his feet. Reason told him that it was the wind—yet there was no wind!

And as he stood there, a sighing arose as though a mournful breeze were blowing through the trees—and again there was no wind!

Louder grew the sighing and within it now faint wailings.

"They come! They come! Farewell, sisters! Sisters—farewell!"

Clearly he heard the mournful whispers.

McKay began to run through the trees to the trail that led out to the fields of the old lodge. And as he ran the wood darkened as though clear shadows gathered in it, as though vast unseen wings hovered over it. The trembling of the coppice increased; bough touched bough, clung to each other; and louder became the sorrowful crying: "Farewell, sister! Sister—farewell!"

McKay burst out into the open. Halfway between him and the lodge were Polleau and his sons. They saw him; they pointed and lifted mockingly to him their bright axes. He crouched, waiting for them to come close, all fine-spun theories gone, and rising within him that same rage which hours before had sent him out to slay.

So crouching, he heard from the forested hills a roaring clamor. From every quarter it came, wrathful, menacing, like the voices of legions of great trees bellowing through the horns of tempest. The clamor maddened McKay, fanned the flame of rage to white heat.

If the three men heard it, they gave no sign. They came on steadily, jeering at him, waving their blades. He ran to meet them.

"Go back!" he shouted. "Go back, Polleau! I warn you!"

"He warns us!" jeered Polleau. "He—Pierre, Jean—he warns us!"

The old peasant's arm shot out and his hand caught McKay's shoulder with a grip that pinched to the bone. The

arm flexed and hurled him against the unmaimed son. The
son caught him, twisted him about, and whirled him headlong a dozen yards, crashing through the brush at the skirt of
the wood.

McKay sprang to his feet howling like a wolf. The clamor
of the forest had grown stronger.

"Kill!" it roared. "Kill!"

The unmaimed son had raised his ax. He brought it down
upon the trunk of a birch, half splitting it with one blow.
McKay heard a wail go up from the little wood. Before the
ax could be withdrawn he had crashed a fist in the ax
wielder's face. The head of Polleau's son rocked back; he
yelped, and before McKay could strike again had wrapped
strong arms around him, crushing breath from him. McKay
relaxed, went limp, and the son loosened his grip. Instantly
McKay slipped out of it and struck again, springing aside to
avoid the rib-breaking clasp. Polleau's son was quicker than
he, the long arm caught him. But as the arms tightened there
was the sound of sharp splintering, and the birch into which
the ax had bitten toppled. It struck the ground directly behind the wrestling men. Its branches seemed to reach out and
clutch at the feet of Polleau's son.

He tripped and fell backward, McKay upon him. The
shock of the fall broke his grip and again McKay writhed
free. Again he was upon his feet, and again Polleau's strong
son, quick as he, faced him. Twice McKay's blows found
their mark beneath his heart before once more the long arms
trapped him. But the grip was weaker; McKay felt that now
their strength was equal.

Round and round they rocked, McKay straining to break
away. They fell, and over they rolled and over, arms and legs
locked, each striving to free a hand to grip the other's throat.
Around them ran Polleau and the one-eyed son, shouting en-
couragement to Pierre, yet neither daring to strike at McKay
lest the blow miss and be taken by the other.

And all that time McKay heard the little wood shouting.

Gone from it now was all mournfulness, all passive resignation. The wood was alive and raging. He saw the trees shake and bend as though torn by a tempest. Dimly he realized that the others could hear none of this, see none of it; as dimly wondered why this should be.

"Kill!" shouted the coppice, and ever over its tumult he was aware of the roar of the great forest. "Kill! Kill!"

He saw two shadowy shapes—shadowy shapes of swarthy green-clad men that pressed close to him as he rolled and fought.

"Kill!" they whispered. "Let his blood flow! Kill!"

He tore a wrist free. Instantly he felt within his hand the hilt of a knife.

"Kill!" whispered the shadowy men.

"Kill!" shrieked the coppice.

"Kill!" roared the forest.

McKay's arm swept up and plunged the knife into the throat of Polleau's son! He heard a choking sob; heard Polleau shriek; felt the hot blood spurt in face and over hand; smelt its salt and faintly acrid odor. The encircling arms dropped from him; he reeled to his feet.

As though the blood had been a bridge, the shadowy men leaped into materiality. One threw himself upon the man McKay had stabbed; the other hurled upon old Polleau. The maimed son turned and fled, howling with terror. A white woman sprang out from the shadow, threw herself at his feet, clutched them, and brought him down. Another woman and another dropped upon him. The note of his shrieking changed from fear to agony, then died abruptly into silence.

And now McKay could see none of the trees, neither old Polleau nor his sons, for green-clad men and white women covered them!

He stood stupidly, staring at his red hands. The roar of the forest had changed to a deep triumphal chanting. The coppice was mad with joy. The trees had become thin phantoms etched in emerald translucent air as they had been when first the green sorcery had meshed him. And all around him wove and danced the slim, gleaming women of the wood.

They ringed him, their song bird sweet and shrill, jubilant. Beyond them he saw gliding toward him the woman of the misty pillar whose kisses had poured the sweet green fire into his veins. Her arms were outstretched to him, her strange wide eyes were rapt on his, her white body gleamed with the moon radiance, her red lips were parted and smiling, a scarlet chalice filled with the promise of undreamed ecstasies. The dancing circle, chanting, broke to let her through.

Abruptly, a horror filled McKay—not of this fair woman, not of her jubilant sister, but of himself.

He had killed! And the wound the war had left in his soul, the wound he thought had healed, had opened.

He rushed through the broken circle, thrust the shining woman aside with his bloodstained hands, and ran, weeping, toward the lake shore. The singing ceased. He heard little cries, tender, appealing little cries of pity, soft voices calling on him to stop, to return. Behind him was the sound of little racing feet, light as the fall of leaves upon the moss.

McKay ran on. The coppice lightened, the beach was before him. He heard the fair woman call him, felt the touch of her hand upon his shoulder. He did not heed her. He ran across the narrow strip of beach, thrust his boat out into the water, and wading through the shallows threw himself into it.

He lay there for a moment, sobbing, then drew himself up and caught at the oars. He looked back at the shore now a score of feet away. At the edge of the coppice stood the woman, staring at him with pitying, wise eyes. Behind her clustered the white faces of her sisters, the swarthy faces of the green-clad men.

"Come back!" the woman whispered, and held out to him slender arms.

McKay hesitated, his horror lessening in that clear, wise gaze. He half swung the boat around. But his eyes fell again upon his bloodstained hands and again the hysteria gripped him. One thought only was in his mind now—to get far away from where Polleau's son lay with his throat ripped open, to put the lake between him and that haunted shore. He dipped his oars deep, flung the boat forward. Once more the woman called to him and once again. He paid no heed. She threw out her arms in a gesture of passionate farewell. Then a mist dropped like a swift curtain between him and her and all the folk of the little wood.

McKay rowed on, desperately. After a while he shipped oars, and leaning over the boat's side he washed away the red on his hands and arms. His coat was torn and bloodstained, his shirt too. The latter he took off, wrapped it around the stone that was the boat's rude anchor, and dropped it into the depths. His coat he dipped into the water, rubbing at the accusing marks. When he had lightened them all he could, he took up his oars.

His panic had gone from him. Upon its ebb came a rising tide of regret; clear before his eyes arose the vision of the shining woman, beckoning him, calling him . . . he swung the boat around to return. And instantly as he did so the mists between him and the farther shore thickened; around him they lightened as though they had withdrawn to make of themselves a barrier to him, and something deep within him whispered that it was too late.

He saw that he was close to the landing of the little inn. There was no one about, and none saw him as he fastened the skiff and slipped to his room. He locked the door, started to undress. Sudden sleep swept over him like a wave, drew him helplessly down into ocean depths of sleep.

A knocking at his door awakened McKay, and the innkeeper's voice summoning him to dinner. Sleepily he answered, and as the old man's footsteps died away he roused himself. His eyes fell upon his coat, dry now, and the ill-erased bloodstains splotching it. Puzzled, he stared at them for a moment; then full memory clicked back into place.

He walked to the window. It was dusk. A wind was blowing and the trees were singing, all the little leaves dancing; the forest hummed its cheerful vespers. Gone was all the unease, all the inarticulate trouble and the fear. The woods were tranquil and happy.

He sought the coppice through the gathering twilight. Its demoiselles were dancing lightly in the wind, leafy hoods dipping, leafy skirts ablow. Beside them marched their green troubadours, carefree, waving their needled arms. Gay was the little wood, gay as when its beauty had first lured him to it.

McKay hid the stained coat in his traveling trunk, bathed and put on a fresh outfit, and sauntered down to dinner. He ate excellently. Wonder now and then crossed his mind that he felt no regret, no sorrow even for the man he had killed. He was half inclined to believe it had all been only a dream—so little of any emotion did he feel. He had even ceased to think of what discovery might mean.

His mind was quiet; he heard the forest chanting to him that there was nothing he need fear; and when he sat for a time that night upon the balcony a peace that was half an ecstasy stole in upon him from the murmuring woods and enfolded him. Cradled by it he slept dreamlessly.

McKay did not go far from the inn that day. The little wood danced gayly and beckoned him, but he paid no heed. Something whispered to wait, to keep the lake between him and it until word came of what lay or had lain there. And the peace still was on him.

Only the old innkeeper seemed to grow uneasy as the hours went by. He went often to the landing, scanning the farther shore.

"It is strange," he said at last to McKay as the sun was dipping behind the summits. "Polleau was to see me here today. If he could not come he would have sent one of his sons."

McKay nodded, carelessly.

"There is another thing I do not understand," went on the old man. "I have seen no smoke from the lodge all day. It is as though they were not there."

"Where could they be?" asked McKay indifferently.

"I do not know," the voice was more perturbed. "It all troubles me, *M'sieu.* Polleau is hard, yes, but he is my neighbor. Perhaps an accident—"

"They would let you know soon enough if there was anything wrong," McKay said.

"Perhaps, but—" the old man hesitated. "If he does not come tomorrow and again I see no smoke, I will go to him," he ended.

McKay felt a little shock run through him; tomorrow, then, he would know, definitely, what it was that had happened in the little wood.

"I would if I were you," he said. "I'd not wait too long, either."

"Will you go with me, *M'sieu?*" asked the old man.

"No!" whispered the warning voice within McKay. "No! Do not go!"

"Sorry," he said, aloud. "But I've some writing to do. If you should need me, send back your man; I'll come."

And all that night he slept, again dreamlessly, while the crooning forest cradled him.

The morning passed without sign from the opposite shore. An hour after noon he watched the old innkeeper and his man row across the lake. And suddenly McKay's composure was shaken, his serene certainty wavered. He unstrapped his field glasses and kept them on the pair until they had beached the boat and entered the coppice. His heart was beating uncomfortably, his hands felt hot and his lips dry. How long had they been in the wood? It must have been an hour! What were they doing there? What had they found? He looked at his watch, incredulously. Less than five minutes had passed.

Slowly the seconds ticked by. And it was all of an hour indeed before he saw them come out upon the shore and drag their boat into the water. McKay, throat curiously dry, deafening pulse within his ears, steadied himself, forced himself to stroll leisurely down to the landing.

"Everything all right?" he called as they were near. They did not answer, but as the skiff warped against the landing they looked up at him, and on their faces were stamped horror and a great wonder.

"They are dead, *M'sieu,*" whispered the innkeeper. "Polleau and his two sons—all dead!"

McKay's heart gave a great leap, a swift faintness took him.

"Dead!" he cried. "What killed them?"

"What but the trees, *M'sieu?*" answered the old man, and McKay thought that his gaze dwelt upon him strangely. "The trees killed them. See—we went up the little path through the wood, and close to its end we found it blocked by fallen trees. The flies buzzed round those trees, *M'sieu,* so we searched there. They were under them, Polleau and his sons. A fir had fallen upon Polleau and had crushed in his chest. Another son we found beneath a fir and upturned birches. They had broken his back, and an eye had been torn out—but that was no new wound, the latter."

He paused.

"It must have been a sudden wind," said his man. "Yet I never knew of a wind such as that must have been. There were no trees down except those that lay upon them. And of those it was as though they had leaped out of the ground! Yes, as though they had leaped out of the ground upon them. Or it was as though giants had torn them out for clubs. They were not broken—their roots were bare—"

"But the other son—Polleau had two?" Try as he might, McKay could not keep the tremor out of his voice.

"Pierre," said the old man, and again McKay felt that strange quality in his gaze. "He lay beneath a fir. His throat was torn out!"

"His throat torn out!" whispered McKay. His knife! His knife! The knife that had been slipped into his hand by the shadowy shapes!

"His throat was torn out," repeated the innkeeper. "And in it still was the broken branch that had done it. A broken branch, *M'sieu,* pointed like a knife. It must have caught Pierre as the fir fell and, ripping through his throat, been broken off as the tree crashed."

McKay stood, mind whirling in wild conjecture. "You said—a broken branch?" he asked through lips gone white.

"A broken branch, *M'sieu.*" The innkeeper's eyes searched him. "It was very plain—what it was that happened. Jacques," he turned to his man, "go up to the house."

He watched until the man shuffled out of sight.

"Yet not all is so plain, *M'sieu,*" he spoke low to McKay, "since in Pierre's hand I found—this."

He reached into a pocket and drew out a button from which hung a strip of cloth. They had once been part of that stained coat which McKay had hidden in his trunk. And as McKay strove to speak, the old man raised his hand. Button and cloth dropped from it, into the water. A wave took it and floated it away; another and another snatched it and passed it on. They watched it, silently, until it had vanished.

"Tell me nothing," said the keeper of the inn. "Polleau was a hard man, and hard men were his sons. The trees hated them. The trees killed them. The—souvenir—is gone. Only *M'sieu* would better also—go."

That night McKay packed. When dawn had broken he stood at his window, looking long at the little wood. It too was awakening, stirring sleepily—like drowsy, delicate demoiselles. He thought he could see that one slim birch that was—what? Tree or woman? Or both?

Silently, the old landlord and his wife watched him as he swung out his car—a touch of awe, a half fear, in their eyes. Without a word they let him go.

And as McKay swept up the road that led over the lip of the green bowl, he seemed to hear from all the forest a deep-toned, mournful chanting. It arose around him as he topped the rise in one vast whispering cloud—of farewell—and died.

Never, he knew, would that green door of enchantment be opened to him again. His fear had closed it—forever. Something had been offered to him beyond mortal experience—something that might have raised him to the level of the gods of earth's youth. He had rejected it. And nevermore, he knew, would he cease to regret.

Golithos the Ogre

by E. A. Wyke-Smith

In the drafts for his famous lecture "On Fairy Stories," Tolkien wrote: "I should like to record my own love and my children's love of E. A. Wyke-Smith's *Marvellous Land of Snergs*, at any rate of the Snerg-element in that tale, and of Gorbo, the gem of dunderheads, jewel of a companion in an escapade."

Snergs are "a race of people only slightly taller than the average table" (they are also described as probably being "some offshoot of the pixies"). They live in "a place set apart" and are exceptionally fond of parties. And they are in fact the direct literary ancestors of hobbits, for after Tolkien's children fell in love with *The Marvellous Land of Snergs* they wanted more stories about the Snergs. Tolkien told them instead the story of *The Hobbit*, with the half-high hobbit Bilbo as the main character.

The Marvellous Land of Snergs tells the story of two children, Joe and Sylvia, and their dog, Tiger, who go on a rambling adventure with Gorbo, a Snerg. In one episode they get lost in a wood of Twisted Trees, which is recalled in Bilbo's adventures in Mirkwood (see note 7 to chapter 8 in the revised edition of *The Annotated Hobbit*). In their various travels, they meet some fascinating characters, including Vanderdecken the Flying Dutchman and Mother Meldrum, a sinister witch who is also a wonderful cook.

The excerpt given next concerns Golithos, a reformed ogre who no longer eats children but has become vegetarian. *The Marvellous Land of Snergs* was first published in September 1927.

THE first glance that Gorbo gave as he came out into the warm sunlight showed him that they were now on the other side of the river.

This was more serious news to him than to Sylvia or Joe. To them it meant daylight, freedom from the subterranean gloom; possibly the prelude to new adventures (it was). To him it meant trouble and danger and the fear of unknown things. The wide deep river, rushing far below between steep cliffs, had been a barrier keeping the Snergs secure from a horror-haunted land, a land of distressful legends of dragons and other fierce monsters, of Kelps and giants, and a ruthless king who tyrannized over his people. No wonder he gazed sadly at the fair green woods on the other side and wished—chiefly for the sake of the children—that he was less of a fathead.

"It isn't such a nice part on this side," said Sylvia, looking about at a dull landscape, dotted here and there with patches of coarse grass and clumps of thorny trees. "But it's jolly to get out of that dark place."

"Yes, isn't it," agreed Joe contentedly. At his age the present time lasts quite a good bit. "I'm jolly glad we got here. Perhaps we'll have some real adventures now."

"I'm thinking we will," said Gorbo.

They went on a little way and, coming to the top of a gentle slope, saw before them a round grey tower some half-mile or so away. It was surrounded by a high outer wall and looked very lonely and dreary. Gorbo stared long and hard at it.

"Yes," he said at length, "that's old Golithos' tower. I can see him outside, doing something to the wall. I know him by his whiskers."

"Then," said Joe logically, "we'd better scoot. Come along, Sylvia!"

"No, don't scoot," said Gorbo; "it's safe enough. Golithos is quite harmless now because he's reformed. We'd better go over and see if he can tell us how to get back. Don't be frightened, Sylvia, I've heard he's quite kind-hearted now. In fact they say he's rather overdoing it."

Though they were not exactly at their ease (what child is at the thought of visiting an ogre?) they were impressed by Gorbo's confidence, and they went on hand in hand with him towards the tower, Joe carrying the puppy.

A huge man, about seven feet high, was working with a heap of mortar and some big stones, repairing a loose part of the wall. As they drew near he turned and saw them; then he smacked his hands together to knock the mortar off and rubbed them in his hair and waited for them with a friendly but weak-looking smile. He had a great silly face and coarse hair and whiskers like bits of a cheap goatskin rug. His dress was the usual shabby dress of ogres in books. It is perhaps slightly unfair to call him an ogre, for as Gorbo had said, he was reformed. Not a child had passed his lips for years, and his diet was now cabbage, turnip-tops, cucumbers, little sour apples and thin stuff like that.

"Aha!" he said as they came up, "you are all heartily welcome. It is long since I had any nice visitors. How are *you,* my little maid? And *you,* my little man? And you also, my dear Snerg? Let me see, have I had the pleasure of meeting you before?" He shook hands with them in a very friendly way.

"I don't think so," replied Gorbo. "You see," he added delicately, "I was quite a boy when they—I mean when you—well, when you changed your address."

"Exactly," said Golithos, with a conscious blush. "Well, come inside and make yourselves at home."

There seemed nothing for it but to go on through his door, though all Gorbo wanted was to ask the way back across the river, not to make morning calls. When they were inside Golithos slammed the heavy door and locked it.

"I get so nervous if I leave it open," he explained. "But come in and I'll have a meal ready for you. You must be tired and hungry after your long journey from wherever you have come."

"Look here," said Gorbo, "we don't want to trouble you too much. All we want to know is how to get back across the river."

"To get back across the river," replied Golithos, bending down and placing a hand affectionately on his shoulder, "is easier than you think. Much easier. In fact I think I am right in saying that however easy you think it is it will prove to be easier still."

"Well, I'm glad of that," said Gorbo.

"Naturally you would be. But come inside and make yourselves at home."

"Thanks, but I should really like to know the way."

"The way?" Golithos looked a bit puzzled.

"Yes, the way across the river of course."

"Oh, yes, of course. What am I thinking of? Well, it's perfectly easy. All you have to do is to—but one thing at a time. Come inside and make yourselves at home."

He led the way up some steep steps to a door in the wall of the tower and into a large round room which took the whole of one story. It was big enough, but the most comfortless room possible. At one side was a great four-foot post bedstead, and in the middle was a big heavy table and one big heavy chair. And that was all the furniture, unless you count an accumulation of mixed litter—old clothes and gardening tools and pots and pans and sacks and barrels and so forth scattered on the floor. Some wooden steps led to a trap-door in the ceiling and in the stone floor was another trap-door, with a big iron ring to lift it by, which led apparently to a cellar. There was only one window, with little round panes of dull green glass.

"This is my kitchen-dining room," he said with a look of pride. "I sleep here too—that structure over there is my bed—so it is a bedroom as well. Please take chairs—I mean, one of you take the chair and the others sit on the floor. But whatever you do, make yourselves at home."

"Thanks," said Gorbo. "But what about the way across the river?"

"The river?" Golithos did not seem to grasp his meaning.

"Yes, the river outside. All that wet stuff over there. We want to get back."

"Undoubtedly. Well, you needn't worry about *that,* because it's a very simple matter. I'll show you how it can be done in the easiest way. But first let's see about dinner." He picked up a pan and a knife and rushed blunderingly down the steps.

"I've heard it said that he's getting very slow since he reformed," said Gorbo after a minute's thinking, "but he's worse than I expected. Somehow or other he makes me feel that I want to contradict him. And I'm not like that usually."

"But he's going to give us something to eat," Joe observed.

"Yes, Joe. But I don't think it will be very strengthening. That's the worst of reformed people. Here he comes."

Golithos came in like a mighty bumble bee, bumping against things and getting his feet entangled with things on the floor and dropping vegetables about and stooping to pick them up and dropping others as he did so. "I'm going to give you the feed of your lives," he said, chopping up lettuce and smiling in his feeble way. "I always think there's nothing so appetizing as fine fresh lettuce and raw onions, especially if they have lots of salt."

In a minute or so he placed a large pan on the table, and then he got two empty barrels and laid a plank across them to make a seat for the children. Sylvia whispered rather anxiously to Gorbo, who had been watching their host with a discontented expression, and indicated that Tiger's contour was losing its curves.

"Look here, Golithos," said Gorbo, "can you give this little dog something to eat?"

Golithos scratched his head. "Let me see—I suppose he doesn't eat salad?"

"No, he doesn't. He's a dog, not a grasshopper. Haven't you got any bread?"

"I may have some odd bits in a sack somewhere. You see I don't eat bread very much. I find it's heating to the blood. But I'll try to find some nice bits for him later. In the meantime, let us eat heartily. Would you like the chair or do you prefer standing?"

"Chair for me, thanks," replied Gorbo, seating himself. "Look here, Golithos, this is all very kind and considerate and jolly of you, but these young ones will want something a bit solider than this."

"No solids here," said Golithos quickly. "It wouldn't do."

"Well, you've got a cow outside. Why don't you give them some milk?"

"Milk? Yes, but do you think it would be good for them? It's rather heady stuff."

Gorbo clapped the table smartly. "You hop out and milk that old cow of yours!" he said loudly. "These children want milk. They can't live on lip and lettuce."

Golithos looked fearfully abashed. "Yes, yes, I'll go," he said. "Don't be violent." He blundered out and down the steps.

"Can't quite make him out," said Gorbo. "He was a wicked old rascal once, but if he was rough he was ready—and a bit interesting if you're not too particular. But I think the watercress diet has weakened his brain."

He felt his responsibility in the matter keenly; if he had not been a born fool he would not have got the children into this mess; and his easy-going disposition seemed to have suddenly disappeared with regard to his host. After a minute he jumped out of the big chair and ran to the window and poked his head out. "Golithos!" he called in a warning voice. "Waiting!"

Golithos appeared, bearing a pitcher of milk and looking highly flustered. "Shall I put some water in it?" he asked.

"Give it to me," ordered Gorbo, taking the pitcher. He looked round the littered table and found two earthenware mugs. "Wash them," he said, passing them over his shoulder to Golithos. "Dear, dear, this is barely decent!"

The milk at any rate was nice and warm, and the children felt greatly refreshed by it. A small bowlful was given to Tiger, who lapped it up and then went to sleep on a sack. Then all set to on the salad, Golithos standing by and pressing them to take more whenever they paused. Gorbo took his portion in a dissatisfied way, sometimes looking at a morsel with scorn before putting it into his mouth (I may mention that they were eating with their fingers; there were no forks in this disgusting ménage). After a time he made a crude attempt at polite conversation.

"Doing well here, Golithos?" he asked.

"Pretty well, thank you. Oh, yes. It's lonely, of course; people seem to shun me so. But I have plenty of time to meditate on my past sins."

"Ah, that ought to fill in the time. Keeping pretty fit, Golithos?"

"Tolerably so, thank you. I suffer from stomach trouble occasionally."

"Only occasionally, eh? That's strange. Sleep well, Golithos?"

"Fairly well, I thank you. I have nightmares sometimes."

"What do you expect? This all you're going to give us, Golithos?"

"I'm really afraid I haven't anything else—Yes, I have! I can give you a fine fresh young cucumber."

"Keep it, Golithos." Gorbo stretched himself and yawned and turned to the children. "Well, Sylvia, what do you think of *this* for a hole?"

Sylvia glanced at the feeble though gigantic face of the once child-eater and felt some pity for him. "Oh, it's very nice," she answered, though not, I am afraid, very truthfully. "Isn't it, Joe?"

"It's fine," said Joe. Then he put his hands before his mouth and spluttered, for his manners were not good. Their host looked very unhappy.

"Just fancy it on a rainy day," went on Gorbo. "Well, Golithos, what's the country like in these parts?"

"I don't know very much about it, because I don't go about very much, but I've heard it's very bad. You see there's the land of King Kul not so very far off, and he's got a very bad character."

"Yes, we've heard of him. What does he do especially?"

"Well, he persecutes the people. You see he makes a hobby of it. And from what I've heard they're the sort of people who ought to be persecuted. But I don't really know much about them because I don't often see any of them. And when I do I lock myself up tight until they've gone. Old Mother Meldrum comes over to see me sometimes and she tells me about the goings-on."

"And who's old Mother Meldrum?"

"Well, she's a witch, that's what she is. She says nothing will go right until King Kul is laid out, and she keeps trying to get me to go for it. But somehow or other I don't feel up to violent exercise since I got reformed."

"You're losing your nerve, Golithos. But why doesn't somebody else try to do him in?"

"I think it's because they're afraid. It's risky, you see. Mother Meldrum says that his castle is three-quarters dungeons. And he keeps six headsmen busy all the time except on Saturday afternoons and Sundays."

"That fits in with what I've heard of him myself," said Gorbo, looking anxiously at Sylvia and Joe, who were taking all this in. "But cheer up, Sylvia, we'll soon get out of it. Now, Golithos, what about how to get across the river?"

*   *   *

The giant took Gorbo by the arm and led him to the window. "Do you see that tree?" he asked, pointing out a tall pine standing far off.

"Yes, Golithos."

"Well, that tree's close by the river, and I pointed it out because it's quite useless your trying to get across the river at that point. Or for the matter of that, at any other point, if you understand me."

"Well, I don't, if you understand me. I can tell you fifty ways how *not* to get across the river. Rouse your wits, Golithos!"

"You make me nervous. And if you do that you'll drive all the fine ideas out of my head. You see the fact is that you don't get *across* the river at all. But, notwithstanding, it's a perfectly easy matter to get to the other side if you know the way how. Now do you see my point?"

"I thought I was something of a born fool, Golithos, but since I've met you I'm quite proud of myself."

"*Don't* speak to me like that; it gives me the all-overs. Look here, all you have to do is to go *under* the river. You go through a little door."

"I thought so. You've been a long time coming to it, Golithos. As a matter of fact we came that way, but the little door shut up tight as soon as we got out of it. And there's another door on the other side. How do we get them open?"

"It's quite easy. But I don't quite remember how it's done—now don't get violent! You see it's not exactly difficult; it's only something to do with some little magic spells. You make a circle on the ground and divide it into six parts—or sixteen parts, I forget which. And then you bring some simple little charms—twenty-eight altogether, I think. I know one of them is the toe-nail of the seventh son of a seventh son born on a Friday. And then you repeat something out of a book—oh, if you're going to look at me like that I shall get thoroughly nervous and forget the rest."

"Look here, Golithos," said Gorbo, "do you think Mother Meldrum has more sense than you?"

"Oh, yes, she's got ever so much more! *She* knows the way to get the door open."

"Oh, does she? Then where can we find her?"

"She may come here at any time. You see she comes because I amuse her—at least that's what she says—and if you wait here a day or two she's bound to turn up. I can give you a lovely room upstairs. I'll move the turnips to one side and give you some nearly clean straw to sleep on. I'd give my own bed to the little ones, but I'm afraid the mattress is rather bumpy; I think some brickbats must have got into it. You see I air the mattress every November, and last November I was doing some building, and as there were a few holes in it, you see——"

"Don't worry, Golithos, we'll take your upstairs room. So come and move the turnips."

The upstairs room was much worse than the one below, which is saying something. It was furnished chiefly with turnips and sacks of lime, and these Golithos began to move to one side in a muddle-headed way, while Gorbo sat on the window-ledge and watched him. At length there was a clear space for the straw, which was spread out in the manner advocated for sick horses.

"There!" said Golithos proudly, resting on his hay-fork, "*There's* a bed for you!"

Gorbo only snorted and said nothing, and there was silence for a time.

"Those are dear little children," remarked Golithos, trying to be amiable and interesting.

"Yes," said Gorbo shortly.

"It's a long time since I saw any. In my bad old days I saw plenty, as you know, but I thought it best—after I reformed—to keep away from them for a good long time."

"Sound idea."

"Yes, wasn't it? But as I say, these are very dear little things, especially the little girl. Do you know," he went on chattily, "it used to be a saying amongst us in the bad old days that the lighter the hair the tenderer the meat—however, I don't suppose that interests you."

"Not a bit."

"Of course not. But I have taken quite a strong liking to these little ones. The little girl is very pretty, and they are both well formed. Not fat exactly. I should describe them as well filled out. Chubby, if you understand my meaning."

Gorbo slipped down from the window and went down the ladder in a leisurely way. "Tidy up the place properly," he ordered as he went.

Golithos obediently went on messing about, crooning a little song about a rose that loved a butterfly and faded away.

It will probably occur to the thoughtful reader at this point that a change had come over the character of Gorbo. A sense of responsibility, mingled with self-reproach, had brought forth qualities hitherto unsuspected, and though he was to some extent losing his natural desire to please all whom he met by conciliatory speech and helpful ways, he was gaining in ability to make quick decisions, as also in verbal fluency and a capacity for what is known among our famed comedians as back-chat.

He found the children in the cabbage patch trying to amuse themselves with Tiger, but not succeeding very well because they were getting very tired of this dismal place. Their surroundings were horrible—all nettles and cheap-looking vegetables and rank grass and stones, and a high wall (on which were lots of snails) shutting out everything but the sky. Sylvia took the puppy to show to the cow, which was the only nice thing in the place and which lived in a rotten old shed in a corner, and Gorbo then had a chance to talk to Joe.

"Joe," he said, "I don't want to frighten Sylvia, but you're a man like me. It seems to me that this is not a healthy place to stay in very long. In the first place we'll get bored to screaming fits, and in the second place I'm having doubts of old Golithos."

"Oo-er!" said Joe, now thoroughly startled.

"Yes, I'm beginning to think he's not so reformed as he thinks he is. Of course it may be only my fancy, but I'm not going to take any risks, and you and Sylvia must keep close by me always. We'll have to stay here a little while because, though it's plain that he won't be able to tell us how to get those little doors open, that old witch may come along at any time, and then I can get it out of her. I'll give her my drinking-horn to tell us how; it's the only thing I've got that's worth anything, but it's got silver on it and perhaps it'll do. But if it's not enough I'm afraid Sylvia will have to give over her little coral necklace. I don't know what witches' charges are, but I should say the two together would be plenty."

"But won't it be awfully risky staying here?" asked Joe. This was becoming rather more of an adventure than he had bargained for.

"Not so much, because you won't go out of my sight and I've always got my bow tucked under my arm. Of course I could make it quite safe by sending an arrow through his hairy old throat, but somehow I don't quite like to do it until I'm dead certain sure. But don't you worry, Joe. And don't let Sylvia know."

The day wore on. They had a light supper of cold sliced turnips and some of the milk that was left over from the mid-day feast. They gave a third part of the milk to Tiger in order to moisten some very hard crusts that Golithos found for him. Tiger did not worry, it was quantity he wanted, not quality, and his little abdomen began to take on bold curves again.

The night passed without trouble. The children slept soundly on their straw; Gorbo had made his bed on top of the trap-door so they felt safe enough. But in the morning there was more than a hint that some good old-fashioned trouble was coming.

Said Golithos to Gorbo (taking him quietly aside by the arm), "Would you oblige me by keeping these dear little children always close by you?"

Said Gorbo to Golithos (removing his arm), "I'm going to. But not particularly to oblige you. What's the little game?"

"It is no little game; it is something more serious. You see I have a horrid fear that I may go back to my old disgraceful ways. The sight of these dear little plump things is a very, very great temptation to me, and I want you to help me to fight against it. I don't want you to go away, because if I don't have the temptation there will be no credit in conquering it—and I really hope and believe that I will be able to. Do you know that last night I wanted to have a look at them asleep, but I couldn't open the trap-door. There seemed to be something heavy on it."

"There was," said Gorbo.

"I thought so. And then, do you know, I came down and sat thinking about them, and after a time I found myself sharpening a big knife in an absent-minded way. It gave me quite a shock. Now promise me that you will help me to overcome this temptation."

"Oh, I'll help you," replied Gorbo.

He called to Sylvia and Joe to come down and to bring Tiger, and then he went with them down the steps to the door in the outer wall.

"Come and open this door, Golithos," he called.

"Oh, you're surely not thinking of leaving me!" exclaimed Golithos, clumping down after them. "I shall be greatly upset if you run away like that."

Gorbo jerked out an arrow and laid it on his bow.

"You'll be more upset in a moment perhaps," he said, "if that door isn't opened before I count ten there'll be three of these sticking out of your silly fat head."

Golithos jumped for the door and had it open just as Gorbo had counted up to six. As the children passed out, shrinking away from him, he bent down and held out his hand to them.

"Good-bye, little dears," he said. "Won't you shake hands with an old reformed person? Oh, this *is* unkind!"

Gorbo put his arrow back in the quiver and stood for a moment looking up at him. "You stick to watercress," he said tauntingly. "Watercress and cold water. A slice of mangel-wurzel for Christmas. That's about your form."

"You have hurt me," said Golithos, drawing himself to his full height (seven feet, one inch). His tone was not without a certain dignity.

"Get inside!" shouted Gorbo, slipping out an arrow again. "I'm not so sure I shan't——"

But Golithos had scuttled in and banged the door and locked it. They walked along a narrow stony track that led towards some rising ground. Looking back, they saw the head of Golithos peeping over the top of his wall. So far as they could judge at that distance it had a wistful look.

A Christmas Play

~❦~

by David Lindsay

David Lindsay is remembered today primarily for his first novel, *A Voyage to Arcturus*, published in 1920. Tolkien and C. S. Lewis read the book in the mid-1930s, and Tolkien remarked of it in a letter: "I read 'Voyage to Arcturus' with avidity . . . No one could read it merely as a thriller and without interest in philosophy, religion and morals." Lewis called it "that shattering, intolerable, and irresistible work" and took its central premise (that a voyage to another world could be essentially a spiritual experience) for his own novels *Out of the Silent Planet* and *Perelandra*, adding a Christian mythic outlook, whereas Lindsay's vision has no orthodoxy.

Lindsay wrote no short stories, but his Christmas play, probably written in the 1930s and never before published, concerns his usual theme of questioning the nature of reality and our perception of it. It is written in a more playful mode than is found in his novels. I am especially grateful to Lindsay's daughters, Mrs. Diana Moon and Mrs. Helen Baz, for allowing it to appear in print at last.

(Scene: Mother Nightshade's Grotto. Outside it is snow, and it is still snowing, Evening dusk. Christmas Eve. The fairy Emerald is moving hesitatingly about the cave, now glancing at its objects, now in puzzled thought, now looking towards the letter in her hand, without re-reading it.)

Emerald.   A letter from the Fairy Queen!—
                    I don't quite know what it can mean.
                    *   *   *   *   *
                    I wished to help three girls I know
                    Because my heart is good
                    And they deserve it—
                    The daughters of a wood-cutter
                    And so I thought it would be
                    Appropriate
                    And nice
                    To give each one a Prince to marry
                    In fact, it is always done
                    Besides pleasing them very much
                    And me, too.
                    But now Titania writes:
                    She cannot manage more than *two* princes
                    This Christmas—
                    Two only.
                    Nor owing to modern social evolution
                    And European revolution
                    And this and that—
                    All which quite bewilders me
                    Because my wits are foolish
                    Although my heart is wonderfully good—
                    But anyway, my plan is spoilt—
                    That I can understand
                    What I *don't* understand
                    Is why she sends me to this dreadful cave
                    All toads, mice, spiders and things!
                    And why must I meet old Mother Night-
                        shade—
                    The wickedest of witches?
                    I'd rather not
                    Yet if I fly the spot and disobey
                    I know—I *know* I'll have to rue the day!
                    Whatever shall I do?

(*Enter Mother Nightshade. She peers into the shadow of the grotto, makes out Emerald, utters a screeching laugh of surprise, and scuttles forward to offer to embrace her—but Emerald shrinks back, and they face each other.*)

Nightshade.   Hail, Emerald!

Emerald.   Hail, *you!*

Nightshade.   I have a name.

Emerald.   I know—a horrid name!
My mouth refuses it.

Nightshade.   Night and shade are praised by all.
When doth set the stupid sun
And the glare of day is done
Shall not magic twilight fall?

Emerald.   But not for wickedness.
You move by night to work men harm—
The sleep of living things you care not for
You'd see them dead.

Nightshade.   When cuckoo calls on winter's morn
When April sees the golden corn
When maid disdains to go in silk
When toper's nose is white as milk
When owl sits by the kitchen fire
When dainty mistress seeks the mire
When foot is shapen to the shoe
When five is made of two and two
When pampered beauty has no moods
When unicorn gallops through the woods
When rich man sleeps on sanded floor
When never in all a house a door
When yellow sun moves from west to east
When water is wine and bread a feast
Then—not till then—
Then will I love all living things.

Emerald.   When old wife huddles by the fire
When Brindle crunches in the byre
When cook tries gravy from the ladle

When fat babe chuckles in the cradle
When ancient hobbles on his crutch
When rabbit's bright eyes peer from hutch
When boy throws stones in chestnut tree
When homeward sails the tired bee
When lark sings unseen in the air
When sewing-maid sews in the sunny chair
When frog hops leisurely to ditch
When cheese makes a banquet and penny makes rich
When yellow sun moves from east to west
When rest moves to work, and work to rest
Then—even then—
Then do I love all living things.

Nightshade.	What want you here?
Emerald.	Nothing, be sure. Titania sent me.
Nightshade.	For what?
Emerald.	Here is her letter. I shan't show it to you, neither can you take anything
	from a fairy. I detest you—I do not fear you.
	I know three sisters
	Fair as the dawn
	And of an age to marry
	Them I would wed to Princes
	But times are changed
	Titania offers me two only
	I fear
	One girl must wed a millionaire
	Of whom there are more.
	And so my Queen has sent me here
	Perchance to use you in the business
	Or else I cannot guess the reason why.
Nightshade.	(*with a screeching laugh*) He! he!
	Fairies can change things
	They cannot make them
	Witches can make them—

	Fairies can season pies
	They cannot bake them
	Witches can bake them.
Emerald.	Pies!
Nightshade.	In honour of this holy time of year
	Mince-pies are eaten.
Emerald.	Spare me your scoffs and riddles!
Nightshade.	Addle-pate!
	Now mark you well my words
	For maybe your simple Queen
	Has told me of your business
	Or maybe
	I know it of myself.
	Wise I am
	Passing wise
	Few things go not
	Before my eyes
	Well! here is the shop
	Where that is sold
	Which you can buy
	With fairy gold.
Emerald.	I have no gold.
Nightshade.	Indeed you have!
	Gold untold!
	Gold in your heart
	Gold in your eyes
	Pay me well
	I'll bake you the pies.
Emerald.	But to what plan?
Nightshade.	In this high season
	Of neighbourly joy
	'Tis merely fitting
	We should enjoy
	Ourselves and our friends
	In one common action
	Whose different ends

(Between you and me)
Will in equal degree
Give us all satisfaction.
I'll bake three pies
For your three maids
They'll eat them, never fear!
In two I'll put your Princes
By fairy spell
The third is mine
Then let them choose by wit
Or lot
Or how they like.

Emerald.   (*doubtfully*) What will you do with yours?

Nightshade. That is my payment!
I can without your will do nothing
And so
There is your fairy gold
To pay me with.

Emerald.   You'll do some ugly work, I know!—
If I refuse—?

Nightshade. I'll then not bake the pies—
Your double-prize
Of Princes
Shall go elsewhere.
You cannot do without my help
Titania knows it
She sent you here.

Emerald.   It's true she sent me here—
You mean to give a husband to the third
Of these poor dears?

Nightshade. Why not?
Should she have none?

Emerald.   Oh, no. But not from you.

Nightshade. A wretch or rogue
You think I'll give!
But what if he has brains—

	Your princes none?
	The world you know not, silly Emerald—
	I do
	To-day men rise from naught
	To be Dictators.
Emerald.	What's that?
Nightshade.	Wizards, too
	But unlike witches
	Their spell moves millions.
Emerald.	How odd! And I have never heard of them!
	But are they good?
Nightshade.	Nobody, nothing, is good for all
	The road for one, for another's a wall
	The slaying of one is another's food
	Bad for you, for me is good
	Dictators are good, if you think them good.
Emerald.	Then is it to be a—a—one of *those*
	For my third girl?
Nightshade.	I did not say so
	And it is not so.
Emerald.	Cease teasing me, unpleasant crone!
	Who shall it be?
Nightshade.	(*impressively*) A man . . . *without a friend!*
Emerald.	(*starting back*) What!
Nightshade.	No more, no less.
Emerald.	(*shuddering*) How *black*—how *wicked* of you!
	No friend!
Nightshade.	Desolation—
	Consolation—
	Between these two
	Men stagger on through life.
	So many friends have some
	They lose *themselves*
	Others have none.
	I did not make the world

	From this man *I* not took away
	His friends.
Emerald.	I will not suffer it!
	I'll leave it all
	And go away.
Nightshade.	Fool! If you dare!
	This is Titania's will.
Emerald.	I'm sure she would not countenance
	A thing so frightful.
Nightshade.	(*searching in her skirt*) Here is her ring!
	She gave it to me.
Emerald.	I see it is her ring.
Nightshade.	Who bears this ring
	May give command
	To all the fairies.
Emerald.	Would I could contradict you
	But it is even so.
Nightshade.	So sensible at last!
	Then do her bidding
	And mine.
Emerald.	(*sadly*) What do you want?
Nightshade.	Beneath this mountain
	Full many a pace
	The cave winds on
	To blacker space
	There is my kitchen
	My oven and pots
	I'll make the pies
	While the fire-stone hots.
Emerald.	What will you make them of?
	Something evil?
Nightshade.	Common flour and common water
	Common mincemeat shall come after
	But then—he! he!—to flavour all—
	One *tiny drop* of cordial
	The witch's magic!

	Then when those three weird mincemeat-pies
	Shall ready be for your fairy cries
	Of other magic—
	I'll call you!
Emerald.	You mean to leave me here alone
	In this dark noisome hole of slime and stone?
Nightshade.	I found you here alone.
Emerald.	Only so lately
	Another Emerald was with me—
	My doing right.
	But now I fear I'm doing wrong
	Although commanded
	And so I am indeed alone.
Nightshade.	At fairy conscience I needs must grin
	Nameless princes heart-ease win
	Nameless *man* is a mortal sin!
Emerald.	I cannot answer you, I'm too unhappy—
	Shall you be long?
	How shall I pass the time while you're away?
Nightshade.	Sing if you will!
	Dance if you will!
	Toads won't bite you
	Spiders won't kill.
	I won't be long
	I'll hear your song
	It will make me smile
	In the midst of my kneading
	A fairy's song
	Should show good breeding!
	(*Exit Mother Nightshade*)
Emerald.	I don't feel very much like singing
	I feel like crying.
	(*She sings*)
	Who praise the fairies little know
	How ill at ease they come and go
	For nothing of the world they see

But bird, and beast, and flower, and tree.
   The human heart they cannot read
What a man loves, or is, or does
And so too seldom they succeed
In helping him where'er he goes
   Who praise the fairies little think
They'd give up sleep, and food, and drink
To know a man's heart and what he needs
In that strange human life he leads.

(While she sings, the three sisters enter the cave from behind her, wrapped in snowy cloaks. Rosa is 20, Violetta 18, and Lila 16. One by one, they absently let fall their cloaks, while staring at Emerald and edging round to see her face.)

Rosa.	Who is it?
Lila.	How beautiful!
Violetta.	How strange!
Rosa, Lila.	Is it a fairy?
Violetta.	It is my dream.
	(Emerald turns round to them.)
Lila.	Are you a fairy?
Emerald.	*(smiling)* Yes.
Lila.	I never thought I should see one.
Rosa.	Tell us, please, what you are doing here
	And who you are
	And where we are.
	Answer *me,* please—
	I am the eldest.
Emerald.	I know you are
	I know you all, and all about you.
	You are in the witch's cave
	But I am here to help you, if I can.
Lila.	The witch's cave!
	I don't like that a bit.
Rosa.	Tell us your name.
Emerald.	Emerald.
Lila.	How pretty!

Violetta.	What was that lovely music That drew us here To this sad eerie place?
Lila.	Though we are miles from home And have no right to be On such an evening.
Rosa.	I hope the Providence that brought us here Through drifts and pathless ways Will see us safely back! I've a responsibility for these two girls— I am the eldest.
Emerald.	I'll guide you home Fear not for that.
Violetta.	What was the music?
Emerald.	Not mine. Perhaps it was Titania's To bring you here.
Violetta.	Have I not seen you in a dream?
Emerald.	Often I've watched you while you smiling slept You three So then you may have dreamt me.
Violetta.	Yes I did dream of you.
Lila.	If it's not impolite, so soon— Why are we here?
Nightshade.	(*faintly, from far recesses of the cave*) Emerald!

(*The girls are startled and bewildered. Emerald also for a moment is disturbed, but then quiets the others with a light motion of her hand.*)

Emerald.	Have no alarm! Only the Witch is there—old Mother Nightshade She needs me for a purpose.

Lila.	(*fearfully*) A witch!
	And you will leave us!
Emerald.	Soon I'll be back, and then what you have asked
	And everything, I'll tell you.
Lila.	Only consider, if she has heard our voices
	She will come out to us!
Emerald.	To-day she cannot harm you
	She does the bidding of my Queen, Titania.
	(*aside*) Would it were *all* the truth
	That I am speaking!
Rosa.	Lila, be more controlled!
	When Emerald promises to bring us home
	What thing can hurt us meanwhile?
	But if it merely is you dread to see
	An ugly beldam, why, at every turn
	In the world coarse horrid sights offend our eyes
	Which yet we govern.
Lila.	Your eyes, I know, are governed
	For your tongue is the eldest.
Rosa.	How can you dare to be so rude
	Before a fairy?
Lila.	I'm sorry, Emerald, if I am rude
	But in this queer dark unexpected place
	My words as well drop unexpectedly
	I feel I'm in a dream.
Violetta.	I fancied music came with the witch's voice
	Like that we have been hearing on the way
	Only it was still quieter and more magic
	And sweeter
	As if it neared its heart.
Emerald.	Mayhap it was Titania's sovereign ring
	She lent the Witch.
	(*She steals an uneasy glance into the darkness of the cave.*)

	If the ring be on her finger
	Here with you must I not linger.
Nightshade.	(*still more faintly than before, from the far interior*)
	Emerald!

(*Lila, frightened, clings to Rosa, who takes her in her arms.*)

Violetta.	Again it sounds!
Emerald.	Stay here for me, dear hearts!
	Go now I must, but quickly I'll return
	When things of high importance you shall learn.
	(*Exit.*)
Lila.	(*disengaging herself from Rosa*) What can she mean?
	What things of high importance can concern *us*
	Who are so lowly born, so humble?
Rosa.	Sometimes I do not feel so humble
	Sometimes I've dreamt of marrying a Prince
	And driving forth in crested open carriage
	With footman tall behind me
	Affably saluting all the people
	(I mean, *I* saluting them)
	Who with their shouting—
	Their joyful shouting—
	Make the day tremble.
	Sometimes I have such dreams, while now they come
	To mind, I don't know why.
Lila.	I would not wish to be a fair princess
	For others' idle shouting, but I'd wish
	To be one for the sake of doing good
	For imagine!
	How many loaves of bread might not one buy
	Even with but ten thousand pounds per year

	Which for a princess—all the world knows— isn't much
	But in each loaf
	Would be new life for some poor starving person—
	North, south, east, west, should roll my emblazoned vans
	While sometimes I'd put money in the loaves
	To add a zest to blessing.

Rosa.   Benevolence of course I never mentioned
            Because I thought it would be understood
            Just as I should wear jewels and a crown
            And be unimpeachable in my private life
            And hold myself from work.

Lila.   But *you,* deep-flowing silent Violetta
            Whose very thoughts are timid to yourself
            Whose words are frightened creatures dragged to the light
            From out of darkness—
            What princess would *you* be, had you the way to it?
            Shyly translated to us your heart's ambition—
            Its fondest, most ambition!

Violetta. I would not wed a Prince unless I loved him
            I'd marry only him who needed me
            His rank, for me, should be his need of me.

Lila.   Who can explain how all my fears for the Witch
            Have quite departed?
            I seem not now to care if she comes out
            I'll laugh, sing, hallo—do anything I please
            I'll *call* her forth, for a wager!
            (*to Rosa*) Let's have what we have often had before—
            A trial of rhyming song. You second be.
            I never fail my part, and you do fairly.

Rosa.	Say what the theme!
Lila.	We'll sing of maids obscure and princely wooers.

(Lila and Rosa sing together. Afterwards Violetta joins in.)

Lila.	Broke the day across the sea
Rosa.	Pale green was the east
Lila.	Sailed a ship was silvery
Rosa.	Like strange phantom beast
Lila.	Heading for the shore it came
Rosa.	Half swift as an arrow
Lila.	On its mast an oriflamme
Rosa.	Lordly, long and narrow
Lila.	Watched it from the darkling sands
Rosa.	Pools and seaweed rocks
Lila.	Maidens three like living wands
Rosa.	Artless wild their locks
Lila.	Of the dawn their unquiet gowns
Rosa.	Of the twilight's glowing
Lila.	On their shadowy faces frowns
Rosa.	Matched their hearts unknowing
Lila.	Strangers three leapt on the shore
Rosa.	Breakers' rude play scorning
Lila.	Gleamed the panoply they wore
Rosa.	Clashed its dreadful warning
Lila.	Bold were they like forest lions
Rosa.	Tall and young and knightly
Lila.	Seemed they well imperial scions
Rosa.	Bearing birth so rightly
Lila.	He whose shield was all dim gold
	Its device, a flame—
	"You who shall marry me,
	I am the Prince of Hungary
	Know well my name!"
Rosa.	He whose moony silver shield
	Held for device a tower—

	"You who shall marry me,
	I am the Prince of Muscovy
	This is my hour—
	Know well my name!"
Lila, Rosa.	"You who shall marry me,
	I am the Prince of (Hungary/Muscovy)
	Know well my name!"
Violetta.	But he whose shield as innocence was white
	And empty of device—
	"You who shall marry me,
	First shall you name me—
	Love bears my name!"
Lila, Rosa,	"You who shall marry me
Violetta.	Know first my name!"

(*The song, when hardly ended, is as if broken by a loud discord from behind, through which, however, seems to sound the same fairy music as before. The sisters start round, to see Mother Nightshade emerged from the cave's blackness. In one hand she bears her long staff, in the other a dish with three mince-pies. Lila retreats in fear, Rosa is struck motionless, but Violetta seems to be drawn step by step towards the Witch.*)

Nightshade.	(*with a cackling laugh*) Well sung, gooselings!
	Featly you've chanted
	Your future ganders
	And bold Alexanders!
	Pity 'twould be
	Were you all at sea
	Your wishes ungranted!
Violetta.	Aren't you the Witch?
Nightshade.	Rich as a witch!
	Witch-rich!
	Here's of my treasure
	For your good pleasure!
	I came myself

Your fay, I guessed
Might allow her affection
For your three chits
To outstrip her wits
And so it were best
This slight reflection
These pies here—look!
Should come with the cook!
(*She sets down the dish of pies.*)

Lila.   (*awed*) But—but what *are* they?
Are they for us?

Rosa.   (*after turning away to cross herself hurriedly*)
If they are for us
We could not eat anything *at all* at present, thank you!
(*aside*) In this repulsive supernatural den—
Mary defend us!

Nightshade. One here
Knows no fear.

Violetta.   What should I fear?
I have not harmed you
Nor have you ever yet harmed me.

Nightshade. Youth harms age
Age is a cage
But youth goes free
Cracks and vices come with years
Blind are eyes and deaf are ears
Heavy are feet and sharp is tongue
Age shall never sing a song
Youth can hear and youth can see
Youth can leap o'er top of tree
Youth rejoices, youth is loved
Age, biting lip, is only moved
By jealousy.

Violetta.   I know you will not harm us.

Nightshade.	How know you that?
Violetta.	I feel no shrinking from you.
Nightshade.	He! he!
	Strange are all new sensations!
	The Witch is loved!
Violetta.	I did not say I loved you—and yet I might—
	I cannot tell so quickly what I feel.
	I do not think you evil.
Nightshade.	Dare you to kiss me?
Violetta.	A kiss is love
	As yet I neither love nor hate you.
Nightshade.	I'll beg a kiss from Violetta!
Violetta.	How is my name known to you?
Nightshade.	The Witch knows many things.
Violetta.	Why should you have me kiss you?
Nightshade.	To show you have no fear.
	(*Violetta kisses her on the mouth.*)
Nightshade.	So sweet it tasted
	As though I were returned to youth itself!
	Your generosity shall be rewarded
	I promise you.
Rosa.	(*to Mother Nightshade*) Please don't ask *me*
	to kiss you!
	I am not mercenary, and really want
	No witch's gratitude!
Lila.	Neither ask *me!*
	So tight and cold and fasting are my lips
	I could not kiss at all.
Nightshade.	My guests you are
	Here in this cave—
	Eat you my food!
	'Twill warm your blood.
	Straight from the oven come these mince-pies
	(*She lifts the dish.*)
	Try how they smell! Look how they rise!
	And what you crave

	May well be inside

May well be inside
With hunger for guide!
(*She sets the dish down again.*)
Eat, I beseech!—
A pie for each.

Lila.   (*quickly*) Rosa, you must refuse for us at once!—
At other times one does not have to prompt you!

Nightshade.   You care not to accept my poor refreshment!
But that can soon be altered—
(*She goes about the dish of pies three times, passing her staff over them, chanting.*)
Pies, forthright
Put out might!
Put forth hunger
Till no longer
Timid hand
Doth you withstand!
Open eyes in admiration!—
Open mouths in expectation!—
Tingle tongues of maidens three!
Eaten be, and eaten be!
She who gave you form and number
Blows you up to flame from ember—
Be your magic nature strong!
Here I end my Witch's song.

Violetta.   (*drawing near her*) May we not hear what is that magic nature?

Nightshade.   Princes your sisters want—
Love, you
Here in the pies lie Princes twain
One for one girl, and one again.
Love lies never within the spell
So choose you wisely and choose you well!

Violetta.	I wish no Prince, but she who finds no Prince What shall she find?
Nightshade.	Quick-stricken was the elf-maid Emerald When I acquainted her before your coming— A man without a friend! Him shall she wed, who does not wed a Prince.
Violetta.	Poor man!

Lila.	(*coming forward*) Most fortunately, however,
	    this falls out!
	For Rosa wants a Prince, and I do, too
	While you're indifferent, Violetta, dear!
	Quite suitable, for all we know, may be the
	    third.

Rosa.	(*to her sisters*) My honesty I need not dwell upon— I freely grant a friendless man for husband Would never tempt me, for I like my friends And do not wish to live as in a desert. You, Violetta, have never thought like that And so it well may be that for this once Lila is right.
Nightshade.	What says my kindest youngling?
Violetta.	For love, I'd marry him who had no friend And think me happy that *I* was his friend— His only friend.
Lila.	So we're agreed! Your heart, my Violetta Is framed for love—it cannot fail to love Whome'er it pleases. No doubt in the world 'twill be A very excellent match.
Rosa.	(*to Violetta*) Indeed unjust 'twould be to with- hold from us The coming of our dream you do not care for.
Lila.	And, sweetest Violetta, pray don't fear That our more splendid marriages shall end

	The affection which has ever been be- tween us. In this one matter—insist he how he will— I'll cross my princely husband.
Rosa.	Why make assurances of our characters To one who is a very part of us? Am I a person—once I shall be in my palace Commanding and arranging everything— To dread to let my sister call me sister? (*to Violetta*) Godmother to your children even I'll be.
Lila.	(*to Witch*) So now that we have settled it, I beg you show us Which of the pies is which, and we can eat them At once, without delay.
Nightshade.	Already I see The hunger works! Reckless as gobblers— Greedy as Turks! One maid only the chant not moves Because her heart already loves When door stands wide And treasure's inside Useless the key!
Rosa.	In short, it's evident which has won your favour Of us three sisters. And she's welcome to it (Meaning no rudeness!) if you will but tell us What she, as well as we, requires to know— Which pie we each must eat, to our desire!
Nightshade.	He! he! Were I to tell you that, the spell were lost! Discover for yourselves!
Lila.	The pies are all alike!

Nightshade.   I go to fetch your Emerald the sprite
                Hers are your Princes (he who's none is
                    mine!)
                It's proper you should thank her for her
                    bounty.
                Taste you no crumb till my return
                When your three choices we will learn—
                Your three lots in the fatal churn
                Churning your fates from dreams to men!
                E'en while you bite
                I'll read the fates right
                But when with maiden's substance is mixed
                The witch-pie magic—fast-fixed! fast-fixed!
                Those fates will be—
                Full willingly
                I'll speak them then!
                (*She points towards the ground.*)
                See yonder snail
                In house of horn
                Hastening slowly
                Like ship in sail
                By zephyr borne!
                Ere it wins
                That stony crack
                Like a man's sins
                I'll be back.
                So delay not to choose
                Which husband is whose
                While to speed your intent
                I'll add one last hint—
                On what shall be bitten
                The names are written!
                (*Exit*)

Lila.   Heavens! what mystery has she spoken now?
                Are they inscribed like ancient monuments
                Or birthday-cakes, these pies?

(*Rosa doubtfully takes up a mince-pie, then utters a startled exclamation.*)

Rosa.   Look! Writing in fire! It's scarcely holy!

(*Lila quickly seizes one of the two remaining pies, first to stare at it, then to turn it round in her fingers while she reads to herself what is written on it. Meanwhile Violetta more quietly takes and glances at the last pie.*)

Lila.   Listen to this!—

"She who me takes
Fortune shakes."

I'll *keep* this one—until I've heard the others.
Rosa, how runs yours?

Rosa.   (*reading aloud*) "She who me eats
Day-dawn greets."

Lila.   It's too mysterious—I like mine better.

(*to Violetta*) Your one has sorcery writing,
too?

Violetta.   (*handing her pie to Lila*) *You* read it—and if
you wish to, keep it
Instead of yours.

Lila.   (*reading aloud*) "She who me chooses
Nothing loses."

I'll keep my own.

(*She returns Violetta her pie.*)

"She who me takes,
Fortune shakes"—

The promise is transparent
For if you shake a tree, down comes its
fruit—
The goodly fruit of Fortune—in my case
A Prince! More difficult are your two leg-
ends.

Rosa.   Because you're young and dull of compre-
hension!
The election is soon made for older me.
Nothing to lose is not therefore to gain

Something—while on the other hand be sure
The day-dawn is to banish hateful night—
My night of hopeless longing for the things
I have not!—This I hold, without a doubt,
Is best of all the choices!

Lila. We dare not lightly guess, and praise our
    guesses—
Too much depends on it. For we shall never
So near Princesses be a second time
In our dim, moveless lives. So, Violetta—
Cool as you are, uncaring as you seem—
Say what *you* think about these oracles!
It often is said that they without the will
Are clear-sighted.

Rosa. (*to Violetta*) We'll trust your loyalty and can-
    dour.

Violetta. I'd help you, but I see no more than you
Into the meanings.

Rosa. You would, but do not, help us!

Violetta. To help you, I am giving up my choice.

Lila. You're most unkind!

Rosa. I hope she is not more than most unkind!
Surely by your strange sympathy, Violetta,
With that old hag, her handiwork you'd
    know?
We only ask which is the unblest pie!

Violetta. Poor anxious sisters! if I knew, I'd say.

Rosa. What use then was it to be her pet, and kiss
    her!

Violetta. Indeed, no *use*.

Lila. (*smiling wryly*) Still you may think you have
    a useful friend
At court! How we decide, little you care—
You won't be left to wander in the cold!

Violetta. You scar your heart, to have such evil thoughts.
Truly I felt her bodily seeming hid

                Another spirit in her. Hardly a witch
                She was. And so I kissed her—for she
                    wanted it—
                Not anything the feeling was to gain me.

Rosa.   Though you may chance to reap a gain from it!

(*While the sisters are contending, enter behind them silently from the cave's interior Mother Nightshade and Emerald. The Witch's face is muffled. For a minute they stand unnoticed, overhearing the talk. Then the Witch takes a single stride to approach the girls swiftly, and stamps her foot. They see her, and Rosa and Lila recoil, but Violetta stays where she is.*)

Nightshade.   (*in a shrill and awful, yet lovely, voice of command*) Peace!

(*There is a hush, while faint music plays, But it soon stops.*)

Nightshade.   (*more quietly*) Peace!—all of you. Emerald,
                be you my tongue!

Emerald.   I may not say I cannot
                And yet, alas! I scarcely have a tongue
                Even for myself!
                Frightened I am—
                Melancholy and miserable
                And everything a fairy should not be.
                I don't know what I've done!
                My ill-considered wish for you three innocents
                Plunges *one* into woe
                And now the moment has arrived
                When, out of hesitating mists,
                Your fortunes shall take solid lasting shape.
                I have no impudence to show you what to
                  do—
                A life I've spoilt!

Nightshade.   (*warningly*) Emerald!

Emerald.   Oh yes, I know!—
                I must be quick to obey Titania's ring!—

	But my heart mutinies

Just like a bird struggling in limy snare!—
However! since it's so ruled—come, dear three!
Divided by a fairy's airy whim—
You hold in hand these pies made by the Witch
Two I have bless'd, one *she* has far from bless'd—
You know about them?

Lila.   Yes, indeed we know.

Emerald.   Two girls shall have resounding marriages,
One, an unkind one—
Have you the resolution now to eat?

Rosa.   Violetta does not want a Prince
Only whether we have chosen right
We're not quite sure.

Emerald.   But now you must decide.

Lila.   Then we'll decide to keep the one in our hand,
Each of us. Please—*please* be quick!

Rosa.   What must we do?

Emerald.   As one by one I shall invite you
Tell me aloud what pie it is you hold
Then, to the last crumb and currant, eat it up!

Rosa.   My privilege is to be first—nor would I shirk it
Though all this weird to-do were much more horrid!

Lila.   For, in the books, the eldest of the sisters
Always goes first!

Rosa.   In those same books, the youngest is most fair
And therefore she's triumphant. Now is *real* life—
Different in all respects, though very strange.

	I'll call you "highness" when you are one, Lila!
	You do the same for me!
Lila.	Mark that the title is in *your* mouth first, Dear Rosa! Let it be a prophecy!
Emerald.	The Queen of Fairies her ring is here— Have care in case it carries back a tale Of wrangling maids! Say nothing more at all Save to my questions. You, Rosa, speak the first!
Rosa.	I am to meet the dawn—such is the message Of *my* pie! *(She eats.)*
Emerald.	Impatient Lila, what does yours announce?
Lila.	I shall shake Fortune. May I do so truly! *(She eats.)*
Emerald.	Since I am back I have not heard your voice, Quiet Violetta! What then promises *Your* writing?
Violetta.	I nothing lose.
Emerald.	So won't you eat?
Violetta.	*(thoughtfully and looking away)* Why must I eat, Thereby to keep the things I'd *rather* lose? Am I so gracious that I have no ugliness Or awkwardness—so saintly that there's in me No trace of envy, spite or meanness—I could lose? But if it says, I am to lose no *good* That may invisibly be reaching to me— Shall I be like a huckster, demanding first To *see* the good?—or like a faithful heart, Adventuring in unknown places, Confiding in the eventual mercy of Heaven? *(She eats)*

(While the three are eating their pies, Emerald steps to the front, wringing her hands softly)

Emerald.   *(aside)* The mottoes are not mine—

Old Nightshade, she has written them in her
     fire!

I don't know which are good and which is
     bad—

I dare not ask her!

*(She walks about, then comes to a stand
again, with clasped hands.)*

There's nothing happening yet!—what will
     be next?

Will the Witch speak?—

Surely these husbands can't appear to-day—

This minute?—

The spell must have a time to take effect—

Except that the Witch knows now, and may
     from malice

Give the bad news for one!

In truth, I overlooked that there might be

This unendurable interval of waiting!

It's hard, and cruel, and mocking!—

These feelings, I think, must be the dreadful
     kind

That mortals have—troubling all their faces!

I may be turning mortal! Perhaps I *am!*—

No! I'm not strong enough—I'd die at once!

(She sings quietly)

He without friend

Cannot love

Cannot defend

Cannot save.

     His heart of love

Dungeoned is—

The day above

Through chinks it sees.

His heart of love
Sickens and dies—
It cannot move
After its eyes.

(*The sisters have finished their pies. Violetta, drawing near to Emerald, gently touches her arm.*)

Violetta.   Now always will your song be my song too!

Emerald.   (*perturbed*) Nearly without knowing what I
                  did,
              I sang it!—
              Yet if its sense has found an echo in you
              Because you've chosen *him* it fits so closely,
              Your song through life I fear indeed it shall
                  be!—
              Dear Rosa and Lila, how is it with you?
              Has the song saddened *you,* like Violetta?

Rosa.   I heard you sing, but not attended well—
              Much louder in my spirit the pie is singing!
              Marvellously gay I feel, and nothing sad!
              My Prince—no doubt of it!—is on his way
              To kiss and wed me!

Lila.   Already mine is here!—or just the same.—
              Poor Violetta! with your sweet emotions
              Of sympathy and pity! Marry *them,*
              Violetta! For *me,* a man of flesh and blood!
              Lovely shall be the flesh, and high the blood!

Rosa.   You're nearest to me, Lila, after all!
              There's something in the failure to aim high—
              Give it the best name we will—

Lila.   Stamps a mean nature!—I know! And that's
                  the way
              Of thinking of the world.
              If we are called upon to set example—

Rosa.   We must be less eccentric!
              Violetta, in the low place she has chosen,
              May be so if she pleases. Almost the only—

Lila.	I know what you would say! Almost the only Right that the humble have, is to *be* humble. She who sits high—
Rosa.	*Must* be as proud as she has been ambitious!
Emerald.	But are you *sure,* dear Violetta's sisters, You've eaten Princes?
Lila.	If I have not now eaten the *handsomest* Prince, I make a vow I'll never eat again!
Rosa.	Mine should be statelier and nobler to suit my years If there is justice in it! And to suit my taste, Handsomer too!
Lila.	If mine's not handsomer, I'll be discontent— And nobler, and richer!
Emerald.	(*to Rosa*) But are you as sure as she?
Rosa.	I'm sure I greatly like what I have eaten! (*Lila throws out her arms gaily.*)
Lila.	The Princess Lila had a dream— She dreamt that she was poor again. Her Prince's eyes with mirth did gleam— "Why, how could that be, foolish wife, When all the days of all your life Within my arms you've lain?" (*speaks*) And so I have! For this wild hour to come Has always been predestinate!
Rosa.	The Princess Rosa had a dream— She dreamt that there was higher bliss. Her Prince's eyes with fire did gleam— "Why, how could that be, witless wife, When all the valleys of your life Are radiant in my kiss?"— (*speaks*) Meaning, there's nothing higher than the sun,

> Which, chasing the earthly shadows of the
>   mountains,
> Gilds every hollow. The sun as well's a
>   Prince!

(*The two girls dance about. Of a sudden the Witch takes another quick step forward, raising her staff.*)

Nightshade.   (*in a high, sharp, weird voice*) Be still and
                   silent, ye senseless ones!

(*Rosa and Lila stop short and face the Witch in alarm. Then
loud music sounds, and while it continues the Witch throws
off her witch's things, standing suddenly revealed as Titania,
Queen of the Fairies. Rosa and Lila drop to their knees before her. Emerald, after making her a low, frightened, yet
very graceful obeisance, likewise sinks to her knees. Only Violetta remains standing before Titania, her feet together, her
hands folded, her head bent in reverence. The tableau endures without change for full two minutes, the music always
playing. But at the last the music dies away.*)

Emerald.   (*in a low, awed voice*) Titania!—dread Queen
                   of Elves and Fairies!

Titania.   In the remotest cave the Witch lies sleeping,
               Beneath my power! Her semblance I have
                   borrowed—
               To-day has no one been here but Titania!
               (*Violetta slowly kneels.*)

Titania.   Rosa and Lila!
               Because you so desire to marry Princes
               And Emerald has begged it for you all,
               Have them you shall—and soon!
               Right were your choices. But the dawn, Rosa,
               Is not full day, and so your Prince as yet
               Must something lack of power.—
               Lila, to *shake* is not to bring down *to* you
               Fortune—so that, for all your princely mar-
                   riage,

	Fortune for you must still remain mysterious.—
	Yet shall these husbands high be very proud
	Young, noble and loving—see you love them well!—
	And still a doom I set against my gift,
	For that you've scorned a poor old wretched woman,
	Witch though you deemed her—and have nearly scorned
	Your sister, too! I'll speak it in a minute.
	(*to Violetta*) The third lot you were told!
Violetta.	(*in low tones*) How shall I beg forgiveness for my kissing you?
	I could not know you!
Titania.	You kissed my good beneath the apparent bad—
	So would I test your heart. For needful is it
	Your husband's wife shall have a loving heart—
	No other friend is his! Are you content?
Violetta.	You will not give me one I cannot love.
Titania.	Then who is he without a friend?
	Beggars have friends in their adversity
	All mortal sufferers of ills have friends
	The base have friends in baseness
	He who would hide from the world still can't escape
	From some one pitying friend—
	Name to me, then, the man without a friend!
Violetta.	I cannot.
Titania.	A *King!*—he has no friend!—

(*Rosa and Lila utter sharp, low exclamations.*)

Titania.	Courtiers a king has, smiling out their lies—
	They're not his friends. Let him be dispossessed

They'll disappear like smoke. Ministers he has,
Each wishing to be a little king beneath
   him—
Neither are they his friends, for every hour
They'd rob him of some royal privilege
To make it theirs. Servants and soldiers he has,
Using his name to colour their own virtues
And glories—but let the king die, another
   king
Will do for them as well. Subjects he has
Honouring his flags and shouting in the
   streets—
Their friendship's like a soul without a body,
They do not know the king.
No friend the king has, for he has no equal
Only his Queen's his equal, and his friend!—
And therefore, Violetta, have I ordered it
That you a King shall marry!
(*Violetta humbly kisses her hand in silence.*)

Titania.	For none of all the women that I see— No one but you—has such a store of love As he must need who knows no other love! So have I tested you this Christmas Eve— Of purest gold's your heart, my Violetta!
Violetta.	(*in the same low voice*) How *know* you I shall love this King?

Titania.	I have so managed it
	That you've both met in Dreamland, and have
	   loved
	Each other passing well! He is not old—
	Singular is his face in shining majesty
	And he is full of care, yet not his own.
	Remember also what your motto said—
	"Nothing you are to lose"—
	But what have you the most of, you might
	   lose?

Love is your chiefest treasure, Violetta!
Therefore you'll not lose love in marrying
    him
I have commanded.
(She turns again to Rosa and Lila.)

Titania.   You other sisters! this now is the doom
I set upon you for your unkind hearts—
Though I've considered, too, you are but
    children.
If ever help you need in earthly life,
To Violetta you shall have recourse
And she shall help you!
So shall your pride be less, when you shall see
Your equal sister above you, dispensing
    bounty!

*(Lila cries quietly, putting her hands before her eyes. Rosa
tries unsuccessfully to control her agitations. Emerald falls
before Titania.)*

Emerald.   Dear Queen! recall this dismal prediction!
Truly their hearts are good—and it is Christ-
    mas,
When love and kindness rule!

Titania.   So far, then, I'll diminish it for your sake—
That while they love, they shall not ever
    need!—
Rise, Emerald!
(Emerald stands up.)

Titania.   To-day you also have been tried, O Emerald!
Obedient to me, I hope, are all the fairies—
Rich in their glowing deeds—
These things are not peculiar to any,
They are the very nature of you all.
But, Emerald, with it—on unknown *her* ac-
    count
Who was to wed a man wanting a friend—
Suffered you have!

	Beautifully with delicate fairy strength This unacquainted pain you have upborne— For which, no less than these three mortal maids, You deserve reward! What then shall it be?
Emerald.	Indeed I was in pain, but could not help it, And did not want it—really, I did not want it! Why should I be rewarded?
Titania.	Light fay! is it your Queen you dare to question? Name what you most desire!
Emerald.	I cannot say so soon. I do not think I want a thing.
Titania.	Consider still!
Emerald.	Unless it were—that I might never do In mortal body!
Titania.	Why that, O timorous one?
Emerald.	I am too weak! This hour I seem to know that mortals' goodness, Unlike that of th' fairies, must be a triumph! Pain and temptation and a host of feelings Are there within the heart, to say it nay! Because I am not warlike, I'd not lose My goodness.
Titania.	Mortal you shall not be until you wish it, I promise you. Some day, dear Emerald, you will understand The high adventure of that arm-ed goodness, Warring with pain, sloth, lies and lovely sin!— Then may you crave of me what now you dread, And I shall grant it!— Meanwhile what other wish have you to ask?
Emerald.	None, great Titania!

Titania.   So I'll pronounce the reward!

                  To-day have not I given you more than you
                      begged?

                  You begged three Princes for your maidens
                      three—

                  Two have I given you, and a King withal!

                  Is not this more?

Emerald.   It's more indeed!

Titania.   Then so henceforward shall it always be—

                  What you shall ask of me in purest kindness,

                  That I will add to!

                  (*Emerald goes on one knee, and kisses her
                      hand.*)

Titania.   Rise, all!

                  (*The three sisters and Emerald all stand up.*)

Titania.   One still awaits her payment!

                  We must not *steal* from the Witch an hour of
                      her life

                  When she's so few!—What shall I pay her in?

(*During a whole minute, while music plays, Titania from
time to time makes mystic passes in the air, towards the inner
cave. At last Mother Nightshade, in true person, comes stumbling in, rubbing her eyes. She squints at everybody in turn,
but starts back a little from Titania. The music ceases.*)

Nightshade.   Hey-day! There's company!

                  I've been asleep, and wake to this!

                  (*She goes up to the three sisters.*)

                  And who are *you,* my dears? You're much too
                      pretty!

                  I'd like to blear your eyes, and blotch your
                      cheeks,

                  And twist your legs in knots!

                  (*She sees Emerald.*)

                  (*chuckling*) *You* I know!

                  The biggest goose among the fairies!

                  Simple they all are, but you're the simpleton!

Who bade you here?—Why do I hold assembly?

Is evil work afoot?

(*to Titania*) Great is the honour, potent Queen,

When you bring your Academy to the Witch!

Perchance you wish instruction in my craft

For these young ladies?

Titania.   Your shape I borrowed for an hour, old wife!

I gave you sleep instead. Now I'd repay you.

Nightshade.   You took my shape!—unheard-of insolence!

Repay me indeed you shall!

What have you *done* in my shape, I'd wish to know?

Who gave you leave?

What tricks have you been up to?

Titania.   Peace, aged woman! Far too rough your tongue is!

Can you not see between your ill and well-wishers?

A gift I offer you, and let that cancel

All talk and memory between us of this hour—

Do you consent?

Nightshade.   The gift must be a good one then!

Titania.   Such as you've never had before!—

Do you consent?

Nightshade.   (*suspiciously*) What is the gift?

Titania.   A magic one—

It will not harm you, but the spell were spoilt

If I informed you first.

Nightshade.   Magic and spells I love! Tell me but this—

Will it take from me life, or power of limb?

Titania.   I've said it will not harm you.

Nightshade.   I'm still in hesitation!

	Why should you make a gift to *me*—your enemy?
Titania.	Dream not, good wife, that you're my enemy!
	I have no enemy but wickedness,
	And you are but its feeble instrument
	That might be made to serve another use.
	Choose you, however, between this gift I offer
	And one that shall be worse!
Nightshade.	Come! come! put by your wrath!
	I'll chance the gift!
	(*Titania makes a pass over her.*)
Titania.	'Tis done!—And what can no more be undone
	Now I may tell you!
Nightshade.	Ay! quickly tell me!
Titania.	I have restored your memories, old dame!
	So that your childhood's earliest happenings,
	As they were pictures, shall return to you
	All painted and vivid!
	About the cottage floor you'll see yourself
	Toddling and waiting for your bread-and-butter—
	You'll see your father coming home from work,
	Lifting you in his arms and kissing you—
	You'll see and hear your mother singing songs
	While she rolls out her pastry.
	Not shadowy and forgettable shall be these things
	But touching you to the quick! And such the spell
	'Twill fiercest work when you are all alone
	Here in this cave—or when at other times
	You're out on mischief.
	Then shall you ask yourself again and again

Which of your days have happiest been, and
    best—
When you were fresh, fragrant, pure, as sum-
    mer morn,
Or now when you are like a human sore,
Offensive to everyone—yourself as well!
Such is my gift, old woman!
It shall begin to move when we are gone,
And have no doubt, before a day is past,
You shall be wondering how your life to
    renew,
Renouncing malisons and black enchantment
And forbidden occupation with the things
Of death and ugly evil!

Nightshade. Should this be true, you've fooled me, Queen
    of Fairies!
Likewise, I shall have lost the only art
I have to live by! Now I must starve, I
    suppose!—
Little that matters to you in a holy action!

Titania. You shall not starve. Each day to this cave
Emerald shall bring you milk and a loaf of
    bread.—
And, till you have changed your character,
    old, old woman,
See that you harm her not by craft or
    violence!—
It will be best for you!

(*Mother Nightshade offers to reply, but Titania waves her down.*)

Titania. Now silent be! I have no more to say.
(*She makes a pass.*)
And be as deaf! while I address these maids.
Your ear must not receive what is not for it—
What do you hear?

Nightshade.	(*in a cowed voice*) I hear that primal silence before creation!
	Quite safely you may speak!
Titania.	Yet you hear my question, cunning one!
	(*She makes a second pass.*)
	Now she'll not hear!—
	(*to the three sisters*) Our meeting must break up.
	Your parents are alone, though I have soothed them
	With a false supposition. Tell them now
	The truth of where you've been, and what has happened—
	Improbable though it seem, they shall believe it.
	Ere Candlemas is come you'll meet your husbands,
	Ere Pentecost you'll marry them!
	Take you no thought to prepare for your three weddings,
	An unexpected letter before long
	You'll have. And also I will send to you by night,
	In bed, my very most distinguished fairy,
	Experienced in human marriages.
	With her you shall consult, and do what's right.—
	Now you must go. A fairy sleigh is waiting
	Outside the cave, with fairy ponies four,
	And fairy coachman—Emerald shall ride with you.
	Before you know that you have started home, You will be there!
	(*making a pass over the Witch*) Now be your ears unseal'd!

(Mother Nightshade puts her hands to her head as if dazed. Sudden loud fairy music sounds, proceeding triumphantly. But in another minute it becomes by transition the different theme of the winding-up song.)

ENSEMBLE.

Rosa, Lila.	'Tis natural that the heart of maiden
	Should dream of marriage proud and splen-did.
Violetta,	Yet when the heart with pride is laden
Emerald.	They say its happiness is ended.
Nightshade.	Unlike your pride, *hate* isn't senseless
	Contrivances it ever knows—
	It's not, like happiness, defenceless,
	But deathless as the tropic glows!
Titania.	The heart of maid was ne'er intended
	To dream of aught else but its loving.
	Before high love her knee is bended,
	Before high love her smiles are moving!
All.	Let each one follow what road she may,
	It will come somewhere, upon a day!
Rosa, Lila.	'Tis fitting that the heart of woman
	Should take a peep where it is going.
Violetta,	Yet when its sight becomes not human
Emerald.	Sad is the token of blood's unflowing.
Nightshade.	Human is *hate,* o'er all the others
	From soul to soul it ever calls—
	The tide of its blood everything smothers,
	In cataracts and fearsome falls!
Titania.	The heart of woman is ever growing
	Towards the love which is its heaven—
	Years shall not stay it, 'tis ever doing
	The same thing o'er, from life's morn to even.
All.	Let each follow what road she may,
	It shall come somewhere, upon a day!

Curtain.

AUTHOR NOTES AND RECOMMENDED READING

This listing follows similarly from the principles outlined in the introduction, the major point being that only authors born five years or more before Tolkien are included. Authors with an asterisk after their names have work included in this volume.

Andersen, Hans Christian (1805–75)

Danish writer, best known for his fairy tales, originally published in four collections. A fine selection, translated into English by R. P. Keigwin, can be found in *Eighty Fairy Tales* (1982), a volume of the Pantheon Fairy Tale & Folklore Library.

Baum, L[yman]. Frank* (1856–1919)

American children's writer and creator of Oz. His fourteen Oz novels tend to overshadow some of his other work of high quality, including the novels *Queen Zixi of Ix* (1905), a traditional fairy tale about a magic wishing cloak, and *The Sea-Fairies* (1911), which takes place in the underwater kingdom of the Mermaids. Baum's *Mother Goose in Prose* (1897) presents some of the stories behind traditional Mother Goose rhymes, while in *The Life and Adventures of Santa Claus* (1902) Baum invented a mythology surrounding Santa Claus, much as Tolkien would do in letters to his own children, collected as *The Father Christmas Letters* (1976, expanded in 1999 as *Letters from Father Christmas*).

Blackwood, Algernon (1869–1951)

British writer of mystical stories, including two classics, "The Willows" and "The Wendigo." Blackwood published many collections, but several early volumes contain his best work: *The Empty House and Other Ghost Stories* (1906); *The Listener and*

Other Stories (1907); *John Silence—Physician Extraordinary* (1908); *The Lost Valley and Other Stories* (1910); *Pan's Garden: A Volume of Nature Stories* (1912); and *Incredible Adventures* (1914). A recent and representative selection of Blackwood's best short fiction is *Ancient Sorceries and Other Weird Tales* (2002), edited by S. T. Joshi.

Buchan, John* (1875–1940)

Scottish writer and politician, best remembered for his suspense novel, *The Thirty-nine Steps* (1915), later filmed by Alfred Hitchcock. Some of Buchan's fantasy and supernatural stories were collected in *The Watcher by the Threshold and Other Stories* (1902), *The Moon Endureth: Tales and Fancies* (1912), and *The Runagates Club* (1928). Of his many novels, the most interesting are *Witch Wood* (1927), set in seventeenth-century Scotland and concerning an ancient and magical forest, and *The Gap in the Curtain* (1932), which deals with fate, free will, and J. W. Dunne's theories of time travel (the latter being as well an interest of Tolkien and C. S. Lewis).

Cabell, James Branch* (1879–1958)

American writer, best remembered for his novel *Jurgen* (1919), which became a cause célèbre when it was put on trial for obscenity. *Jurgen* is the slightly bawdy tale of a poet/pawnbroker in Cabell's fantastic medieval French province of Poictesme, a place about which Cabell would write many volumes, later collected in the eighteen-volume set *The Biography of Manuel* (1927–30).

Carroll, Lewis (1832–98) [pseudonym of Charles Lutwidge Dodgson]

British writer and mathematician, author of the children's classics *Alice's Adventures in Wonderland* (1865) and its sequel *Through the Looking-Glass, and What Alice Found There* (1871). Tolkien did not consider the Alice books to be fairy tales because of their dream frames and dream transitions, yet he considered them successful stories. Tolkien was also fond of *Sylvie and Bruno* (1889) and its sequel, *Sylvie and Bruno Concluded* (1893). Christopher Tolkien has written that his father knew these works well and occasionally recited verses from the books.

Coleridge, Sara (1802–52)

British writer and editor, daughter of the poet Samuel Taylor Coleridge. Her novel *Phantasmion* (1837), about the travels of a prince in Faerie, was the first fairy-tale novel written in English.

Coppard, A[lfred]. E[dgar]. (1878–1957)

British writer, who specialized in the short story, many of which fancifully describe rural England. While Coppard published numerous collections, his own selection of his best work, *The Collected Tales of A. E. Coppard* (1947), was very successful, and it provides a good introduction to the author's writings.

Crockett, S[amuel]. R[utherford]. (1859–1914)

Scottish writer. His thirteenth novel (out of fifty), *The Black Douglas* (1899), was read by Tolkien in his youth. In a letter Tolkien remarked that the episode of the wargs in *The Hobbit* was in part derived from *The Black Douglas,* calling the book "probably his best romance and anyway one that deeply impressed me in school-days, though I have never looked at it again." An excerpt from one chapter ("The Battle of the Were-Wolves"), showing Tolkien's indebtedness, can be found in note 10 to chapter 6 of the revised edition of *The Annotated Hobbit.*

de la Mare, Walter (1873–1956)

British writer and poet. De la Mare's *The Three Mulla-Mulgars* (1910) is a children's fantasy about three royal monkeys on a quest, which some have considered a precursor to certain elements of *The Hobbit.* De la Mare's strengths are most evident in his short stories, many of which contain fantastic or supernatural elements. A series of three volumes will collect his entire short fiction, *Short Stories 1895–1926* (1996), *Short Stories 1927–1956* (2001), and *Short Stories for Children* (forthcoming).

Dunsany, Lord* (1878–1957)

Anglo-Irish writer, dramatist, and poet. Several of Dunsany's earliest collections of short stories contain the very best fantasy stories in the English language. These collections include *The Gods of Pegana* (1905), *Time and the Gods* (1906), *The Sword of Welleran and Other Stories* (1908), *A Dreamer's Tales and Other Stories* (1910), *The Book of Wonder* (1912), *Fifty-one Tales* (1915), *Tales of Wonder* (1916; U.S. title *The Last Book of Wonder*), and *Tales of Three Hemispheres* (1919). Of Dunsany's novels, the best are *The King of Elfland's Daughter* (1924), *The Blessing of Pan* (1926), and *The Curse of the Wise Woman* (1933). The recent British omnibus in the Fantasy Masterworks series *Time and the Gods* (2000) contains six of the aforementioned collections. Another sampler of Dunsany is *In the Land of Time and Other Fantasy Stories* (forthcoming), edited by S. T. Joshi.

Eddison, E[ric]. R[ucker]. (1882–1945)

British writer and civil servant. Eddison's first novel, *The Worm Ouroboros* (1922), is perhaps his best book, a fully imagined secondary world described in an ornate and dense prose. His later books make up the Zimiamvian series, *Mistress of Mistresses* (1935), *A Fish Dinner in Memison* (1941), and *The Mezentian Gate* (1958). These are much more ambitious and difficult than Eddison's first book and only partially successful. Yet they remain Eddison's major works. Eddison's second novel, *Stybiorn the Strong* (1926), is an excellent historical work whose subject matter is similar to that of an Icelandic saga. In 1930, Eddison translated *Egil's Saga,* one of the major Icelandic sagas. In 1957, Tolkien wrote of Eddison as "the greatest and most convincing writer of invented worlds that I have read."

Forster, E[dward]. M[organ]. (1879–1970)

British writer, predominately of realistic fiction, including *Howard's End* (1910) and *A Passage to India* (1924). Forster's short stories include a large number of excellent fantasies, collected in *The Celestial Omnibus and Other Stories* (1911) and *The Eternal Moment* (1928).

Garnett, Richard* (1835–1906)

British writer and librarian, prolific scholar, and biographer. *The Twilight of the Gods and Other Tales* (1888, sixteen tales; expanded 1903, twenty-eight tales) contains Garnett's only fiction.

Grahame, Kenneth (1859–1932)

British writer and banker, author of the classic children's book *The Wind in the Willows* (1908), which Tolkien called an "excellent book." Grahame's other books, including *The Golden Age* (1895) and *Dream Days* (1898), are explorations of Edwardian childhood. The latter includes Grahame's famous fairy story "The Reluctant Dragon."

Haggard, H[enry]. Rider* (1856–1925)

British writer and civil servant. Haggard was a very prolific novelist and one of the most successful writers of his time. He spent much of his early life in South Africa, and a number of his writings have African settings. His two most famous novels were *King Solomon's Mines* (1885) and *She* (1886), each of which has been filmed several times. Another of Haggard's novels that interested Tolkien is *Eric Brighteyes* (1891), written in the style of an Icelandic saga. In a lecture, he referred to it as being "as good as most sagas and as heroic."

Hodgson, William Hope* (1877–1918)

British writer. As a youth, Hodgson went to sea and found the sailor's life to be one of misery. Much of Hodgson's fiction is supernatural and shows an obsession with the sea, as in *The Boats of the "Glen Carrig"* (1907), *The Ghost Pirates* (1909), and the collection *Men of the Deep Waters* (1914). His best book, however, is *The House on the Borderland* (1908), about a remote house haunted by hog-like creatures from another dimension.

Hoffmann, E[rnst]. T[heodor]. A[madeus]. (1776–1822)

German writer and music composer. Hoffmann wrote a large number of literary fairy tales, some of which have been made into ballets and operas. Good selections are found in *The Best Tales of Hoffmann* (1967), edited by E. F. Bleiler, and *Tales of E. T. A. Hoffmann* (1972), edited and translated by Leonard J. Kent and Elizabeth C. Knight.

Housman, Clemence* (1861–1955)

British writer and wood engraver. Clemence Housman published only three novels, each of which is a Christian fantasy. *The Were-Wolf* (1895) is a minor classic of werewolf literature, while her final novel, *The Life of Sir Aglovale de Galis* (1905), remains her supreme achievement. It is a remarkable psychological reconstruction of the life of Aglovale, a minor rogue knight in Sir Thomas Malory's *Le Morte d'Arthur*. Out of print and largely unavailable for many years, it was reprinted by Green Knight Publishing in 2000.

Housman, Laurence (1865–1959)

British writer and dramatist. Laurence Housman was by far the most prolific of the three writing Housmans, who include his sister Clemence and his brother A. E. Housman, the poet. Laurence's original fairy tales were collected in several volumes, some of which contain wood engravings by his sister, including *A Farm in Fairyland* (1894), *The House of Joy* (1895), *All Fellows* (1896), *Gods and Their Makers* (1897), *The Field of Clover*

(1898), *The Blue Moon* (1904), and *The Cloak of Friendship* (1905). *A Doorway in Fairyland* (1922), *Moonshine and Clover* (1922), and *The Kind and the Foolish* (1952) are reprint collections.

Kipling, Rudyard (1865–1936)

British writer and poet. Kipling's fantasies for children, including *The Jungle Book* (1894), *The Second Jungle Book* (1896), and *Just So Stories for Little Children* (1902), are rightly acclaimed as classics. Also of interest to Tolkien readers would be *Puck of Pook's Hill* (1906) and *Rewards and Fairies* (1910), which involve mythological characters and the history of England.

Knatchbull-Hugessen, E[dward]. H[ugessen].* (1829–93)

British writer and politician. Knatchbull-Hugessen (the first Lord Brabourne) wrote fourteen books of fairy tales, beginning with *Stories for My Children* (1869). Another tale out of this collection can be seen to have resonances in Tolkien. The story "Ernest" presents a slight analogue to Bilbo's speech with Smaug in *The Hobbit* (see note 5 to chapter 12 of the revised edition of *The Annotated Hobbit*). "Ernest" has recently been reprinted in *Alternative Alices: Visions and Revisions of Lewis Carroll's Alice Books* (1997), edited by Carolyn Sigler.

Lang, Andrew* (1844–1912)

Scottish writer and editor. Lang is perhaps best remembered for editing (with significant assistance from his wife) twelve volumes of colored fairy-tale books, ranging from *The Blue Fairy Book* (1889) through *The Lilac Fairy Book* (1910). The series was immensely popular. Lang also wrote some original fairy stories, including *Prince Prigio* (1889), which Tolkien found "unsatisfactory in many ways" but which he felt had some admirable qualities.

Lindsay, David* (1876–1945)

British writer. Lindsay's major works are all attempts to combine philosophy with various types of the novel. His most imaginative work, *A Voyage to Arcturus* (1920), uses Wellsian space travel to another planet as a template for a spiritual quest. Lindsay's other novels are more conventional but still powerful. *The Haunted Woman* (1922) is a kind of haunted house story, where some people are at times able to see and enter a staircase leading up to a nonexistent part of the house. *Devil's Tor* (1932) concerns the worship of the Great Mother and the reunion of a magical talisman associated with her worship that was broken in ancient times.

MacDonald, George* (1824–1905)

Scottish writer and minister. MacDonald was a prolific writer of novels for adults, but only a few are fantasies, including *Phantastes: A Faerie Romance for Men and Women* (1858), his first novel, and *Lilith* (1895), his last. His children's novels include *The Princess and the Goblin* (1872) and *The Princess and Curdie* (1883), both of which were influences upon *The Hobbit,* particularly in the depiction of goblins. MacDonald also wrote a number of fairy stories, recently collected as *The Gifts of the Child Christ and Other Stories and Fairy Tales* (1996), edited by Glenn Edward Sadler. The volume edited by U. C. Knoepflmacher and published as *The Complete Fairy Tales* (1999) contains only MacDonald's shorter fairy tales.

Machen, Arthur* (1863–1947)

Welsh writer and newspaperman. Machen wrote both supernatural fiction and fantasy, including *The Great God Pan & The Inmost Light* (1894), *The Three Imposters* (1895), and the collection *The House of Souls* (1906). Machen's best book, *The Hill of Dreams* (1907), is a kind of spiritual autobiography, written in a superb style. An omnibus containing much of his best work is *Tales of Horror and the Supernatural* (1948).

Macleod, Fiona [pseudonym of William Sharp] (1855–1905)

Scottish writer and editor. In the 1890s, Sharp's shadowy double, "Fiona Macleod," emerged, though Sharp pretended she was real for the rest of his life. Macleod's writings, unlike Sharp's, are mystical Celtic fantasies, heavy with nostalgia and atmosphere. The best tales are collected in *The Sin-Eater and Other Tales* (1894) and *The Washer of the Ford and Other Legendary Moralities* (1896). Her allegorical novels include *Pharais* (1894), *The Mountain Lovers* (1895), and *Green Fire* (1896).

Merritt, A[braham].* (1884–1943)

American writer and editor. Merritt published only a handful of novels and short stories, most of which appeared in pulp magazines. The best of his works are *The Moon Pool* (1919), which concerns a mysterious portal activated by moonlight, and *The*

Ship of Ishtar (1924), in which a man is taken by an ancient ship to an alternate world.

Mirrlees, Hope (1887–1978)

British writer and poet. Mirrlees's sole fantasy novel is the excellent *Lud-in-the-Mist* (1926), which tells of a town near the borders of Faerie and its problem with the illegal trafficking of fairy fruit.

Morris, Kenneth* (1879–1937)

Welsh writer and theosophist. Morris reworked stories from the Mabinogion into two companion novels, *The Fates of the Princes of Dyfed* (1914) and *Book of the Three Dragons* (1930). His supreme achievement lay in his short stories, ten of which were collected in *The Secret Mountain and Other Tales* (1926). His complete short stories can be found in *The Dragon Path: Collected Tales of Kenneth Morris* (1995). An excellent Toltec fantasy novel about the coming of the god Quetzalcoatl is *The Chalchiuhite Dragon* (1992).

Morris, William* (1834–96)

British writer, artist, and poet. Morris is perhaps best remembered for his association with the Pre-Raphaelite movement and for the textiles, furniture, and wallpaper he designed. Morris was also especially interested in medieval literature, translating *Beowulf* and various Icelandic sagas. Though he wrote some fantasy short stories when young, he returned to fantasy in the last decade of his life, writing seven prose romances with medieval settings: *A Tale of the House of the Wolfings* (1889), *The Roots of the Mountain* (1890), *The Story of the Glittering Plain* (1891), *The Wood beyond the World* (1894), *The Well at the World's End* (1896), *The Water of the Wondrous Isles* (1897), and *The Sundering Flood* (1897). Some of these were printed in gorgeous editions at Morris's own Kelmscott Press. Morris's pioneering works had a profound influence on J. R. R. Tolkien and many other fantasy writers.

Nesbit, E[dith].* (1858–1924)

British writer. Nesbit was an extremely popular writer for children. Her first fantasy novel, *Five Children and It* (1902), concerns a "Psammead" or sand-fairy. Tolkien certainly knew this work, for he refers to Psammeads in the early drafts of *Roverandom*. Two sequels followed, *The Phoenix and the Carpet* (1904) and *The Story of the Amulet* (1906), in which the Psammead returns. Another Nesbit title of special interest is *The Book of Dragons* (1900).

O'Brien, Fitz-James (1828–62)

Irish-born American writer and poet. O'Brien published no books during his lifetime, and the posthumous collections of his short stories were often severely edited. The authoritative two-volume edition *The Supernatural Tales of Fitz-James O'Brien* (1988), edited by Jessica Amanda Salmonson, restores the texts to their original versions. Volume 1 is subtitled *Macabre Tales;* and volume 2, *Dream Stories and Fantasies.*

Pain, Barry (1864–1928)

British writer and editor. Pain was one of the most popular humorists of his day, but his fantasy and supernatural stories, written throughout his lifetime and sprinkled through numerous volumes, are the basis for his reputation today. A collection of these stories, *The Glass of Supreme Moments and Other Tales* (2003), has recently appeared from the small Canadian publisher Ash-Tree Press.

Pyle, Howard (1853–1911)

American writer and illustrator. His most famous works are illustrated retellings of Arthurian legends, but his original fairy tale *The Garden behind the Moon* (1895) deserves to be better known.

Ruskin, John (1819–1900)

British writer and art critic. Ruskin's *The King of the Golden River,* written in 1841 but published ten years later, is probably the first English fairy story written for children. Influenced by the German *Kunstmärchen,* it still manages to create an identity of its own and remains a supreme achievement in the literary fairy tale. The original illustrations by Richard Doyle are also very striking.

Stephens, James (1882–1950)

Irish writer, primarily remembered for *The Crock of Gold* (1912), about an Old Philosopher and his problems with leprechauns and Irish gods.

Stevens, Francis* [pseudonym of Gertrude Barrows Bennett] (1883–1948)

American writer. Stevens published only a small number of

stories. Her *The Heads of Cerberus* (1919) is a pioneering work of alternate history. Many of her stories mix elements of fantasy, horror, and science fiction. A long overdue collection of her work is *The Nightmare and Other Tales of Dark Fantasy* (2003).

Stockton, Frank R[ichard].* (1834–1902)

American writer and editor. Stockton was a prolific writer of novels and short stories, but it is for his children's stories that he is remembered. His collections *The Floating Prince and Other Fairy Tales* (1881), *The Bee-Man of Orn and Other Fanciful Tales* (1887), and *The Queen's Museum* (1887) were very successful. A recent omnibus is *The Fairy Tales of Frank Stockton* (1990), edited by Jack Zipes.

Tieck, Ludwig* (1773–1853)

German writer. Tieck was one of the primary figures of Romanticism, and many of his best tales were collected in the three volumes of *Phantasus* (1812–16). Translations of Tieck's stories have been widely anthologized, but only an incomplete translation of *Phantasus* has appeared in English, as *Tales from the Phantasus* (1845), translated by Julius C. Hare, James Anthony Froud, and others.

Wells, H[erbert]. G[eorge]. (1866–1946)

British writer, best remembered for his early scientific romances, including *The Time Machine* (1895), *The War of the Worlds* (1898), and *The First Men in the Moon* (1901). Wells's short stories include a number of fantasies. The best omnibus is *The Complete Short Stories of H. G. Wells* (1998), edited by John Hammond.

Wilde, Oscar (1854–1900)

Irish writer and dramatist. Wilde's two volumes of fairy tales, *The Happy Prince* (1888) and *A House of Pomegranates* (1891), contain nine tales, two of which, "The Happy Prince" and "The Selfish Giant," are considered classics.

Wyke-Smith, E[dward]. A[ugustine].* (1871–1935)

British writer and mining engineer. Wyke-Smith published eight novels, four of which were for children. *Bill of the Bustingforths* (1921) is, like *The Marvellous Land of Snergs* (1927), a delightful anti–fairy tale. Of Wyke-Smith's adult novels, *The Second*

Chance (1923) is science fiction, concerning an old man rejuvenated to his youth by a drug made from ape glands.

Young, Ella (1867–1956)

Irish writer and poet. Young published three volumes of stories retelling Irish folk tales, *Celtic Wonder Tales* (1910), *The Wonder-Smith and His Son* (1927), and *The Tangle-Coated Horse* (1929). Her *Unicorn with Silver Shoes* (1932) is an original children's fantasy and probably her finest book.